Crazy Good

Local Author - Crystal River

Rachel Robinson

CRAZY GOOD
Copyright © 2014 Rachel Robinson
All rights reserved.

Cover design by Kari at Cover to Cover Designs
http://covertocoverdesigns.com/
Cover photography by Tatum Kathleen Photography
http://www.tatumkathleenphotography.com
Edited by Wendy Callahan
http://www.wendylcallahan.com
Formatted by Polgarus Studio
http://www.polgarusstudio.com

For the wives. You know who you are. (Hint: you have dead hooker bags and cold weather gear filling your storage closets.)

Chapter One

Windsor
Present Day

My mother is a bitch. Was, is, will always be. It's never been a question of love. She's my mother. I grew in her body—she loves me. But for her, it's always about instilling something more simple. Something more primal.

It's about survival.

You do what you have to do to get by and you don't let anyone look down their nose at the decisions you make. Actually, if I were taking a page from the Kathy Forbes playbook, it would be to not even spare a passing glance at anyone else. They don't matter. Only look forward. Only look up. Always be competitive. Always snatch up opportunities that come forth.

I realized the dose of tough love she was imparting when she moved onto her third husband. I was twelve years old, angry, and made up of half her DNA.

Everything she was, was everything I would not be. By the time her fourth marriage was in shambles because I was *irrevocably unhappy*, I'd learned well. I knew I caused the fourth divorce, maybe even the third. I'll give her the credit for that one, though. You don't marry a vegan and request steak at the wedding reception. At the tender age of fourteen even I could see doom and gloom when shoved in my face.

When I reached adulthood I knew it didn't matter what I said or did with regard to her past conquests. She ruined relationships all on her own. You see, it was all about the competition. The opportunity. From one relationship to the next, she took what she needed or wanted and then left. They say people come into your life for a reason. I know my father came into my mother's life to give her me. I know husband number five came into her life to bring her back down to reality. He ruined her. He made her fall in love with him. Then he started giving her a taste of her own medicine. He threatened to leave her every chance he got. He still does it. If you've been there, you know it's a horrible place to be. With the help of a wine bottle, and her emotional scars she morphed into a person unrecognizable.

I'm not sure what I want out of life, but I know it's not what she has; a charade game and marriages of no consequence. When she finally did find herself it was too late. Number five locked her away and swallowed the key. I don't visit. I can't visit. All I know is she is a bitch who finally got something that drowns out what she couldn't find. I can't tell you what she learned along the way. All I can tell you is she survived. She taught me well because right now, in this moment, all I want to do is survive.

People always say life is too short to be unhappy. If you don't like something, change it. There's a beauty in change that can't come from anything else. Like all positives, there are also negatives warring on the same front. Not that I'm an unhappy person, but I don't deal well with change…of any kind. Changes in my cycle, changes in the weather, life altering, glaring mistakes that force a huge life change—all of these things are a recipe for my own personal kind of disaster.

It's been one year, eight months, twenty-one days, and fifteen hours since the first time I laid eyes on Maverick Hart. It's been eighteen days and twelve hours since I last heard from him. Numbers and time are tangible things I can make sense of. Nothing else in my life is that easy to compute.

Honestly, after meeting Mav, I don't think I want *easy* anymore. Right now, I'm worried, but worried doesn't even begin to describe the sick feeling coursing through my body. It's not just my stomach that turns and flips with anxiety; every particle that makes up Windsor Forbes is affected. I'm not sure I'll make it through this particular survival course.

The white, sterile hallway is cold. Goosebumps prickle my skin, and with each step forward toward him I feel dread. *What will be left? Will he be the man I remember? Will he even remember me?* I say a silent prayer, promising to give up everything if only he'll survive this. I'd give up everything, anything for him.

The big, burly nurse comes out of nowhere, her sensible white shoes as drab as her grim features. "Can I help you with something, ma'am?" She's blocking my way to the rooms. Normally I'd cringe, play by the rules, and this would be the end of my task. Not now. I focus my eyes on the large, black wart on her chin.

I tuck my long, deflated, brown hair behind my ears and square my shoulders. "I'm here to see Maverick Hart. I'm his s…significant other," I say, knowing full well only family members are allowed in the hospital rooms. The lie of *sister* just wouldn't pass my lips. Burly Wart Nurse clears her throat. She looks to be contemplating something and then merely shrugs, shaking her head. "Second door on the right. Good luck, honey." *Good luck?* She ambles back to the nurse's station and I'm left staring at her wide back, not believing she is just going to let me go in. I didn't even have to lie. Wrapping my sweater around me a little tighter, I head for his room. It should be a good sign that he's on this non-ICU-floor of the hospital, but all I feel standing in front of his door, room number 143, is stone-cold terror. *Just survive,* I think.

Good luck? I push open the door and a melody of beeps ambushes me. The room is dark—of course, because I flew all day to get here, it is now night.

"Who are you?" The voice cuts through the darkness. It's not a familiar voice and I automatically assume it's another nurse. I swipe my sweaty palms down my jeans. I can't talk yet. It's physically impossible until I see him—his face, his lips, his hands. I want to see all of him. My heart thumps wildly, taking away my breath, thinking of the last time I saw him. I shuffle my feet forward, bringing me closer to the bed in the middle of the room. I see the monitors casting an ominous glow on the white sheets.

A side-light clicks on. Not even caring what or who turned on a light, I take in Maverick. He is battered and bruised, but he's here. He's alive. He is so perfect. Light brown hair peeks out from beneath the bandages around his head. His strong jawline has a sprinkling of scruff surrounding his pink lips. His hazel eyes are closed, but best of all, his chest rises up and down. A woman clears her throat. I startle.

"I'm going to ask one more time before I call security. Who the hell are you?" she says. I see her then, her long blonde hair piled on the top of her head in a messy topknot. She is sitting on a cot, covered in a sheet. I have obviously woken her up. I also realize I have no clue who in the hell she is either. I take a step closer to the bed.

"I'm Windsor," I say.

"Forbes," the woman finishes for me, knowing eyes narrowing as she takes me in. Her voice is acidic. I'm not even sure how I know, but I do. With one word the woman has said everything. She's involved with Maverick in some way.

"Who are you?" I try to stop my shaking hands because I don't want to disturb Mav. I know people in a coma can sometimes sense or hear things. As horrendous as it sounds, I just hope he stays sleeping for a little bit longer. "I'm his girlfriend," I proclaim. I never would have said something so bold before. The man unconscious in this hospital bed taught me to stand up for myself.

She laughs.

I should have called. Why didn't I call before I came here? I feel so stupid. And now, standing in front of another woman I'm panicked, the sheen breaking across my forehead as proof.

"Sweetheart, I'm his *wife*," she says, motioning to her bed, and her obvious family status.

At once, it's like I am the one with a body full of shrapnel. A swift shock of pain starts in my stomach and creeps up to my heart, wrapping around it like a plague. That one sentence from her perfect lips chokes me of air, robs me of everything. I want to call her a liar, but I know she's not.

I look down at Maverick, still breathing, machines beeping all around him, and tears blur my vision. I knew he was messed up—really messed up–and I still got involved. This is what I get.

All the memories of us wash over me at once. The tender touches, the sweet words, the molten gazes from across the room, and the silent words we exchanged simply by looking at one another. I clutch my stomach in physical pain.

I hear her sheets rustle as she comes to stand on the other side of his bed. I meet her angry gaze. Staring each other straight in the eyes, we have a silent standoff. I know who loses these things. The other woman. The diamond and solid band sparkling on her left hand signifies my status in this duel. I feel the tears rolling down my cheeks like hot traitors. Worrying about what his wife thinks doesn't even register. The sting of Maverick's betrayal is all-encompassing. *You knew he was fucked up,* my inner voice whispers. A wife? He's married. A wedding. A bride. Another life I have no clue about. Lies. I shudder. Nothing but lies.

"Why?" I ask. The question is involuntary; it just comes garbling out of my mouth on its own.

"Because he asked me to marry him five years ago. Why else?" She doesn't realize I wasn't talking to her. I look down at Maverick.

My fists balled so hard I think my nails are slicing me, I try to swallow down the bitterness. "Why? Why didn't you tell me? You asshole! You lying asshole! You promised me honesty! Why?" I scream. It's loud and echoing and I don't give a shit. Silent, complacent Windsor is gone. I suck in air trying to fill my lungs, but they refuse to fill.

The wife backs away from his bed and sits on the cot. The self-satisfied look on her stunning, make-up free face causes my blood to boil. I take a step away from Mav's bed too, like maybe more of his horrible lies might seep out of his comatose body and enter me.

I stab my finger toward her. "He never mentioned you. Not once," I rasp. Her smile disappears. Finally the in control Windsor seems to be making an appearance. I take another step away from him. I latch onto the only thing that strikes as true. He never mentioned her, a wife, not once. Surely, I'd have taken off at a fast pace the second he did. "What's your name?" I ask. I know my anger should be directed at Maverick, but there are too many unknown variables.

She raises both arms over her head to fix her hair and sighs loudly. She wants me to think I'm inconveniencing her. "Monica Hart." She enunciates her last name thoroughly. *Bitch.* She ignores the accusations. She stands again and grabs his hand. "Did you really think someone like Maverick would be with someone like you for long?" She motions to my bedraggled appearance. I am already acutely aware of all of my shortcomings; I don't need the lying bastard's wife pointing them out. I feel like the broken woman I was the day I met him. Broken, untrusting, and freaking vulnerable.

"I guess everything comes full circle. Doesn't it Maverick?" I say, my voice still louder than prudent in a silent hospital in the middle of the night. Aware that Mrs. Hart is watching my every move, I approach and lean over Mav's bed.

"Take a leap, Windsor. Trust me, Windsor. It's always only going to be you, Windsor. Forever," I choke out the words. "I love you, Windsor." I raise my gaze to Monica's. My words horrify her. As I give all of his words straight back to him, I feel the black pit forming inside. Lies. All of them. "I'm in, Windsor. I'm all in. That's what you said, Maverick." I straighten up and swipe under my eyes with my fingertips. "I guess he was only half in," I tell his wife, shrugging my shoulders. She just stares, wetness glazing her eyes. I grab Maverick's hand. It feels heavy…wrong.

"Guess what, Maverick?" I stutter, unable to answer my own question. I rub his knuckles knowing this will be the last time I see him. Or touch him. My stomach is warring with my heart. I know I'm doing the right thing, I just feel stupid. This is my fault. I took a leap and Maverick Hart let me fall flat on my face. Stroking his jaw with my thumb, I silently say goodbye. He was never mine to begin with. The realization hits me full force. I want to cry and pummel something at the same time.

I glare at Monica. "You won't mind if I break up with my boyfriend, will you?" She doesn't respond, doesn't nod, or remove her eyes from Maverick's face. She looks like a zombie, albeit a pretty one, from a bad horror flick. I kiss his cheek and whisper the words I promised him I would never say.

"I'm out, Maverick. I'm leaving."

Knowing I can't look at him again I speak to a now tearful Monica.

"Good luck, Mrs. Hart. You need it more than I do," I say. With that I turn and walk out of his room. As the door clicks behind me, I hear his monitors beeping wildly. A second later Monica screams for a doctor. I walk past the bustle of nurses flying to room 143. Burly Wart Nurse meets my eyes and offers a weak, apologetic smile. I mouth the words *thank you*.

As I exit the hospital darkness greets me. Darkness of all sorts. *I will give up anything if he'll survive.*

Guess ole' Mom had the right idea.

Chapter Two

Windsor

The Past

One year, eight months, twenty-one days,
and eighteen hours ago

I slick the second coat of nail polish over my toes slowly, making precise strokes. I blow on them even though I know it doesn't speed the drying process; it just gives me something to do while I wait. "Spontaneous," I say out loud, reading the name of the shade I selected. The second I say it I immediately regret it.

"Even your damn nail polish is trying to tell you something," Gretchen snaps from the other side of the room before she turns on the blow dryer. She has one foot propped on the kitchen counter while she dries her self-tanning spray. She glances up from her furious work and widens her eyes to make sure I've heard her, urging me to acknowledge her.

I roll my eyes. "Yes, yes," I scream over the hair dryer's dull roar. She smiles, switches legs, and returns to her Friday night ritual. I'm just glad she finally found something that makes her look island tropical instead of Oompa Loompa orange. That was a bad few weekends. I shake my head at the memory as I swipe a cotton ball with nail polish remover around my cuticles. *Perfect,* I think, standing from the old, leather couch. I hear the dryer shut off and know I'm about to be privy to an official Gretchen-knows-best-rant. I tighten my thigh length robe and heave a sigh as I watch her walk toward me, clad in her black lacy underwear and matching demi-cup bra.

"Seriously. You need to have fun tonight," she says, fanning her six-pack abdominals, even through the spray is already past the tacky stage of drying. "You are in desperate need of just letting loose, Win. The type of fun that you let happen during a night out—the kind that you don't worry about what will come next month, next week, or even tomorrow morning." She's right. She's unfortunately, perfectly right. I sigh, clutching the belt of my robe, twisting it half to death.

"It's just hard. You know I was with Nash for four years. We were planning our wedding, Gretchen. I can't just pretend that didn't happen. I can't act like I wasn't ready to settle down. I'm over the bar scene," I tell her, hoping playing the sympathy card will make her shut up. Even the Gretchen machine has boundaries when it comes to my botched engagement and the downward spiral that almost landed me in the looney bin. "I'm over the hapless fun and, frankly, men are just skeevy these days." I look down at my toes, making sure they aren't touching. "They only want sex."

Gretchen leans in and hugs me, her lean arms wrapping around my shoulders, and light brown hair sticking to my glossed lips. "They aren't all skeevy, honey. Some are good and you will find a good one because you are good," she whispers.

"You smell like a baked potato, Gretch," I counter, trying to figure out the exact scent of her spray tan. I already know for a fact all men are skeevy, and all the good ones get snapped up quickly. She giggles, then pulls back and plays at mock outrage, one hand splayed across her chest.

She sniffs a forearm. "It's vanilla passion," she says, lacing her words with a slight French accent. It sounds more like a Crocodile Hunter accent, but I don't say so. I know she is trying to lighten the mood, to force my focus to the present. "How do you expect to get Johnny Nash out of your head if you don't fuck him out of it?" Gretchen smarts.

Her question is crass, but I can't deny the truth in her words. It's been years since Nash and I can't stop dwelling on the monumental birthday I have coming up. Thirty. I am alone. I shudder.

"You don't want to be alone when you start to get wrinkles. You have to find a man now, so he'll think your wrinkles are adorable when you do get them. These are your prime years," she says, cocking one eyebrow, urging me to disagree. The obscene wisdom that trickles out of her mouth at times such as this reminds me why we've been friends for so long. I puff out my cheeks and pretend to swallow down a mouth full of vomit. Then I smile.

She folds her arms under her breasts, not amused by my joke. "Seriously though. You're giving him all this power over you just by acting like a stick in the mud." Gretchen pauses. "Meeting someone new will help."

I sigh. Meeting someone new will only mute the dastardly sorrows for a brief time. Thinking maybe I do want a mute button, at least for the night, I decide to agree with my best friend, the dictator.

"Fine, Hitler. I'll go out. I'll try to have fun. I'll dance *from the windows to the walls until sweat drips down my balls.* Happy?"

Gretchen nearly chokes on her own spit before she replies through hysterics. "I'm going to go find that song on my iPod and you are going to get your hot little ass into that very dark corner of your closet. Find that dress – you know the one. Then we are taking our hot, professional asses to the club. I need to stalk Benji and you need…to get out. I'm going to introduce you to some people and I won't let you self sabotage either, so don't even think about wearing cotton briefs." She pats me on the ass and, just like that, my best friend, the Gretchen machine is back in action, our tender moment gone. Her outrageous attitude and her inability to lie made the decision to move into her Virginia Beach condo the easiest decision I'd made in a long time.

"Professional. Ass. Club. Words that don't go together for a thousand, Alex," I quip at her retreating back. I add, "You have a brown smudge on your professional ass!" Gretchen merely laughs and adds a little extra jiggle as she struts down the hallway to her room.

Benji wants her. I know he does. What I'm not sure of is why she doesn't act on her feelings for him. Then again, I obviously don't know much about love and relationships. The only guy I've ever loved wriggled his way into my heart and then ripped it out. When I thought the worst was over, he had his new, much younger girlfriend prance on it in her daddy-bought Louboutins.

Breaks weren't something thrown my way often. When you want something so badly for so long, it takes a very long time to get over it. I don't expect anyone else to understand, but I've been grieving for the life I didn't get. The life I probably won't ever get with my rapidly deepening wrinkles. I scowl at my full-length mirror as I pass by to the dark place in my closet.

When I exit my bedroom wearing the tight black dress and a pair of sky-high heels, I see Gretchen waiting for me by the door. She looks up from digging in her clutch and smiles widely. She squints her eyes, then nods fiercely one time. She approves, thank God. I roll my eyes as I brush past her to open the door.

She puts her pointer finger all the way into her mouth and then pulls it out, effectively removing the red lipstick that could potentially get on her perfectly white teeth. She wipes her finger off on a napkin and throws it on the counter before wrapping her hand around my waist.

"Let's go. Jess is out front waiting. She's the DD tonight," Gretchen admits with a smile. With one sentence she is also letting me know she expects me to get crazy-pants-wasted with her tonight. I slide into the passenger seat of Jess's BMW and strong perfume assaults me at the same time as the artic blast from the air vents.

"Hey Jess," Gretchen exclaims from the back seat, as the car pulls away from the curb.

"Hey, guys," Jess says as she points the vents in front of me onto herself. She continues, "I don't want my makeup to get shiny." I laugh because her makeup is the least of her worries. I look over at her and drop my eyes to her barely there white mini-skirt. Like *barely* there. She doesn't have a slutty bone in her body, so how she dresses when she goes out confounds me.

"I can see your underwear," I tell her, laughing. She doesn't even attempt to pull her skirt down.

She shrugs. "I'm not going to be sitting down tonight. It's just us girls right now." Her flawed logic is painfully refreshing. Because dancing won't make it ride up more than sitting. *Sure.* Jess cranks up her rap music to a level that makes me wince. Always the ghetto booty rap when in the world of Jess.

"Good point," I say, peeking into the side mirror to see Gretchen stifling a laugh. When we arrive moments later and the valet guy opens the door for Jess, I don't try to hide my sniggering when his eyes widen briefly. Jess hands him the fob with a small wink and finally readjusts herself.

When people say age is only a number, I don't think they take into account the difference a few years can make. As I watch all the newly minted twenty-one year olds dance around with full cups splashing vodka everywhere, I wince remembering those days. Finding yourself, losing yourself, and then finding your real self. That's what happens in only a few years. Unfortunately for me, I get to lose myself one extra time. Here I am, warped back in time, mixed in with twenty-one year olds, trying to find it again.

Being almost thirty and supposedly wiser, Gretchen called ahead and reserved a table for the night; not that Jess will be sitting at it, but it is a reprieve all the same. I slide into the booth and wedge myself toward the corner, deciding to make it my home for the night. I watch Jess meander closer to a few of our other friends just as Gretch sits down next to me.

I bump her leg. "Total hottie checking you out at twelve o'clock," I say in her ear. She just smiles like a person mad. At Benji. Who just so happens to be the bartender at the club she chose for the night. Which just happens to be the club she chooses every weekend. "I don't get why you give him the run around. Go on a date with the poor guy already. Your wrinkles are getting uglier as we speak." Benji waves at our table, knowing full well we're talking about him.

"I'll go get drinks. Morganna is on her way. Keep an eye out," Gretchen says, disappearing into the crowd of swaying bodies and flashing lights. We got here later than usual because *good spray tans take time.* The drunkenness in this place has already peaked.

Through a crowd of stumbling babies I see her. Our friend. As she approaches my mind plays the song from *Mean Girls.* You know the one where the Plastics walk in a fierce group down the high school hallway? Then everyone stops and stares? That's Morganna in one song.

Morganna comes from a small southern town where people talk more than they listen. When they do listen they take their careful, manipulative time to listen to the undercurrents laced throughout the words. Innocuous statements turn into gritty rumors that spread like wildfire in the parched forests of California. Morganna caught more than a thick southern drawl growing up in her hometown; she caught a fearsome, incurable drive to succeed. Nothing is more potent or dangerous than a woman with something to prove and proving things, no matter fact or fiction is her favorite past time.

After obtaining scrupulous grades throughout her stint at an Ivy League college and passing the BAR with ease, Morganna became a divorce attorney. She is feared, revered and, most of all, wildly successful. I've never seen Morganna cry nor have I ever seen her show any emotion that she hasn't planned out at least fifteen days in advance. She is untouchable, beautiful and her confidence knows no bounds. It's easy to forget Morganna's southern roots. I know she only lets her country accent slip when she is furious with her husband or when she's had a few too many glasses of red wine.

You go to her when you need help organizing a party, if you need advice about your stepbrother's DUI arrest, or if you need directions on how to cook and serve a fifty course, organic based meal. The fact that she wears designer, five-inch heels in her home office is a testament to everything Morganna stands for. Simply put, Morganna gets shit done.

She has an assistant named Phillipe that I can't help but feel bad for. The first three months Phillipe was employed by Morganna, I assumed his name was *Phillipe Get* because his name was always followed by a direct order.

"Phillipe get Mary Saunders on the line."

"Phillipe get my calendar book."

"Phillipe get me the client's number." Freaking relentless, but you only feel bad for so long. I bet a million gays would scratch eyes out to be Morganna's assistant.

I smile sweetly at Phillipe when I visit Morganna at home because I know he is the one who pencils me in. His returning smile says, "You better hurry up, bitch. I wrote in a thirty minute slot for you and it will be my head if you stay any longer." I know better though; she doesn't care how long I stay. She just likes to bitch at him to assert control. Control is huge for Morganna because the one thing she can't control is the most important to her. Her husband, Stone Sterns. Who happens to be absent tonight.

Why is any of this important? Well, Morganna has everything I want. She is the person I would choose to be on any given Sunday.

The waters part and she struts to our table. "You look gorgeous Morganna. I wouldn't expect anything less," I say. "Where is Phillipe? Did you give him the night off?"

She raises her eyebrows as she notices my tight black dress. "Finally," she whispers, red lips twitching in a mischievous smile. I shake my head as she sits down next to me. "Oh, that regurgitated piece of human flesh is typing some documents for me tonight. I don't want to talk about him anyway. I want to talk about you." True to form, she switches the focus back to someone else almost immediately. *She's your friend.* I have to remind myself.

I nod toward the bar where Gretchen stands. "Gretch is grabbing us drinks. Want one? I can go…" I plead for an escape. She knows it.

"I'm going to set you up," Morganna demands. It's not a question. I laugh a little to try to diffuse the situation. It's the same situation every time I hang out with her in a *single* atmosphere. You might wonder why I don't let her set me up. Someone I idolize so much has to have some taste, right? Well, I don't want anyone's help replacing the Nashhole. Call me a romantic at heart, but I want it to happen organically. Like in the bread aisle. Because he needs to know up front I like and eat carbs like a duck in a pond. They're hopeless aspirations, but they are my own.

"Where's Stone?" I utter the only name I know will shut her up.

She fluffs her already high hair even higher. "He's with the rat pack tonight. Actually I suspect they may have already slithered their way here somewhere." She glances around the bar slowly. "The guy I want to set you up with is with him."

I start shaking my head the second the words leave her mouth. No way. Not one of them. One of *The Guys*. I'd rather meet a vegan on the veggie aisle. I don't hang out with Stone very often as he has a lot of work trips, but I know all of his friends are the same as him. Crazy. Reckless crazy, not deranged. Not fully deranged anyway. One glance and I know Morganna is merely waiting for me to continue, knowing I'm not done rejecting her ludicrous idea.

"I love you, but you're absolutely crazy and there is no way. No way." I make my arms into an X in front of chest and open them up. "You know when I'm ready – and I'm not saying I'm ready – that I want to stumble into a guy. There will be slow clapping, and heart palpitations. If I go out with one of The Guys there will only be heart palpitations because I'll be in a near death experience, I'm sure. I'm here tonight because Gretchen thinks I'm on the fast track to inhabiting a library with cats winding around my feet. Oh, and I'm wrinkly in the un-cute way."

"You are," Morganna says, unapologetically. I flinch a little, but they are both right. And I can't hate the haters. Nash has made me the ultimate hater. "Well you aren't wrinkly and Botox can fix that, but it's time. That's the end of it. You either want help or you want to fend for yourself. Which is it?" she asks.

I look away, honestly considering doing what she wants. I want to please her and do something decent for myself at the same time.

I decide to head to the bar. "I'll think about it. Meaning I will really consider it, but not tonight, okay? I'm not ready to dive into the deep end." I smile. She nods. "One dose of Benji and Gretchen has forgotten all about us. I'm going to grab us drinks. Warn me if *your* rat pack arrives so I can duck in a corner." I shake my finger at her as I teeter away. A red nail brushes the bottom of her chin. She's conspiring, God dammit.

I hear them before I see them. Voices commanding. Laughter booming. A drunken baby turns to look at the commotion and splashes half her cup onto the top of my foot. A wet high heel—perfect. I don't even bother looking. I know it's The Guys. I glare at Morganna, and she just laughs. I know the exact moment her sights lock on Stone. Her face morphs into a puddle of slush. I walk, with my heel slipping out of my shoe all the way to the bar, and grab a cocktail napkin out of a stack. I slip my foot out of my shoe and start drying it. When I look up, I see him.

Muscles are everywhere. He's so large he is the only thing my eyes can possibly be drawn to. I think the rest of the bar is probably looking at him too, but I wouldn't know because I'm staring at him. Like a deer in freaking headlights.

Except he hasn't even noticed me. His black dress shirt is cuffed up his forearms and dark tattoos peek out. His dark wash jeans fall to that exceptional place on his narrow waist. Usually, I'm not so into physical things about the opposite sex. Right now, though, all I can think about is sex. Him. Muscles. On me. I'm hot all at once. I can't breathe.

He throws his head back and laughs at something one of the trophy women around him says. I want to thank whoever made this creature laugh because it reveals perfect teeth, and I now know his eyes crinkle when he laughs, and it looks like perfection. He is perfect. He probably knows how perfect he is and that is the number one thing that I do not want or need in a man. Not that he'd have plain ole' me anyways. It looks as if he could have his choice out of the entire bar—perhaps even the world. Stone claps the guy on the back, looking directly at Morganna, and then retreats to his wife. Of course he is one of *The Guys.*

Off limits, Windsor, I remind myself because my damn traitorous body has other thoughts.

I notice his black watch, the tattoo that creeps out of the neck of his shirt, all tell tale signs. I know what he does; I also know exactly how long he can hold his breath.

Mr. Sexy meets my gaze. I suck in a sharp breath when he rakes his eyes over my body once and then again. A predatory smile creeps its way up the lower part of his face. Dimples. Two of them—one on each side. They aren't cute either, like little boys with dirt smeared on their faces.

These dimples are *hot*. What makes them smolder is that they don't go with the rest of him. The juxtaposition of the dimples on something so unfathomably masculine is…mouthwatering.

Even as embarrassed as I am, I can't look away. He leans his head to one side trying to hear the girl talking next to his ear, but his narrowed gaze doesn't stray from mine.

Someone jerks my arm. "Put your fucking shoe on, Windsor," Gretchen hisses from behind me. "That man, and he is a fine ass specimen, is coming over here. By the way he's looking at you I think he might want to eat you for dinner." One crude sentence is all it takes. I'm back on guard, minus the fluttering heart. Gretchen knows it.

"Good thing I don't like to be munched on then." I fix her with my icy stare. The wall is up. This guy could be Kellan Kyle mixed with Channing Tatum, and he wouldn't have a chance in hell with my wall.

Awareness of everything on and inside my body hits me. I don't even need to turn around. I know he's there. I sense it. Every hair on my neck rises as I take in his sweet, musky cologne.

"Maybe I can fix that," Mr. Sexy says, voice licking each syllable like he invented the damn English language. I still don't turn around. I stare at Gretchen's face, transfixed by this man's presence. Her face breaks into a huge grin.

"Damn. That is best line I've heard in a long time," she says to him, slow clapping and shaking her head to drive the point home. "Fix that? Munch on you? Get it?" Gretchen snorts.

All I'm aware of is the heat permeating my body and the frantic pace of my heart. I turn around and face *The Guy.*

Chapter Three

Maverick

This chick looks completely mortified. She would look less shocked if she walked onto an airplane naked. Or got caught fucking in public. Her huge blue eyes are scared shitless, like a wounded animal. I know what scared shitless looks like. I deal it out as a profession.

I turn on my smile and watch her study my face. She's guarded…I see it. A challenge. Not an easy fuck. Not my type at all. I glance at her cute friend who looks easy as poker with a blind man. She's exactly my type. No strings. I'm not even sure what drew me to the doe-eyed girl in the first place.

The friend chuckles a little and pushes her toward me. The friend must be taken. "No…thank yo-u," Blue Eyes stutters, finally responding. Sinking my hands in the pockets of my jeans I narrow my eyes.

"Are you sure? I'm good at fixing things." Her cheeks are so red I think she will turn into flames any second. I laugh. I could let my little charade go on all night. When she stays silent, I nod at her bare foot and then the shoe she clutches in her hand. "Your shoe is broken. Do you want me to fix it?" I ask, putting her out of her misery. She visibly relaxes when she realizes I'm not talking about munching on her. The joke was too easy.

Balancing on one foot, she slips her shoe back on. I catch a glimpse of her purple toes before she does. It reminds me of how all women get dressed after I'm done with them and my dick gets hard. I readjust it through my pocket. Her eyes dart down to my crotch. Perfect. It's exactly where I want her attention.

"My shoe is fine. Some idiot spilled on me," she says, as her gaze wanders back up to my face. I make sure the smile is in place when she does. I like to watch them squirm before I leave them in the dust. She's different though. Her expression hardens even further. "I won't be needing your services tonight."

Ouch. Blue eyes isn't even pretending; she doesn't have any interest. Which pisses me off because that means I'm wrong. Mentally, I lower my woman targeting percentage. I'm intrigued even more. Studying her small frame, hugged inside a tight black dress, I want to see more. Because I know the challenge is steep, I want it that much more.

Her friend peeks over her shoulder. "Or maybe you do need fixing tonight, Windsor?"

Her name. Something as small as a name holds a huge part in seduction. I use it to its full advantage. If the friend thinks she needs fixing, it must be really bad.

Blue Eyes shoots her friend a death glare and hisses something under her breath. She yanks down her dress. "Despite what my bitch best friend says, I don't need fixing. Especially the brand of *fixing* you are skilled at dealing out," she says. Her eyes don't waver. Her shoulders don't slink. She stands proud as she shoots me down. The problem is I haven't even propositioned her yet. Not really anyways. Not flat out. Game fucking on. Challenge accepted.

"I'm not sure what you're talking about, Windsor. I was just going to ask this fine bartender to *fix* you a drink. What is your pleasure?" I ask. I don't take my eyes off hers as I throw my hand in the air to get Benji's attention. Surely she won't turn down a drink. She is out at a bar after all.

Her poker face is tight. Better than some of the guys. I think she will turn me down and it pisses me off. Her friend leaves and starts dancing with a girl in a tiny skirt. Blue Eyes looks at them longingly. She bites her bottom lip. The thought of my dick in her mouth pops into my mind.

"A martini. Vodka. No ice. No olives. Dirty," she says, leaning in. Barely suppressing a groan, I order her drink and motion for her to take the seat next to me at the bar. Sitting is the only thing I'll be able to do while I'm around this girl. The supreme cock tease. That's exactly what the guys would call this one.

My goal tonight is to figure out just how challenging this will be. One should always know exactly what they're fighting for. Once I fixate on something I don't stop until I get it perfected. I want to perfect fucking Blue Eyes. Then, once I reach that goal, I'll find a new one. Something or someone more complicated. The women shouldn't be offended. It's how my entire life is. One set of hurdles followed by more and more and more. Now, at almost thirty I'm pretty perfect at a lot of fucking things. I may not be a good guy, but I am fucking perfect. Maverick Hart's luck doesn't ever run dry.

"Name?" she asks, staring into her martini glass. I chuckle.

"What do you want it to be?" If looks could kill, I'd be doubling over in pain.

"I don't want it to be anything. It is rude not to introduce yourself. After all, you've already offered the rental of your mouth and/or dick for the night without even telling me your name," she says, grimacing. Damn. She reads between the lines better than I thought.

"I don't rent out my body parts, Windsor. I loan my services. My name is Maverick and I do not want to loan to you. I don't think you have a large enough down payment. Too much liability," I tease. Her face drops. She looks surprised by my cavalier sex talk. So, she's guarded *and* innocent. "So what does Windsor, who does not like to be objectified, do for a living?" I ask.

She runs her forefinger around the rim of her glass. I shift in my seat. She notices. A smile crosses her lips. "I balance risks and liabilities," she says, tilting her head to the side. Her brown hair swings around her shoulder. I smile so she'll continue and so I can hide the God damned lust I feel. "I'm an accountant, Maverick. A CPA. I deal with other people's money for a living. What about you?" she asks.

Cock Polishing Assistant. The abbreviation wiggles in my mind, but the second she says what she does I'm already trying to think of what I can do to force her to see me again. The ideas are endless now that I know her profession.

She raises her eyebrows as she waits for me to tell her what I do. I think she already knows. She saw the guys I arrived with. It's not really a secret. Just in case she really is clueless, I play the subtle card. "Oh, you know. I'm Navy," I say, sipping on water.

She nods, smiles, and brings her lips to her glass, draining it in one large gulp. "I knew it," she says, after taking a large breath. I raise my eyebrows. She glances over at Stone and his wife Morganna, lifting her small hand to wave in their direction.

I follow her gaze and see a stony-faced Morg. She knows I'm a womanizer. She knows my game. Windsor must be her friend. Shit. Shit. Shit. Bad news. Stone smiles and then forces Morg to kiss him, all tongue and groping hands. Only Stone has that kind of control over that wild card. I'll have to ask him to smooth my way with

Windsor. I want this and I want her more than anything I've wanted in a while. It confuses me and excites me at the same fucking time. A new, shiny toy.

Windsor clears her throat. "Well, I think I've had enough fixing for tonight." She stands to go and I grab her wrist. She's warm and soft against my huge calloused hand. Delicate. Fragile. Perfect for fucking. I stand in front of her, towering over her slight frame. I know the masses of easy fucks are just behind me, but I want this one. I want Windsor. I study her profile as she looks out the dancing bodies, searching for someone. Her friend? A man? The questions are endless and I feel helpless. I need to talk to her more. Her glossy lips shine in the dim lights. I want to know exactly how she can use them. On every square inch of my body.

"Number?" I ask in the same manner she asked for my name. I never get phone numbers. There's no need. I fuck em' and forget em'. I can't even believe the word just came out of my mouth. I hope I don't sound desperate. Actually, maybe it will work to my benefit if I do. This is a game, after all.

"I don't do dates. I don't give numbers. I work with them. Let's not pretend this is going anywhere." She motions between us with a swift flick of her hand. "I know what you're after and, frankly, I'm not giving it up. Not to anyone and especially not to a Navy SEAL who shoots just as precisely with his gun as he does his dick," she says.

I can't help the chuckle that escapes. Humor, innocence, and guarded like Ft. Knox. She smiles over her shoulder as she walks away, her perfect ass moving in the wrong direction.

I only know a few things about this woman, but I'm left with one damn thought: Windsor wins this match, hands down. I rearrange my hard-on for the millionth time in one night. Mother fucker.

Chapter Four

Windsor

I spent Sunday sulking because I didn't pull the damn trigger on the guy at the bar. I had him. I saw it in his eyes. He isn't my type at all. He's dangerous. Breaking hearts is probably one of his perfected skill sets. I should have just taken him home and beaten him at his own game. Sex and skedaddle. Hormones have completely taken over my body since coming in contact with Maverick. Horny doesn't even begin to describe what the mere thought of him does to me. And I didn't even see him with his shirt off!

I can't concentrate on my computer screen in front of me because of the color of the damn numbers in my program. They are like this bluish black color, and I wonder if it's the exact color of his tattoos. I'm sick. I don't even think banging Garrett, the hot CPA in the office next to mine, all lunch hour would work. No. Only a Maverick or someone similar would do for my wanton needs. This is what I get for going years without sex. One sexual laced conversation with a sex God, because I know he is a sex God, and I'm a panting dog. I bet he even knows his effect on women, which makes this all the more horrible. A maybe-solution pops into my mind as I hit speed dial number four.

"Hey, Phillipe. Is Morganna super swamped? I need to talk to her," I say. I hear the hiss of an iron and cover my giggle. He's doing her ironing.

"Of course she's busy, Windsor, but I'll ask if she wants to talk to you if she isn't screaming on her head set." I laugh again. He remains quiet. He isn't joking.

She picks up almost immediately. "Morganna Sterns," she breathes in a huge rush of air. I get up to close my office door as tightly as it will go.

"I need that date you were talking about." I cut right to the chase. No need to mince words or beat around the damn bush. That ship sailed the second Maverick asked for my phone number. "Who were you going to set me up with last night?" *Please be Maverick, please be Maverick.* My silent pleas are freaking pathetic and I inwardly chastise myself.

"Happy Monday to you too, Winnie. Hard up are you?" I hear the smile in her voice. I suddenly know exactly why Morganna is wrapped around Stone's finger if she deals with this insane sex drive just from looking at him.

"Hard up doesn't even begin to cover the bases. Date. Phone number, e-mail address – whatever you have. *Now*!" The phone line she has on hold chirps. I hear papers shuffling.

"Mav Hart is bad news. Stay away from him. I wouldn't fix you up with him unless you were my mortal enemy. He has a really twisted back story. It's not my business to discuss this with you. Just please, accept this warning, Winnie."

My heart sinks and a pit forms in my stomach. It's not like I didn't already know it; it just sucks to hear someone else say it.

"I was going to set you up with Steve. He's a good guy. Maybe a little more tame than some of the others in the rat pack."

Tame. Ugh. I don't want tame. That definitely won't do for what I have in mind: amazing barbarian sex that makes me forget I ever preferred missionary sex with the Nashhole. Who wants eye contact anyway?

"Okay. I'll e-mail him." I scribble down Steve's phone number and e-mail address with half effort, still undecided if I want to date him. Morganna's warning about Maverick was like dumping a huge bucket of ice water on my libido.

"Shut up with your useless drivel and do it!" Morganna yells. "That was to Phillipe, not you, honey."

"Are you always such a bitch to him?" I ask, laughing. It makes me feel a little better knowing Phillipe is having a bad day, too.

"No, only when he questions me," she deadpans. "I'm serious about Maverick, too. He-e…" she trails off.

"He what?"

"Might as well tell you, you'll find out soon enough. He called me this morning trying to get your information. I didn't give it of course. But I'm sure he'll find another way. He's persistent at his worst."

"Oh," I say. I'm sure she knows I'm disappointed, but if she says it's for the best I have to trust her. Especially with something like this—something she deals in. She knows The Guys.

"Thanks, I guess. I'll let you get back to work."

"When he finds you, because I know he will, don't get upset with me when I say 'I told you so'. Gotta go, darlin'." Her accent slips at the end. She was being sincere.

Click. The line is dead.

I scribble doodles all over the notepad with Steve's number. I feel like a traitor because I secretly hope Maverick gets in touch before I make this phone call. Then I won't have to worry about anything except hot sex. Morganna doesn't know that I already know what type of guy he is. I tried the good guy for a long time and it ended up biting me in the ass. A bad guy was exactly what I needed all along. A villain—a nasty one with hot hands and wet lips. I'm not trying to find insta-love, or even insta-lust, even though the last one is probably part of the deal.

A shiver shoots down my spine and my core clenches. It's ten a.m. and I've gotten nothing accomplished. I pick at my barely living desk plant. I dump the remnants of my water bottle onto the soil. "You never had a chance," I whisper to the inanimate object.

"You have two afternoon appointments. New clients. One and Four," Hannah drones through my phone's intercom.

"After lunch? Why one, Hannah?" I had plans to go home for a long lunch and have a long drawn out date with Bob, my battery operated boyfriend. I sigh. "E-mail me the info," I say.

My inbox chimes almost immediately. One is just a tax consult, which is normal and boring. The second email, the one o'clock appointment with T.H., is a full consult. My boss has an asterisk next to the subject line, which means money. Lots of it.

I beep Hannah back. "How much are we talking?"

"No details. He requested you. Even after I told him you prefer morning appointments."

The ad I placed online must be working if I'm getting people requesting me personally. I fought an internal battle after the woman in marketing told me I'd get more business if I posted a photo of myself with the advertisement. Like a freaking personal ad or something. I guess I should thank her if it's actually working. Our accounting firm is large, and there are plenty of other accountants with a lot more experience and with substantially larger resumes. John Nash is also an accountant in this firm. He works a few floors up and I never run into him. I think it's purposeful. I went a little crazy the months, and probably year, after his cheating scandal. My co-workers went out of their way to make sure I'd never see him again. I don't even see Nashhole's car. His parking garage is on the other side of the building.

"Thanks," I yell a little too loudly before shutting off my intercom. I'm intrigued to find out what I'll be working with. Who I'll be working with. The giddy thoughts of advancing because of a large account make me forget why I didn't get anything done all morning. With a new purpose I start plowing through my work, balancing accounts and calling clients. On a roll, I work straight through lunch, clearing my workload so I can leave directly following my four o'clock. It startles me when Hannah's voice echoes in my small office.

"Your one," she stutters. I narrow my eyes at the phone, wondering what the hell is making the iron-willed Hannah fumble words. "Your one is here, Ms. Forbes." Recovered completely. Even addressing me formally in front of clients like our boss requests. I straighten my desk so I don't look like a complete paper slob.

"Send them back, please," I tell her. I comb my fingers through my hair and plaster the fake, friendly smile on my face. The same smile that is on my ad. The one they expect. I'm discovering new levels of vanity I never knew could exist.

All vanity goes directly out the window the second Mr. T.H. enters my office, closing the door behind him.

"Windsor Forbes. You were far easier to track down than you should be," Maverick says. I should be scared because he obviously stalked me. I should be angry that this asshole didn't take no for an answer. I should beep Hannah and tell her to send security up to my office, even though I'm sure the rent-a-cops wouldn't stand a chance against the muscle wall that is Maverick.

But I don't do any of those things. I shake my head out of sheer feminine cattiness. Inside? My stomach is doing flip-flops and my heart is pounding, sending jolts all the way down to my sex. The things that flit through my mind are all lewd. Crass. We are both naked in all of the images. Sweating, skin clapping, hair pulling. I want him. His dimples are out in full force, because I still haven't spoken. He knows what he's doing to my insides.

"T.H.? Well who would have thought," I say, extending my hand to shake his. I'm suddenly a little disappointed it's Maverick when I was expecting to land a huge account. Granted, I will land some other huge object straight between my thighs. He must see the displeasure on my face.

He takes my outstretched hand, shakes it, and then folds his large arms across his chest. "Expecting someone else?" he asks.

"Yes and no. I spoke with Morganna today. She told me you wanted my information." As I say the words, paranoia hits me. Maybe Maverick really does have a lot of money and he does want me to manage it for him. Maybe he's not interested in dating, screwing, insert sex act here, with me. He wants my professional services. I'm not sure what is worse. Not getting a large account or not getting him, Morganna's warnings aside.

"I want your information, huh?" He stalks around my office like a predator. Which is what this man is. Fully. I love it. His eyes heat when he looks me up and down, not trying to hide his appraisal. He drags the office chair that sits in front of my desk next to my seat.

His proximity heats me, wetting my panties and blushing every part of me that isn't covered by clothes. I cross my legs. His unreadable gaze darts to my legs and the black pencil skirt that covers my desire. This much man, and how he affects me, should be illegal.

"Well, you've found me. What can I do for you," I say, glancing down at the paperwork he laid on top of my keyboard, "Mr. Thomas Maverick Hart?" Trying to ignore the way his arm brushes mine, I scan the numbers on the paperwork. The large numbers. Maverick is loaded. Not loaded like a Navy bachelor who has a couple re-enlistment bonuses in his account; he's loaded like a trust fund baby who never has to work a day in his life. I feel his gaze boring into the side of my head as I read. It's unrelenting. I look at him and hold up the top page, pointing at the bottom line.

He shrugs his shoulders and the top of his neck tattoo peeks out of his polo shirt. "Can you help me with it or not? You are a CPA." He rasps my title a little too excitedly.

If this is a ploy to get me to date him, he is sorely mistaken. Money won't win me over. If anything the exact opposite is the case. I know what type of people have this kind of money and I stay away from them. They are the ultimate assholes that don't care about anything except number one. I shudder. Maybe Maverick isn't even worth a one-night stand if he's pushing this in my face on purpose.

He lays his hand on top of mine. "I wanted to see you, Windsor." He says my name and my stomach drops. He might as well have ripped off my clothing, for the reaction it causes in my body. I suck in a determined breath. *Be professional, God dammit.*

"I need to know exactly what you want me to do with this money. We could diversify some of it. Use the bulk of it in a more aggressive nature. You are younger. What rates were you getting before? Do you have any ideas or expectations?" I ask, trying to keep my voice from going all freaking raspy with desire. This might be impossible.

"I have high expectations, Windsor," he says. I want to scream at him to be straight with me. Snatching my hand out of his, I get up and walk to the window overlooking the parking lot of Food Lion. Women juggling kids and groceries distract me.

"Color me stupid. Could you spell it out for me?" I ask without turning around to face him. It's a little better when I don't have to look at him, or know he's in touching distance. I cross my ankles to try to fight the fire between my legs.

"I did my research. I know that you aren't only a CPA. You are also very good at making money for people. I'll up the percentage you make on profits if you go out with me. One date," he says, his voice growing closer as he approaches. I turn around wide-eyed and supremely pissed off.

"Are you seriously trying to buy me? I'm not a prostitute for God's sake!" I scream, and then slam a hand over my mouth, praying Garrett didn't hear my outburst.

Maverick laughs. He has the fucking audacity to laugh at me. He shakes his head.

I interrupt him. "Even though I'll probably get fired for doing this, I'm going to have to say no thank you. You should take your copious amounts of money elsewhere to be managed." My blood is boiling. I can't believe he thought buying me out would be the only way to get a date with me. Walking around him, careful not to brush his arm as I pass, I sit down at my desk. "Did you even think to just ask me out?"

He has the good sense to look mortified. He bites a corner of his lip and blows out a breath. "It didn't cross my mind. I thought it would be much harder than simply asking. You didn't want to give me the time of day Saturday night." He cocks his head to one side. "I figured if I sweetened the deal a little, maybe you'd be more receptive to my advances." Hands in his pockets, he approaches quietly, stealthily. I shuffle his papers on my desk, feeling ill. Ill that I have to send his accounts away and sick because I can't sleep with him. Not after this show of stupidity. Even my libido has IQ standards.

"You know what they say about assuming, I assume? It makes an ass out of you and me. Plus, it would be a conflict of interest if I handled both your money and your…" I trail off, and let him assume whatever he wants. He's good with that.

Now he looks really pissed off. Dragging a hand through his longish brown hair, he continues his head shaking.

"I'm sure you have plenty of options, especially given your financial situation. You don't want to date me," I tell him, hoping to make him feel better about my rejection. Because I'm insane and I honestly feel bad because he thought this would work. Women don't tell him no. "I'm all messed up. Ex-fiancé drama and all. Add in your womanizing and it's a recipe for disaster," I admit. I'm honest even though he doesn't deserve my honesty, and even though my crazy heartbeat and the throbbing between my legs tell a different story.

"I'm sorry if I offended you. You're good. I did my research. I want you on my accounts. No date. I never should have tried that tactic," he says, looking remorseful. He doesn't even meet my eyes. He looks down at the floor as he speaks.

Morganna's words bounce around in my head. *Bad news, Winnie. Bad news.* I can't even help it. I'm still inclined to throw myself at him. Thank God my brain speaks before my body does.

"My associate, Garrett, will be happy to manage your accounts," I say. Garrett will be more than pleased to have this pushed his way. I'll have to make up some lie about not being able to comfortably deal with the amount, because I sure as shit can't tell him the real reason I don't want to deal with the money or T.H. I smile. "He's good. Just as good as me, I assure you."

Dimples flash at me. They look less mouthwatering and a little more menacing. Eyes narrowed he asks, "That's two no's then?"

"Yes," I tell him as I extend his paperwork out to him. "I have an afternoon appointment. I appreciate *all* of your interest. Garrett's office is out my door, first door on the left." I take one more look at the assets and liabilities on the page before he takes it from my hand and strides out of the door like a freaking Viking called to war.

I should have just accepted the date, because now I feel like all I managed to do is poke a grizzly with a long stick. I won't be able to find that long of a stick next time. I don't want Steve. I don't want anyone that will make me think of Maverick. I need to get him out of my system…and fast.

*****

Maverick

She sent me away like a diseased leper. Not only that, but she did it easily. She didn't even consider fucking me, even when she saw the money. No dollar signs flashed in her eyes like a normal woman. No. She said "No." And she even tried to make me feel better about her rejection, doling out some story about how messed up she is.

I passed desperate asshole status a long time ago. Hanging out in this level of embarrassment is new. I had no intention of going to visit Garth's office. I'm so fucking pissed off and frustrated. To top it off, my dick is hard. It didn't get the rejection memo yet. The tight skirt, the flawless skin in daylight, the blue eyes that show every emotion she has. If I saw another guy I'd probably end up doing something stupid, breaking something or saying something really incriminating.

It took more self control than I knew I possessed to walk out of that woman's office without saying anything else, or just bending her over the desk and fucking her senseless. This pit in my stomach would be gone if that had happened. Of course it wouldn't be that easy, though. The challenge to bag her while she screams my name is now the only thing that consumes my thoughts.

A new layer to the game surfaces—I want her to care about me. I want her to give a shit. I want the very thought of my absence to cause her physical pain.

"You know what?" I whisper to myself as I pass Garth's office. "What the fuck. Why not?"

I turn around and grip the doorknob to his office and blast inside. I cock my head to the side at Garth's startled appearance. He holds his desk phone to his ear.

"Uhh," he says into the receiver, "he just got here." He pauses again as he listens to the female voice on the other end, a voice that can only be Windsor's. Garth holds up a finger in the air. Seriously? This little prick is telling me to wait? "Sure, Win. Drinks sound good. Tonight?"

Windsor shoots me down and asks this asshole out? Not even minutes after I leave. *Win?* He uses a nickname, too and it sounds intimate and familiar. I want to crack his skull against a wall. I want to use her nickname.

Reel it in, Mav. Why do I care what he calls her? I don't give a shit. Garth is fucking with my game. That's why it pisses me off. That's it. Nothing else.

"Captain's at 8 o'clock," he whispers, probably trying to be discreet because I'm staring him down. He hangs up the phone and smiles a goofy fucking smile. Because Windsor asked him out. I'd have that smile if she said yes to me. Now, I get to see what it looks like first hand.

"Ms. Forbes said you'd be coming over," he says.

Now she's Ms. Forbes. Fucking convenient. My hands are shaking at my sides. I can't control them. When I hear the papers I still carry rustle, I know I have to get the fuck out of here before I explode. I want a drink.

No you don't.

I need to fuck something. I know getting laid won't even appease me. The game is now fucking with my head and my damn dick. I realize I haven't said anything to this pansy prick.

"I already got everything I need," I say, confusing him. I turn around and blaze out of the stifling office building as quickly as I can. I slink a leg over to mount my motorcycle, the only thing I'll get between my thighs today, and shake my head. This whole afternoon is shot to shit. The rumble of the engine does little to soothe me, so I push the accelerator faster, urging it to take me where I need to go.

Captain's at 8 o'clock.

Chapter Five

Maverick

"Just screw her, dude. It's easy. Pull the thong down or rip it off and shove your dick in there and bump it around. Ahh yeah," Stone says.

Soaping up my hair I let a chuckle slip. We're in the showers after a long ass workout. I hit it hard. My shoulders are sore and no matter how long I stand in the lukewarm water, my skin burns. Images of Morganna and her thong flit through my head and I wince a little. Won't be telling Stone that. Windsor wasn't at Captain's when I casually stopped by the night of her date with Garth. Her absence only made me think she was probably screwing him at home in her bed. The thought of him in her bed enraged me. If I couldn't have her, I didn't want anyone else to either.

"Why are you doing this to yourself? The Maverick fuck club is extensive. Bag one of your many admirers.

Don't get bent dicked about the one who won't have you."

After the no-show date I fucked four girls this week, but I didn't tell Stone that. I wanted to prove to myself and to Windsor that I was fine. That it didn't matter what game I was playing, I still had *it*. Each chick was equally excited to be worked over and I just didn't care. I wasn't into it. I got off…barely with the last one.

You know what I had to think of to get there? Blue Eyes on her knees, whale eyeing me, lips wrapped around the base of my cock, while she fingered herself and hummed my name. I tossed the girl out of my hotel room the second I ripped the condom off my dick, so disturbed with the mental image of Windsor. I jacked off three more times that night to the same mental image, or some variation. Always Windsor. Always saying my name. Always her hands on me. I choke on the mental image now.

I shut off the water and wrap a towel on my hips, before I pop wood and have to ante up my mental images of Windsor, because I'd have to offer up something to Stone as explanation. "I need to talk to her. I just need to talk to her," I say. I half hope he doesn't hear me sounding like such a pussy. I already have her cell number and I've almost dialed it a few times, but I haven't. I'm stronger than that. Or so I've told myself.

It's Saturday morning and I haven't seen her face, in person, since Monday. I paused the game for the week so I could try to figure out what exactly I wanted or needed from her. Why the game? What was it about her? Could I fuck someone else and get over her? When the last one didn't work, I knew I had to try to see where this went. I have to fucking date Windsor on the regular. Try to get to know her and do my best to find something wrong with her—something really awful that I can't stand. Then she won't be this unobtainable dick-sucking queen. She'll just be another bag I can forget.

Stone groans behind me, still in the shower. "Morg will fucking kill me if I tell you this. Look," he says.

I turn. My eyes are drawn down because he has his dick and balls tucked between his legs. His pubes are the only thing visible. It's called *the goat*. The fucking asshole got me. He laughs loudly. I meet his eyes, smiling, and shake my head. I'm going to belt buckle that son of a bitch the next chance I get. He knows it, so he makes the most of his jab.

"Do you want to fuck me, Mavvy? My vagina is so tight, it's like a magic twat or a vice grip wormhole," he says in a high, fake girl voice. "I walk dogs on Saturday mornings at 10 on the beach in front of the Hilton." He rubs both of his hands over his large pectorals and cups them, circling his damn nipples. His voice sounds like a fucking transvestite with throat cancer. "Maybe you can come make me into a sugar cookie?" Stone purrs.

That's it. I lunge forward and lay a fist into his stomach and retreat quickly. He curls into himself, his shoulder hitting the back of the shower room wall, laughing through gasping breaths.

"You're a fucktard, Stone. If you wanted to homie glide, all you had to do was ask," I say. I don't really want his dick gliding between my butt cheeks, but I'd do almost anything else for him. He's my bro. He's got my back always. Down range and home and pretty much anywhere else. He's known me my whole life. Not only do we share the same legal first name, Thomas, but I dealt with his vagina dick way before we decided to be professional badasses. It's why I would do anything for him. We went through BUD/s and SEAL qualification training together; bitching and moaning about night sweats and the inability to sleep, and how Hell Week was for pussies. Which it wasn't; it was torture, but we'd never say that to each other. We are the same—him and I, strong for each other and strong for our teammates. You fuck with him and you are automatically fucking with me. It's like that with all my brothers. They are the closest things to family I've ever really had.

My real family only gave me a trust fund and a nice pat on the ass out the door because I wasn't like them. I would never be like them. Of course I appreciate the money; it affords me to do whatever the fuck I want. I can follow my dreams. I can kick ass for a living.

The money doesn't make Henry and Barbara Hart my family, though. It makes them large donating entities to fund my fucking. Because I never bag girls at my house. Ever. Hotels are my first choice and their place comes in second. My house is too personal, says too much about me. I don't want them to know anything about me.

Except that my dick is hard and they should do something about it.

Cruel? Yes. The way my parents raised me facilitated that, but the SEAL Teams are where I found the only family I felt like keeping. That's what matters.

I grab some of my shit and get dressed.

"Thanks for the info, asshole," I throw over my shoulder as I bust out of the locker room. I have new plans this Saturday morning.

*****

I lean against the Neptune statue like a real fucking creeper. The statue is a beacon. If you're at the beach, you can tell someone your location by using Neptune. Today though? I'm hiding behind the damn thing so I can watch Windsor without her knowing. Not yet, at least. I just want to see my prey in her natural habitat—before she feels threatened by a predator. I see her in the sand by the water.

Windsor is wearing the tiniest, tight, black shorts possible. They are made of that stretchy shit. I wouldn't even have to take them off to fuck her; I could just yank them to the side. Her smooth legs are miles long. I picture them wrapping around my face and my dick gets hard. Her body is so damn fuckable. She is in shape, but not in the gross Crossfit-crossover man way that so many women seem to think looks good. Windsor has curves. Banging fucking curves. She holds a pair of running sneakers in one hand and a leash in the other. At the end of that leash is a huge German Shepherd. I recognize the dog and smile. This is going to be too easy. She pets his head and lets it lick her in the face. I grimace. She stoops down to pay the dog more attention and I figure it's show time.

The dog sees me coming, but she doesn't. "Steh," pronounced shtay, I command using a rough voice. Windsor startles, falling back on her ass. The dog? Well he stops what he's doing and looks at me, ears down, ready to obey. "Sitz," I growl. Her head swivels the second she realizes what's going on. The dog sits, completely submissive to my German commands. This dog works with us, here and overseas. I only know a few simple commands, because it isn't my job, but I know it'll be enough to impress her. I extend my hand down to her and the dick sucking, doe eyed image pops into my head. Fuck. She wraps her hand in mine and pulls herself up, dusting off her shorts that look like panties. If I can't pull my head out of my dick I'm going to be in trouble. *Date her. Get a date with her.* Reminding myself of the ultimate goal, I swallow my fucking pride.

"What are you doing here? I mean, I guess I shouldn't be that surprised," Windsor says, staring at the dog instead of looking at me. This woman infuriates me. I don't even get eye contact, but Garrett gets a date. What the fuck does that douche have that I don't?

Since I can't answer her question without diming out Stone, I ignore it. I pet the dog on the head, just so I can brush her with my arm. She twists out of my way, trying to play it off by rearranging the leash. I make her squirm. It gives me a small amount of hope. I push up my *Gatorz* sunglasses so they rest on my forehead. I'm about to go 100 percent charming-panties-off on her.

"How was your week, Windsor?" I ask, making sure to draw out *Windsor*. At her name her head snaps up finally, looking at me and really seeing me. I lick my lips. I smile, tilting my head in question. Glossing over our meeting in her office seems a good idea. I don't want to remind her of that asshole move. It still embarrasses me.

"It was fine. Normal, really." She looks down at the dog, still alert, awaiting his next command, and then looks back at me. "Do you want to *walk* with me?"

I can't believe my fucking ears. She narrows her eyes, but she looks hesitant and maybe a little scared. Of what? Does she think I'll turn her down? I am so fucking thrilled right now that it scares me. I feel my adrenaline spike like it does when I'm about to shoot something or jump out of a damn plane. This feeling that I have right now is what I live for. What I thrive on. Except the origin of it now makes me very fucking wary. *Play it cool. Be smooth, you fucker.*

"I'm walking him for one of my friends. I didn't realize he belonged to *you guys*," she says. Her voice goes a little caustic at the end.

I nod my head. Lowering my voice I say, "Fuss," pronounced Fooss. The dog immediately heels and we start walking down the beach. I take the leash out of her hand. She looks at me sideways, very quickly, but doesn't object. I tap my sunglasses so they fall back over my eyes. "I missed you this week," I say. As the words pass my lips I look around to make sure no one else heard me. She stops walking and faces me front on.

Crossing her arms under her perfect tits, she fixes me with an angry glare. "Seriously? You missed me? You offer me a cool million for a date and then don't call me all week? For someone who wanted something so badly, your follow through sucks."

This is why I need my sunglasses on. We have a joke about the huge, fucking ugly sunglasses chicks wear in San Diego. SCUBS. Southern California Ugly Blockers. My sunglasses have a different acronym. LB. Lie Blockers.

I grin. "I needed time to reassess. I made a huge mistake. I want to get to know you." I reach out and hold the side of her face in my hand. So fucking soft—perfect. I'm obsessed with the game. It's like a drug. "Go on a date with me. Tonight," I plead.

I see my touch affecting her. Her breathing speeds up. Her cheeks flush. A few more seconds and I'd be able to smell her wet pussy. For me. Only me. The dog yanks on the leash, but I don't dare break eye contact. I see the second she decides. It flickers in her blue eyes. With her unspoken *yes* I see the whole thing play out. A date. Fucking like rabbits in a couple different hotel rooms, because once probably won't be enough, and then tossing her away like empty casing. Game. Set. Match.

"One date. One date. Dammit. Morganna is going to kill me. You realize that right?" she asks, turning from me to face the ocean. I watch her brown hair blow to the side, and then let my gaze fall to her tight, round ass. Maybe I'll need a few hotel rooms. "Why are you so bad, Maverick. Why?" She turns around, hands on her hips and hurt in her eyes. "I won't sleep with you. Just a date."

It even sounds like a lie to me. I have to shift my over excitable dick. Fumbling for her phone in her jacket she pulls it out and dials, ignoring me completely.

"I need to talk to Morg," she barks, turning to block the phone from the wind. My heart picks up. She said yes, and all my plans are about to get crushed by the ball-busting Morganna.

"I'm standing here on the beach with Maverick, who conveniently knew where I'd be walking the dog, and he asked me on a date. Tell me the worst thing about him. Right now, or I'm going on a date with him," she says, looking right into my eyes. I stop breathing. Morganna knows all my dirty secrets. I snatch the phone from Windsor.

"Hey Morg. This isn't like that. I want to get to know her. Just a date...nothing more," I promise. Windsor looks shocked, her hand still up where the phone was just moments before.

"I swear to god I'll eat your balls for dinner if you fuck with her, Maverick," Morganna says. She sounds exasperated. I can't blame her, really. She knows me better than any woman because of Stone. She didn't have a choice in the matter. Lucky bitch.

"I like her," I return. I smile so wide my face hurts, when Windsor's eyes bug out of her fucking head.

"Bullshit," Morganna whispers. The line goes dead.

"Great. Thanks, Morg," I say, then hand the phone back to Blue Eyes. She still looks shocked when she grabs the phone from me.

"Morganna is fine with a date," I say, already planning to call Stone to have him control his wife for a few days while I lure Windsor into my web. I can't have anyone else influencing her decisions except me. I want her to only see me. Eat me. Breathe me. Drink me. I want to consume Windsor Forbes.

"Looks like you have a date, then," she says, breaking me from my triple X visions. She grabs the leash from my hands. Indecision lights her face for a second. She pulls her hair to one side using her free hand. The rush and adrenaline are still going strong, pumping through my veins thicker than blood. I never feel like this about a girl, not even when I'm pumping inside them about to blow my load.

"The only man I ever loved cheated on me. I found out about his two-year long affair while I was trying on my wedding dress for the final time. I don't want you to feel sorry for me." She pauses and shakes her head. "I just want you to know so you don't expect much from me," she says.

Adrenaline crash. Baseline. Some dickhead had her perfection almost locked down and he fucked it up? I wouldn't believe it if she hadn't said it. Her blue eyes break a little as she admits it. This is going to be way more complicated than I thought. In fact, I feel fucking sick. I want to kill the guy for doing that to her, making her eyes look so sad. In the same breath, I don't want to care, but I do.

I also want to kick my own ass because what I want to do to her is not much better. I wince a little when she starts walking away. I haven't even responded. I can't. What lie would I counter to that blatant honesty? I'm going to have to open up to her completely if I'm going to gain any headway. I should walk the hell away. Turn around now before I fuck her up even more. I can't though. I'm a lot of things and a quitter isn't one of them.

"Fooss," she says to the dog with a smile on her face. "Pick me up at seven," she hesitates, "I'm sure you know where I live."

I do. I watch her walk for a little while and I'm so pissed off. At whatever this chick is making me feel. Because for a small, fucking second I think I want Windsor Forbes to consume me right back.

Chapter Six

Windsor

"You're just going to bang Benji all night anyway. Why do you care if I have a date?" I ask Gretchen. She's standing in my bedroom wearing black lingerie and brandishing a riding crop. She whips the foot of my sleigh bed. She finally gave Benji the time of day. And night. And every other time they are free and aren't working. I'm happy for her, if not a touch jealous of all the sexual attention she's been getting.

"Let's get this straight. I was okay with you banging Mr. Sexy Badass. Like a one night stand. I did not say you should go on a date with him. You saw him." She fixes me with her gaze after the crack of the leather ceases. "He is not the dating kind of guy. He's the guy you do anal with because you plan to leave after you bang him and never see him again. Not exactly the bring home to mom type." She's right.

"Good thing I don't bring anyone home to meet my mom then, huh?" I don't even visit her. It's been so long since I've seen her, I'd be meeting her for the first time again. My inability to lock up a husband really pissed her off. Gretchen looks a little embarrassed, but I don't blame her for the mom comment. Mom comments are normal for most healthy adults. Unfortunately, I don't fall into that category.

The doorbell rings saving me from Gretchen's pity party. I rush out of my room to get the door, slinging my high heels on as I go. "Get out of my room," I yell over my shoulder. She shoots me a dirty glare and disappears down the hallway. Nervousness hits me in spades.

This is the first date I've been on in a long time. I canceled my drink date with Garrett last minute. Like so last minute that he's still pissed off at me. I tried to make amends, but his butt hurt over the flaky date night combined with the fact that neither of us landed Maverick's account mixed like oil and water.

I yank open the door expecting to be knocked flat on my ass. "You're early," I admonish. I don't plan to make anything easy for Maverick. Everything in his life seems easy. He wants a date. I'll give him a date, but that's it. He thrusts a small bouquet of flowers into my hand.

"For you," Maverick says, peeking into the condo, gaze darting around like he's taking inventory.

When his gaze lands on me, he smiles. Dimples. Scruffy jaw. Just a date may prove to be harder than I thought.

I wedge the flowers into a vase on the entryway table that already contains a bouquet from Benji. He looks a little put off at the placement of his gift. "Thanks, they're pretty. Ready to go?" I glance over my shoulder hoping Mistress Gretchen doesn't show her face…or weapons.

"You look absolutely stunning tonight, Windsor. I like your dress."

God, I hate when he uses my name. It does things to every part of my body, mostly everything below my belly button. I smooth the yellow dress down and smile. It took me a while to decide on something that said "I like you and I want to have sex with you, but it's not going to happen."

"My dress thanks you," I say, shutting the door behind us. I hear the tail end of a whip cracking and have to stifle a laugh.

"What was that?" Maverick asks, eyebrows raised, looking back at my door.

I pull his hand to lead him toward the exit. "Just your warning," I admit. He smells so delicious now that we're in such close proximity that it makes my mouth water.

"I figured I shouldn't bring my bike tonight. Although, it would have been the highlight of my week to see you get on it. In that dress," he whispers in my ear, and goose bumps prickle all over my damn body. He nods to his car. Which is a completely awesome, obviously old, and totally refurbished Chevelle. The paint is a deep blue and the racing stripe that spans the car is a light silver. The car is as hot as the owner.

"Nice car," I tell him, ignoring the comment about the highlight of his week. Hardly. I bet he's seen multiple panties this week. His answering smile is, as always, breathtaking. I'm glad nothing covers his eyes tonight. I want to see all of him.

He opens the door for me and I slink down into the buttery leather. Watching him walk in front of the car, I fight the urge to tear off my dress and have my way with him, right here, in my parking lot like a dirty hooker. So I focus on my surroundings instead. His car is pristine on the inside—insanely clean and meticulously kept. I assume when you have a car this nice, it's what you do. Or pay someone to do it for you is likely the case with Maverick.

I pull down the visor to use the mirror, and I sense his eyes on me, watching my every move. I brush at a loose eyelash and turn to him. "Where are we going? I guess I should have asked earlier, before I dressed up."

"We're going to Swordfish. You look perfect," he says. Not perfect. Overdressed. His dark green striped shirt is buttoned almost all the way up, concealing his tattoos. The sleeves aren't rolled up either, so nothing shows there either. I'm momentarily disappointed. I may not be able to sample this perfect piece of trouble, but I really wanted to ogle him.

He keeps his eyes on the road, completely aware of everything going on while he drives. I've never seen anyone so focused while doing twenty-five on a residential road. "I want to apologize for the day in your office. I want to start over. Starting tonight," he says.

His cell lights up, but he doesn't make a reach for it. I can't help but see Jessica's green text bubble flashing in the center cup holder. Who doesn't have an iPhone? Ugly jealousy rears and I tell myself only a horrible person would read the text, so I don't. Though If I read more texts, I would have known about Nashhole's affair. It was right under my freaking nose. I think he got off on parading it around without me discovering it.

"I'm okay with that," I say, leaning toward him. "I'm going to completely ignore all of Morganna's warnings and have a nice date with you. Because she has me thinking you're a crazy prick. I really just want to walk into her office and stick my tongue out and tell her I'm still alive, and you weren't a complete Neanderthal—which you do kind of look like. So, please don't disappoint me. Let me win this round with her," I ramble. "One condition though."

"Anything," he says.

"Forget what I said on the beach today about the Nashhole, okay? I feel like by telling you, it gives him power over me...still," I admit, trying to keep my voice strong, even though the mere thought of my former life makes me feel weak. "I'm embarrassed I told a complete stranger my woes." He laughs and the sound makes me jump a little.

"What exactly is a Nashhole?" I forget normal people don't know what a Nashhole is.

"Sorry, yeah. That's my ex-fiancé's name. Not really. It's John Nash, but Nashhole fits him a little better," I confess. His eyebrows scrunch together, and I regret saying his full name. "I really don't want to talk about it anymore. We're both starting over tonight. I'll pretend you didn't say crude things at the bar...among other things, and you'll forget I've lost the ability to love anything except numbers and my routine." Another rumble of laughter buzzes around me, consuming the entire car. His voice...his laugh is like a stick of dynamite to my willpower.

We pull into valet parking and he finally grabs his over-worked cell, but he doesn't look at it. He slips it into his pocket instead. I shouldn't give a shit, but I want to see his face when he sees the text. I'm sure it's one of his many *call* girls. The specific, non-enviable term is *frog hog*. Women that only have sex with SEALs.

"I can agree with that. Wait here," he says getting out of the car. I see him take a huge breath as he slams the door and approaches the teenager eye fucking the Chevelle. The boy has his hand out waiting for the keys. I don't even think he's seen the Maverick wall yet. A quick exchange that leaves the teen completely somber finishes, and Maverick opens my door and offers his huge hand.

I'm impressed with his manners. Not that I was expecting him to club me over the head and drag me into his cave, but it's almost like he has a refined touch that I never expected to find in a man...a SEAL, like him. He doesn't let go of my hand as we walk in, or when we take a seat at a small candlelit table. I narrow my eyes and peek at him sideways as we settle in. I see his jaw work as he surveys the restaurant around us. His eyes dart around, but when his gaze lands on mine, he smiles.

"The room has been mentally cleared?" I joke. I've seen all the movies about SEALs. Living in Virginia Beach, I'm surrounded by the allure of it. I've picked up some of the terminology…and I might have Google searched just because I was curious. It garners a small smile. No more SEAL terms. Check.

"Tell me about yourself. Tell me something no one else knows," he says. Wow. Cutting to the damn chase, was he? I shouldn't balk, I wanted this—his interest in me…with clothes on, but I'm not prepared.

His lips are pursed completely. It's like he has major issues even asking me personal details. It's not his regular M.O., I realize. "There isn't much that everyone doesn't know about me. It's sort of obvious…you know, you probably already know the worst," I pause. "I'll tell you some important things though."

He glances over my shoulder. "Perfect. Let's hear it."

"I come from a small town in Georgia. Which is where I met Morganna in college. I like dolphins and the beach, which is why I moved to Virginia Beach. I prefer animals to people, because you can always trust them without question. I go to the animal shelter at least once a month and can't take home a puppy because the uncalculated risks are way too high," I ramble, taking a sip of my wine that just arrived. "Running is my favorite form of exercise, and I hate gyms and gym rats with a passion. Everything outdoors is my jam. I'm probably the only person that has a classic rock station and a 90's one hit wonders station on my Pandora. Gretchen is probably banging Benji reverse cowgirl on my bed as we speak," I admit, take a deep breath, and continue, "I believe in romance and one true loves despite everything I've been through."

Maverick wears a huge goofy grin when I finally look his direction. I had to avert my gaze to be able to admit these things.

Time passes as we chat about everything I just rambled on about. He seems interested in every aspect of my life, like a detective trying to gain as many details about it as he can. When it gets to the awkward level, I switch the focus off myself…or try.

"Now, you tell me about you," I demand, looking him straight in the eye.

He rubs his hands together, and the image is so youthful that it actually takes me back a little. "Not yet. Speed round. I ask a question and you give me a one word answer," he growls. With his playful eyes and dimples wreaking havoc on my entire body, there is no way I'll say no.

"Go," I say, smiling.

"First thought that came to mind when you saw me at the bar." I can't control my mouth. It pops open in surprise and I start to stutter, but he silences me with a swift shake of his head.

"One word, Windsor," he says, leaning toward me. His delicious smelling cologne trickles into my senses.

"Trouble."

He pauses, but his poker face is tight, unreadable. "Second thought after that one."

I want to say "bad news" in one word.

"Stop thinking so much. One word. It's easy," he says.

"Predator," I whisper. I know he hears me because that wild smile licks up and I automatically retreat into myself a little. He looks exactly like a predator should look. It should warn me off or send me running with my tail between my legs, but it doesn't.

"Third thing." He's fishing. The almighty Maverick Hart is fishing for something. I grin a little.

"Hot," I admit, trying to keep the blush from my face. I already know what I'm going to say if he asks for a fourth. "But that doesn't negate predator. That came before."

"Way more than one word," he says. "Number three is always number one. You lied." I fold my arms across my chest.

"How do you know that?"

"I have my ways. You'll just have to trust me." It's something in the way he says it, but I do.

"You're wrong. I mean yes, I did lie. Number three wasn't the first thing I thought when I saw you," I tell him. I take a deep breath and get ready to shock the hell out of him. He folds his hands on the table in front of him and waits expectantly. Our food came during one of the lulls, so I shove some vegetables around my plate.

"Go ahead. First word you thought when you saw me."

I meet his hazel eyes full on and say, "Wet."

He doesn't even look surprised. He smiles at me, but this time it's different, calculated. It's a half smile, one side pulling up more than the other. One dimple. He nods his head a couple times and I swear between those two things alone, I am actually wet right now. I'm also blushing and totally embarrassed.

"Someone spilled a drink on my shoe…remember? Literally, I was wet," I say. His lips press into a firm line, but his eyes are still amused. Thankfully, I remember that part of the night to fall back on. "I want to know about you. You've already accrued enough information to stalk me for the rest of my life." His gaze darts behind my shoulder again, but this time I turn around to see what has his attention. A massive guy, who could only be one of *The Guys*, is wobbling, very confidently, from the bar to our table.

"Wining, dining, and then sixty-nining? That's not your style, buddy. Introduce me to your friend," the guy says, as he eye fucks every corner of my face and body in the most uncomfortable way possible. He's good looking, but not nearly appealing as the guy sitting next to me.

"Get the fuck out, Steve," Maverick says. "Go back to the bar." He doesn't tell the guy my name. Shit. This is the guy Morganna is trying to set me up with. I'm uncomfortable in the worst kind of way.

"Hey darlin', you're hot with a rockin' body. Come find me when you want a real man," Steve says. Maverick makes some inarticulate noise from behind me. Morganna is going to hear a rash of shit from me the next time we speak. This guy is totally skeevy. Worse yet, he thinks I'm a freaking *frog hog*. "See ya buddy," Steve says as he ambles back to the bar.

I am absolutely mortified when I see a bleached blonde girl grab his crotch and smile. She. Touched. His. Dick. In. Public. When I finally turn back to Maverick, I'm not sure if I'm mad, sad, or thankful he didn't mention my name. He has his head in his hands.

"Jesus Christ, Maverick. Who the fuck are you? I know what you do, but honestly if that," I wave my hand over to Steve and his public mauling, and then gesture to myself, "is what you want or expect from me, then you have the wrong girl." I shut my mouth and refuse to say anything further. This is his life, he can do whatever he wants. I am the variable for tonight. "Just one date," I remind myself out loud.

He takes my hand, swallows hard and sighs. "Please, forgive me for that. He's a real jackass. I'm sure he didn't realize I was on a real date," he says, defending the caveman.

"What the freak is a real date?" Now, I'm mad. I've settled for mad. I want to say anything to make him angry, too. "I have that guy's phone number. Morganna has been trying to set me up with him!" I point at Steve without looking back, because the sight nauseates me. Maverick's eyes widen a little. I swallow the rest of my wine in a large gulp and stand. He just looks at me from his seat, his gorgeous eyes lingering on my body for a touch longer than I'm comfortable with.

He doesn't stand. He takes another bite off his plate. "You can't go out with him. You know that, right?"

"Excuse me? I can go out with anyone I please. Maybe a public show of sex is exactly what I need to get my head straight," I say, pushing in my chair, making it obvious I'm ready to leave. He sips his water and looks at me over the rim of his glass. When he doesn't say anything I tell him, "At least I know what he wants from me. That's more than I can say about you, Mr. T. H."

For the very first time, his tough guy front fades. He actually looks a little hurt. It disappears a second later as he brings the cloth napkin across his mouth, wiping away any trace of emotion. He stands up, places some cash on the table, and tucks his chair in. The quickest dinner on planet earth just took place.

"Thank you for dinner, Maverick," I nearly spit, a fake smile plastered on my face. If my venom affects him, he doesn't let me know. He does grab my hand unexpectedly and leads me from the restaurant. The valet boy scurries when he sees us exit the building.

"I'm sorry again. I never should have brought you here," he says, confusing the hell out of me. I'm offended, my blood boils. I feel hot, and not in the fun kind of way that he had me feeling on the way here.

"I'm sorry you brought me out, too. I'm obviously more of an idiot than I previously thought. I deserve this."

He just shakes his head, not even attempting to correct what I'm inferring. So, he's sorry he took me out. Everything that means crushes me at once. When he opens the door for me, I honestly consider asking the valet boy for a ride home. Surely, he wouldn't turn me down. Maverick's eyes look sad, and it's the solitary reason I get in. Like maybe he's just as dejected as I feel, though I don't see how that's possible.

The silent drive to my condo is awkward. I watch his phone pop up with a zillion text messages in the cup holder between us. Again, he doesn't even glance at it. I wonder how many messages he got while we were at dinner. The thought sickens me. I never should have assumed this would be a *real* date. I never should have told him anything about myself. But, what the hell, he doesn't give a shit about me. When he makes a move to get out of the car when we arrive at my condo, I hold my hand out to stop him.

"I'm perfectly capable of walking myself to the door. I wouldn't want you to regret that, too. I'm sure you have a lot of texting and calling to catch up on anyway," I tell him, motioning to the glowing iPhone in between us. I chance a stealthy look at his face. He is pissed off. Angry doesn't even begin to cover it. I'm glad.

He picks up the phone and shakes it side to side. "This? This is what you're worried about? The fucking electronic device full of random women and faces that mean nothing to me?" Rolling down the manual car window, he throws the phone across the parking lot. It hits a telephone pole and pieces scatter everywhere. "I don't give a shit about those texts or the phone calls." He runs a hand through his hair and pulls on the tips before releasing them. Throwing his big hand out, he motions to me. "You are the one sitting in my car, Windsor. Women don't sit in my car. You are the one I wanted to take out to dinner. Even as fucking disastrous as it was…I don't see anyone else sitting here, but you. Do you?"

I stare at him wide-eyed in disbelief. I'd be lying if I said I wasn't scared down to my bones. Maverick flying off the handle is terrifying.

When he realizes I'm not going to speak, he continues. "I don't regret taking you out. I regret that Steve made you upset. I regret that I took you somewhere where my friends might be. In all honesty, I regret the moment I ever laid eyes on you." The gasp that fills the car is my own. The nice things he says are buried deep in the ground after utters his last sentence.

"In all honesty," I use his words, "I regret the fucking moment you took your first breath." I exit the car and don't look back. The meanest thing I've ever said was directed at a person I barely know. It feels good. It feels bad. It feels like I wasted my whole night on a crapshoot. At least maybe I'll be able to forget about him and his body. I'll even tell Morganna she was right. I'm *that* relieved it's over.

I hear his car door slam and then muttered profanities under his breath. He catches up to me fast. Too fast. He grabs my arm to spin me around.

"You didn't let me finish," he breathes.

"No, I finished for you."

"I regret the moment I laid eyes on you because you ruined everything, Windsor." His grip lightens on my arm.

"That's so much better, Maverick. Really," I say, my anger wearing off and pure annoyance blistering to the surface. I'm annoyed that his touch is warm, and his words are confusing. I'm annoyed with myself that I can't just walk away.

"I want you," he says. "You said you didn't know what I wanted from you. I'm telling you. I want you. I want you to be mine. That's all I know for sure."

I bite my lip and shake my head. "Unbelievable. I need a night to sleep on this epiphany of yours. The hot and colds are almost too much for me to keep up with," I admit, still shaking my head. Denial. He's said the words. Some part of me wants to believe them, but the skeptical part of my brain whispers other things.

He brushes a strand of hair away from my face and cups my bare shoulder with his other hand. The magic shivers start again. He leans down and I have to work at controlling my shaking body. *He's going to kiss me. He's going to kiss me.* He swallows and the tattoo on his neck dances. I want to lick it. The desire is back in spades. I tilt my chin up, waiting.

And he hugs me. He gives me the awkward freaking hug. The one I give my boss when she gives me a gift card to Starbucks on my birthday. When he leans back, the one-dimpled smile is on his face. Even though I'm still mentally sorting out *the hug,* I want to lick that, too.

"I'll call you. Bye, Windsor," he says. It's okay for him to fuck my name with his voice, but he definitely doesn't want to have sex with me tonight. I am seriously in need of my therapist.

I watch him walk back to his car, which is still running, and try to decipher the Maverick code. I can't. I probably won't ever be able to. When I enter the condo I come to the conclusion that with a man like Maverick, you don't try to decipher, you just ride the waves as they come and hope like hell you can hold on tight enough to enjoy the ride— or at the very least prevent yourself from drowning.

As I try to fall asleep several agonizing hours later, my phone chimes with a new text.

Are you awake? I got a new phone and number. It's miraculously silent.

I stare at it blindly, trying to decide how best to respond.

I type back, *I wish my head were as silent as your phone.*

A second later. *Go out with me tomorrow. All day. I'll pick you up at 9.*

Only if you promise not to awkward hug me ever again.

Chapter Seven

Maverick

I've killed men before. I watch their heads explode through the scope of my gun. I hate to break it to you, but it's nothing like how it happens in *Call of Duty*. Blood sprays like a halo of red and then nothing. The crackle of life that hums in the air gets a little duller. Less life exists in the space surrounding me than it did only moments before. I don't know how I can tell; it's just like breathing, but death really is another sense.

After that trigger pull I feel release and a huge sense of accomplishment. After years and years of practicing, I get to do exactly what the Navy trained me to do. Of course directly following, I question my fucking sanity for the exaltation that comes with a snuffed life. It's not about whom you kill. It's about what you save. My brothers are beside me—like they always are, chasing down the same sense of enlivenment that only comes from this line of work. If the monsters on the other side of the scope don't die, one of my brothers could. Or worse, an innocent.

Windsor is an innocent. She is so good that the opposite sense of death has reared its head. I have the urge to protect her. I want to protect her from all the bad around us. I get so caught up in her good and in the way she makes me feel that I forget that the main thing I should protect her from—that she should be fearful of—is myself.

I've made the decision to try to be with her…whatever that really means. There isn't another option. I can't think of anything else. When I close my eyes I see huge blue eyes, her cheekbones, her white smile. Oh, I still think of her sucking and fucking, but now it's more. Way more. I'm worried if I don't get whatever the fuck this is out of my system before deployment, I might not be as focused as I need to be. I'm losing my normal precision control and it scares the shit out of me. I'm afraid to kiss her because I'm afraid to fuck her because I'm afraid of what that will mean. I know enough to know I can't fuck Windsor Forbes out of my system. The tiny glimpses I've gotten into her world only intrigue me and make me want to know more.

For the first time in my entire life I want more from another person and I can't give what I take. It's a mutual relationship with my teammates. What I give, they give back. It's symbiotic. I can tell Windsor wants more from me, and that's the scariest fucking thing of all. Because I know I'll eventually give it to her. And it will wreck her completely to pieces. The damage will be catastrophic. Worse than death. The biggest halo of dark red blood spray will come from the right section of my own God damned chest.

Currently, my pulse resides in my cock. She's in the passenger seat of my car wearing the smallest jean shorts I've ever seen. Her long tan legs are stretched in front of her. Tiny gray Converse shoes tap along to music. The white tank top rides up every time she leans over to mess with the radio, and I pray that static will fuzz out a song every couple minutes so I can catch a glimpse of exposed skin. With her hair down and her face almost bare of makeup, she looks like a walking water board created especially for me. Torture on every level. I haven't even figured out what exactly it is about her that makes her so different from every other girl I've met in the last five years. *What holds my interest? What keeps me engaged?* I have no clue. I actually sat down and made a list of pros and cons of dating Windsor. The only cons were all things that dealt with me. Things that I can't change, that are my fault. Not hers.

I put Steve in place the second I bought a new cell phone. He knows exactly where I stand with her, even if he doesn't understand it. On a whim, I decided to change my number so my phone wouldn't be blowing up with texts and calls from all of the insignificants. I meant what I told her. I really don't want anything to do with anyone else. That said, I need to get laid badly. My cock saluted Windsor the second she came bouncing down the stairs when I picked her up. I've had to work at keeping it at bay as I drive, but even her damn voice gets to me. This is our fourth date since the horrible dinner date.

A pop song blares out of my speakers, causing me to wince a little. "I love this song," she says, curling her legs underneath her. "How can you drive without glancing at me even once?" she asks. "I mean, I'm glad you're a safe driver, but what gives? Are you worried about crashing this beautiful piece of machinery?" I chuckle. Little does she know my peripheral vision has been studying her every subtle curve for the past twenty minutes. She refers to my car with such reverence. I love it.

"Some things demand your full attention," I say. To make a point I turn my head and look directly at her. She startles and her full lips part. I make a show of running my eyes down over her cleavage and back up again. She smiles.

"Just drive, please," she says, her voice a little breathy. I love that I affect her. "You should tell me where we're going, too." I focus my attention back on the bare road. Sunday mornings are always like this. I'm usually on my bike, by myself, but this…with her, feels good. She rubs her hand on the bottom of the seat, feeling the leather.

I grab one of her hands in my right hand and squeeze. "It's a surprise. I owe you. You granted me multiple dates so I have to make every second count," I say, rubbing my thumb over the dip between her fingers. She sighs a little. A jolt runs from my stomach all the way down to my dick. *A nun or my grandpa on a cold, wet day. A nun or my grandpa on a cold, wet day.* The mental distraction works.

She captures my hand on top and starts rubbing my fingers back. "Good. I don't want to have to call Steve for that date anytime soon," she says, voice teasing. Jealousy. A feeling I'm not used to hits me like a brick wall. Even though I know she's joking, I can't stop it. We've shared girls before, more times than I'd like to admit, but the thought of Windsor with anyone else makes me crazed. One of my brothers? Fuck no. "Well, at least I know he wouldn't awkward hug me after a *real* date," she finishes, and I feel like she's hit me in the gut. I've avoided touching her as much as possible, even going as far as not walking her to the door so I'm not tempted to kiss her goodbye.

"I can let him know you're interested in non-awkward hugging if you want?" I tell her, my tone far too sharp to be joking, which is what I was aiming for. She laces her fingers in between mine, fitting our hands together perfectly. Mine big. Her's small.

"I was joking. I'd rather awkward hug you than anything with Steve. You have to tell me though…you said you wanted me and then you hug me and then you nothing me. What's that about?"

"I want to take it slow, that's all," I admit. It's a truth, just not a whole truth. I'm not sure why exactly I don't want to bag her just yet.

"Because you've never gone slow before?" she asks. I think she's joking, but one look at her face says otherwise. I guess it makes sense she'd think that. I know the general public expects us to keep up fast-paced lifestyles. I'm sure everything she knows about me and my profession came from either Morganna or Dr. Google.

"Yeah. I guess that's about right," I admit. "Don't think I don't want to fuck you five ways from Sunday, though. That would be a lie. I don't do lies…ever. In perfect honesty, I've never wanted to insert my penis into a body more than I do yours." I do look at her after I speak. I have to see her face. Sure, it was crass. I mean it.

Eyes wide, she just glares at me. The thought comes perfectly, sanely—Windsor wants everything I just said. She wants to fuck me. And for all her talk of not wanting sex with anyone or me, she just gave herself away. It's so obvious. A little of her innocence slips away in this moment and I couldn't be happier. I turn the steering wheel into our destination –a huge barren patch of land with tire tracks leading to a small building surrounded by airplanes.

"It's okay to want to be fucked five ways from Sunday, Windsor," I say, turning off the car. She swallows audibly. I watch the top of her breasts as they rise up and down. She is so fucking beautiful I can't stand it. Sitting in this car, which is now off, I can focus on her completely.

She is still trying to respond to my non-question. I smile. The one I know affects her. I'm pulling out all the fucking stops right now. For some reason I want to hear her admit what she feels.

I graze her knee with my fingertips casually, running them lightly up her smooth thigh only stopping when my fingers hit jean. She closes her eyes as her breathing speeds up. "As long as I'm the one doing all the fucking," I whisper into her ear, making sure my lips graze her earlobe as I speak. She turns her head, searching for my lips. I pull back and stroke the inside of her thigh again. "Today though? You're going to jump out of an airplane strapped to my chest," I say, making sure she looks me directly in the eye.

Blue Eyes is all mine. Even though she looks shocked at today's choice of activity, I know she wants me and that stupid knowledge makes me so fucking giddy.

"S-s-skydiving," she stutters. It sounds more like *fuck me*, than a recreational sport. My dick, who has been tenting my pants since I removed the key from the ignition, is on high alert. I know I need to take it slow; he doesn't. Poor bastard. "Are you even qualified to do that?"

I laugh loudly. "Of course I'm qualified to do that. Who do you think I am? You think I'd break the law?" I grab a bag from the backseat.

"I mean of course you can do it, but you can do it with me under you?" She shakes her head. It looks so cute. I know what she means, but I want to go there anyway. The sexual tension is so thick I'm about to choke on it.

"Windsor, you can be in any position you want to be in. Today, for tandem skydiving, you will be under me. I'll make it good…fun. I promise," I tell her. I've never gone tandem with a woman before. Usually it's one of my buddies swinging under me during training trips.

"I'm scared. This is not on my bucket list, Maverick. Do you know how many things can go wrong? I mean there must be at least a thousand glitches that could happen. We'd career into the earth so fast we'd explode!" she says, her voice rising. I can just smile and reassure her that I won't let anything happen to her. Because I won't. Her worries do distract me from her ass, which is a good thing.

*****

We're up in the small, rickety airplane ascending to twelve thousand feet where we will jump out of a perfectly good flying machine. She made me check her harness twenty-two times before she agreed to board the plane. I indulged her mainly because it meant my hands were all over her—in between her legs, her waist, her shoulders. I went over the procedures and what exactly I expected of her. She paid attention, her eyes wide, as if her life depended on it. She thought it did, which made me laugh. Her life depends on me. Windsor got a little pissy when I told her that.

"I hate this part," I whisper into her ear. She's sitting on my lap because she's officially connected to me. She turns her head to the side and her eyes go wide.

She clutches my pants in her hands. "Do not say stuff like that, Maverick!" she yells back over the whir of the engines. The buildings on the ground are getting smaller and smaller. I wrap my hands around her waist and drag her back to my chest. She tenses for a second, then relaxes completely into me. When she leans her head back against my shoulder and turns it to look up at me, my head swims. The trust in her eyes gives me a high I only get from a couple other places.

"I got you," I say, and hope it's not a fucking lie. I want to have her not just now as we hurl toward earth, but for as far into the future as I can comfortably predict.

She nods her head, though her heart is hammering. I feel it thumping into me, and I know exactly what will take her mind off everything. I want to kiss her so badly I can already taste her lips. I've been so close so many times in the past weeks that I think I know what her lip-gloss will taste like when I lick it off. I've memorized her every curve and have predicted what she will feel like in my hands as we make-out furiously, no caution—just tongues and skin and sweat.

"Take a leap, Windsor. I won't let anything happen to you," I tell her as I lift her to stand in front of me. She nods once more, but I believe it this time because she smiles before she turns around, her back still pressed against my front.

A muffled voice fills the cabin of the plane, announcing that we've reached our jumping altitude. We're the only two so we walk together, like we practiced in unison, so we don't trip, to the door. Mannie comes over and unlatches the hatch exposing the blue sky. A whistle fills the air and Windsor lets out a little scream. I chuckle to myself, remembering the first time I jumped out of an airplane, the adrenaline consuming me. It really does go against every self-preservation defense mechanism the human body has. My heart picks up, like it always does, and it's like a fucking jolt of life entering my bloodstream. This is it. This is what I live for. And with this woman strapped to me I don't think there is a better feeling in the world.

I inch up to the edge of the door, keeping my hands on each side of the hatch. I look down over Windsor's shoulder to see the landing zone. It looks like a speck of something, but I know it's where we need to end up. Another scream, but this time accompanied with laughter, hits me. She's excited and that makes me even higher.

"On three!" I shout. It's hard to hear anything with the engines and now the wind whipping us, calling me to it.

She nods her head. "Yes!" she screams back, her hands tensing on the hatch door. I glance at Mannie and he gives me a solid nod, with a huge smile.

"One," I say, and rock forward a little bit in preparation for three when she'll go out completely. "Two." Another rock forward, a little bit further, extending my arms almost fully. "Three!" I yell and I push forward all the way.

The wind hits us like a punch and then we fall.

*****

Windsor

There is no sense of falling, only air hitting me. It's like the air is trying to hold me up, but gravity wins out in the end. I know this because the things on the ground get bigger as we fall. I focus all my energy on keeping my arms out to the sides and bent just like Maverick taught me. It's hard, because I scream every few seconds and I'm sure I move from the correct position.

The scared shitless feeling left the second we left the plane. Now, I just feel free. Adrenaline pumps and my heart hammers, but being one with the air makes me feel unrestrained in a way I never imagined possible. The risks are moot; I'm in the air, falling rapidly. Nothing matters except the way this freedom feels.

I'm confident in Maverick's abilities. I never for a second questioned whether I'd be safe. His confidence is enough for both of us. When he wrapped his arms around me and told me to take a leap, I knew this was what I needed. I see his arms in my peripheral vision and the sight of his big arms, wrapped in tattoos, hovering over me just confirm my safety. I am safe.

"One," Maverick shouts. He's going to pull the parachute on three like we practiced. Two comes next.

"Three," he says. I ball up my legs as much as I can, which isn't much, and we are rising up, up, up in the opposite direction we were just going. I look up and see the huge blue parachute opening. All falls silent as Maverick grabs the handles and begins guiding us down.

I pant a few seconds, just catching my breath from the thrill of it all. He laughs. It's a laugh I haven't heard before. It's completely unguarded and carefree. "Oh my God. That was insane!" I squeal. It really is a squeal, too.

"Insane good or insane awesome?" he asks through his laughs.

"Freaking insanely awesome. AHHHHHHHHHHH!"
It's contagious. I laugh so hard that I don't know if I'll ever stop. A few pulls on the handles and we're spinning around in circles that make my stomach drop.

"We'll get down quicker this way," he explains.

The scenery is unreal—so beautiful from the vantage point at the top of the world. We are so small. The ground moves toward us fast now. I don't realize how quickly we're dropping until I see trees get larger.

"I want to stay up here as long as possible," I say, reaching back to grab on to his leg with one hand. I lean my head back and rest it on his chest.

"Remember to bend your legs when we land," he says. I do and we're on the ground in a perfect landing in a large open field. In another moment, he is unclasping the parachute from his back and detaching my harness.

I'm still breathing hard and the adrenaline I feel is buzzing so wildly that I think I may pass out or scream again. Maverick turns me around to face him. His one-dimpled smile is out to play. His brown hair is air tousled. He looks more amazing than I ever remember him looking. He's in his element. This is the real Maverick.

I prop my hands on my hips, but he pulls me against his chest in a quick jerk. "I should have done this weeks ago. Now, I can't wait another second." Cradling my head in his hands he smashes our lips together. He bends down and scoops me up. I wrap my legs around his waist without removing my mouth from his. His tongue is soft as he pushes it into my mouth with skilled flicks and twirls. Mint flavor hits me, mingling with his cologne and I think I might devour him forever. And ever. And ever.

I wrap my hands around his neck and pull his head toward me until our teeth click together. The sound makes him groan and clutch my ass tighter to him. His fingers splay on the edge of my shorts. It annoys me that my clothes have the audacity to stop this man from touching every inch of me. When Maverick bites my bottom lip, I shut my eyes and gasp. I love how sweet gentleness laces his roughness. I turn my head so my lip breaks free. Bringing my lips to his neck, I lick the frog tattoo that peeks out of his t-shirt. I drag my mouth up to his ear, and then very slowly along his scruffy jawline. His stubble tickles my tongue.

"Smile," I order, looking directly into his *fuck me* eyes. He knows exactly what I want, because *that* smile breaks across his face. Dimples. I shut my eyes and my tongue finds one of those sweet little dips all on its own.

Maverick loosens his grip on my ass so I slide down his body. He presses my sex against the bulge in his pants. It is so freaking hard and so large, I can't ignore it. I circle my hips, grinding against him, feeling him where I want him so badly. A growl that seems to rip from his chest echoes in the wide-open air around us. His noise of raw need makes my pulse speed. He traces the curve of my lips with the tip of his tongue before plunging it back into my mouth. Claiming my mouth like no one else has. This man is owning me. And I want it so badly that I'll let him own me in every way possible in the middle of a field.

He smiles against my lips. It forces me to open my eyes. "This is even better than jumping out of airplanes," he says, his voice so low, I'm so freaking turned on that my hips automatically rock against him again.

I smile against his smile. "This is better than anything else, Maverick." I say his name in a sexed up tone and drag my tongue over his other dimple. He sighs loudly. "It's way better than awkward hugging, isn't it?"

He draws back, his lips pink and swollen from kissing. He shakes his head a few times as he just stares at my face. "You," is all he says. I know he's looking at my eyes and lips. It's a back and forth game.

"You," I say back, as I watch something flicker in his eyes. "That was some record breaking first kiss."

A cocky grin plays on his wet mouth. "I only do record breaking, Win. One word," he says.

I bite my lip, which now feels a little swollen from his teeth. A shiver of delight runs up my spine at the use of my nickname. It sounds so much better coming out of his mouth.

"Amazing," I say, but his lips descend back to mine before I can ask him for his one word. He brings us to the ground and we make-out like teenagers in a field for a long time. He doesn't let it go further even though I think I beg him once or twice.

I may have had reservations about the type of person he was when we first met, but the person who is with me today isn't that guy. This Maverick Hart is sweet, compelling, fifty shades of hot, and so into me. He is amazing. I've trusted him with my life today, and with that came a tiny piece of my heart.

Chapter Eight

Maverick

I pull off the sand colored headphones that act as ear protection. "Nice fucking shot, dude," Stone says. Two shots in the heart. One in the head. The perfect combo. Stone's a better shot, but I'd rather stick my dick in flames than admit it.

We're at the range shooting paper terrorists and zombies. My favorite target practice is steel targets, but today the guys had other ideas. I love shooting at the range. It's one of the few times when my head clears completely. I can think only about my forefinger hovering over the trigger and the solid, cool weight in my hand. The best shots are always when you don't over think it. You just let your body do what it's done a million times before. Pure instinct.

I ignore Stone and Steve's loud ass conversation about which bad guy the holey cut-out looks more like. I sit on a bench and start taking my gun apart to clean it. The focus and concentration are gone so my mind switches back on. I think of Windsor. An instinct of a different kind leads me to walk to the one fucking corner in this whole building that gets cell phone service.

I can't wait to see you tonight. I send off the text message half hoping she's busy and won't respond right away. If Steve realizes I'm texting a chick right now he'll bust my balls for days.

"Fine. We'll just agree it looks like Hilary Clinton and be done with this shit," Steve chortles as they walk over to me. "What is Maverick the Pussinator's opinion?"

I laugh. "Yep. For sure," I reply. I know the second Stone's gaze lands on the phone I'm trying to hide in my palm. He smirks. Then he looks at Steve. Fuck.

"Who you talkin' to, Mavvy?" Stone starts rattling off every girl name in the history of girl names...with a Boston accent. I start walking toward the high bay, knowing full well he will follow me all the way there, and possibly for the rest of the day. We enter the huge open, empty room just as Steve figures it out.

"Are you still talking to that chick? The same one from forever ago?" To him a month is a long ass time. Until recently it was a long time for me too. Now every day doesn't seem long enough. "Please tell me I'm wrong, dude. You can't seriously be banging the same chick. If you are there isn't any hope for the rest of us."

I slump down on the worn leather couch, and Stone and Steve head to the bar. Yes, we have a bar at work.

Multiple ones, actually. I just need to fucking say it and stop being such a pussy. Then the questions will stop and no one will think twice about my weird ass schedule. Stone thrusts a Solo cup into my hand, his back to Steve, and nods. He fucking knows and he's trying to make me admit it—either to myself or to the high bay full of plaques and photos of our fallen brothers. There's only three of us, but it feels like all eyes are on me.

I take a sip of my drink. "I'm inviting Windsor to my house," I admit. I don't need to say anymore. They both know exactly what that means, or what it doesn't mean. Stone specifically is probably choking on his fucking tongue right now.

Steve snorts then says, "You haven't bagged her yet?" Stone clears his throat. Tongue choke. Just what I thought.

"It'd be best if you don't talk about her and bagging in the same sentence, Steve," I say, feeling a bit defensive.

"He told you to back off her, man. That should have told you everything you needed to know. Our buddy Mav here actually gives a shit. For the first time in his life," Stone says. "I fucking knew it. I knew it!" He fishes his cell phone out of pocket and pounds out a text. I shake my head.

"Morganna owes me a blow job all-the-way tonight. I fucking told her you weren't going to bag and bash on Windsor, but she didn't believe me." With good reason. I have huge dickhead status when it comes to Morg. She's seen or heard about them all. I do mean *all*.

"Don't bet blow jobs on my fucking life," I tell him, but I'm laughing. It feels kind of nice to beat Morganna. She never loses. Anything. Steve has already lost interest, wandering away and shaking his head as he goes.

As far as Steve is concerned I'm just like Stone, one of the few other guys who only fucks one woman. Except I'm worse—I'm not fucking anyone. I feel nauseous when I think about fucking one woman for the rest of my life. But isn't that what this is? I can't even look at another woman the way I used to. I compare them to Windsor, and there is just no comparison. I haven't even gone past second base with the woman and I know she's going to rock my God damned world like a hurricane when I finally get inside her. The anticipation is almost too much. That says something because I thrive on the feeling of not knowing what comes next, yet knowing I'll be able to conquer it completely.

"What's the S.O.P for this? I'm in the dark," I ask Stone as he flings himself onto the couch. I'm more nervous about letting a woman into my world than going down range with bullets whizzing past my head. I can do bullets. I can do bad guys hiding in closets with AKs. I can't do this. "I don't even know what this means. I feel crazy, man," I whisper. I can tell Stone anything. And admitting this is fucking hard.

He flicks on the big screen television to create noise. "There is no standard operating procedure for this. This isn't something you can control, like every other facet of your meticulous fucking world. That's the point. That's why you feel like this. You're taking a risk in something that you've never dabbled in before. It's something you didn't even do with her." He says the last part with mock disgust. We don't talk about *her*. I don't even like to think about *her*. She's known as the biggest mistake of my life in a tiny, bitchy, blonde monster package. I'll pay for that blunder for the rest of my life. Literally.

I sigh. "Maybe I'm too fucked up to get into this with her. I should just back off now."

"Is that what you want to do?"

"No. I don't even think I could if I wanted to," I say. Lacing my hands around the back of my head, I look up to the ceiling. "I hired Tawny to go clean my house. I haven't even asked Windsor to come over yet. She might freak the fuck out and say no. She knows about my hotel thing. It's probably too big of a step." Stone is shaking his head before I finish.

"You really haven't bagged her?" he asks. I wince at the word, but figure if I hear him talk about bagging his wife, I shouldn't correct the word now. In my mind I've fucked her every way imaginable. Even a few ways I'm not sure are possible while having a spine.

"No," I admit. "And not because she hasn't wanted it. She has begged me a million different ways. I can't say no anymore, dude. It's killing me. Just the aftermath...and everything that will change when it's a done deal. Fuck!" Stone points the remote at the TV and changes the channel. I can't explain how just being with her, not touching or kissing or even talking, is enough. It's enough for me. Fucking that up isn't an option. She's open and honest and all at once it fucking hits me: that's probably one reason, if not the main reason I can't push her away...why I don't want to push her away. She doesn't hide a thing from me.

Even if she tried, I'd see it as clear as the blue of her eyes. I've only had that with one other person. And he has a vagina dick, so I can't put them in the same column. She wants to have sex with me, but that's not all she wants from me...like all the other women. They say they want more...I never believed them, though.

"You can do this, Maverick. You got this. You deserve this. I'm not gonna go all homo on you, but if it's easy...then it's right. That's how I knew with Morg. Granted she's as predictable as a snake, but I don't think around her...it just is. I'm not up in your business but I see enough to know that whatever you have with Windsor is good," he says. The word again—good. She is so fucking good. Stone's right.

I feel like a pussy, but I need to hear him say these things. Call it a weakness from growing up in a family that never accepted or appreciated anything about me or my life, but there it is. I get what I need elsewhere. From my brother.

"Tawny's probably all up in your shit at the house. I can't believe you let her in there." Stone laughs. It's over. The moment passes but everything remains. Everything.

Steve jukes his way toward us wearing boxing gloves and an American flag speedo. "Who's fucking Tawny?" he asks while upper cutting the air.

"No!" both Stone and I say at the same time.

I stand up and hold my hands so Steve can punch them. "Johnny got the clap from Tawny last year, remember? No one fucks Tawny anymore," I say. Steve slams a gloved fist into my palm. "She's cleaning my house," I explain.

"She cleaned my pipes when I was going through BUD/s," Steve says with a smile. "Tawny was a Phantom." That fact, I did forget. During training there is a phone number you call in the middle of the night and a girl comes to you wherever you're at and blows you. You can't look at them because their identity is supposed to be a secret. Tawny has a tongue piercing and long fingernails. Steve, like any good SEAL, sleuthed her out after she sucked him off. She worked at the coffee stand in Coronado where we were going through training. Secret Phantom no more. She followed one of the guys over to Virginia Beach, and somehow that woman is still a staple in our community.

I'm shopping with Morg Gretch n Jess. Need a 'dress' for tonight ;) Windsor's text comes through. The damn winky face is enough to make me anxious to see her in whatever "dress" she gets.

My big thumbs tap out a text before I even think. *I need to see you before tonight. Meet me for lunch.*

Where? I love that there's no pause or hesitation.

Cappy's. In 30? That will give me enough time to go home, make sure my shit is still there and change.

Can't wait to see you ;) ;)

I'm smiling like a ten year old when I realize Steve and Stone are staring at me. "What?" I ask, knowing full well they won't say anything.

Stone coughs and says, "Pussy whipped," at the same time.

"No dude you have to tap the pussy before you can be whipped," Steve says, calmly, like he's quoting scientific data.

"And on that note, I need to make sure she's cleaning the proper pipes," I say, bringing the conversation back to Tawny as I grab my duffel bag off the ground. It's Frogman Friday. It's always a light day at the office. Soon my days will be anything but light. I'm deploying in a month. My new unspoken challenge, that has flipped and reversed since Windsor walked into my world, is to make her mine before I leave.

*****

"Morganna," I say under my breath, like a curse word. I see her standing in front of Cappy's. Her huge handbag on her shoulder like a suitcase, and her Bluetooth studded in crystals—or are they real diamonds?—in her right ear.

"Hey Maverick. She told me she was meeting you for lunch and I just had to see this for myself," she tells me, waving her hand toward me. "On a date in the daylight hours. And with the intentions of a second date tonight. With the same girl. It's unbelievable, really."

I smile so fucking big and shake my head. "No welching on your bet, Morg," I say. I even think about calling Stone to let him know Morg didn't take his word for truth. She had to see it for herself. So typical. I decide against it because I need her on my good side. She has the ability to destroy all my chances with Windsor.

"Morganna Sterns does not welch on bets." She slits her eyes. A fucking tiger about to attack its prey is what pops into my mind. I recognize the look.

"I told you before. I like her," I admit, trying to keep my voice down in case Windsor is outside. I think it's beyond liking, but I don't know what comes after that. "You have to trust me this time. I know I've given you every reason to think I'm a horrible person, but Windsor just might make me a little less horrible. Come on? Give me a break?"

She taps her ear to either hang up a call, which wouldn't surprise me, or call someone. "I don't give anyone breaks. You need to tell her," she says, her voice twanging on the last syllable. When the country accent slips it makes her seem more human.

"Tell her what exactly?"

"About *her*," she says through her teeth.

I shake my head. "There's nothing to tell. She's gone. She doesn't matter anymore. She never mattered," I say, just as heated. "I'm not going to fuck this up, Morg. If I do, let it be my own fault. Don't intervene. I want whatever this is becoming with Windsor," I pause, swallow loudly and continue, "I want it more than I've ever wanted anything else." Normalcy. A real relationship with a woman. Stability. Warmth. Someone to come home to. Someone to fight for.

I see Windsor walking toward us, weaving her way through cars in the parking lot. She's dressed like she just came from the office—high heels, white button up shirt, and all. I sigh, thinking of how I'll be undressing her in my head throughout lunch. *Button. Pop. Button. Pop. Boobs. Button. Pop. Button. Pop. Hard stomach. Belly button.* She waves when she sees me, but it falters a little when she sees I'm talking to Morganna. Windsor is Morg's friend and even she is wary of her. I laugh.

"Fuck it up on your own, then. I've already warned her, so I'm washing my hands of this," Morganna says.

"And Stone will be washing out your mouth later," I say.

She laughs a little as she turns to snatch up Windsor in a hug. The women exchange a few words and smiles, and then Windsor's bounding into my arms smiling, making everything okay.

I pull her to my side as she wraps both of her arms around my waist. "Light day for you too?" I ask.

"I usually have Hannah clear my schedule on Fridays," she replies as I lead her to a table way in the back where there is no possible way we'll see anyone else that might interrupt us.

I hold the chair out for her and take my seat facing the door. Always facing the door. I'm uncomfortable if I'm not able to see the entry point. The male waiter, who looked at Windsor a touch too long, took our order and we're finally alone.

"I do have to go back to the office after this. I have to finish up some work. I have a training conference next week in Richmond." She's giving me her schedule. I take that as a good sign.

I grab her hand. "I missed you," I say.

"You just saw me last night, Maverick. I feel like if I don't give you a chance to miss me, you're going to get sick of me," Windsor tells me, rubbing my hand. It feels so good. I smile. But not the big smile. It's a sort of sad smile. Because she thinks I'll get sick of her.

I look over my shoulder for a few seconds, intentionally averting my eyes from her completely. When I turn back, I say, "I missed you! I didn't look at you for two seconds and I missed you. Of course not seeing you all night would make me miss you." She shakes her head and her wavy brown hair swings around her shoulders. She laughs a little and her smiles reaches her eyes. She squeezes my hand.

"I missed you more. I miss seeing you and talking to you. Everything. For someone who doesn't do relationships, you're pretty good at them. I don't think I've ever talked to someone so much in my life," she admits. It makes me squirm a little, because I know she's comparing me to her Nashhole, and also because she mentioned the word relationship. It's what this is. I just never thought about defining it before now. Several dates and hours of calls and texts is definitely a relationship.

"A relationship, huh?" Maybe she won't balk at coming to my damn house then. Asking her would be a step in the relationship direction. Wouldn't it? Fuck. I am so out of my element. Her blue eyes flick down to our joined hands. She opens her mouth to speak, and then closes it again.

"Well, yeah. That's what this is, right?" she whispers holding up our hands. "I mean you refuse to have sex with me, so I can't be sure because healthy relationships usually involve sex..." she trails off, cutting short one of her rambles. I know her rambles contain nothing except truths, so I actually encourage them.

I lean over and kiss her cheek. "This is most definitely a relationship, Windsor. Just because I'm taking it slow doesn't mean I don't want to have sex with you. It just means I want everything else Windsor Forbes before it," I whisper in her ear.

Exhilaration hits me in a rush. I admitted it. Out loud. That I wanted a relationship; that we are in a relationship.

The asshole waiter with his impeccable timing brings our salads at this moment. I know it will startle Windsor, because she's shy. I could kill him for his timing. Instead of leaning away from me because we're in mixed company, she grabs the side of my face and smashes her lips into mine. I forget everything. Where we're at, what my own fucking name is. It's easy.

As she pulls away from the kiss several seconds later, she pulls my bottom lip with her teeth. It snaps back into place with a pop. So fucking hot. Blue eyes bore into mine and like always, the truth is right there. It doesn't flicker subtlety, either. It's as blatant as a hand grenade.

She recovers quicker than me this time. "One word, Maverick," she whispers, her lips brushing mine as she says my name.

"Mine," I growl. Taking one more swift kiss that leaves her breathless is my intent, but I get a little more wrapped up in it than I should. My hands find my way to her waist, her legs, then wrapped in her hair that smells like damn womanly, sweet perfection.

"Tonight?" she asks. It's her one word. It's a loaded fucking question. One I don't know how to answer, because I'm not sure I can delay fucking her for much longer. If I get her in my house, naked on my own bed, the sight alone will make me spill it before I get within ten feet of her. I ask the question before I lose my nerve.

"Will you come to my house tonight?" She leans back into her chair and looks me squarely in the eyes. She looks confused, like maybe she didn't understand what I said.

"I want you to come over," I say again. Windsor bites her lip. The hesitation makes my pulse skitter all over the place. She usually doesn't pause to consider anything when it comes to me.

"Depends. Why are you asking?" She looks away. "Is it because you think it's something I want? Or do you really want me to come over? I know that's not your standard protocol." Skittering heart now turns to pounding heart.

"I want you to come over. I want you in my space. In my house. In my world, Windsor. There is no standard protocol when it comes to you. I'm just going with what feels right," I reply, making Stone's words from earlier my own. She studies me, eyes narrowed, like she's trying to psychoanalyze me. I've been analyzed plenty of times so I know what that looks like.

"I'd love to come over, then." Windsor smiles and it blinds me and melts me at the same time. For the first time in a few minutes I can breathe again. I can hold my breath for about three minutes while underwater. Somehow waiting for her response was worse than drowning. Now I'm elated. I want to skip the Halloween party tonight and go straight home now.

She starts eating her lunch without taking her eyes off me. Like she's eating me instead of lettuce. "We'll head there after the bar tonight," I say.

"What are you dressing up as?" she asks.

I laugh. "I don't dress up for Halloween anymore, Win. I look scary enough already," I tease, running my hand up her leg. "Boo," I whisper when she squirms.

"You certainly do scare me. That's for sure," she says removing my hand from her upper thighs. Begrudgingly, I start eating.

"What are you dressing up as?" I ask, curious what exactly "dress" means. She grins. Oh, I'm in for it.

"You'll have to wait and see. Should I pack an overnight bag, then?" Sex. It's all she's thinking about. It's all I can think of. It's the one thing I don't think I want to do with her yet. The heat in her eyes forces my answer.

"Of course, if you want, but you won't be wearing much while you're there," I say. Every word was worth it to watch her fuck me with her eyes. I won't have sex with her tonight. I'm not ready for that. I'm not ready for her to leave because there's nothing left to do. I will indeed use my hands and mouth on every square centimeter of her body. We've never done that before and I think it will be enough. I'll deal with blue balls for at least a week, but it will be so worth it. My gaze lands on the buttons of her shirt. She notices.

"That, my friend, is exactly what I wanted to hear," she says. My cock twitches. "I guess I can tell you then. I'm going to be a devil tonight," she whispers, biting her lip and then resting a hand on my thigh. She's out for blood. I like it. I hate it. I'm not in for it. She's out for it. I'm in trouble.

The waiter clears his throat and asks, "Do you need anything?" I need something alright.

She doesn't take her eyes off mine. "Check please," she mumbles.

I glance at the guy and nod. "Yes, the check, please. Everything was great," I say, remembering the decent manners drilled into me by my parents since birth. He scurries away, leaving us alone again.

She's shaking her head back and forth when I look her way. I narrow my eyes and cock my head in question. "You have no idea the effect you have on people, do you?" she asks. I smile. This causes her to shake her head a touch more furiously. I laugh.

"I only care about how I affect one person," I admit.

"Fear not. I don't think you could affect me any more unless you came in alcoholic drink form," Windsor says. She crosses and uncrosses her legs.

"Drink form can be arranged," I say, smiling so wide it hurts.

Chapter Nine

Windsor

I'm lying on the formal dining room table, legs spread wide open—naked except for a shirt. I shut my eyes as tightly as they'll go and wait for it. This is a bad idea. I've said as much at least twelve times.

"Scoot your ass closer to the edge of the table." Only one other person has said this to me: my gynecologist.

I do as I'm told. "I'm counting to twenty and you better be done," I say through gritted teeth. This is painful—torturous on so many levels.

The hot wax meets my bikini zone and I jump from the unexpected heat.

"Ow, Gretchen. God, be a little more careful would you?" I can't believe she talked me into this. "I feel like wax shouldn't be where I feel it right now."

She puffs out a sigh. I make the mistake of tilting my head up to glimpse her camping headlamp shining on my nether regions like a beacon from heaven. She's biting her lip in extreme concentration. All I can do is groan and hope she ends this with my sex organs in tact.

"You need a fucking landing strip, Win. Don't deny it. Your first kiss happened after you jumped out of a plane. It's so poetic I'm a little jealous honestly," Gretchen explains. "He needs to fuck you the first time with a landing strip." I roll my eyes even though they're closed.

"Jesus, you're so crass. Just hurry up, will you?" I lift my butt and put it back down. I pull my t-shirt down to gain some modicum of modesty. Gretchen smacks my hands away.

I hear the front door to our condo open and close. Morganna's working voice echoes down the hallway. "Stay still. I'm going to rip this last one off. It's on the side so it's going to hurt," Gretchen warns. I throw my arms over my face, completely embarrassed, and brace for the pain.

"This is the beginning of a horrible porno," Morganna drawls from the doorway. I groan.

"It was her idea!" I bark out, my eyes still closed.

Gretchen rips the last of the wax off. The screaming pain rips down my leg and then all the way up to my head.

"Damn it! Damn it! Damn it!" I grab my throbbing crotch and pull my shirt down to cover it before I sit up on the table. Morganna, dressed like a nun, is stifling a giggle. Morg isn't the giggling type, so that says a lot about this situation. Gretchen is just staring at me with huge eyes, like she's waiting for me to swing a baseball bat in her direction.

"Assholes! Everyone is assholes," I say, dashing for my bedroom. One look at my landing strip and I know that I need to turn on the hazard lights to ward off airplanes from landing in this airport. I am so pissed off at Gretchen and myself for agreeing to her absurd plan.

I pull the sexy lingerie out of my over night bag and stuff a silky pajama top in its place. My plans are completely ruined. My crotch is throbbing with an unwelcome sensation. I'm not sure I can even dance, or walk in high heels without looking like I have a stick up my ass.

"God dammit, Gretchen!" I yell. She told me she knows how to do this. The only reason I let her do it was because I'm so worried about everything being perfect tonight. Sex with Maverick has been on my mind constantly since, well, since the first day I laid eyes on him. Now, it's different. I can tell he has feelings for me, I also know he's fighting them off. It's the only reason I can come up with for a straight man to hold out on sex for so long. He wants me. I've ruined the damned night. I've ruined everything.

As I shimmy into the red, sequined mini dress, I vow not to let a burning crotch ruin his night. I will power through this like a Navy SEAL. I will not complain or whine. I won't even beat the shit out of Gretchen for it. Right now, at least. I also realize I cannot wear underwear. It adds to my devil appeal. Right? Completing my look is a pair of devil horns and red lipstick.

Gretchen is nowhere in sight when I exit my room and find the sexiest man alive sitting on my couch. He looks out of place in a setting so plain, mundane. It's like even my subconscious knows he should be doing something more manly, more dangerous, something more like…me. He's dressed from head to toe in white. Both dimples are out as his gaze travels over my body. He stalks over to me in only a few strides. I wince a little when he picks me up and places a dry kiss on my lips. He sets me back down, letting my body slide down his. No panties. I have to remind myself, before I unwillingly give the world a peep show.

"I went for a pure look. To balance you out," he rasps in my ear. Goosebumps break out all over my body. I feel another kiss on my neck. He backs away, holding my hand, to better appraise me. I laugh.

"You are far from pure, T.H."

"I like when you call me that," he says, following me back to my bedroom. I know he's watching my ass, so I make sure to stick it out a little further.

"Well let me get my bag so I can spend the night at your house, yelling T.H. all night long," I say, peeking over my shoulder. He's not looking at me, though. He's looking at my room and my things like they are artifacts in a freaking museum. "Like my room?" I ask. He nods, runs a finger over my dresser, and then faces me.

"I like it a lot. They say a room says a lot about a person. But I'm inclined to say a dress says more about a person."

I slip on one of my red heels. "What does this dress say about me?" I put my other foot in the shoe, and Gretchen's hack job throbs a little. A tiny cry escapes. His eyes immediately narrow. I won't let a little tender skin ruin my night. I smile through the pain.

He pulls me tight to his chest. "It says you want to torture me all night long," Maverick growls. His eyes flick to my bed. "It says you don't even want to go to the party." He backs me up to the edge, his hands skimming the bottom of my dress. Oh God. It can't happen right now. I need the night to recover a little. I can't do this now. I want to, but I can't. Gretchen made sure of that. I push back on his broad chest. He lets me. I slip past him and grab my leather overnighter off a chair.

"Actually, I do want to go to the party," I say. He takes the bag from my hands, but looks insanely confused. It's better than him knowing I have a second-degree burn where I want his dick. "Later though." God, it even sounds like a lie. He catches on right away and his confusion turns into something else.

He asks me at least five times if I'm okay during the ride to the bar. I reassure him I'm just excited to see his house and for the party. He peers at me while he drives, something he never does. I realize I won't ever be able to get anything past Maverick. He's not calling me out on my lies, but he knows I'm dishing them out. I wonder what he thinks is going on. I know with women what we think is always way worse than what actually happens. It's just our way. I feel guilty. My cell chimes with a text from Gretchen as we pull into the valet parking.

Ur mom called the house after you left. U need to give her ur cell #, Winnie. PS) so sorry. I hope M can still engage landing gear.

I'm surprised my mom called. She never calls anymore. I didn't think she knew how to work a phone anymore. I thought number five did it for her. Hell, maybe he did tonight, too. I type back to her as I exit the car, feeling where every hair follicle once was.

No landing gear tonight. I can barely walk. What did Kathy want? You owe me anyway.

She was upset. U need to call her 2morrow.

Great. That sounds like a freaking nightmare. She probably drank too much and wanted to talk about how my life was turning into her poor, miserable existence. It wouldn't be the first time. I debate texting Gretchen back, but realize Maverick is studying me. He glances at my phone. No more confusion in his eyes. He looks angry. The hairs on my neck rise at the sight of him.

"Ready to go in?" I smile and put my cell in my clutch. I'll talk to Gretchen later. My mother…maybe never. My focus should be on the man I'm with right now. The man who looks absolutely edible. The man who I am going to have to confess Gretchen's mortal sin to.

"Are you done with your phone?" he asks, with more irritation than I've ever heard from him. Maybe even a hint of sarcasm too. I just nod because we're already in the club, and it's loud and full of sparkles and wigs and all the crazy-ass slutty costumes that are typical on Halloween. Air conditioning blows to keep all the swaying bodies cool and a slight chill blows up my dress. It gives a little relief. I tuck my hand into Maverick's elbow and let him lead us to the back where we have a table in the VIP section. The nun and the pope are already there. The pope has the nun pinned to the back of the booth, his hand groping her boob. I scoff.

"You are going to hell. The both of you!" I yell. Morganna looks at me, startled, but her eyes float right back to Stone and go all gooey. It's one of the few times she doesn't have her phone in her ear.

"Speaking of going to hell. I need to talk to you." Maverick pulls me to the other side of the curtain to an empty booth shielded from both the dance floor and from Morganna and Stone.

He forces me against the wall just by proximity. The smell of his soap envelops me. I inhale greedily.

He runs a warm hand down the side of my body and stops on my hip. "Now, are you going to tell me what's wrong? Or are you going to make me guess?" I think for a second that making him guess will be a fun game, but think better of it.

"I'll tell you later. I just want to have fun now," I say leaning up to kiss him on his lips. He shakes his head. I wedge my tongue in between his lips in protest. There's no fight. He opens up and lets me in with a loud groan. He shifts me a little and I shut my eyes a little tighter when I feel the pain return.

"You fucked someone else," he whispers in between kisses. I pull away, stunned at what he's said.

I shake my head and say, "No!" at the same time. For him to be able to pinpoint exactly where I'm hurt is amazing. The fact he's acting like he wouldn't care if I did have sex with someone else is even more disconcerting. He disconnects our lips and waits for an explanation. I sigh. "There was someone in between my legs today," I say, thankful for the dark. He can't see how furiously I'm blushing.

He takes a few steps away from me and looks at me like I've burned him. "I knew it." He pulls the ends of his hair, something I now know he does when he's frustrated. I could let this go on all night. But I won't.

"Stop it," I say. I'm angry he thinks I would do anything with anyone else, my chest rises and falls rapidly. Does he not see himself? It's like a death wish for any man who comes after him.

He stares at me blankly. Hurt crosses his face.

"Gretchen, Maverick. Gretchen was the one between my legs." His eyebrows pull inward, and his mouth forms a grimace. Confusion etches every surface of his face. I laugh. "Come here," I crook a finger a few times. He hesitates, but walks over to me very slowly. I peer left and right to make sure we're absolutely out of eyeshot of anyone and grab his hand. "Trust me," I say.

I guide his palm to the hem of my dress. His eyes are fixated on his hand, like he can't believe what's happening. Eyes wide, he lets me be in control.

"Don't move," I tell him. He swiftly nods.

I flip his hand over so his fingers are up and I bring two fingers to my sex. His eyes flutter closed as I use his fingers to trace the lips, avoiding the center, and also the sore side. A guttural noise escapes his throat as his forearm muscles bunch, wanting to take control. I know he won't and the power he gives me makes me so freaking hot.

"She waxed me," I breathe, so incredibly turned on I might just burst into flames. "She also hurt me." I pull his fingers closer and circle them around the sensitive area that joins my sex with my leg.

His eyes open and meet mine, then dip down to watch his hand and my hand joined, under my dress. The sight alone is almost enough to send me over the edge. His hand twitches and I know his control is waning. You can't ask that much from a man who has his fingers near a wet hole.

"It's just you, Maverick. This," I move his hands around the smooth area, getting closer to the center, "it's yours and yours alone. I'm just sort of out of commission for the night," I admit ruefully. I know for a fact my face is a shade of red. I bite my lip. The music is blaring in the background, but I can still hear his breathing.

"I thought that was you, Mav," a woman slurs from behind him. I try to jerk his hand away, but he keeps it firmly planted right where it was a second ago. His huge frame masks the fact that I'm even standing in front of him, luckily. He turns his head to the side. "I've been trying to call you," the female voice bites out.

"Yeah. I'm a little busy right now," he says. He is quite busy, though my curiosity is insanely piqued. I glance around his shoulder and find a tiny blonde in a cop costume. Irritation courses through me. I see the way she's looking at him…and me. Her face falls a little when she sees he isn't going anywhere.

"Later then?" she asks. I have to balk at that. Maverick is standing here, obviously with me and she asks "later"? Seriously. Women have no self-respect. Then I remember his hand is on my sex in a public facility. I'm not much better than she is. At least she knows exactly what she wants. Him.

I look up to his face. I desperately want to know how he's going to respond to her, if at all. He sighs. Pulling his hand away, and tickling every sensitive area as he does, he wraps his arm around my waist. Cop chick is still standing there, waiting for him to respond to her. Waiting for the time of day.

"Not later, no. This is my girlfriend," he says, nodding his head to me.

Her eyebrows scrunch together in confusion. She doesn't believe him. Or she doesn't know what the term "girlfriend" means. I'd place a wager on either. She takes a step closer and stares directly at me. It's more than a stare; this bitch is scrutinizing me from head to toe. I pull at my hem, suddenly extremely self-conscious. I have to remind myself that he just called me his girlfriend and she is the other woman.

"Have a good night, Nic," he says loudly. And she is dismissed. I wince at his tone. He was polite at first, I give him that.

She lets out a high-pitched giggle. "You're serious?" she asks. "Maverick has a girlfriend? So what hotel do you take an official girlfriend to?" She air quotes on the word "girlfriend".

My cheeks are red. I know it. I feel hot from my head to my toes, and I know it's obvious to anyone who sees me. I'm jealous this stranger knows things about Maverick. How many pieces of him are scattered around Virginia Beach? The US? The world? I feel sick.

Maverick laughs. It's caustic and bitter. "Jealous?" he asks.

My stomach flips again. This is the cocky Maverick I met at a bar. The one who oozes sex and knows it. This is how he treated me before he knew me. She folds her arms under her huge fake boobs. I notice she doesn't say she's not jealous.

"She's my girlfriend. She stays at my house," he says, finally putting her out of her misery. He pulls me tighter to his side. He has no idea that I am so put off by this reminder of "bad" Maverick, that I might just tell him I don't want to see his freaking house. But I do. Of course I do. I'm just so baffled by all the feelings I have in this moment. Being with Maverick is like sharing him with everyone. There's no flying low on any radar. He owns everything surrounding him.

Blonde cop rolls her eyes. "Right," she mutters, turns on her pointy boot heel, and stalks off. I watch her perfect figure vanish behind the curtain and wonder how many other women behind that curtain there are. I pinch the bridge of my nose and exhale a pent up breath.

"How many," I ask. It's simple. I shut my eyes because I don't want him to see how much I truly want to know this answer. He must know. He must have a black book somewhere with all of his conquests. If there isn't a name, there must be a number. He did remember this girl's name, so does that make her a *good* one? I groan when I realize where my thoughts have taken me.

Stone pops his head around their curtain. "Drinks are here. Want one, Windsor?" he asks, a perfect gentlemen. A freaking façade. Both of them are scrupulous actors. I see how easily Maverick turns it on and off.

"Yes please," I say sweetly, breaking from Mavericks grasp. Even though my crotch feels like it's on fire, I don't break my stride or let on to the pain. I sit next the nun and pour a huge cup of vodka with a tiny splash of Sprite. Morganna looks at me oddly.

"Trying for black out drunk tonight?" she asks.

Maverick peers around the curtain, looking at me curiously. I force a smile. He narrows his eyes. I put the cup to my lips and suck down half of it. "Like back in undergrad?"

She laughs, already a little tipsy. The memories I have with Morganna in college are my favorite. It's before she became the shark. I understand that a lot of her personality probably has to do with dealing with Stone.

A slutty robot winds her way to Morganna's husband and starts talking to him, all flirty and Bambi-eyed. He doesn't look interested, but she is. Morganna doesn't even bat an eye. I'm jealous for her. It's such an atypical marriage. It's a whole different way of life. A life I'm not sure my skin is thick enough to handle.

I cough and meet Maverick's eyes. Concern creeps onto his face and I'm not sure if he's worried about my wax burn or my shift in demeanor. I guess it doesn't really matter. It's concern nonetheless. "Let's go dance, Morg," I say, pulling her up to her feet, mostly so I have leverage when I stand up.

"You're up for dancing?" I'm sure right now she has a vision of me spread eagle on my dining room table, hot wax on my bits. So I just nod and then shake my head when she starts to laugh. Emboldened by my anger and the vodka, I pull her into the mass of swaying, costumed bodies. I feel ridiculous being at this type of soiree. I am done… Correction, I was done with this lifestyle. I tired of it years ago when I was planning a wedding and perusing *Parenting* magazine. Look at me now.

"How many people has he slept with, Morg. I need to know what league I'm in here. It's been obvious that I'm in over my head from the start, but I'm feeling like a freaking Little Leaguer right now. I'm in this bar," I dance a little, just to fit in, and wave around the room like it's the most disgusting thing in the world.

She purses her lips and shakes her head. "My lips are sealed. He's bad news. I told you to should stay away," she says joining in my one-person dance fest.

"Bad how?" I'm desperate for any reason to run. Like I know I should.

"He does seem different with you," she leans in and blurts into my ear, ignoring my question. The music is blaring. "If you only knew how much that costs me to admit, I think you'd feel hopeful about the status of your...arrangement with him," Morganna says, slurring every other word.

This was my last hope of getting anything out of her. It's already too hard to deny my feelings for him. A quick glance to our VIP section shows several scantily clad women all vying for Maverick's and Stone's attentions. Maverick's talking to them, and he even smiles every once in a while, but his gaze hasn't strayed from me. I wish I could change what I see. I wish I could change what I feel for him. I shake my head sadly and try to disappear into the crowd.

Two young guys dressed as prisoners circle us, with huge, goofy grins on their faces. Morganna laughs and shakes her head. I think I hear her tsking as well. These guys are really young. Dancing with their shoulders and thrusting their hips. Babies, really. They haven't lost themselves that final time quite yet—it's obvious.

And Stone is here, buzzing up to us like freaking Patrick Swayze in *Ghost*. The baby men widen their eyes when they take in Stone. He's huge, all muscles and tattoos and confidence jacked up so high that it probably needs its own zip code. He rests a hand on each of our shoulders.

"You boys like my girls, huh?" Stone growls. "They are pretty smokin'."

Morganna hits him in the arm playfully. "Don't scare them, honey," she yells.

"Do you know what I like to do with prisoners?" Stone asks the boys, who are now just standing there, glued to the floor, dumbfounded looks perched on their faces. One guy shakes his head. The other turns around and runs away. He actually runs. I'm impressed with his feat in such close quarters.

I crane my neck and find Maverick sitting in the VIP area surrounded by even more woman than when I looked a few moments before. His elbows rest on his knees and his hands are folded together. I notice the blond cop, Nic is among his fan group. He's totally into his conversation, not even looking my way anymore. My heart hurts worse than my waxed crotch. The other prisoner retreats, trying to escape Stone's wrath.

I yank on the sleeve of Morganna's costume. "I need to get out of here. Can you take me home?" I ask.

She looks up at Stone. "How much have you had to drink? Windsor wants to make a quick exit," she explains. He shakes his head like she smacked him.

"I don't want an ass beating tonight. Plus, Mavvy's the only sober one here. He'll kill me if I bring her anywhere," he admits. He grabs Morganna's waist and pulls her to him and starts grinding on her. I swear they're more like twenty-one year olds than married adults.

Maverick is still busy with his admirers so I make my own freaking escape.

"He'll find you," I hear Stone rumble over everything else.

The vodka has numbed my pain, but it also makes me teeter in these sky-high heels. Somewhere inside me, I know I'm probably overreacting, that he's just talking and that's not a crime. The overwhelming sense that this thing with Maverick is only going to end badly forces my feet one in front of the other. His past is never going to change. My past is never going to change.

I slam into another blond cop with fake boobs. It's the same exact costume. Tears sting my eyes as her drink splashes down the front of my dress. Finding a side exit, I push my way out and take off my shoes. Clutching them in one hand, I run down the side of the building, the pavement cold on my feet. A security guard sees me and stops me. I grab his jacket.

"I left in taxi. I went home," I plead with him, nodding my head as I speak. "Please. The girl in the red dress got into a taxi and went home," I say again.

"You're sure you don't need help?" he asks. I shake my head. I must look wild, out of control, but he nods and walks off. I duck into a back alleyway just as my phone starts buzzing. Maverick. I ignore his call and text Gretchen to come get me. I hear rather than see when Maverick blazes out of the building. A loud bang resounds and a string of profanities travel to my hiding spot. His car revs to life only a few moments later.

Gretchen the fairy and Benji the pirate pull up in her car fifteen minutes later. I rip off my devil horns.

"Take me to Jess's house for the night, please," I command quietly the second I slip into the back seat. I adjust my position when my vagina burns in protest. Gretchen doesn't ask or say anything. She just drives. She knows something went horribly wrong and the fact that she nearly dismembered my lady bits tonight gives me the trump card. She won't even ask.

I flip on the silent button on my cell, which has been blowing up non-stop with texts and calls from him.

"Thank you," I whisper. I'm sure she thinks I'm thanking her for rescuing me. I'm actually thanking her for more than that.

Chapter Ten

Windsor

I had to shut off my phone. I also had to move from Jess's house to Morganna's on Sunday because Maverick found out where I was. Morganna would never, in a million years, rat out my hiding spot. Stone was too scared of Morganna to go against her wishes. Or so I thought. Gretchen brought me a suitcase full of everything I listed in a text, because I had to leave for my training trip today.

"Take her suitcase for her, Phillipe," Morg barks to her assistant. I'm dumbfounded at the early morning hour he arrived at their house. I haven't slept well, so I was up drinking coffee and surfing the web on my iPad when he came in at the ridiculous hour of five a.m.

"Sure," Phillipe says, rolling my bag down the long, beautiful corridor that leads to their garage. We hid my car in there, at Stone's suggestion. I also called the hotel early to request early check-in so I could leave here super early to try and avoid any contact with Maverick. Stone stops me in the hallway.

"He knew you were here, Win. I can't keep shit from him. He's my brother. He stayed away because he knew it's what you wanted. Please give him a break. This is all new to him. If you saw him when he found out you left…well it probably wouldn't have been a good thing for you to see," he says, pausing. "I've known him his entire life. I've never seen him struggle with anything…except with whatever this is he's trying with you." All I can do is close my eyes and try to keep the image of a heartbroken Maverick out of my mind.

"The women. This life he's cultivated. All of it. I'm not sure I can deal with it," I tell him honestly.

"Did you know he walked away from his entire family. All of them? They haven't spoken since he made the decision to become a SEAL. They're against everything Mav represents. It's like he doesn't even exist to them. Walking away from them was easy for him," he says and my heart does break a little…for him.

I can't fathom a person who doesn't respect his career path. I mean, the lifestyle might be a little much, but the profession? Serving and protecting America is the most prestigious and respectable job possible. A tear slips down my face. I know exactly what it feels like to be outcast from a family, but not for the same reasons.

Stone interrupts my tormented thoughts. "But walking away from you is impossible for him," he whispers.

"Why me?" I ask. Morganna is already dressed to impress when she waves from the other side of the hallway. I give her a small wave and smile back. She yells at Phillipe to bring her something and she's off to conquer the world.

"Because you're something he thought he'd never get. You're someone he thinks he doesn't deserve," he says. And I think he's lying, except the truth that shines in his brown eyes is blatant. He cares for Maverick a lot. "You can't question everything. Sometimes a spade really is a fucking spade, Win."

"I want to believe you, I do. Because I don't think I've ever been so completely had by someone who refuses to have me. It's maddening. Can someone like Maverick really change? A tiger changing stripes and all that." All the girls. His fan club will always be there waiting in the wings. Waiting for me to mess up so he can choose a good one for a hotel date.

"Who said anything about stripes? He does have some badass fucking tats though," Stone says, smiling wide. My returning smile is weak, there is no happiness behind it. "If you tell him I said anything, I'll deny it. You're doing exactly what he thought you'd do, except he hasn't bagged you yet," Stone says, retreating down the hallway. My head swims for a second and my brain scrambles.

"He thinks I'll leave him?" I ask, completely shocked. My stomach lurches. It's normal for people to turn their backs on him. His own family did it. It makes perfect sense, but I don't know if it changes how I feel.

Stone looks over his shoulder as he continues to walk away. "What the fuck are you doing right now?" It looks like I'm running, but really I'm just thinking. Sorting. I'm recalculating my liabilities.

I grab my suitcase and load it into the trunk blindly— not aware of anything except the new knowledge rolling around in my head. Everyone has a little bit of a messed up past. The challenges make you who you are, whether you end up good or bad is up to you. Maverick has a lot of good. And a lot of bad.

During the entire drive to Richmond, and while I unpack my suitcase in my hotel room, and while I eat breakfast, I think about Maverick and the things Stone told me. Guilt hits me square in the chest. The problem is I'm not sure if I feel bad for leaving him at the bar that night without so much as a goodbye, or if I feel bad for teenaged Maverick who left his home to begin a life no one approved of.

I'm dwelling somewhere in between self-loathing and pride when I hear a voice from my past. The voice. I feel like I may fall over. I have a cup of coffee in my hands. It shakes. I put it down on the table in front of me and turn around, trying to portray some semblance of confidence. I must be able to do at least that.

"Nash," I say. Nashhole almost came out instead. The sight of him makes my heart pound. Silly thing has no idea, he's the same one who crushed it to bits.

I glance over his shoulder and see Garrett smiling like the cat who caught the mouse. He did this. He scheduled us to attend this thing together. I shoot him a death glare. I knew he was pissed off for the missed date, but this is bad form. Though a meeting was bound to happen sooner or later.

"My, my, my, Winnie, time has been kind to you," Nash says, checking me out, his eyes narrowed and his bottom lip caught between his teeth. I have to take a deep breath to steady myself.

"At least something has been kind to me. How's your girlfriend?" I ask. I really know nothing about him these days. I'm also surprised my words flow so freely. Granted, I've wanted to talk to him face to face for a long time, but never had the courage.

An emotion flickers across his face. "We broke up," he admits. That bitch must have broken his heart. I can't even help it...I smile. I head to one of the conference tables and take a seat. Somehow I take solace in knowing Nash's bimbo screwed him over. It makes it easier to be around him.

Karma. Maybe it does work after all.

He sits next to me. "What about you?"

I know he's asking if I have a boyfriend, and I really don't want to take on that question so I respond vaguely, "I'm good. I'm really good. Happy," I say.

He scoots his chair closer. His proximity feels so comfortable, normal, but I'm also aware it's not. It's funny how the body reacts to familiarity. It's been years, and I have no clue who this man is, but every fiber in my being wants him to engulf me in a hug and apologize for ruining everything. That's the weak Windsor. I know that, but I can't help feeling that way.

Maverick pops into my mind. His face, his kindness, the way my body responds to his. The pull to Maverick is different than the pull to Nash. I have the urge to call Maverick right now. I want to apologize for being so flighty.

"I miss you, Winnie. It's been hard for me since Stacey left me," he says. Oh, God. I dreamed about him saying those words for a year straight. I would have taken him back then. I would have forgiven him for everything and married the bastard. I was a lunatic back then.

I shake my head and get up from my seat. I can't hear this. I dumped many hours and a lot of money in my psychiatrist's office because of this man. "No, Nash. You don't get to say things like that to me. You cheated on me for a very long time," I tell him through shaky breaths. I start to walk away, but he grabs my wrist and follows me. I have to get away. The tears come and I know I won't be able to stop them.

I enter the elevator and slam my finger on the number five at least ten times. "Come on, Winnie. I'm sorry. I am. I know now that Stacey is the kind of girl you date. You are the type of woman you marry. I should have married you. I'm so stupid. I'm so stupid," he says. His blue eyes are pleading. That look used to get him whatever he wanted from me. I want to hug him. I want to smack him. My heart wants to forgive him. I feel like I might choke on my own shallow breaths.

"Why then? Why did you cheat?" I ask the question that tortures me the most. I hear the elevator ping and the door open. I get off, tears still pouring down my face. Nash follows me down the hall. I spin on him. "Why, Nash? You owe me the fucking truth!" I scream.

The wave of depression I fought through slams me. Every horrible thought about myself floats around me, taunting me. How his cheating was my fault. How I was a horrible person. How I couldn't keep one man. How I was destined to end up just like my miserable mother. It took a long time to realize I was normal and Nash was the fucked up one. It still didn't make the black hole that swallowed me whole any smaller.

He blows out a long breath and I know he's about to say something horrible, but I don't care. I need to hear it. I need to bury this in the ground so I can get over it, instead of burying it inside.

He takes my hands in his. "I was bored, Winnie. It was always the same with you. You were too predictable. Life got boring. You never took any risks," he says.

There they are. The words I needed to hear, yet they are tearing me into two. I look down the hallway to the right, where my room is and see him—Maverick sitting on the floor in front of my door. He just looks at me, searching my face for something. Nash is oblivious that anyone else is present. I pray Maverick didn't just hear Nash's words, like maybe he'll think that's the person I really am.

"Take a risk, Winnie. Come back to me," Nash whispers. I turn and look at the man who ruined my life, even though I can barely see him through my flooded eyes.

I decide to do something he'd never expect from me, because I know…I just know I have back up. Even if I ran away from him, even if I abandoned him and thought the very worst of him, I know Maverick cares.

So, I rear my hand back and smack Johnny Nash's freaking face so hard that my palm burns like a million bees just stung me. I've never felt a better feeling. That was what I needed while I was lying in bed, pondering the worth of my life. I don't need Nash. I don't need anyone. I want someone, and it's not the man who cheated and lied to me.

Like I suspected, Maverick is by my side quicker than seems humanly possible. He has Johnny by his collar, pinned up against the wall. His feet dangle off the ground like a little child. The sight actually calms me. Nothing about Maverick is calm. He is a ball of fury, anger probably directed at both Nash and I. His breathing is harsh and the muscles in his tattooed forearms bunch. It looks like he's trying to stop himself from killing Johnny on the spot. A button pops off Johnny's freshly pressed shirt. Maverick wears a stretched out black t-shirt and jeans. The difference between them is great. A stranger looking on would think good and bad. Except they'd pin the wrong guy as bad, I'm sure of it.

"What the fuck, Winnie? Who the hell is this guy?" Nash asks, his face turning a bright shade of red.

Maverick doesn't speak. He just looks at me, like he wants to know what I'll say just as much as the Nashhole. It breaks my heart even further. His hazel eyes are glistening. He is enraged to the point that every emotion is blistering to the surface. And I'm the one who did this to him.

Without looking away from Maverick's gaze I say, "He's a risk worth taking." I speak just loud enough for both of them to hear.

Maverick lets Nash's feet touch the floor. He closes his eyes, trying to reign in whatever it is that affects him so greatly. One deep breath later, he's back.

"Meet Nashhole, Maverick," I say, when he looks at me grinning the mean spirited, scary as hell smile.

Nashhole clears his throat. "You're here to kill me? Aren't you?" Maverick, who has yet to release him, turns that same look on him.

"No, even though I think it would be therapeutic for me at the moment," Maverick says.

Johnny whimpers a little. "Winnie…" he whines.

"Don't say her fucking name one more time," Maverick growls. Speaking directly to me for the first time, he says, "What do you want me to do with him, Win?"

The instinct to protect the foul human that once held my heart in his hands appears, but I shove it back down and remind it how insane I was for a long time. The Nashhole looks at me with a crazed look in his eyes. He thinks I'll order his death or something. The prick obviously never knew me—not even one bit. The whole thing is so sad.

"Hit him for me," I command. There's no inflection in my tone and it scares me.

Maverick punches once. Once is all it takes, and it looks like he held back. Actually I'm sure he did. Bones crunch and blood trickles down from his nose and lips. Johnny slinks to the floor holding his face in his hands. I've never seen him that low. He was on a pedestal so high, for so long, that it's like I'm looking at someone else. The sight flips my stomach and shatters my heart, but then I glance at Maverick and he's staring at me, looking for my approval. He doesn't give a shit about anything else, just how I feel. If only the simple, bloody one treated me the same way.

I walk over to my hotel door. I hear Maverick actually helping the Nashhole up, uttering heated words under his breath. Threatening I'm sure. Johnny scurries down the hall like a beaten dog. I don't turn around, but I know he's there. My skin prickles with awareness, like it always does when he's close.

"Thank you," I whisper softly. "I'm so sorry." I don't say exactly what I'm sorry for because it's supposed to encompass so many things, including the things I'm not supposed to know about. I slide my key into the door and walk through. I hold it open for him. He doesn't stop looking at me, my face—trying to read what's in my head. "Come in," I say, though it sounds more like a question.

He hesitates a few more seconds, but must come to a conclusion with his case study because he strides in. He stops in the middle of the room, hands on his hips, his back facing me. The sun hits at the perfect angle, silhouetting him —like an avenging angel or something equally as impressive.

"What did I do, Win? You just left. You were supposed to come to my house. If it was too much, too soon, you should have told me. I'd never pressure you to do anything you didn't want to do. That's it, right? That has to be it."

He has no clue why I left. Even more guilt comes up, twisting my stomach into knots. All weekend he thought I ran because I was scared of sex...or of furthering our relationship. I shake my head, even though he can't see it.

"I don't know if I can handle your past. Seeing you with all of the women reminded me of the person you are," I say quietly.

"Was. The person I was," he says a little more loudly. He turns and faces me. He freezes me to the spot with his accusatory glare. "I can't change my past, Windsor. Trust me, I would if I could, because it obviously is an issue for you. I move forward." He points at the door behind me. "You can't change your past either. You move forward. You trust again."

I fold my arms around my stomach to hold myself together. "It will kill me," I whisper. "I can't go through that again."

I'm engulfed in his warm arms in the next breath. I sigh, relaxing for the first time in days. He smells so incredible. He feels so perfect. His words hit the right spot in my heart. He sighs, leans his head down, and inhales deeply.

"I've got you. I'll never do what he did to you. I won't abandon you, Windsor. I'd rather kill myself than hurt you," he says, still breathing in my hair by my ear. I wish there were a handful of guys in between the Nashhole and Maverick. Then I'd be ready for this. "I have no self-preservation awareness when I'm around you. My happiness is directly dependent on you," he says.

He pulls me away and holds my shoulders. He looks so shaken by his confession that I actually see his shoulders shake. I want to kiss him. I want him to know I'm his. I lean toward him, but he immediately backs away.

"Please, just…can we leave here?" he says, stuttering. He notices I'm aware of his verbal trip up. "This," he waves his arm around the hotel room, "is something out of my worst nightmare," he says stonily. "You upset. Crying. Standing in front of a bed, in a fucking hotel room." He shuts his eyes tightly, trying to erase the image from his mind. "I never wanted to see you like this. Especially here, Windsor. You have to understand—you have to believe me when I say you're different." His voice drops lower.

I close the gap between us and hold his big bear paws in mine. "I'm getting that. I'm sorry, I just saw all of those girls all over you and I got jealous, and they are all so flawless and want to give you whatever you want. I don't even know what you want me to give you," I admit. My face flushes. He still looks extremely uncomfortable in this room. "You do know you are eventually going to have to have sex with me in a hotel room, right?" I ask, trying to lighten the mood.

The corner of his mouth wedges up, but the dimples don't come out to play. He shakes his head. I sniffle loudly. He picks me up with ease and carries me to the bathroom. I wrap my legs around him when he places me on the counter, to hold him to me. He reaches for the tissues and hands me one. I wipe my eyes and then my nose. He just stays silent, happy just to be with me. I lean my forehead against his chest.

"Why are we so messed up?" I whisper. I feel him kiss the top of my head. Every touch he gives is so full of feeling. It's like he knows I need everything he gives without even asking. Being with him is effortless.

"I don't know, but know this, and remember this, you shouldn't be jealous of anyone, I only want you and because of that I'm about to ask for the most selfish thing I've ever asked for," he says, pausing, waiting for me to respond.

I nod my head. He couldn't possibly ask for anything that selfish. I mostly think this because I'm currently in a state of hysterics.

"I want you to give me you," he says, like it's the most obvious thing in the world. His words line up with everything Stone told me earlier this morning. He doesn't think he deserves me, or a relationship. I wrap my arms around him a little tighter.

"I'm not going anywhere, Maverick. I promise. I meant what I said out in the hallway. Well, I said a lot of things, but when I said you were worth the risk…I want give this a chance," I confess, placing my hand over his heart. He blows out a giant breath. "You couldn't possibly think I'd deny you that request? You did just defend my honor. I did the one thing I've dreamed of doing for years now." I lift my head and meet his hazel eyes. One dimple pops up. I laugh.

"What? Crack his face in?" he asks. "Because technically I did that."

"No," I say, tracing his smile with my thumb. I place a quick kiss on his dimple. "I took a risk. I tend to do that a lot around you." A hot rumble of laughter echoes in the small space.

"Don't run away again. Please. Just talk to me. We'll work it out. I'll be what you need me to be. Okay?" he says the words quickly. He doesn't want to say them, he needs to say them. He seems more calm and rational in here…away from the bed. So, maybe he doesn't hotel date in hotel bathrooms?

"I promise," I say, crossing an X over my chest. "Only if you kiss me right now." One of his hands comes up to caress my neck, the other pulls in my hair. A view of both dimples and a huge white smile is all I see before his mouth crushes mine. His lips move with mine, his tongue mimics mine and I am in control of everything. His caution only enlivens me.

I lace my hands around his neck and hold him to me even tighter. Butterflies invade my stomach when he grunts in male satisfaction. His lips leave mine and I feel a little lost. Then I feel his lips and tongue grazing my jawline and then down my neck. I tilt my chin back to give him easier access. He licks a trail from behind my ear and down to my collarbone, and then back up. He nips my earlobe.

"Let's leave. Come to my house," he growls. It really is a growl, too. I grab the sides of his face and force his mouth back to mine. Unbuttoning my shirt, I tear it off and throw it on the bathroom floor. The blue lace bra is sheer and my nipples are puckering through the material. The heat of his lips disappears when he pulls away.

I reach around my back and unfasten my bra and throw it away as well. "Take off your shirt," I command.

My voice doesn't even sound like my own. It's all breathy and sexy, and I would totally want to have sex with me right now if I were him. His eyes fixate on my chest and it looks like he's going to attack me. I want him to do his worst.

"Are you going to say no to me, Mav?"

Chapter Eleven

Maverick

The sexiest woman in the world is half-naked and begging me to fuck her—just shy of serving herself on a silver God damned platter. She called me Mav. I feel like I should fuck her right now just to reinforce the good behavior. I never thought it would go down like this when I came to the hotel.

She repeats herself. "That's a no, then?"

I'm so lost inside my own head and consumed by just looking at her bare chest that I forgot to answer the first time. I grab the back collar of my shirt and pull it over my head, baring my chest to her. She immediately starts tracing my skin, my tattoos, with both of her hands. I know I have to stop this because I can't go much further here. In this fucking hotel room. She is so much better than this. I have her on a bathroom counter like some random bag.

She leans over to lick the bone frog tat on my neck and her nipples buzz across my chest. Everything she does feels like it's the first fucking time. I don't even know how many mouths have kissed my tats, but right now all I care about is that her mouth is on me. She's the only mouth I've ever wanted on me. *Stop her. Stop her.* Her wet tongue trails over my nipples.

"Fuck," I rasp. My dick is so hard, the second she touches it I'll lose it. Along with self-preservation, my self-control is shot to fucking shit. Her blue eyes rise to meet mine. A smile crosses her delicious mouth and a piece of her brown hair gets in her face. I brush it away. She bites her lip. Then she places a kiss on the right side of my chest, directly above my heart. There's no tat there. She kissed me there because she wanted to kiss me, not my ink.

I take my t-shirt, which I held onto for good reason, and put it over her head. She puts her arms through the sleeves, and then crosses her arms over her chest and juts out her bottom lip. So fucking hot.

"My house?" I ask, taking her pouty lip in between my teeth. I pull it out a little, like she does with mine. She sighs. "Please don't beg me today, Win. I'm not strong enough to hold out. I've missed you. I want everything to be perfect. I want to take it slow," I say again. My excuse seems weaker and weaker each time I say it. She hops off the counter.

"Your house. Now. I'm the most sexually frustrated person on the face of the planet," she says.

I blow out a breath, happy she agreed to come home with me. I never thought about how she was feeling sexually. I've been neglecting her because I don't trust myself. It's one thing for me to have perma-blue balls, but I need to please Windsor. I feel like a complete dickhead. I'll have to remedy that the second we get out of this hotel room. It's making me jumpy now that we're back by the bed.

And with her wearing my shirt that falls to her knees she's like a walking wet dream. Her eyes linger on me while she waits for me to respond. My cock is still hard and standing at attention like it has been since the second I walked into the hotel. It's like Pavlov's fucking dogs. It knows what these rooms mean.

"How's Gretchen's handiwork?" I ask. I can't keep the smile off my face at her mortified expression.

"Why don't you come check it out for yourself?" Zing. I feel like a weak pussy for not being able to take her up on the offer right this second.

"Let's go. I'll get up close and personal with it," I look at my watch, "in one hour and fifteen minutes. Follow me back?" I ask. I hate that she can't ride with me, but we can't leave her car and honestly, staying here with that asshole here isn't even an option.

When I saw them in the hallway, I knew it was Nash. I looked him up after the first time she mentioned she had a cheating fiancé. I know where he lives. I know he works in her office building. I also know his social security number and that he leaves his house every day at 8:25 a.m. I won't tell Windsor any of that though.

"Turn around," she mumbles. "I'm going to take off your shirt. If I look at you for another second looking like you do, I'm going to slam you down on that bed and have my wicked way with you, issues or not."

I laugh, but a fucking pit forms in my stomach. She said I have issues. I guess I do. I definitely do not want to see her naked in this room. The fact she knows, and is trying to prevent it, makes me happy and fucking angry. I turn around and fold my arms behind my head. The whole situation is hot and incredibly unfair at the same time.

"Change," I order. "I guess I should have asked if you need to stay here for this conference first. That would be the gentlemanly thing to do…do you?"

My black shirt lands on the bed in front of me. "They can't pay me enough to stay here with him," she says, stopping mid-sentence. "I'll call my boss when I get in the car. She'll understand. Maybe I can make it to the office later today, too," she says.

"Or maybe you won't," I say, shrugging on my shirt and turning around. She has her suitcase in her hand, ready to go. Her face is still a little red and her hair is all fuck-me-now. Very deliberately she skates her gaze down my body and back up. God damn, it does things to me I never knew one look could do.

"You're right. I probably won't," she whispers. I grab her suitcase from her, because I will be keeping it with me for collateral. She doesn't object. Grabbing my free hand in hers, she hugs herself to my side, like it's where she's always been. When we arrive in the lobby there are way too many people standing around. It makes me nervous. I glance at the exit out of habit.

Windsor tenses beside me. The guy from her office notices us and actually has enough balls to approach. "I'm sorry, Windsor," Garrett says, looking directly at me. "I guess I didn't realize how upset you'd be if Nash was here at the same time. It's been what? Two years?" he asks, and it pisses me off for a few different reasons, but I want to see how Windsor handles this without me interfering.

"It's fine, Garrett. You did me a favor. I never asked anyone to walk on eggshells about Nash with me. They did it all on their own. So whatever, thanks," she says. "I am taking off with my boyfriend now, though. I'll check in at the office."

I think my chest rose a few feet the second she called me her boyfriend. I grin at asshole Garth, because now I know he's the reason Nash and Windsor were here together. He's on my growing shit list. I'm just glad he hasn't ran into the Nashhole yet. I scan the room one more time.

"Yeah sure, of course," Garth says. "Mr. Hart." He nods at me and walks off. Windsor laughs, causing me to chuckle.

"Mr. Hart is my father. Doesn't he know that?"

She basically drags me out of the building without saying another word. I walk her to her car, because I know exactly where it's parked. I parked mine right next to it. "So…" I start to say, but Windsor cuts me off with a wave of her hand.

She twists the front of my shirt in her hand and brings me to her. "I guess you forgot how badly I want you. No more talking. Your house. Now. I'll follow you there," she tells me, releasing me and grabbing the handle of her door. On a second thought, she goes up on her tiptoes to kiss me.

Her words have had their intended effect. My adrenaline is spiking through the roof with the anticipation. I lean down and kiss her. She smells like a flowery perfume and me. This kiss is all tongues and teeth and promise.

"Fuck, Win. Drive," I command. I gently push her away from me, because the image of fucking her in my back seat pops in my mind. That might even be worse than having sex with her in a hotel room. She doesn't even say goodbye. She gets in her car, starts the engine and fucking tailgates me all the way to my house.

I pull into my driveway and punch the code into the gate box. I watch her follow me in the rearview mirror. She is looking around, like all chicks do when they're supposed to be driving.

My house comes into view and I watch her blue eyes widen when she sees it. I wish I could be with her, to know exactly what she's muttering to herself in this moment, but I'm not so I settle for facial expressions. Facial expressions tell a lot about a person. If you're good enough, like I am, you can tell when someone is lying to you. With someone as honest as Windsor, I don't have to use any of my talents. It's almost a relief. I park my car behind one of the four garage bays and she pulls up next to me. I hop out as quickly as I can to open her car door before she can.

"I should thank you for that one really awkward time when you came into my office trying to get a date," she says before she exits her car. That was over a month ago, but I still cringe at the memory.

I scrunch my brows together. "Why is that?"

"Because if you didn't flaunt your money in my face that day, I wouldn't have expected this." She gestures to my house, which is larger than average, sure, but nothing that fucking special. Nothing like my parents wanted for me. I'm happy here, though. "And then I would have been flabbergasted, or weird. Because I knew to expect something like this I don't have to go through those emotions," she explains. I laugh.

"I'm glad my asshole could be of service to you. Weird wouldn't be good, would it?"

She shuts her eyes and shakes her head. She takes my offered hand and we walk up the paved walkway to the front door. I unlock the door and hold it open. I throw my hands forward, ushering her in first. Windsor looks at me and smiles an impossibly beautiful smile, and then she walks into my world. And I never remember being so happy.

She slips off her shoes before I take off mine. Her bare feet make a soft noise as she wanders over to the sofas in the living room. She doesn't sit down. No, she drags a few fingers over the leather, just touching it. I follow behind her, my hands behind my back to control the trembling. It's the opposite of the trembling from earlier. Now that she's here in my space, I want her so fiercely that my body is taking over.

"It's beautiful," she whispers, standing in front of a mixed media piece of art that hangs in one of the hallways. "This isn't the bachelor pad I expected…it's more," she says. It's more now that she's in it.

"I'm glad you approve. Something to drink? The kitchen is down here," I point at the end of the hallway. The need to touch her wins out and I wrap my hands around her waist and pull her back against my chest. She sighs a contented sound and my pulse skitters. I know she feels my hard cock against her. There is no hiding it now.

"First, a drink," she says, spinning to face me. "Then, a tour of your bedroom." She slips her hands under my shirt and runs them up my chest. "I want to see all of this again."

I flex my abs and my pecs. It's an automatic reaction to touch I can't control unless I'm thinking about it. She grins and squeezes my muscles. Then she bites her fucking lip. I drag her into the kitchen and show her where the refrigerator is. She stands in front of the open door for longer than is normal, crossing one ankle over the other.

"Do you cook?" she finally asks. I tell her I do and she seems even more shocked at that fact than anything else. That says a lot because I told her my official job description, not Dr. Google's definition. Finally, she decides on a bottle of water and turns on me, eyes narrowed. "What else can you do?"

I pull my shirt off. It distracts her. Just what I was going for. "I can do many things, Win. You want me to show you a few?" My dick strains against my jeans. Maybe confused, because we are at home, but excited nonetheless. She stays quiet, just studying me. I'm reminded of how I study her when she doesn't know I'm looking. Except, of course, Windsor wouldn't be sneaky or vindictive about anything. It's all out in the open for me to see. Her honest eyes telling me all I need to know.

"One word," I say, voice low.

"Bedroom," she mutters.

I grab one of her hands and pull her onto my back piggyback style. I run down the corridor that leads to the master suite and her sweet laughter fills the space, echoing off the cold walls. I dive into my king sized bed and trap her beneath me. Her hair fans out, spreading all around her. I kiss her mouth. I kiss her forehead. I kiss her nose. I kiss her neck. I kiss her mouth again. Because I can't help it. My mouth wants to be on her.

"Look at me," she whispers. I open my eyes. Blue eyes shine back at me. "Thank you for showing me this. It means a lot to me." Her wet lips crash into mine, but this time I keep my eyes open because she wants me to look at her. A fine sight it is, too.

She breaks free from the kiss, breathing hard and staring at me. She squirms her way up to a sitting position. I roll off her to let her up. Walking away from my bed, Windsor looks around my room curiously. It's not until she turns around do I know she's fucking taking off her clothes. Her shirt is completely unbuttoned.

"I know you want to take things slow. I can respect that even if I don't want to participate in the same restraint." She smiles, then lets her shirt float to the ground. She reaches behind her back to unzip the skirt and steps out of it, exposing a blue lacy thong that matches the bra I saw earlier. Her body is tight and beautiful, kissable, more than fuckable. "You do owe me, though," she says, more confidently than I thought her capable of. All I can do is nod my head up and down like some sort of Neanderthal. I'm focused on the panties—that match my sheets, that match her eyes.

I swallow and shake off the fucking trance that is Windsor Forbes. I have a damned job to do. And by the looks of her, I better do it well or I'm in fucking trouble. She drags one finger over a chaise in the corner of the room and my gaze is glued to her every movement. I couldn't look away if I had bullets flying at my head. It's like she's a mirage or something perfect my mind conjured. This woman is made for me. She looks at me sideways, and continues her slow walk around the room. Like she's at a museum instead of in my fucking bedroom walking around practically naked. A growl rips from my throat.

"Get. Over. Here. Now," I order, standing from the bed. That gets her attention. Her slim body glides toward me. And it's like this slow motion moment.

It happened once when I was down range. The convoy in front of us hit an IED and the Humvee blew into a million pieces. It was a moment of pure clarity when I knew exactly what the outcome would be. When the bomb blew, I knew everyone in the vehicle would be dead. Now, watching Windsor approach, I know the outcome of whatever is happening between us. I'm falling for her. And there is no fucking stopping it.

Standing in front of me, she takes off her bra. She hooks both of her thumbs onto the sides of her panties and pulls them down slowly. She's bare. Her creamy, tan skin is flawless. This sight—of her naked in front of my bed –is my new favorite thing in the entire universe. She merely stands there, hands by her sides, a half smirk on her face, waiting for me to make the next move. She's handing over the reins. Fortunately for her, I'm more than willing to take them.

I cock my head and push my lips to one side. "Guess it's time to settle old debts then?" The display of mock irritation makes her laugh out loud. She throws her hands out in a *what can you do* motion. Windsor crawls over and kneels in the middle of my bed.

I change my mind. This is my favorite thing. The tiny landing strip at top of her pussy is mouthwatering. I keep my jeans on and walk on my knees to meet her front on.

She gives me a little frown. I brush the tiny crease between her eyebrows with my finger. "Slow," I remind her. Her cool fingers grab the front of my jeans and underwear and jerk me forward. One of her fingers rubs the tip of my dick. I suck in a breath through my teeth. "If they come off, I'll be buried in you before you take your next breath," I whisper.

"Maybe that's what I want," she replies.

"Kiss me," I order. I know I can distract her with my mouth. She leans up on her knees and presses every inch of her bare skin against me. Tracing my lips with her tongue, she rubs her tits on my chest. It is so fucking hot. I grab her sweet ass in my hands, rubbing it at the same tempo she's moving. She moans into my mouth. I bring one hand around and find her sweet, wet pussy. Her mouth stops moving against mine at first contact. Her blue eyes open and her gaze meets mine. She spreads her knees to give me better access to her.

Carefully, I dip a finger into her. She is sopping wet and tight. Too tight for my dick, I'm sure of it. Not that I plan on putting my dick anywhere near her pussy. At least not today. Which is unfortunate because I want her so bad it hurts.

But this is about her and her alone. She's breathing with her mouth open, tiny pants of pleasure. I drag my middle finger against her channel making a *come here* gesture with my finger. A tiny whimper escapes between breaths. My cock twitches. Leaning her head on my shoulder, she rocks her hips into my hand, trying to get my finger to go deeper.

"You're so tight, Win. You feel so fucking good," I say, crooking my finger, creating the perfect pressure against her wall.

She pulls away from me, her hands still on my shoulders and moans. I look down, because now I can see everything. My finger disappearing inside her, the way she grips my finger when I pull out a little.

Windsor makes some indistinguishable noise and I know how good I'm making her feel. If my finger wasn't dripping wet, her face would give it away. Her gaze falls down to watch me work my finger in her, and I fucking love that she's watching. "You like that?" I ask. All she can do is nod her approval. "Lay down," I say, inhaling the scent of her hair. I want all of her scents in me, on me, smothering me.

She makes a move to slide back but pauses. "Don't move your hand," she breathes. I can't help but smile— the big one.

"I wouldn't dream of it, baby," I say, pushing in my middle finger as far in as it will go. The moan that comes this time is loud. Her back hits the bed and I am on her in an instant. Her pink nipples are hard. Which means they need to be in my fucking mouth. I lick and suck each one. And just because I can't help it, I cover her mouth with another kiss. I want to taste all of her whimpers and moans. Memorize them.

I circle her wet clit with my thumb and really start the tempo. Brushing my tongue down her throat and back to her perky tits, I make my way lower. When my mouth finds her belly button, I lift my gaze to find her watching me. It's always like this. It's the silent asking for permission to go downtown. Some women are funny about it.

"Yes, yes. My God, yes," she says in one rushed breath. Access granted. I smile up at her, but she just throws her head back and whimpers. I never stop moving my fingers and I know she's close. I can see it.

I replace my thumb with my tongue. I suck on her clit and flick it with the tip of my tongue at the same time. She raises her hips. I push them back down to hold her in place. Very slowly, and also very carefully, I insert another finger into her. I can feel her hips trying to move.

"That feels so good," she moans, grabbing my hair, pulling my face closer to her. I work my fingers a little faster, but always keep the same tempo with my tongue. That's the key. My mouth is so wet from her, and she tastes so sweet that my head is clouding. Usually when I go down on a girl I can think about other things, not right now though. I have single-minded focus.

When her whimpers grow a little more quiet I know I'm about to make her fucking thighs tingle. I hook both fingers and rub her spot. She yells out. It echoes in my room, and I think it's probably the loudest and sweetest sound that has ever come from my bedroom. Her whole body stiffens, and I let her hips go so she can fuck herself with my fingers to her heart's content. Her pussy grips my fingers over and over and over; it's the orgasm that went on and on and I'm the one who gave it to her. She flops down, totally spent, breathing hard, her eyes closed tightly.

I slip my fingers out of her, after the spasms stop. I leave my mouth on her, knowing how sensitive she is right now. She sighs, this contented, happy fucking sigh, and it rocks me to my core. I lick her wet slit, wanting to taste it directly. I grab under her thighs and drag her to me until her legs rest on my shoulders. I drive my tongue into her and the taste is indescribably good. She shudders. I look up to find her arms propped behind her head, her eyes on me.

"Do you have any idea how good that feels?" she asks. I lick her from the bottom all the way up to her clit in one stroke. A quiet moan escapes her mouth. Her cheeks are flushed. She looks perfectly fucked. My bulging dick contests that idea.

"Not exactly, but I have some idea," I reply, lapping a few more straight trails up and down, only stopping to stick my tongue in her as far as it will go on my way by. Her pussy looks like perfection. "Do you know how good you taste?" I ask. She shakes her head.

Making sure my lips and tongue are coated in her, I slide my body up to come face to face with her. I smile. She smiles. I kiss her. She sucks my lips more than she kisses. When my tongue enters her mouth, she sucks that too. She grabs my fingers, the ones that were just inside her, and she sucks them. It's like my fingers are directly connected to my cock because when I feel her warm mouth sucking them, my hips rock into her, hoping to find a wet hole to play in. She bites my fingers a little. I rock into her again.

"You should take your pants off and try that," she says. I lick her neck and bite her ear lobe.

"Slow," I remind her. Even though right now I want nothing more than to bury myself in her and call it home, lock the door, and never leave.

"You're the first guy I've ever let do….that," she says, pointing down and then licking my mouth.

Pure male pride courses through me at the thought of being the only one. It's like I own it. Just because I feel like it, I drop down and kiss her directly on her pussy lips. I smile my widest smile when I see her smiling at me.

Sighing, she says, "Also, do you have any idea how your dimples affect me? Not only can I not think straight, but I can't tell you no either." I run my hands from her breasts all the way down the sides of her body, stopping at her thighs. Goosebumps rise on her skin everywhere I touch.

"I like responsive," I say.

"Too responsive?" she asks, furrowing her eyebrows. I shake my head in disbelief.

"You can never be too responsive. You probably can't help yourself now that you know what my tongue can do,"

I joke. Something mischievous flickers in her eyes. "Not even if you beg," I say, reading her mind directly correlating with the look in her eyes.

"It's only fair that I reciprocate, Mav," she says. Dick twitch. He's raising his hand. His turn. His turn. If her face gets an inch away from my cock, I'm sure I'll explode and embarrass the hell out of myself. That's not a problem I've ever considered. I'm breaking all the fucking rules today. I have more problems now than I've ever had.

Windsor grabs my jeans and has them unbuttoned and unzipped before the word "no" can come out of my mouth. Which is just as well, because I may be able to stave off putting my dick inside her, but a blowjob is something I don't think any male can refuse.

"Please let me suck your cock." Especially when your girl is begging for it.

Standing I pull off my jeans and boxer briefs in one swoop. I stand there, giving Windsor the opportunity she gave me. Her lead. This is her show now. She bites her fucking lip. Another dick twitch. My balls are in her hands and my cock is in her wet mouth a few seconds later.

I immediately regret standing up because my knees feel like they're going to buckle at any second. I fist her long hair, but I don't push her down, I let her swallow it at her own pace. And it is a fucking perfect pace. I look down and there it is. The sight a million wet dreams were made of. Blue eyes, full of emotion, staring up at me, sucking *my* dick. Her tiny hand pumps the bottom of my shaft and the other hand grazes my ball sack. It feels even better than it did when it was only a mental image.

I can't resist; I push her head a little bit and she takes my cock deeper. It's so warm and so wet. Her mouth was made to suck my dick. She keeps her hand moving and licks the sides, the bottom, the tip, around the edges, like a fucking lollipop before sliding it back in her mouth, all the way to the back. There's no way she can fit my whole package in her mouth; it's big. Windsor gets an A for effort. She gets an A for everything because I'm already about to fucking come. I knew it would be quick, but this is a new Maverick record.

I rock my hips into her mouth and tighten my grip on her head. Should I give her the gentlemanly tap? Usually I don't. I tap the back of her head a few times, the telltale I'm-going-to-blow-my-load-any-second signal and she speeds up her pumping hand. Green light. I tilt my head up and close my eyes as I come, like a fucking geyser, down her throat. My legs feel weak. I look down to watch her swallow the last of it. Sex, even almost sex, is the best damn kind of messy. Her spit and my come are all over her…and me. Windsor stands, wipes her mouth off the back of her hand, and then leaps into my arms. I collapse back on the bed, taking her with me.

"That was the best not sex of my life. Just so you know," I say, still trying to rein in my breathing. She props herself up on her elbows to look at me, a huge smile stretching across her satisfied face.

"Seriously? That really means something…given your extracurricular activities. I'm sort of honored," she replies. She does this tiny fake bowing motion. What I want to say is that she could have given me the worst blow job of my life—all teeth with no clue what the fuck she was doing – and it still would have been better than a deep throating porn star. Because it's her. I don't say that though.

"I'm serious," I say, kissing her shoulder because it's bare and it's right there taunting me. "You are amazing." She kisses me back, whispering sweet things in my ear. She gets under the sheets and lies down on my side of the bed. I change my mind for the third and final time. This is my new favorite sight. This time though? It scares me.

And then I know. I've fumbled with my fucked up thoughts long enough to know why I can't fuck Windsor. If I do, what I feel would be too real—because it won't be fucking or bagging or laying pipe.

It will be making love. And then she will own me forever without even knowing it.

Chapter Twelve

Windsor

"If I knew you could cook I probably wouldn't have disappeared on Halloween," I say, teasing. I feel like a real bitch for that move. Making fun of it makes me feel better. Hopefully it makes him feel better too.

I'm sitting at his dining table, an industrial chrome masterpiece, wearing only his t-shirt. He's making lunch. A very late lunch. We just left his bedroom for the first time in three hours. I'm all weak-limbed and deliriously happy. We didn't even have scx. Oh, but now I can picture it so vividly that it's almost enough. Almost. I have never thrown caution to the wind like I did with Maverick. The liberating feeling was a rush. I didn't worry about if I was doing something right or if my butt looked big. He made me feel comfortable in my own skin without even trying.

"How exactly did you disappear that night? A security guard told me you left in a taxi, which I'm beginning to think is not a fact," Maverick says.

"Your human lie detector must be off kilter." I smile. "Gretchen picked me up. She owed me that night for…well, you remember what happened," I trail off. So damn embarrassing. He turns back to the stove and I take this opportunity to check my messages.

"You should really be a little more thankful. I think she does fine work," he says, laughing. I groan.

It's not because Maverick seems to have forgotten about the second-degree burns Gretch graced me with, but my mother called and texted me today. One of them reads *I need you.* She's stooping to new levels to get my attention. She couldn't be bothered to call or visit or be a mother during most of my formative years, but now she needs me. She wants me to visit her.

I sigh. "I have to visit my Mom soon. I read on Google that Navy SEALs go through some pretty horrible, intense training. You don't sleep for days, they torture you, and so on." I swallow. I'm about to ask him something I never thought I'd ask anyone else for the rest of my life. "I know you have some time off before you leave, you know, to deploy. Do you want to partake in my personal brand of torture? Maybe visit Kathy with me?" He's leaving in a month. I think it's the first time I've said it out loud. It's sort of scary, and odd because I have no idea what I expect when he leaves. Will he pause the relationship and we'll just pick back up when he returns? "I have no idea why she wants me to visit. We're like oil and water. She's horrible, Maverick."

Still shirtless, he comes over to me. He lifts my chin up. "I would be delighted to meet your mom. If she's half as horrible as you make her sound maybe I can scare her a little for you. Throw off the bad guy vibe," he tells me, flashing his dimples. "I wanted to ask you to come on a trip with me before I left anyway. We can stop in Georgia before we head out. If you say yes."

I scoff. Is he serious? "A secret trip and you're wondering if I'll go? Of course I'll go. That actually makes me feel a little better about visiting Kathy. I know it's just a means to an end. I even have vacation days to use. Where are we going?" I ask.

"I have a training trip in San Diego. There'll be a lot of down time though, so I want to take you with me. You like the beach and dolphins right?" He remembers my long ramble from our horrible first date. He sits down in the chair opposite from me.

"I love the beach and dolphins. Do you love the beach and dolphins?" I ask, but he knows I'm asking a much bigger question. What the hell does he like? I feel like he never gives out details unless I ask for them. He's so internal in all ways.

"I actually do like the beach, even though I've spent many a nights freezing my balls off in it. I won't go in the Pacific without a wet suit, though." The huge smile crinkles his eyes. "Dolphins are okay, but they can be mean too. We have trained dolphins that help catch bad guys in the water. Training with them is painful. I got a cracked rib one night," he explains and I just kind of stare at him blankly. Normal isn't something that will ever be associated with Maverick. Getting used to that will take some time. "I can show you them when we visit, if you want."

"Wow. Okay," I reply. I look around his spectacular home filled with very expensive, yet tasteful furnishings, and wonder what exactly I'll find if I can peel away a few more layers of Mr. T. H. Stone told me things that makes some of it make sense, but I feel like there has to be more. I chew on my lip a little bit, searching my thoughts for the right question. He gets up and walks back to the counter.

"I'm sort of a Renaissance man, Windsor. I try to do a little of everything," he says. I look up at his unexpected confession. When I smile, he goes on, "I built the Chevelle from the bottom up. I enjoy cooking and can even do a little sewing. I can speak a couple foreign languages. During my last deployment I finished up my Masters degree. I appreciate good art and music, electronics make me happy, as does playing a little guitar," he says. He puts a plate with a pressed Panini sandwich on it in front of me. He takes his seat again in front of me. "I also know that you never button the bottom button on a suit jacket. Tell your friends that tidbit."

Maverick takes a deep breath.

"I have a bad past, but I don't like talking about it." He takes a bite of his lunch and stares at me as he chews. He's trying to decide what to say next.

I stuff a bite in my mouth, hopeful he'll keep his mouth running. It's so uncommon. He swallows.

"My favorite things vary because I get wrapped up in whatever I'm trying. Whatever I'm doing at the moment is my favorite. I want to perfect things. Make them better, make them my own," he says.

"You're sort of an anomaly. You know that? You're not the average Joe," I reply.

"I don't deal well with comparisons. That's something else you should know. I only care about comparing when I'm at fucking Best Buy picking out a new television," he says. I laugh.

"Don't compare you to other men. Check," I say. "I like this free flowing information. It makes me less self conscious about my verbal diarrhea problem."

Maverick grimaces. "I'm eating, Win," he says, shaking his head. I guess that was sort of gross.

We finish lunch in silence and I just process everything he's said. He is so unlike anyone I've ever met that I'm not sure what to label him. I suppose he gets his own label. I'm sure he'd appreciate being in that mental category anyways.

"I'm going to jump in the shower," he says, leaving me alone to process his confessions.

I'm cleaning up his kitchen. It's so nice and everything is so modern that it's sort of like a playground figuring out how to conquer the appliance. The minute after he leaves me alone, I hear knocking on a side door and I freaking panic. I don't have much time to decide what to do because Stone blazes into the house.

I yank down the hem of Maverick's shirt when he sees me. He stops in the middle of the living room, raises his hands over his head, and screams. I cover my ears because it's so loud. "Fuck yeah!" Stone cries. "Morg, get your pretty little ass in here." The door still wide open, Morganna walks through and closes it behind her. She shakes her head.

"God, Stone. Leave her alone," Morg says to her husband, who seems to be in the middle of some weird freaking touchdown dance. To me, she says, "There's rules, Windsor." She sighs. "Even if I don't agree with them I guess it's time to spill them. We'll talk later."

I just stare at her. Rules? What in the hell does that even mean? I'm so shocked I forgot what I'm wearing and what I look like. This looks like I'm having a sex-filled romp at Maverick's house. Of course they would assume the worst. Even though I feel like what we did was just as hot, and just as intimate, it still wasn't sex. We're going slow. Because Maverick wants to, and I think maybe that's best for me too.

"I told you she would be here. I told you!" Stone says, pointing at Morganna. She swats at his outstretched hand. "Who is the king, baby? Who is the fucking king?" His dance shifts to some sort of robotic sway. Morganna looks to the ceiling, like she's lost all patience and faith in humanity. I almost wish I wasn't here so she didn't have to endure Stone's…dance moves.

"You're the king, honey. You are," she says, exasperated, merely placating him to save time.

I take this opportunity to flee into Maverick's bedroom. At some point he grabbed my suitcase out of his car so I have all my things. I hear his shower running so I poke my head in and let him know he has guests. He seems surprised, but not really shocked. So, he does have houseguests that are "just friends." It's just the slutty variety he doesn't allow in his personal realm.

The sight of him naked gives me pause. I don't think I'll ever tire of looking at his perfect body.

His narrow waist frames his perfect V. You know the one. The caboose that belongs at the bottom of every mouthwatering ripple of his abs. All...six, no all eight of them. He told me working out is part of his job, that his body is a like a machine because it's his craft, his tool, for doing anything that is required of him.

For all the hard curves I can't help but know how easily a human life can be taken. With a deployment to God knows where looming, it makes it so much more real. Sure, I could die in a car accident on the way to my boring accounting job. But I don't deal in death and danger as a profession. His calculated and uncalculated risks are so high they can't be deciphered. I offer a weak smile and strip off my shirt, and enter the enormous shower with him. It's a wet room, with showerheads everywhere. The solitary bottle of some sort of body wash or hair shampoo is on a shelf by his head. I have to laugh. He's still just a guy.

His gaze is hungry as he watches me walk toward him. I brush against him as I grab the green bottle. There are a few other showerheads I could choose from, but I grab him around his waist instead. He pulls me against him as the hot water cascades over both of us. Every bone in my body softens against him.

"Morganna is pretty pissed. You should probably go corral your friend," I say against is chest. He kisses me on the top of my head, then dips down and kisses my shoulder.

"You just got in here. Can't I corral you first?" he asks. I shiver. Not from the cold.

His hard-on presses on my stomach and moves. "You're so responsive," I say. He cuts me off with his lips on mine. His tongue slides into my mouth and works in and out. I lean up to grab his face in my hands. It's scruffy beneath my fingertips, so perfectly manly. He slides his fingers very slowly up the sides of my neck and then into my hair.

Morganna's giggle finds us in the bathroom. Maverick pulls me, super quickly, behind his back. Sure I'm hidden, but Mav and his huge, manly, beautiful dick are on full display for her.

"She's giggling," I say quietly.

"She is. In my bedroom," he replies tersely. I stifle a giggle myself.

Maverick yells, "Not in my bedroom, Stone!" He palms my breasts in his hands a few times, making my nipples stand at attention, and then shakes his head. "Later," he rasps, even though his eyes say *right now.*

"Later," I answer. He grabs a towel off a hook on the wall and wraps it around his waist, in that perfect way guys do. I finish showering, using the sole bottle of soap on my entire body and my hair.

When I enter his room it's blessedly free of Morganna and Stone. Dressing in a dark red shift dress, because I only have work clothing, I put my hair in a messy side-bun. I brush my teeth, do my makeup, and pray I've taken so long that Morganna isn't here anymore. Maverick hasn't returned so that's a bad sign. I'll be answering to Morg about ignoring all her warnings about Maverick. A phone conversation or even a texting match would be preferable to talking face to face with her about whatever awkwardness this is going to be. I glance at Mav's bed before I exit the bedroom and I get hot and shiver at the same time. I have a goofy grin plastered on my face when I find Morganna sitting on the couch, tapping furiously on her laptop. She's talking to someone on her blue tooth, of course.

"I don't care what she says. She's the one who got herself into this fucking mess to begin with. I can't help her if she doesn't keep her collagen filled duck pout shut." Morganna pauses her tirade. "Of course you can tell her I said that. I'll fire her ass, I will." She looks up and smiles at me when I sit on a chair opposite her. The smile on her face looks insane because of the obviously very brash words coming out of her mouth—Jekyll and Hyde in her element. She clicks off her call without saying goodbye. "They're in the garage doing whatever it is that men do in garages. Getting dirty, trying to add to their appeal," she says still typing on the computer. "He did tell me you will be joining us on our trip." She stops typing and looks directly at me, gauging my reaction or trying to tell how I feel about it. Morganna probably has the same lie detecting skills Maverick does.

"Yeah. I'm bringing him with me to see Kathy first," I say. Morg knows about my mother. She listened to me whine and complain about not having any family while we were in undergrad. My dad died when I was in my teens, leaving me alone. She also knows about the string of stepfathers. All of this adding up to my foolish trust issues. It's probably why she's tried to keep me from dating Maverick. Maybe she thinks he's just bad news for me, not necessarily in general. "The crazy lady has been calling Gretchen to try to get to me. I may be a lot of things, Morg, but I can't ignore her if she's actually asking for me. God knows I'll regret going, but having Maverick there with me will make it a little better." She hasn't stopped staring at me since I first opened my mouth. "What?"

"You're falling for him," she says. It's not a question, just an observation. Like she would tell me the color of my dress, or what she had for breakfast. I look down at my hands folded neatly on my lap. "I already told you I'm done meddling, Windsor. You don't have to be afraid of what I think. I'm starting to think it's for the best anyway." She huffs. "He seems better for it and if I lose one more bet on his expense, my jaw may come unhinged," she says, smiling a perfect grimace.

It would make me a new brand of crazy if I admit I'm falling for a guy after several dates, I'm more cautious than that, but I can't deny it. I shrug.

Morganna laughs. "Let's go get them. I have to get back to my office. Phillipe is probably downing purple pills as we speak. Sometimes I feel like no one does what I want them to," Morganna says. I have work to get done, too.

"If you want something done," I muse. She brushes me off.

"I know, I know…do it myself," she says. "I can't hold the whole world on my fucking shoulders though." She laughs a little at her own expense. And it's in moments like these that I see the old Morganna. The person who would laugh at how serious and mean she's become.

She leads me down a corridor on the opposite side of the house. I haven't been on this side. Or upstairs. There are a ton of rooms that need exploring. Naked explorations come to mind. Morganna prattles on about a case she's working on and how Stone is giving her a hard time about working too much. The subject of my affections for Maverick has fallen off her radar all together. Broaching the subject isn't in my best interest, so I nix my questions about the *rules*. Morganna pushes open a heavy door and we walk into the garage.

It looks like a full on, very organized mechanic's shop in here. Two full garage bays are devoted to tools and random pieces of equipment that I can't name. Maverick and Stone are standing together talking, their voices low. Their conversation stops completely when we get within earshot. It's obvious they weren't doing anything in here, just talking. Maverick smiles. Stone, still exuberant, just stares at me with a creepy gleam in his eye.

"I'm going back to work. Drive me please," Morganna commands in a sweet voice. I'm not sure why I keep my distance, but I do. It's not like Morganna and Stone don't know what we've been doing here in his house. Where women don't go. They know. I want to hug him and kiss him because he's standing there, in the middle of heavy machinery. I feel like I'm on display. The freak at the sideshow. The one Thomas Maverick Hart let in. They say their goodbyes and with a swift clap on Mav's back Stone is gone.

Morganna goes to leave, then pauses mid-step. "Rule number one. Don't forget your pants," she says. Being Morg, she leaves before I can ask what the hell that is supposed to mean. I shoot a puzzled glare at Maverick. He hikes his shoulders.

"Seriously. You come with rules?" I ask, mortified. His life is different, way different than the average person, but can I really be expected to follow rules? That could be the only possible explanation for Morganna's statement. Michelle Obama can't wear shorts. Windsor Forbes has to wear pants. It is ludicrous.

He laughs a rumble of low laughter as he approaches me. He grabs both sides of my face while he traces my lips with both of his thumbs. "No rules. Never any rules with us. Okay?" he says.

"How can I argue with her? I didn't have on any pants!" I answer.

"With good reason. Stone won't be making any more surprise visits. I made sure of that. Morganna probably made up a set of damn rules herself," Maverick says, closing the space between us, trying to reassure me.

Shivers shoot down my spine. I don't think I'll ever get enough of his touch. It seems silly to want something so badly that you've lived your entire without, yet there it is. Now I'm wondering how I'll go without it. He seems to be thinking the same thing. He replaces his thumbs with his mouth and kisses me passionately. His hands slide down to rest on the curve at the bottom of my spine.

"Plus, if they were rules for *me*, number one would be that you *never* wear any pants," he says against my lips. "Or anything else for that matter."

"Fine. I'll go to work naked," I joke. "I do have to go check in. Especially if we're leaving shortly," I say. I can't help the smile that hurts my cheeks. I'm so excited to go anywhere with him—to get to know him more. We are officially a couple who vacations. I notice the frown on his face.

"You really have to leave now?" he says. I've been around him long enough to realize he's at his own "office" only when he has to be. It's either short days, because he went in to work out and shoot, or long days where I have no idea what he did all day and night. I don't ask, either.

He gives me vague answers when I do ask. "Diving." "Meetings." "Speed ball." "I got some new gear." "Monster Mash."

Oh, he's going to make this hard. "I can come back over after…if you want," I suggest.

"Yes." He answers quickly.

"You have a lot of house to show me. I haven't even gotten the official tour yet," I say. Chewing on my lip, I think of all the things we can do during the tour. He shakes his head, his dimples coming out in full force. It's like felony assault, I swear it. I lean up and kiss him. "I can't wait. Goodbye," I say, leaning over to whisper in his ear.

He cuts me off before I can finish. "Never say goodbye," he demands. His smile fades. "I'm making my own rules. Never say goodbye. That's rule number one."

I nod. "I'll see you later."

Chapter Thirteen

Maverick

Cocaine is less addicting. Windsor fills every waking thought, and my dreams at night? She's fucking starring in them. The rest of my life is merely subtitles at this point. That's not necessarily a good thing either. At least all the years of doing nothing except training, or thinking about training will probably kick in. I'm counting on autopilot coming in for the win.

"I swear she is trying to kill me," Windsor says. She's sitting in the middle of a pink, frilly bed. We're at her Mom's house in Georgia, in Win's childhood bedroom. Kathy wanted Windsor here because husband number five—I'm not even sure if she's said his actual name—left her...again. "He'll be back. He's gotta come back." She turns to face me. Her eyes are wild. I know what she's thinking.

"You don't live here anymore. She's not going to ask you stay here. Kathy knows you have a job and a life," I say. Windsor is like a ball of fucking nerves. Her leg bounced the entire flight to Atlanta. I tried to get her to join me in the airplane bathroom, but she was too wound up to respond. That's when I knew this wasn't just an issue of conflicting personalities. Whatever went down between Windsor and her mother, the scars from it are deep. If it were possible, I felt an even tighter connection with her for it.

She runs her hands through her hair and collapses back onto her bed. A white teddy bear bounces off. It seems Kathy had a hard time letting go, because this bedroom looks like it hasn't been touched since Windsor left.

"I keep telling myself that. She is a fucking mess, Maverick. She can't take care of herself. What kind of daughter would I be if I left her here by herself?" she asks. It's almost rhetorical. We both know what kind of person she is. She's good.

"I could make some phone calls and see if we could get someone to come over and check on her every day," I offer.

She shakes her head. "She's always had a man around. That was always number one for her," she says sadly. Fuck. Now Windsor looks miserable. I sit on the edge of her bed, feeling a little apprehensive because It's like I'm sitting on a child's bed and that's just fucking weird.

I run my fingers through her hair. I'd take away whatever she's feeling if I could. God knows I'd take it all away. Because I know what feelings like this do. She hides her face in a fuzzy, heart shaped pillow. I don't even know what to say. Nothing can fix it. Words aren't a magic cure for anything. Words only take the sting off the surface. Deep down, everything is still shredded and bleeding and aching.

"I have to stay here," she says, the pillow muffling her words.

My pulse picks up and I try to calm myself. I'm not mad. I take a deep breath. The rational piece of my brain starts connecting the dots. Being separated from Windsor makes me nervous. My body has an actual physical response to the mere mention of me going and her staying. It is fucking insane.

"I know," I say. Because I do know. It doesn't change how I feel. If she didn't stay, she wouldn't be the person I fell for. She turns to look at me and a tear slips down her face. I wipe it away with my thumb. She is so God damned beautiful that I can't stand it. Even in a child's bed with a red face, she is the only sight I've ever been addicted to. I want to look at her and really see her in every possible way. When she's sad, happy, coming, when she's angry…I'll take it all.

Windsor groans and flips to her back. "Tell the dolphins 'hi' for me," she says, sulking with her arms folded across her chest. "That's why I'm upset you know. I know Kathy will be okay…eventually. I'm upset that I won't get to spend this time with you."

I lean down and kiss her square on the mouth. I do it because I'm not sure what to say. Hopefully my mouth says everything it needs to say without actually speaking. "It's a shame really. I was going to take you to get a dolphin tattoo on your ankle," I offer, rubbing my lips across hers. She laughs and sniffles a little. It was the reaction I wanted. A cute grimace crosses her face.

"You never see a bumper sticker on a Bentley, Mav," she says. "Forbes women don't mar their bodies with art. We prefer it on the wall. It's not the 1990's either. A dolphin?" she laughs even louder. I smile. "You get a dolphin tat," she counters. I kiss a tear that is about to roll down her cheek.

"You think I should? Maybe one diving over my dick?" I reply.

Her laughter fades a little. "If anyone is going to be diving by your dick, it's going to be me," she whispers.

It is so hot I actually consider a dick diving dolphin. God, Stone would love that. That's a vagina dick image he'd never be able to burn out of his mind. I chuckle.

She stands from the bed, but not before running her small hand over my jeans-covered cock. Tease. Cock fucking tease. "I have to go talk to her," she says. "I'm sure that's what is expected from me. Dance monkey, dance!" she yells.

I grab her waist from behind and pull her ass to my dick. "While you're obeying commands lets do bad things in that bed. I want to defile it tonight," I say, already picturing her naked in it. The weirdness of the pink, child's bed has completely disappeared the second I imagine her naked. Dick twitch. Schwing! "I need to take a run. I'll pick up some groceries. Seems she doesn't get out of bed all that much. I'll make dinner tonight?" I ask. She bends down to pick something off the floor and the angle is so perfect I can almost feel her pussy through both my jeans and hers. "Or we can defile it now," I grind out.

Windsor sighs. "What exactly is your definition of defiling? It can't be all that bad if we're still *taking things slow*. Or are you finally going to show me a new talent?" she replies.

Fuck. I don't know how much longer I can hold her off. She told me she was glad we were waiting to have sex, but I'm not sure if that's because she knows I have some weird fucking hang up about it, or if she really doesn't want to either.

"You're ready?" I ask. Fuck. Fuck. Fuck.

She turns around to face me. "I've been ready, Mav," she says, using my hard-on inducing nickname. She pauses, bites her lip, and then continues, "In fact I'm ready right now. I'm ready any second you're within eyesight or ear shot. Everything about you makes me want you. I've wanted your dick inside me even when I only wanted a one night stand with you."

What. The. Fuck. This particular ramble enlightened me, that's for damn sure. I narrow my eyes. "When did you want a one night stand?" I ask. That would have made things even more fucked up than they are now. I'm also so turned on that I can't see straight. A one night stand is what most of my bags want. The fact never bothered me in the least, or had any affect on me really. Now the same words out of Windsor's mouth? She might as well say, "Come in me, big daddy." That's what it does to me.

She folds her arms across her chest and smiles a knowing smile. "Don't play coy. You know the first night I met you the effect you had on me. I would have had sex with you on the second date. But you went and propositioned me with money instead of a hotel date," she explains. "I was already wet before you walked into my office. Because I was thinking of you all weekend long," she admits. My stomach flips a little. "The question of the month is are you ready?"

I swallow loudly. Am I? She is so honest with me about everything. Should I just tell her how I feel about her? Do I tell her that I think sex will change everything? That I'm so fucking mad about her that the second I stick my dick inside her, I might proposition her with marriage? That would scare her off for sure. Because Johnny Fucking Nash screwed her over. I sigh. I can't give in to her. Not yet. Not until I know that she's ready to accept all of me. All of me forever. That's a huge thing to ask. I settle for a half-truth. "I want to fuck you so badly that it hurts me." I run my hand down the front of my jeans, over my engorged, miserable cock. "Everything in my life is fast and fleeting. Is this so wrong?" I kiss her, rubbing all the way down the sides of her body. She lets out a small moan. "I want to do one thing slow. Not crazy…just good and right." If she only knew how much I just admitted.

Windsor slides her hands under my shirt and up my chest. "I'm not going anywhere. I promise," she professes. The way her blue eyes are locked on mine scares me and excites me. I think she's going to say it. She's going to tell me how she feels about me. If she admits as much that will be it. Game over. I'm hers. That's what I've been waiting for. Just a tiny, little something to let me know she feels just as fucking crazy as I do. She closes her eyes and looks down. I feel sick.

She pulls away from me. The moment turns to complete piss. I'm a pussy. She's been burned. This is fucking dismal. I smile to try to hide the disappointment. I lift her chin. "I'm yours. You are mine. Okay?" I tell her. This much we can both agree on. It's safe territory.

"Mine," she repeats. I nod. She's way more than mine. She's everything. Fuck.

She leaves me in her room to go visit Kathy in a room down the hall. I told her I was going for a run, but I still can't shake the fucking moment. She can't say it. I wonder if she'll ever be able to tell me how she feels. I will wait forever for her to get on the same page as me, but what if she never gets there? What if I'm this dumb fucking idiot trying to get the girl who will never want anything more than sex from me? Most guys would be thrilled at this prospect. Hell, a couple months ago that'd thrill me, too. Now it just makes my stomach hurt. I walk out of the bedroom, leaving the J.T.T posters to have a staring contest with her cheerleading trophies. I hear Windsor's voice and I can't help it...I walk toward it, toward the cracked bedroom door, and I listen.

Her voice is muffled a little bit and I can tell she's crying again. I have to remind myself that I'm fucking eavesdropping, so I can't go in and hold her. The urge is so powerful that it surprises me.

"Why, Kathy? Why?" Windsor begs. Well, when in Rome...right? I walk a little closer and stand just to the right of the door, completely out of sight. Stealth is one of my favorite tricks. I can disappear into night like a ghost, but the thing driving me now is the ability to discover something about Windsor that I didn't know before. Something she isn't comfortable telling me. It's like a fucking unicorn or something. You wouldn't look away if one crossed your path. You never know when or if you'll see it again. Fuck. Even my rationalizing is becoming insane.

"You would never understand, Windsor. I did what was best for you. After your father died everything was...different," Kathy says, sighing.

"What you really mean to say is that *you* were different." Windsor sobs a little, but she seems to be pulling it together. Less tears, more anger. "You and dad broke up when I was small. Why would him dying while you were married to number three affect you? It doesn't make any sense. You were remarried. You didn't give a shit about him anymore!" Windsor cries.

"Bite your tongue," Kathy says. Windsor scoffs. "The numbers you give them only show your bitterness. It's no wonder Johnny cheated on you." I've never hit a woman, but I have the urge to fucking bitch slap Windsor's mother so hard that she ends up in a different country.

"Johnny cheated on me because he is an asshole, Mo...Kathy. I didn't do anything wrong. If you don't agree with me, maybe you can talk to my psychiatrist who says the same thing. Nash is a self-centered prick who doesn't deserve someone like me," Windsor says. My chest swells with pride. Pain changes people. Some people don't rise above it. She has.

"If that's what you have to tell yourself," Kathy replies.

"Why did you want me to come here? You wanted me here and all you do is say nasty things to me. If you haven't noticed, I've moved on. Nash is fucking history. I'm with Maverick. And he is one hundred times the man Nash is." There is a long, silent pause. My pulse pounds in my ears at her admission. She speaks again. "I take it back. Maverick is one million times the man Nash can ever hope to be. He would never do what Johnny did to me," Windsor says, lowering her voice. I think she knows I'm still in the house. She has no clue I'm listening, though. Kathy makes some noise, and I can just see her sarcastic expression. Windsor doesn't bring up my job, or tell her mother what I do. She only speaks of my character. It hits me hard. She's defending me as a man. Not a glorified SEAL.

"Don't fool yourself, honey. You will never be able to keep a man like that. You're merely a plaything—a flavor of the week. Maybe if you had some of my wiles you'd be able to lock him up," her mother says. A small sob, one that I recognize, hits me directly in the heart. Kathy clears her throat and says, "Let's be honest, though. You're weak. You'll never fight for what you want. He'll crush you just like Johnny did…maybe even worse."

"I hate you," Windsor cries. She doesn't try to defend me anymore. Windsor thinks her crazy mother is right. I feel like killing something. Shooting something. Doing something reckless. I hear a glass with ice rattle. "Are you seriously drinking bourbon right now?" Windsor sounds completely shocked.

"You've upset me. It's 5 o'clock somewhere. Always remember that," Kathy spits out.

"It's also always 9 a.m. somewhere," Windsor replies. I'm starting to feel guilty for invading her privacy like this, but there is no way I can turn away at this point. I know what I need to reassure her of. All of the complete bullshit Kathy spews can help me convince Windsor of my feelings. Her fears are supremely unfounded. I vow right now to make her mother know this too. Whatever it takes. Whatever it fucking takes.

I hear a footstep and get ready to bolt. Kathy speaks. "Stop, Windsor. Just listen for a second please." This bitch has the nerve of steel.

"What, Kathy?" Windsor returns. Ice rattles. She takes a large gulp of the liquor. I almost feel the burn in my own throat just hearing it.

"I'm going to try to explain something to you." More ice rattling, a bottle glugging out more truth juice, then a sigh. I want to protect Windsor from this. From the type of person this is, because I know what a person like this is capable of. Windsor sighs. It's long and heavy and full of emotion.

"When you can't have the person you want the most, you start to find pieces of that person in other people. That person, the one you're in love with, is like your favorite song," Kathy says. She takes another sip and then continues on. "You try to find sections or pieces of your favorite melody in others. Some will have the same chorus line, others will seem so similar you might be able to forget it's not your favorite song, just a welcome imposter. You take the new songs and you sink down into them. They wrap around you and take away everything else, changing you to accommodate. You end up changing so much that the one person you wanted so badly wouldn't recognize you at all—inside or outside. Then nothing matters. You give up. You're left with snippets of mismatched melodies and emptiness. I do what I do to get by. I do what I do to forget. Because Windsor? Remembering is far worse than forgetting," Kathy explains. Windsor clears her throat.

"Your father was my favorite song. After he died all of the possibilities died with him," she tells Windsor. "This," I hear her ice rattle. "All of this is just imposter. This is what you will have," Kathy says.

"I will never be like you," Windsor bites back. Her voice holds more anger than I've ever heard. I want to see her face. I want to know what this looks like for myself. "If it's the very last thing I do, I will make sure that my life never turns out like yours," she says.

"Then my goal in life will be reached. Be strong enough to take what you want," Kathy says. "Don't be a weak girl. Be a noble woman." I can't listen to this fucking shit anymore. I wish I never came here. Never hearing those horrible words would be preferable to knowing exactly who...or what Windsor calls family. I sneak away from the door just as quietly. I dress quickly in my running gear and walk downstairs. Guilt washes over me for leaving Windsor with the damned monster upstairs for any amount of time. Her good is so good, that she would choose to stay here and help the woman who never gave her anything except heartache and bad advice. It disgusts me almost as much as the bad guys I kill. A rat in the house is far worse than a rat in the attic.

I want to do anything I can to reassure her that I won't burn her the way Nashhole did, but I can't. I started dating Windsor with the intentions of breaking her fucking heart. I knew I would and it didn't matter—at the time, of course. It still doesn't make me any better than him. That doesn't make me any better than the person Kathy thinks I am. It makes me think of my own family, something I try to do as little as possible. We're not so different, Windsor and I.

My precise control slips and I'm flooded with the insecurities I never let anyone see. Maybe I am the fuck-up everyone thinks I am. I try so hard to cover up who I am with what I do, that I get lost inside. Pushing my jog into a fast run, I let everything in. All of it. It doesn't break me like it used too, but it still fucking hurts. It always hurts.

Chapter Fourteen

Windsor

My mother didn't eat dinner with us and, damn, it was so delicious. Maverick is a fantastic chef. He doesn't have to measure anything and only glanced at a recipe twice.

He was a little out of sorts when he came back from his run. I pray to any deity that will listen that my crazy ass mother won't scare him off. It would be fitting if she did though. He has been so sweet to me since we've been here. He knows I need something to balance out the ugly. He brought home two bouquets of flowers when he returned. One for me and one for my mother. Obviously overkill, but who was I to deny my boyfriend motherly bonding with Krazy Kath? I have to keep reminding myself that I'm used to being an emotional bomb when I'm near the beast. Maverick has no clue this is how it is every time we're together. I'm sure he's catching on.

Kathy drank herself to sleep before 4 p.m. Fitting. Now Maverick and I are snuggled in my double bed, staring up at the plastic glow-in-the-dark stars stuck to my ceiling. No matter which way we lay, we're touching. It's only now that I feel gratitude toward number two for buying me a double bed instead of the queen that I'd asked for. This has always been my room. It feels strange now. My mother always lived in this house. Husbands came and went through the revolving door downstairs. I guess I should be grateful I didn't have to move constantly, like some of my friends with divorced parents. I think she promised my Dad she'd give me a stable home life. I scoff at that crazy notion.

I roll to face Maverick. "I'm going to miss you so much," I whisper, turning my head to kiss his neck. He breathes out a contented sigh. I can't help the giggle and then kiss a little more wantonly—my tongue licking, lips brushing, and teeth trailing. He rolls on his side, one hand splayed on my ass, the other behind his head. Of course I'm insanely turned on because Maverick is in a five-mile radius. It's so unfair, the effect he has on me.

"Where's your accent?" Maverick asks, surprising me. He is so trying to distract me. I'll let him…for a little while. I smile.

"Do you wish I had a southern drawl? I've never had an accent. I think this state has pockets of country. Does that make sense?" I ask. In the city no one has accents, but in the smaller counties you'd think we were in Kentucky or somewhere where good ole' boys rule the world. My parents don't have an accent, so I lucked out. Maverick shrugs.

"The women at the grocery store had thick accents. I was just wondering," he explains. I lean over and place a dry kiss on his mouth. His hard-on pokes me in the stomach.

"Were you wooing women in my hometown grocery store, T.H.?" I ask, wiggling a little bit to let him know I feel his erection. I see his white smile in the dark. He grazes my earlobe with his teeth. "You were all sweaty and probably all mouthwatering. It's hardly fair. These women aren't used to men like you," I whisper. It comes out breathy, and his gentle licks send shivers directly between my legs.

"I only care about wooing you," he says, still too close to my ear for me to think straight. "Men like me?" he asks. Does he want reassurance? Surely a man like Maverick knows exactly how people perceive him.

"Consider me wooed. I'm gooey and pliant and completely at your disposal," I admit, turning my head to catch his lips against mine. I speak against his mouth, "Men like you. The type that are so magnificent and perfect that women aren't sure if we want to turn around and run for the hills, or strip off our panties and demand retribution for living in such an unfair world." He chuckles a little. I trail my hand over the side of his neck and over his large, hard bicep. "Put me in the second category." He groans. I haven't stopped moving my hand on his body. I'm now grazing over his rippled stomach and further down.

Quick as lightening he rolls me over, his weight pressing me on the bed. Even in the dark his perfect hazel gaze finds mine. "I wish I was as perfect as you think I am. I wish I were good. I'm not. I want to be good enough. For you," he says, his voice cracking a little bit.

Instead of replying, I kiss him. I was just playing around. Maverick's words are serious. They hang in the air like an unspoken question. He's leaving tomorrow for a week and I don't want him to remember a serious conversation. I entwine my tongue with his. I pull on his thick bottom lip with my teeth. I keep my eyes open because he likes to watch me kiss. I like him watching me kiss him.

I don't beg him for sex anymore. It will be obvious when he's ready. He'll be inside me. He always makes sure I come...at least once. His tongue and hands rival the average guy's dick. I try not to dwell on how many women he's practiced on, but it's hard not to be thankful when I'm screaming his name in complete ecstasy. I do wonder what exactly he thinks will happen after we do the deed. Personally, I think I'll be so happy that I won't think straight for a few weeks, and then I'll make him screw me a million more times until I can't walk. Then I'll have to stay in his bed forever. It will be perfect. I wish he knew that. I'm open about everything with him. But something holds me back from telling him these things. My pride wants him to come to the conclusion all by himself. I won't beg, but I will tease him unmercifully. I get an idea. I break the kiss. I lick his neck tattoo and across his jawline.

"I have an idea," I tell him. I jump up from my bed, click on a small light, and start digging through my old dresser. There is some seriously creepy clothing from the 80's—ugly t-shirts with Bob Saget on them, back when he was a father to DJ and Stephanie, and not some skeevy old guy. There is also, in the very back of the bottom drawer, a lacy piece of lingerie. It was my in case of emergency item when I was a senior in high school. Of course it never got used.

"Why does that sound like a horrible idea and a bad case of blue balls?" Maverick growls from the bed. I can only laugh. He already knows what's inside my head— what I want to do to him. Maybe along with his lie detecting he can also read minds. Nothing would surprise me at this point.

I tell him to turn away and not to look until I tell him to. I slide off my nightshirt and pull the scrap of lace over my head. It hugs me like a glove. I remove my panties because to be the ultimate tease, I plan to show him everything he's refusing to partake in...and dance on his lap. A little dirty, but I'm sure he can handle it. A box catches my eye. It's poking out of Maverick's leather overnight bag. He's not looking so I investigate further. Because it looks like a box of condoms and I know it can't be. But it is. A 24 pack of extra large sized schlong wrappers. I feel like I just found my Christmas presents and I'm about to get busted. Shit.

"I'm ready for it. Whatever depraved act you have planned...I'm ready," Maverick says, his head still turned away. With the knowledge of the condoms my confidence falters a little. Dancing or stripping or doing many of the sexual things with Maverick are things I never, ever did in my past. All of it comes from the need to be creative—no sexual intercourse makes for interesting, hot foreplay. Dampness creeps between my legs at the mere thought. Turning him on equals turning me on.

I yank on the bottom of the stretchy black lace. "Okay. You can look n-o-ow," I stutter. Real freaking sexy, Windsor. Why did I have to see the box? I would be dancing with the same confidence as the pros at the Spearmint Rhino if I didn't look in his bag. Crap.

Maverick shifts in the bed and stares at me. He continues staring at me. And he also looks like he wants to devour me...and I haven't so much as moved an inch. I shoot him a weak smile.

"Depraved enough?" I ask, running my hands down my sides. He nods. He moves to sit on the edge of the bed, his feet planted solidly on the floor. His abs flex when he moves, and even just sitting there shirtless, they are on full display.

Mustering courage, I bite my lip and sashay up to him, using my best sexy walk. The seventeen year old me who slept a thousand nights in this room would never believe the almost-thirty year old me has this man in this bed. She'd demand photographic evidence.

He reaches both his arms out the second I get close enough to grab. I shake my pointer finger at him. "No, no, no. Touching isn't allowed," I say. He makes a big show of folding his hands in his lap and flashing his fucking dimples. No fair.

"You are so fucking hot, baby," he says. I feel hot. He makes me feel it. I bring both of my hands up and run them through my hair. His eyes cut to my thighs that expose the millisecond I raise my arms. A few more centimeters and he'll see my goods. I sway my hips back and forth, my bare feet on the wooden floor making the only noise. "Hold that thought," he growls.

Maverick grabs his iPhone off the nightstand and turns on a classic rock song. Smiling, using both of his freaking dimples again, he sets the phone back on the nightstand. He nods at me. I never stopped moving in the first place. Now I let my hips rock back and forth, swaying and moving to the beat. Rubbing the side of my thigh, I bring my hand in between my legs and caress myself. I bite my lip, but never take my eyes of his.

He lays his hands on the top of his head and watches me in that predatory way as I move. I turn around and bend all the way over, baring myself completely. He lets out a whoosh of air. I peek at his face. It's a firm mix of indecision and lust. His eyes are glued to my ass, while his chest works overtime to keep up with his rapid breathing. "You like?" I ask.

"You just passed depraved and moved into wicked territory," he whispers so low I'm not even sure if I'm supposed to hear. "Come here," he says a little more loudly.

I couldn't tell him no if I wanted to. His voice sends a shock of wetness right between my thighs. The promise of his hands on me forces one foot in front of the other. I leave the hem of the lace riding high and straddle his lap, facing him. His hard-on is on full display, tenting his black boxer briefs, begging to be touched.

Finding one of the few appropriate places, he rests his hands on my arms. "What are you doing to me?" He lays his head against my chest, buzzing his nose and lips against my skin.

"Dancing for my boyfriend," I reply innocently, grinding down a little further on his lap and pushing my tits into his face. "What are you doing to me?" I ask.

"Whatever the fuck I want," he growls, pulling my hips and my exposed sex down onto his lap. I feel his dick through his underwear and it does crazy things to my head. The classic rock song finishes. Lacey black nighty is gone the next second.

He kisses me furiously, like he's going to starve without me. He's crazed. And I know why. This is it. He's finally going to make love to me. He can't hold back anymore. His mouth finds my nipple the same time he pulls my hips against him, against his cock. Creating the perfect friction his tongue flicks one nipple and then the other, before closing his mouth fully around one. Throwing my head back, a long moan escapes. He makes me feel so good. Tingling pressure spreads inside and outside of every cell in my body.

"Do whatever you want, Mav…whatever you want," I cry. His tongue is on my neck, my ear, my jaw, and then finally back in my mouth, twisting with mine. I thread my hands around his thick neck and press my body against his. He lays down and I'm on top of him.

"What do you want?" he asks, but it's more of a freaking growl. I've never seen him this turned on. His huge hands are like vice grips on my hips. I couldn't get away if I wanted to. He twitches underneath me every few seconds, reminding me he's there. I think I want to suck him right now. That's what I want. I catch my bottom lip between my teeth and give him a knowing smile. I kiss down his chest, over his heart and down his abs. He stops me. "No, Windsor. What do you really want?"

"I want to suck your cock, if you'll let me," I say, confused. Isn't it obvious I'm going downtown?

"Just say it," he says. A light switch is thrown. I know what he's asking. He wants me to beg. He wants me to tell him I want him to make love to me. I can't be the voice for both of us.

I exhale, placing a wet kiss on his hard, lower stomach. "What do you want me to say, Mav? Do you want me to beg? Is that what you need?" The stupid questions sound pathetic coming out of my mouth. "I saw the condoms," I admit, averting my gaze and tucking my hair behind my ear.

Maverick releases me and brings his hands up to tangle in his hair. He runs his palms down the front of his face, and heaves a huge sigh. He looks tortured and I don't want to see him like this. Not now. Not ever. So I give him the reprieve of not having to answer me. I yank down his underwear and stick his dick in my mouth. He hisses out a breath.

"Not like this. Come here," he orders. He grabs me by my waist and twists me so my knees are on each side of his head. Roughly, he parts my legs with one hand and pulls me down to sit on his face with the other. I cry out once, as the sensations assault my body all at once. Several long seconds pass as he licks and sucks, and thrusts his tongue before I remember I'm supposed to be doing something too. Not that he cares. Maverick is ravenous as he goes down on me. The biggest turn on is how much he enjoys it.

Leaning over, I put him in my mouth and try my best to focus, but every few seconds my eyes go a little blurry with complete lust haze. I lick around the tip and try to keep the same tempo as Maverick. He pushes his tongue into my sex; I swallow his cock as deep as I can. I close my eyes and try to picture us having sex. Spit is everywhere and his mouth is making me so wet that I'm sure he's covered in me. I almost want to pull away and just sink myself onto his dick, just to feel it inside me as I come. Maverick's fingers find my sex and work overtime to bring me over the edge. Slamming my eyes shut, I have to stop sucking; I'm about to come. I'm on the brink, and I know it's going to be strong, because it always is with him.

He flips me so I'm laying on my back, his head still between my thighs. I throw my arms over my head and scrunch the comforter in my hands for something to hold on to. My thighs tingle.

Then he stops all together. I was right there, and he stops. I groan and force myself to peek at him. "Ugh. Who's the depraved one? Please don't stop," I beg. I could just touch my clit and go off like a firecracker at this point. "Don't stop, Mav. Go…go. Come on," I say, raising my hips, like he can see how badly I need to come. His face is grim, determined, so fucking turned on that I might just come from looking at him.

"Beg for it *now*," he commands. There it is again—an order because he can't pull the damn trigger himself. God, how I want him to bury himself inside me and never leave. He wouldn't even get all the way in before I'd start clenching around him, I know it. This is the point in our normal sexcapades that I beg him to make love to me. Every time without fail. This time is different because he'll actually do it. I'm so horny I can't even think straight. He's giving all this power to me, when I'm feeling like the weakest person in the universe, only craving release.

I speak without thinking. Because I'm not. Not really. "Fuck me, Mav. Fuck me like I'm one of your bimbos. Make me come," I plead. I can't even believe the words that came out of my mouth. "Is that what you want to hear, baby?" The silence that fills the room is beyond deafening; it's murderous. He punches the bed next to my thigh. The slam reverberates in my chest.

"Fuck, Win!" Obviously not what he wanted to hear. Damn. I sit up. His huge body looks even more enormous in my tiny bed, scrunched at the bottom. "You couldn't just say what you say every other time...could you?"

I'm horny and angry. "You couldn't just take matters into your own hands? You know I want you. You know I'm not going to leave you no matter what. I've promised you!" I yell, not even worried about waking up my drunkard mother. She's slept through a hurricane before. I make up my mind about something. "When we have sex—if we ever get to that—I want *you* begging *me*." I stab my finger into his chest and leave it there. Touching him isn't a good idea. Now I want to throw myself into his arms. He merely smiles at my anger, his fading at the same time. I huff.

"I'm sorry about what I said about your bimbos," I mutter. "I was just so close and you stopped," I admit ruefully.

"You were so close and yet you couldn't just say 'make love to me?'" Maverick replies. The tone of his voice crushes me. It's disappointment. I really messed this one up. But he is the one enacting cruel and unusual torture, bringing me on the brink of a mind-numbing orgasm and then requesting me to speak certain words.

I hide my face in my hands. "You have me like a ticking time bomb. There aren't niceties anymore. Maybe after you work me over a few hundred times I'll be down to make love. You do this to me," I explain, groaning an embarrassed sigh. My sex drive slams into park. He pulls my hands down.

He's right in my face. No hiding from him. "I made a decision. If you beg me one more God damn time to make love to you, I will. That's why I bought the condoms. Because I want to make you happy. I'm willing to give up on going slow if it's what you want, Windsor. At this point we're just denying the inevitable anyway. I'm a fucking firework and you're the fuse," he says. "Denying you has been the hardest thing I've ever done. I'm a selfish prick. I'm no good."

There are a couple things I picked up on, the first being telling me no sex was the hardest thing he's ever done. He's a freaking Navy SEAL for fuck's sake. So that speaks volumes. So does denying the inevitable. It gives me pause. I just stare at him, willing the answer to come to me. Do I just tell him to have sex with me or do I respect what he obviously wants and hold off?

"I'm only trying to protect you," Maverick whispers.

"I don't want protecting, Mav," I say, laying my palm on his chest. "I want you here." I bring up my other hand to muss his brown hair. Then I tap him lightly on the side of his head. "I want you here, too," I admit. I straddle his lap and feel his large, hot member nestled by my sex. Even though his boxer briefs are on, it's the closest we've been to sex. "Those are the important things you should know. Everything else can wait."

Maverick stares at me, trying to figure out exactly what I mean, even though I've made myself perfectly clear. He's such a man. Both dimples and the smile that crinkles his eyes and dampens my nether regions blazes on his face.

"You sure everything else can wait?" he asks, his tone low, sarcastic. I realize I'm rubbing myself against cock, my wetness creating the perfect friction against my most sensitive spot. "I won't do that again. I won't deny you. I'm sorry," he growls slipping two fingers into me, realizing just how worked up he had me.

Finding the rhythm that will take me over the edge doesn't take long, I have his hard body underneath me, his tattoos wrapping his huge muscles like a freaking gift. His fuck me eyes and tousled hair are the icing on the Maverick cake. Everything inside the man is what makes me the most turned on. I slide up and down on his fingers like they're his dick. I can almost pretend I'm having sex with him just by watching the look of lust and awe in his gaze. He breathes out deeply every few seconds, and his neck muscles look strained. This man is hungry.

"Come for me, Win. Come for me," he says while watching my tits bouncing up and down. His other hand finds my clit and his thumb circles furiously. His words alone cause me to grip around his fingers and release like a wild animal, rocking up and down in time with my clenching sex. His fingers. Oh. My God.

I slump over on him. My nipples feel sensitive and hard as they brush his bare chest. I love everything about the moments after, with Maverick. I want to remember every bliss-filled second. I hear him sucking, so I look up.

"What's that taste like?" I ask, as he licks a finger he just fucked me with. He offers his forefinger to me and I suck the salty, tangy taste off. His eyes close and his nostrils flare. He pushes his hips up, forcing his hard-on exactly where we both want it. "Mmmmm," I hum around his large finger.

He chuckles, but there is no humor in it. His body is tense. He's like a freaking tiger about to attack. Except he doesn't want prey. He wants to fuck. He wants carnal. He is denying himself for crazy reasons. But they're his reasons, so I have to respect them.

"I taste pretty delicious," I murmur, before bending over to drive my tongue into his open mouth, and wrap both of my hands around his throat. He groans, and grinds his erection between my sex lips. He does it again. And again. His dick is so firm and he's pushing down on my hips so hard that it almost hurts me. He's playing rough. I tighten my grip around his neck, and kiss him harder. My mouth burns, but the pain is sweet. I want more of it. I pull his bottom lip with my teeth.

"Fuck," he moans into my mouth. One more swift thrust and I feel him explode underneath me, warm wetness spreading all over the entrance of my sex, drenching his boxer briefs. "Fuck," he whispers again, his voice hoarse.

I wiggle on top of him. "That was *not* dry humping, Mav. You don't do anything normal, do you?" I tease.

I am so turned on that I have the ability to drive this animalistic man to orgasm without the use of normal means. I didn't use my hands or my mouth. My sex clenches with the knowledge. It's sultrier than sex—mind bending hotness, in every aspect. Maverick is so into me that he just creamed his panties. I could make a million jokes about it, but I don't. Because the way he's looking at me right now makes my heart hammer.

A sweet smile plays on his lips, and his hands caress me with the softest touch. No one has ever looked at me like this. Not even the man I was going to marry. This is new and butterflies automatically invade my stomach. I watch his throat as he swallows, his neck tattoo dancing.

He ignores my question completely. Stroking the side of my face he simply says, "You're everything."

If I didn't know any better, I'd say Maverick Hart was in love.

Chapter Fifteen

Maverick

Something happened after I left Windsor in Georgia. I watched her drive away from the Atlanta airport after she dropped me off curbside, by my request, and I knew she'd forever changed me. I sat in that crazy fucking airport and thought about everything. I started to feel a little bad for John Nash, which pissed me off. Because I know Windsor is the type of person who is hard to get over. Maybe you never get over her, actually. You'd have to push the memory of her to the back and let her live there, quietly tapping your shoulder at any given second. Forgetting her completely isn't an option. You need the reminder of her, and of how she affects you, to feel alive. At least I do and I assume any person who is close to her needs it too. I never want to try to get over her. My ultimate weakness has been exposed, ripped open so wide that I'll never be able to fill the fucking gap with anything or anyone except her.

Stone grunts beside me, as he shifts to a seated position on his surfboard. "Fuck, I can't wait to get back to Virginia tomorrow," he says. The Pacific Ocean is fucking freezing cold, even through our 3-millimeter wet suits. The waves in Pacific Beach, San Diego are worth it, though. We finished the dive training we came for, squeezed in a few skydives in Otay just for fun, and now we're killing our last day catching some waves.

I paddle past him and stop. "Me too, dude. Me too." I'm actually ready to get the hell out of California and this water. Not because I'm cold, but because I want to check my cell.

Windsor and I have been texting back and forth every day I've been gone. She tells me the crazy shit her mother says, and I tell her tiny snippets of my day. How deep I can dive. To which I responded, *Just wait and find out.* What type of flippers I use. What diving in black waters at night actually feels like. She asks me a lot of questions, and I secretly love it. No one has ever taken any interest in what I do. Certainly not my fucking family. The only people I care about are next to me doing the same damn thing, so that steals my thunder. Windsor wants every gory detail. Of course I can't tell her most things about what I do, or what I'm training to do, but the fact that she cares is enough. She's more than enough.

Stone rattles on next to me about how we're going out to a bar tonight to meet up with the rest of the guys. The same guys that give me shit because I'm no longer bagging pussy every night I'm out. I'm not bagging *anything*. My cock hurts. In the beginning of my relationship with Windsor, I thought that not having sex was going to be the biggest challenge. How can I keep my dick to myself when the woman who I'm most attracted to on earth is bouncing up and down on my dick, only separated by fucking underwear? That night I thought I'd break, but I didn't. Windsor knew something changed that night. Blue eyes told me so. The hardest thing is keeping my fucking mouth shut. If I tell her how strongly I feel about her, I know she'll run. I should give her more credit, but I can't. I can't control her…I have no power over the situation. Scary fucking shit.

"You are always out in fucking space, Bro," Stone says. I look at him. He's not smiling. Fuck. He starts paddling for shore and shouts, "Should I grab a helmet and join you out there?"

Sometimes it blows dicks he knows me so well. I swear we live in the same mind sometimes, so alike in so many ways. Running my hand over the wax on my board, I try to come up with something to say—an excuse to placate him for the moment.

I paddle my long board behind him. It's silent this morning. "I'm not in space. I'm just ready to get back. That's all," I explain, coming up next to him. He glances over and smiles that asshole fucker smile.

"You need to bang her out, Mavvy. You really fucking do. Bang her out real good. What's going to happen if Windsor pussy is on your brain when we load out?" He splashes me. I stop paddling and sit up. It's still too deep to touch the bottom.

"I can't fuck her, Stone," I say, pausing. I take a deep breath and let it fly. "I'm in love with her." This can go one of two ways. He doesn't start cackling, which is a good sign.

"I know you are. Usually you fuck em' if you love em'," he explains, a serious expression on his face. Of course he knows I'm in love. My fucked up past always makes me feel like he feels sorry for me, but I know better. He cares. In his own demented way. "Tell her you love her and bang her out a few times every day until we leave. I promise you'll feel a million times better. Then maybe you can come back down to earth with the rest of us."

"She'll leave me. Look at my fucking life, man. I'm gone all the time, not to mention my shit past. If I bag her, there'll be nothing left for her to wait for. She'll leave," I repeat, swallowing all my fucking pride. "I just need her man. I just fucking need her to be with me," I say.

We've reached the shore. Rolling off my board I lay down in the sand. I hear Stone settle next to me.

"I've never wanted anything the way I want her. I've also never sucked at anything more," I admit. I can't think straight when I'm around her. I'm an intelligent man. I know a lot of things, but it's like half my brain is missing when I'm around her. My hands start shaking, right now, on this fucking beach 2,000 miles away from Windsor, just when I think about touching her. It's really God damned bad.

"You remember how long it took me to tame Morganna into submission? Years, man. You know that. She loves me, but I sucked so hard at dating her that I honestly thought I'd lose her a time or two. You're also forgetting that I'm gone all the fucking time too and Morg waits. A good woman will always wait. If you love her, she's a good woman. For as big as a fucktard as you are, you have a solid heart. You always have. I'm a little jealous someone else penetrated the cement wall you have wrapped around you," Stone says. I feel his fat fingers brush my upper thigh. I smile and swat his hand away. Now, he cackles.

I laugh a little as I grab my backpack and fish out my cell phone from the plastic bag I put it in. Stone's already chattering away on his own phone. It's definitely a guy, and not Morganna by how many *fucks* and *pussies* I hear flying out of his mouth, to balance out our heart-to-heart conversation, no doubt. What happened to the days where we talked about work and my weekend fucks? I've complicated everything. It's affecting every area of my life. I have one new text. I click on it so fast you'd think it was about to self-destruct.

It's a long message from Windsor. *I'm safely back in VB. Krazy Kath has a friend staying with her for the time being. Still no sign of #5. Can I pick you up tomorrow? I can't wait to get my hands (and wet mouth) on every single inch of you. Mainly, the 10 inches that reside below your belt. I'll come to your house?*

I text her back. *Yes. To all of the above. Especially the wet mouth part and the you at my house part.*

Stone's words rattle in my skull. I wonder if he's right. If I should confess it all, put it out there and let her do with it what she will. Maybe she won't be scared. Maybe the Nashhole didn't ruin her completely. Before I lose my nerve I type another text. *Stay at my house until I leave.*

Like move in with you? How I wish I could interpret the tone of a text message. I've never wanted anything more. Fuck.

Yes. I want you sleeping in my bed every night.

A long few seconds pass. *Sleeping sleeping? Or sleeping?*

Sex is always there. In every single moment we're together or just merely talking. It's the elephant in the fucking room. *I promise to make you come twice every single night. I want to be little spoon.* I grin as I shoot off the text. Stone's waving me to the truck, trying to pack up to leave the beach.

Okay. I'm bringing my other boyfriend with me then. I ignore Stone's shouts, because I only see red. Before I can type a text back and hit send another of hers comes through.

Battery operated boyfriend, Mav. Get yo' panties out of a wad. He has no problem going Windsor diving. Maybe you could help me with him? Sometimes he gets out of hand. :)

Fuck yes. I pop wood just thinking about it. *Yes. Please.*

I miss you so much. I want you in my arms. I miss your smile. You're so miss-able. My heart does that weird hammering thing it always does when it comes to Windsor. I read the text a few more times. And I smile, because if she misses it, I'll do it constantly to make her happy. I want to text her back and tell her how missing her is worse than any sort of torture I've had to endure in my life. I want to tell her inside her arms are where I'm happiest, where I want to call home. I should tell her I love her and that I want to make love to her the second I'm back. But I still can't say any of those things. Time is running out, too. I'll be down range trying to do my job and I'll be drowning in all the words that I couldn't say. Stone is right. I need to clear my fucking head.

I say the only thing I can that encompasses it all without actually saying it. I've said it once before and I think she knows what it means. *You're everything to me. See you tomorrow, baby. 5 p.m. Airport.*

I unzip the top of my wetsuit, pull out my arms, and sit on a towel in the passenger seat. A few minutes pass without a message back. We're rolling down the freeway, the beach passing alongside us as we head back to Coronado. Stone is hammering the steering wheel pretending it's a drum, beating along to an old rock song. I smile. My phone chimes a few minutes later.

Her message reads, *You're everything, too.* There it is. Just as good as I love you, too, but it's not. And it's my fucking fault.

"Let's go get new tats," Stone says, breaking up my thoughts of Windsor and my inability to tell someone I'm attached to them.

A new tat is exactly what I need. The sting of the needle, something permanent etched on my body. It's fucking genius. I can *show* Windsor how much she means to me. Pulling out the big guns is what needs to happen. I'll be gone for six months. That's a long ass time for her to wait for me in the real world, with every male clawing for her attention. She's oblivious to her beauty. It only makes things worse. The dolphin dick tattoo was a joke.

I pull out my phone and Google search something. I know exactly what tat I want to get and where. This will be a grand gesture she can't ignore. She'll know I'm hers. All hers. Forever. Permanently.

Stone screams out a few lyrics. "I want to get a lobster body with Morg's face. She'll fucking love it," he says, patting his forearm where he plans on getting the monstrosity that Morganna will surely hate. She'll come around, like she always does with his dumbass body art, but I would pay money to see her face when she sees a lobster with her head. Fuck yes. Hell fucking yes.

I smile wide. "That's the best idea you've ever had," I tell him. It probably is. He usually comes up with stupid fucking schemes. Like the time he wanted to hold donkey races at our camp in Afghanistan. Or when he thought bringing a filthy puppy from a surrounding village back to our base would be a good idea. We had fleas in our tent for weeks. Fucking asshole dropped the dog off at least eight miles away after everyone got pissed at him. Do you know that damn dog came back? It was in Stone's bed one morning weeks after he'd dumped it. He said it was because it was a female puppy—woman can't resist him, even dogs. Idiot. Tattoos are always a better idea than anything he comes up with.

We hit up our favorite tat shop in San Diego. We both left with white bandages and huge smiles. I paid for both of the tats because I lost credit card roulette. We threw our cards in a hat and the artist drew one out. Of course it was mine. I don't mind. I owe Stone more than I could pay him in a damn lifetime.

"She's going to drop her panties the second she sees it," Stone drawls. I clap him on this shoulder, still smiling.

"Panty dropping isn't the problem, man. It's keeping them on her that's the issue," I tease. Windsor dancing naked pops into my head. I yank out my phone to check for messages. I glance at Stone's bandaged forearm and shake my head. Morg is going to shit when she sees his new *art.* "Morganna is going to sue your ass when she gets one look at that." I point to his arm.

The artist did a good job. The best he could have done. It still doesn't negate the lobster wearing a bikini with his wife's face and hair. He pulled a photo off her attorney website to show the artist. So Morganna looks like a fucking shark, no smile, all serious bitch face. Both are underwater animals at least.

My tat is understated and small. It means something. It's on my body, but it's not for me, nope. It belongs to someone else.

*****

The bar the guys chose is so fucking loud. It's a good blend of people. The girls in San Diego are always a mixed variety. There are the surfer girls with the jean cut-off shorts so short you see ass cheeks. Then there are the ones who wear mini dresses and fifty-inch heels to a bar.

I'm not checking them out. Steve and a few of the other guys are pointing them out, telling me I should go fishing for them. When I told them they could get their own bags for the night, they got pissy. We're in a corner of the bar, all fifteen of us, surrounding the largest table. Security looks at us every other second. We look like a bunch of drunk swinging dicks with more muscle than they can deal with. They're praying we don't fight each other. Or anyone else for that matter. They won't fuck with us. We're loud. We're obnoxious and we can be. That's end of fucking story. A few mini dresses approach the table. They're decent looking. I would have bagged them. Maybe even at the same time. Before. Way before. Steve swoops in and makes some loud joke, and offers a compliment to each one of them. They blush and giggle. Putty. It makes my stomach hurt at the haunting reminder.

I got you a present. I text Windsor, my heart racing—half from thinking of her reaction and the other half is adrenaline, coursing through me like my favorite drug.

You are my present. (But I'm excited for a gift too!) I'm in a late meeting right now. Ugh.

I'll let you unwrap it. Is my friend Garrett Garth there? It's like 11 p.m. on the east coast. I'm immediately suspicious. I glance up. I feel eyes on me. One of the mini dresses is smiling that smile. Directly at me. The one that says she wants my attention, now and later. I'm not a dickhead, so I smile back. I wish I were smiling at someone else. Old habits die hard. The blonde woman walks toward me; her heels and obvious drunkenness cause her to saunter more than walk. Steve gleams at me over his shoulder and I know he sent her over here as a fucking test. Still no return text from Windsor.

"Hi, I'm Lexi," the blonde woman says. I glance down at my phone when I see that Windsor's typing back.

I meet her gaze. "I'm Maverick. Nice to meet you," I say extending my hand for her to shake. My hand engulfs her tiny one, her bright pink nails standing out.

"Your girlfriend?" she asks, nodding at my phone. She's cutting right to the chase. You have to admire a woman who knows exactly what she wants. It's easy.

I smile the big smile. I slide my cell into the pocket of my jeans. "It is my girlfriend," I admit. It feels good to call her my girlfriend. But I find myself noticing other things about Lexi.

She tilts her head to the side, letting her gaze land on every part of my body at least once. My cock? She went there twice. "I can be your girlfriend for the night," she says, taking a sip of her drink. Like I said. She knows exactly what she wants. She's taller than Windsor and her eyes are brown. They're nice eyes. Her lips are full, covered in a nude colored gloss. It reminds me of bare skin. Windsor's bare, tan, naked, skin.

Remember what I said about old habits dying hard? I start thinking maybe I could just take Lexi to a hotel and bag her. Maybe a few times just to get sex out of my system. It wouldn't mean shit. It never means shit with the others. It's like working out. Or cooking a meal. Or taking a shower. Something you have to do everyday for your health and survival. I'd go home and I'd be a better man for Windsor. I wouldn't be wound up like a fucking top. She'd want that, right? I should fuck Lexi. She's giving it up so easy that it's meant to be. No attachments. Just raw sex.

I'm attracted to this girl, but I'd have to picture Windsor to get off. I know it. And how fair is that to the girl or to Win? Stone hooks his arm around my neck.

"How's that tat feeling, man?" he asks. I'm snapped out of my weird fucking hotel fantasies, and disgust takes their place. Fuck. What is wrong with me? Stone stares down Lexi.

"I have a girlfriend," I repeat to the girl, but mostly for my own benefit. The definition of girlfriend runs through my mind. I thought about cheating on Windsor. I did more than think about it. I had the whole scenario planned out—a mental cheat. Stone knows it too. He gives me a knowing look.

"Fine," Lexi says, hiking her shoulders and walking off to the bar. I'm all but forgotten, written off her list of conquests for the night. I'm fucking relieved. This will happen again. It always does. I need to get used to rejecting the old Maverick norm.

"Let's get out of here," Stone says. He slams his beer and we leave. I drive back to our hotel. My cell phone chimes a few times in my pocket but I can't take it out and look at it. I feel like an asshole. I haven't had a sip of alcohol, but my stomach churns and my throat feels thick. I don't deserve to see her kind, sweet words. I don't deserve anything from Windsor. Not even her fucking trust.

I rub my chest with my palm. Tomorrow can't come soon enough. I'm a walking fucking disaster.

Chapter Sixteen

Windsor

I've moved some of my things into Maverick's house. I want to surprise him when he gets back from his trip. Hesitantly, Morganna gave me a key to his house. I'm positive she called to ask him first, which totally ruins my surprise.

I have candles scattered around and I put some of my clothes in his closet. I also filled the shelves in his shower with all of my girl products. I love being in his house. It feels like I'm with him, even though he's not with me. The house suits him perfectly. He's right, you can tell a lot about someone just by looking at where they live. Albeit a few girly touches, I wouldn't change a thing.

While he was gone I missed him more than I'm comfortable with. It's like a warm-up for when he leaves for six months. The thought makes me tear up and cringe at the same time. It's an odd sensation. I don't know if I should feel this proprietary after the short amount of time we've known each other. I know he feels just as strongly, but he won't admit it to me. He tells me I'm his everything. I think that is secret code for *I love you*. I think.

Do people like Maverick Hart say I love you? Do they only think it and assume women should know? He's good at everything. That fact is obvious when you look around his house...and his garage. And also one glance in his bedroom has my knees shaking, but that's just me.

It's unreal I get to call him my boyfriend. Not only that, but the fact that I actually have a relationship after the Nashhole makes me happy. I thought for a long time I'd never get over him. Maverick makes that easy too. I barely even remember Nash and his adulterous ways.

Kathy calls and texts to bitch about how she is lonely, and needs me to come and stay with her again. She misses me. Or she misses someone to drive her to the store when she's too drunk to drive. I'm sure she doesn't ask her girlfriends to do that for her. That'd be too embarrassing. It's a daughter job. You shit on the people you're closest to. Even though she assures me money isn't an issue, because she *made out* during the last divorce, I still worry she's going to end up living in my spare room any day now.

My cell phone chirps at me from the kitchen counter. It's a text from Maverick. *We got in early. Stone is giving me a ride home. Meet me at my place?*

I text back, *Sure.* I'm disappointed. I wanted to pick him up from the airport and have that run into each other's arms moment. I hope he feels my irritation through my text. I laugh because that's insane. Nothing else from Maverick comes through.

I do get a text from Gretchen listing a bunch of crass, dirty sex positions, because she can and that's Gretchen. I had an actual professional wax my landing strip this time, much to Gretchen's dismay. My hair is freshly blown out and I had my makeup done—nothing crazy, just simple and pretty. It's my everyday look enhanced by a professional's hand. I chose a black, casual cotton dress. It hugs my curves and boosts my chest. I reapply some clear lip-gloss and scrutinize my appearance in a large gothic mirror that hangs on a wall in one of the corridors.

I didn't snoop through his house, as I'm sure most people would. I want Maverick to show me everything. I want to know what he finds important about his house. What will he show me first? What does he like the most? These things will all help me crack the code. Sleuthing for details about him and his personality take creativity. I think I know something about him and he does a complete one eighty. I never know what to expect from him.

The front door opens. I don't hear it close. I run down the hallway, my bare feet padding against the solid wood floors. Maverick drops his leather bag from his shoulder and stares at me. Okay, maybe Morganna didn't tell him she gave me a key. He looks delectable, like always. He looks even bigger than I remember. But the last time I saw him we were in my small, pink bed. Shock crosses his face, mixing with raw emotion. His hands tremble by his sides. I feel my smile fading from my face, praying to God that this is a surprise he's okay with.

I give him a little wave. "Surprise?" I say, my voice wavering a little.

His gaze hasn't strayed from my face...my eyes. He's doing that weird thing when I know for sure he's trying to get a read off me. I cross over to him, walking slowly but purposefully. He crushes me against his body, leans down, and inhales deeply. His heart is pounding. I actually feel it on my cheek—solid, steady, obviously not the slow normal pace of a heart.

"Is this okay?" I ask hesitantly.

Dipping his head lower, he places his face in my neck. Taking another long, deep breath he says, "This is more than okay. I missed you so much, Win. I missed you," he whispers into my ear, causing my insides to quiver.

Sweeping my hair away, he kisses my neck, and then my ear, cheek, and now he's looking at my lips. He doesn't kiss them. He just stares at them. I smile after a few awkward seconds of lip staring pass.

Then I kiss him, interlocking my hands high, around his strong neck. He slams his eyes shut, almost as if my kiss pains him. I coax his lips open and deepen the kiss, pressing my body as close to his as I can. Candles melt when you light them. I melt when Maverick Hart kisses me. Into. A. Puddle. Of. Mush. His lips give me small doses of delirium. I pull away before I lose myself completely.

His head follows me back and his lips are almost back on mine. "I missed you more. I also made dinner. Morg gave me a key. I moved some of my stuff in while you were gone. I hope you don't mind," I give him all the important details in a Windsor ramble. Finally. Finally, the smile appears. He narrows his eyes. "We only have a few weeks until you leave. I wanted to be thorough," I deadpan.

"My, my. You've been busy...and sneaky." He nips the tip of my nose with his teeth. "I like it though. I like it a lot. You here. Your stuff here. Coming home and you're here. All of this. I love it all," Maverick growls. He said the L word. Why do I even care he said it? I wouldn't notice that word coming out of any other mouth except his.

He picked up on the fact I noticed right away, because he does what he always does when he wants to move past something. He kisses me. Closing the door with a free hand he backs me toward the couch, his lips never breaking from mine. We crash down on the sofa and the scent of expensive, worn leather wraps around me. My hands go to the edge of his shirt automatically. I want it off. I want his skin and all of his glorious muscles as close to me as humanly possible. The second my fingers touch his skin, he pulls away from me.

I scoff at him. "What? I'm not allowed to touch you now? I thought you missed me?" I ask. I'm smiling, so he knows I'm not totally serious. He runs a hand through his crop of hair.

"I want to talk to you. Can we just talk?" His eyes look a little worried, which only worries me. The last time someone told me they wanted to talk with that look on their face was when one of my friends was telling me about Johnny's affair. I try to avoid *talks* as a general rule. I nod, tuck my legs under me, and face him on the couch.

"Lets talk," I urge.

He exhales. "When I'm around you, I don't think straight. I just want you. I'm crazy. Do you understand that?" His eyebrows knit together. "We don't talk enough." A man admitting that we don't talk enough. Shit. This must be really bad. My pulse skitters, still between my legs, but now also at my throat.

I bite my lip. How best to proceed with this? "You're not crazy, Mav. We should talk more. I agree. You start," I tell him, stifling a stutter. Crap.

He shakes his head. Then he launches into a speech about how he doesn't speak with his family, and how Stone and the guys are the only people he has relationships with. He tells me his past haunts him, that he relives the day he told his father he was going to boot camp in Illinois and then to San Diego to become a Navy SEAL. He rehashes the different ways that conversation could have gone, and then has nightmares because it was the moment when he lost the people he cared most about. Maverick goes into gory detail about how letting people into his life isn't acceptable. How keeping women at arms' length in a hotel room is preferable to letting them inside his house and heart. He takes several deep breaths and continues on, connecting all the dots for me. I realize I'm shaking when he places his large hand on my shoulder. He's talking about me now. About how he knew I was different the first moment he saw me.

"I wanted to let you in. Maybe I was just ready, Win. Maybe you were sent here just for me—because that's what it feels like to me. I have never been more afraid of fucking something up," he says, hanging his head to break eye contact. "I have a confession."

Oh, shit. He can't even look at me when he admits it.

"A girl came up to me in a bar last night. She offered herself to me within seconds of saying hello," he says.

I swallow. Please don't say you accepted. Don't say it. I'll break. Just like Kathy said. He'll break me beyond repair with just a few words. He wouldn't. Maverick couldn't do that to me. Could he?

"Say it, Maverick. Just say it," I mumble.

He looks me in the eye. "I planned the whole thing out in my mind. How I would take her to a hotel and fuck her senseless. So I could come back here to you with a clear head. I didn't. Of course I didn't. But I thought about it, and I feel like it's just as bad," he grinds out. Thank God. I can deal with this. I can deal with this.

I grab his hand in mine and squeeze. "You didn't do anything wrong. I have sex with Channing Tatum in my head anytime I scroll past his photo on my newsfeed. You don't even want to know what I do to Zac Efron in my mind when I watch his movies. You can think whatever you want, Mav. You don't act on it. There's a difference. It's a very large difference," I explain. He seems to relax a tiny bit. "I want you just like this." I lay my hand on this side of his face. It's a little pink from time spent in the sun. "Foggy head and all. I want you like this. If you need to fuck someone, I know a willing participant." I smile at him. He shakes his head, one dimple disappearing.

"I'm no good. I'm telling you I'm crazy. Nothing in my life will ever be what you deserve. I internalize everything, and don't tell anyone how I feel. I'm reckless where others are careful. I'm also completely at a loss. I have no idea how to keep what I want most," he says. He didn't use the word "fuck" once. He's honestly telling me how he feels. "You." He finishes his sentence and it's like a punch to my stomach and heart at the same time.

My palms feel a little sweaty. "If I tell you one more time I'm not going anywhere you're gonna start thinking I'm lying. I've promised a million times, maybe even once while your dick was in my mouth, that I won't leave you. I'm the one who should be worried, Maverick. You have girls propositioning you on the regular. My prospects are non-existent. I'm just plain Windsor with the boring job and a cheating ex-fiancé. You make me special."

He pulls me into a hug. It's warm and comforting and not the least bit sexual. It's refreshing just to have him reassuring me, with all our clothing on. I crawl into his lap and entwine my body with his.

"Don't worry. Please. I only told you to try to warn you how messed up my headspace is. I guess I won't frighten you off after all I've admitted. So let's just be together. I've missed you," he repeats for the fourth time. It's like a plea.

"I've missed your more, I bet. I wasn't swimming with dolphins or surfing. I was stuck in my office," I say. I kiss his cheek because it's right in my face.

He smiles and his boyish good looks appear. He's two people—the person he turns into when he talks about his past and his issues, and then this one—the most attractive man on the planet who teases, laughs, and just happens to be all mine.

"God, I'm so glad you're mine," I whisper. "Even if it was an accident, or weird cosmic powers, I'm glad you picked me. You make me so happy." His heady gaze locks on mine. He opens his mouth to say something, but then closes it again, sighing. "Where's my present?" I squeal, when I remember. I love presents and something from Maverick makes me insanely giddy.

A straight white smile assaults me before his lips kiss mine. One hand twists in my hair and the other pulls my waist closer to him. I'm wearing a dress, a fact I didn't remember until this second when my panties begin to stick to me. My breathing speeds up, his touch sparking every nerve ending to life. God, his hands are like a magic freaking wand. I shudder. He feels it. His lips form a smile against my mouth, his front teeth meet my tongue instead of his own tongue.

"I actually have two," he whispers.

I shiver again, because I can't freaking help myself. Having him close completes me in some odd way. I didn't even feel like this when I was engaged to Nash—something that scares the shit out of me. I would have lived an entire life without *this* feeling.

He glances over my head into the kitchen. "Lets eat first. You cooked," he says, raising his eyebrows.

"I can cook, Maverick. I use a recipe like a normal human, but I can cook. And no," I tell him, shaking my head. "Give me the present now. I hate surprises and I don't do well with anticipation." I smile. He laughs.

"It seems to me you do quite well with anticipation." He disentangles our limbs and grabs a scrap piece of paper from the side pocket of his bag. "I hate to drag it out, but you're going to have to wait a few more minutes. I have to go grab something," he confesses with a lazy smile. I nod. He disappears into a hallway. When he returns he's holding a beautiful wood-grain acoustic guitar.

I'm pretty observant, but I still won't believe what I'm thinking until it's a done deal. A scrap of paper and a guitar? A song? For me? Holy shit.

My stomach gets all light when he levels me with his gaze and says, "I wrote you a song." He clears his throat. This. Is. Real. "I've never done this before. I usually just jam with my buddies. Bear with me." His face is a mask of frightened anxiety. His eyes are a little wider than they usually are and the crinkles by his temples are absent. I'm sure the smile I beam back at him is the goofiest, most unattractive thing my face is capable of, but I can't control it. Or my mouth.

"Are you serious? Oh my God. Oh my God. I'm totally about to have a heart attack over here…or maybe vomit…or something unsightly and embarrassing. You wrote a song for *me*? That's the type of thing that only happens in movies and passionate romance novels. It definitely does not happen to me," I gush.

Damn it. I realize I'm bouncing on the sofa like an animal at the zoo. Not quite at Tom Cruise on Oprah level, but still bad. Trying to assemble some degree of control, I cross my legs and scoot to the edge of the couch. He drops down in the leather chair directly across from me. He's chuckling under his breath as he twirls some of the knobs on the end of the guitar. I memorize the way he looks right now because I never want to forget this. If it ends badly, which I don't even think about anymore, I'll always have this moment. I'll lock it up so it stays untainted by anything that happens after it. It's mine.

He strums the strings a few times and then continues fiddling with the knobs. More strumming that already sounds like perfection fills the room. He lays the paper in front of him on the table. Keeping his head down, his eyes flick up to meet mine. Dimples arrive a second later. I squeal. "You're starting," I guess. He does.

A haunting guitar solo fills the air. My huge smile fades as I listen to him play. His eyes close as he gets lost in the melody. It's beautifully simple in pattern, but something bittersweet laces the notes. I find myself leaning toward him, the sensation to comfort him uncontrollable. The muscles of his forearms stretch and flex as he plays. It's soft, not like bench pressing heavy weights, or carrying big, manly guns. This is a whole new side of Maverick. It's sensitive. His fingers buzz over the strings with ease and grace.

Then he begins to sing.

His voice is low, soothing, and raspy. It's freaking hot.

If I asked for forever would you run from right now?
If I gave you a promise would you want to know how?
I need to breathe you inside me til' I know you can't leave.
Forever is too long but it's what feeds my greed.
You twist me in knots, you break me in two.
I want you. You're everything.
I want you.
I do.

His lips curl around the last words and he looks at me. His gaze steady, questioning.

If I asked you for forever would you run from right now?

My jaw is practically on the floor. His long fingers glide over the strings, repeating the melody from the beginning of the song. I'm glad. It gives me a few seconds to absorb his words, or control my rapid-fire pulse. His song. His gift to me. Maverick looks down to watch his hands work, and I realize he's giving me time to be alone with my thoughts. His song, my song, says everything I need to hear.

"No," I say, realizing I have a few tears leaking from my eyes. He looks up, pulls the guitar closer to his body, and slumps over it, his arms dangling over the top. "I won't run, Mav. I won't leave," I clarify.

"Promise me," he growls. Still with this?

I take a deep breath. "Put the guitar down," I command.

He props it against a small table. Folding his hands together in his lap, he fixes me with his gaze. I feel my breaths come faster and faster. I fling myself over the coffee table separating us and into his lap. Grabbing his face with both hands, I kiss him quickly once.

"That was for the song. It was seriously perfect," I admit. Then I kiss him a bit harder. "That's a promise." I hug him tightly, fitting myself to him like a puzzle piece. He holds me to him. I pull back and look into his eyes. "Make love to me, Maverick," I say.

Indecision lights his face. He told me if I begged, he'd cave. I don't want to beg.

"Because you want to. Not because I beg for you to," I explain. He stays silent, his eyes drinking in my mouth as I speak. "And because forever isn't really that long and we've wasted too much time already. I want you. Right now. Tomorrow, too. Next year? I'll want you then as well," I ramble. The thought comes like a freight train. "Now, you promise me you won't leave me." It has to be both ways. My heart is already his.

He shakes his head, disbelieving. Maverick grabs the back of his shirt and pulls it over his head. My heartbeat picks up. This is it. Finally.

My gaze lands on a white bandage on his chest, above his heart. He peels it off to expose an obviously new tattoo. It's a vertical line of black ink reading 36° 40' N 076° 36' W. I trace it around the edges avoiding the raw skin.

"Now you're always with me. You can never leave. No matter what," he says, grabbing my wrist. I glance up to his face. "It's the exact location I fell in love with you," he whispers.

The tenderness in his eyes breaks me. A tear slips out of the corner of my eye as I lean in and gently press my lips against his. It's a salty, tear-laced kiss. He pulls my hand to his chest…his heart, bloody, healing tattoo be damned.

"I promise," he confesses against my lips.

"Where?" I reply. I want to know when. Let's be honest, I need to know *exactly when* he fell in love with me.

"Twelve thousand feet in the air, of course." Date four. Maverick was in love with me after four measly dates and he's just telling me now. To say I'm shocked is an understatement.

This tattoo is permanently on his body. I can't stop starting at it. You get a tattoo when you want something on your body when you're old and wrinkly. When you want to look at it and remember a certain moment. Maverick picked this moment.

He tilts my chin up. "Windsor the rambler is speechless?"

If I started talking now I wouldn't stop for days. He brushes a tear off my face with his warm thumb.

"Say *something* or I'll think you hate it and think I'm…"

I cut him off with a finger against his lips. When he silences I lay my hands on his stubbly face and bring his forehead to mine. "Thank you," I whisper. "I don't think you could have done anything more…perfect. This means the world to me—it means more than words ever could." I rub my hand down to his chest once more, making sure it's real. His eyes stay locked with mine. The untouchable place inside Maverick is open. To me. "You make me look bad. All I did is make dinner," I say, giggling a little. The big smile is on his face and doesn't seem to wane like it usually does.

He stands from the chair, picking me up with him, like I'm a throw pillow. I wrap my legs around his waist and lock my arms around his neck. "I am pretty hungry. Baring my soul really takes it out me. I want to eat whatever smells so delicious, then take a shower to wash off the airplane," Maverick says, setting me down on a bar stool in front of the plates I've set out.

"Then what?" I ask, not releasing his neck.

He leans over and places a scorching kiss on the hollow of my neck. "Then I have a lot of fucking begging to do," he rasps in my ear, tickling me and sending a thrill directly to my sex.

Tonight is going to be a trifecta of awesome.

Chapter Seventeen

Maverick

"What exactly are in all of these bottles?" I ask as I yank off my pants at the entrance of the wet room. The only answer I get is a bout of her sweet laughter. I fucking love the pink bottles crowding my solitary green one. I'm on top of the damn world right now. Windsor loved the tattoo. It took a little longer than it should have for her to respond after I revealed it, but the wait was worth it. I'll replay her response constantly. I've also decided I should write her a million songs because of how she reacted to that. The emotion was almost too much for me to handle. I rarely crack, but that was the closest I've come.

"Where did you learn to sing and play like that?" she asks. Her tiny frame, barefoot, is leaning against the shower wall, away from the showerhead I have turned on. She's eyeing me like musical talent is the last thing she's interested in. I work the soap in my hands and rub it on my body, sliding it down my legs. Her eyes are glued to my dick when I cup my junk and wash it.

Long seconds pass. "I taught myself mostly, but I played when I was a kid too." I clear my throat. "Like what you see?"

"Huh?" Windsor glances up, eyes round. Caught. Just her eyes on my body make me hard. She's fully clothed and I can't help but remember last night when I saw the woman, Lexi in the bar. I didn't feel like this, my body didn't have this reaction to her. In fact, my body has only reacted like this to Windsor. Especially my damn heart—beating like a drum. I want her. I'm going to have her. She will finally be all mine. Tonight.

She swallows hard. "You know I do. It's probably my favorite sight…better than the Alps or the Grand Canyon; possibly even a quaint town in France." She grins. "I actually have a small confession to make, too. It's nothing crazy, but with your streak of confessions it makes me want to tell you everything. I sort of do anyways. Whether you want me to or not."

"I love when you ramble," I say, washing the soap out of my hair. She bites her lip. My self-control teeters on the fucking edge. I want to pull her in, clothing and all, and have my way with her. I've said the word "love" more times in one night than I have during my entire life. "Ramble on. Confess your sins. I'll tell you how many Hail Mary's you need to do after." I grab one of her bottles, open it, and give it a quick sniff. It smells like her hair. Fucking delicious. I pour some in my hand and scrub it into my hair just for good measure. Windsor shakes her head, laughing.

"Nash has been calling. He called a few days ago to apologize. He wants to be friends. Just friends. He knows how out of line he was at the conference. Well, you showed him exactly how out of line he was. He knows we're together."

Fuck. I haven't even left yet and he's moving in. I know his game—I know exactly what angle he's playing. I nod because I don't trust myself to speak.

"It's easy to talk to him about my Mom. He's known her…and our avalanche of problems for a long time."

And there it is, a history I can't compete with. The past is the only thing you can't control. I know this all too well. I might have to make a visit to the Nashhole before I leave. He's obviously not clear on what's mine. I'll make it crystal clear.

I shrug, playing at nonchalance. It's important she think it doesn't bother me in the least. "That's fine. At least he apologized for all of his shortcomings," I say, reminding her exactly why she didn't talk to him for years. Though I'm sure she knows. My hard-on took a nosedive the second she mentioned his name. His dick has been inside her. I can't even say that. I slam the lever to turn off the water. She jumps a little at the noise.

"You're not mad are you?" she asks. If I were mad, she wouldn't have to ask.

I run a towel over my head to dry my hair and cover my face. "No. I'm just surprised. You told me how badly he hurt you and yet you throw him a bone? It doesn't make sense. If it makes you feel better then do what you want. I'll kill him if he hurts you again." I will.

She snaps the towel out of my hands and throws it to the bottom of the wet shower. I can't help but cringe a little. My obsessive-compulsive tendencies circle around cleanliness and organization. A towel on the floor fits both of those categories. Forgive her Father, she knows not of her sins.

"I don't want him, Mav. I want you," she says, running her hands over my biceps. She knows I'm jealous even though I haven't breathed a word. "Whenever you forget that remember this." Windsor drops to her knees and pulls my dick into her warm mouth. The sight of her fully dressed inside the wet room is odd, and a gigantic turn on. My dick in her mouth? Well, that's just complete fucking nirvana. My head falls back without my permission as she works me into frenzy. Her tiny hand wraps *almost* all the way around my cock as she sweeps the sides with her tongue and lips. The gentleness is just for show because when I look down and meet her gaze, whale eyeing me, it's completely evil—in the best kind of way. I give her the smile she loves and it makes her work my dick even better. Hand. Mouth. Tongue. When I pop out of her mouth and she laps at my balls I groan. It echoes through my bathroom. I fist my hand into her hair, which she didn't want to get wet, and guide her mouth back onto my dick.

"That feels so good, Win. Lets take this into the bedroom. Come on..." I grind out. The last thing I want is for her to stop, but if I have any hope of lasting tonight, I need to her to.

"Are you sure?" she asks, humming the words around my dick. No. I'm lying. Yes I'm sure. Thinking with both heads at the same time blows. Literally.

With effort, I nod. She stands up, a string of spit connecting her to me. I wipe her bottom lip with my thumb and kiss her. I taste Windsor. I want to bottle this fucking flavor and drink until I'm drunk. Her blue eyes are heavy, glazed with lust, her pupils almost completely dilated.

I ask, "Can I have you?" It's a loaded question.

Resting her hand over my new tat, she says, "I thought you'd never ask." She pushes away from me, her wet feet slapping the floor. She doesn't turn around or take her eyes off my body as she backs into the bathroom and then into the bedroom. I don't take my gaze off her either. Adrenaline hits me in spades as I watch her, the innocent way she moves, not even knowing how fucking hot she is. The way her black dress hugs certain spots of her body each time she takes a step back, the way my breathing speeds up to control all the chemicals in my body trying to rear up to do what it's good at. I want to dominate her. I want her to know she's mine. I want to erase any guy who has ever been inside her. I will fill her so completely that there's no room inside her heart for anyone else.

Her dress falls to the floor in front of the bed revealing a deep red corset and matching panties that I. Will. Tear. Off. With. My. Teeth.

If she's nervous, it doesn't show. "How bad do you want me, T.H.?" She swings her long brown hair around to cover one shoulder. "Beg for it," she commands. I couldn't resist if I tried. I take a few more steps and hit my fucking knees in front of her. This, right now, is a moment of unfettered weakness I've never known the likes of. Whatever it takes to make her mine. No cost is too high.

I swallow, because I've forgotten to do that since she undressed and because she is the fucking definition of mouthwatering. I wrap my hands around her smooth, tan thighs. "I want you, Windsor. Let me have you," I say, looking up into her huge blue eyes. The doe-eyed innocence is gone, replaced with need...desire. It's like nothing I've ever seen. And I've seen a lot. She bites her lip and narrows those same eyes, calculating something. "I'm begging you. Let me have you," I plead, my tone harsh. "Please make love to me."

"One condition," she replies.

Anything. I'll give her anything she asks for: Diamonds, marriage, screeching kids, an ugly white fucking picket fence—all of it hers if she has me...and keeps me. These thoughts don't even scare me anymore, because they're true, honest. I would do anything for her. Not just to have sex with her either—because I want to. Because I need to. Because she is my future. Fuck me, I'm *attached*.

"Anything," I breathe, already primed to say yes to whatever comes out of her perfect fucking mouth next.

"Always be honest with me. I can deal with a lot. You just have to be honest with me."

Fuck.

"You don't want me anymore? Tell me. Don't cheat on me. You have something to say? Say it. No lies. Lies are deal breakers. Agree?"

I pause for a few beats, because how do I tell her I began our relationship on lies? That my past is full of blonde monster lies? I can't. I'd lose her. So I give her the last lie to fill the jar and seal it tight. "I promise," I say. And then a truth, "And just to be clear…I will always want you, Windsor. Always." I stroke her legs travelling up to her red, wet panties and pull them aside to look at her perfectly sculpted landing strip. I scoot a little closer and kiss the top of it. The scent of her arousal hits me. My balls tighten and, if possible, my dick gets even harder.

A hot little noise exits her mouth. "We have a deal then," she moans. "Now get off your knees and get on top of me. Where you belong." No one can ever accuse me of not taking orders.

Standing, I back her into and then onto the bed. I notice a pink toy? Vibrator? Dildo? Sitting on top.

I pick it up. "Bob," she explains. "My boyfriend. You remember." I roll it around in my hand, contemplating. It could be fun—if I wasn't strung out on the idea of being inside her. Nothing is going to take my place tonight.

"Let him know he doesn't get to Windsor dive tonight. You and he are taking a break."

She bites her lip, and it's more suggestive than being straight up propositioned for sex. I stalk toward her on my hands and knees. I see red. Not only her fucking lace underthings, it's connected to passion...lust, and God be damned...love. I drop my head and kiss her shoulder, then her chest above the swell of her breast, all the while sliding her panties off.

She throws her arms above her head, wiggling the fucking dick blockers off and kicking them across the room. "Nice distance," I whisper into her ear.

Windsor grabs my face and forces me to kiss her. "I've dreamed about doing that forever. Never say I don't go the distance for my man." She rolls over. "Get this freaking thing off me. And fast," she cries. My fat fingers work the laces and I'm struck with a thought. Other than the fact that her round ass is the finest specimen I've ever seen.

"How did you get this on?"

"Gretchen," she breathes out, trying to help with the laces but only tangling them more. Premeditated seduction, then—I never stood a chance.

"They should sew emergency releases into this these things." If I wasn't so focused on fucking her, I'm sure I'd be coming up with a new corset release system in my head. She rolls onto her back.

"Break it. Just get it off me. I need you now." I stare at her and the remnants of what covers her and I come to the only one conclusion.

"You didn't have any kind of attachment to this did you?" I reach over to my nightstand and grab my black, extremely sharp knife and a condom, which is a new mainstay in my house. Straddling her slim legs, I think about the combination of the two things. A condom and a knife seem really fucking strange, but I don't have the patience to think about it long.

Windsor sighs. "This ole' thing? I hate it." I flash the knife. She giggles. You laugh when someone holds up a knife when you're crazy or when you have the upper hand. Windsor has both. Crazy good, of course.

"Don't move," I order. She licks her lips. I grab the fabric with one hand and slice it at the bottom. I toss the knife back on the stand and then grab each side of the tear and pull it apart, like a fucking stripper. It makes the most satisfying ripping sound that I can't help the smile on my face. Now she's biting her lip in that impossibly hot way of hers. I yank down and her breasts pop free. I slide it over her ass and toss the thing away, making sure it lands further away than her panties. I win.

She notices. "It's not so much about distance as speed…and length," Windsor confesses. My dick twitches to prove her point. There's too much talking, not enough action. Grabbing the condom off the bed and waving it like a white flag, she whispers, "Is it wrong that I am so turned on right now, and I'm not sure if it's because you're naked or because you used a knife to cut off my lingerie?"

We're on the same page. Same fucking word. With her lying beneath me, naked, and looking at me like I'm the fucking Hope diamond, I know I don't deserve this.

But I'm going to take it anyway.

I snatch the condom out of her hand and have it rolled down my dick in the next second. Our lips crash together in furious need. All these weeks…months of denying each other have turned our bodies into machines, desiring only one thing: each other. Running my hand down the side of her body, down her leg, and then landing right at her soaking wet pussy, I feel so fucking stupid for not taking her sooner.

"You are so wet," I say. I slide down and replace my fingers with my mouth. She writhes against my mouth like she's trying to get it inside her. She tastes so good that I can't lick up enough of her. She pulls her knees up, exposing herself in that awesome porno kind of way. I'm seconds away from losing it completely and plunging inside her.

"Maverick," she cries. She's begging now, and I can't fucking stand to hear it after what I put her through to fight off my own God damned demons. She waited because of me. She got me. I kiss up her stomach and chest.

"I'm here, baby. I'm here," I say, kissing her lips. Making out with her delicious mouth almost makes me forget how close to taking her I am. She raises her hips and my dick hits her opening, warm and inviting and my wildest fucking dream. Her blue eyes fly open at the contact and I see the sweet tenderness that resides there. She reaches between our bodies and grabs me with her hand, guiding me up to her clit and then back to hot center over and over.

I have the fleeting thought that I should lay down and bring her on top of me so she's in control of this. So she's the one responsible for the whole thing. Windsor will be the one controlling it, but I don't because I want this—to know that I have complete control over her, and because somehow I feel like I owe her this after denying her for so long. I'm choosing her.

With her free hand she grabs the side of my face. "Make love to me," she says. It's a simple request, though I somehow know nothing will ever be simple when it comes to us.

She lifts her hips up and the head of my dick slides into her. Arching her back, I feel her hands slide down to grab my ass. She pulls me into her a little more. I hiss in raw delight. My head falls into the crook of her neck. I can't control my breathing or my body. Thrusting until I hit the back, I start moving, like really fucking moving in this tempo that feels so good that I know I'll have to switch it up soon so I don't blow my load during the first minute of sex.

"You are so fucking tight. You feel so good," I rasp at her throat, kissing her, worshipping every centimeter of skin my mouth can find. I'm so consumed with how good she feels that I barely hear her moaning and panting. It's like the chorus to my favorite song. Windsor's song. She tilts her hips and meets me thrust for thrust, like we were made to fuck each other. Skin slaps as I change the pace, a pace I know she loves because she's holding onto my ass to keep me moving.

She turns her head searching for my lips. I kiss her while I fuck her. I've never done this before. Well, maybe before I knew what it meant. It feels good. Her tongue licking my tongue while my dick is inside of her makes me feel connected to her in some different way. She's not a bag. Windsor isn't a one-night stand with a wet hole and fake tits. I love her. I fucking love her.

Against my lips she moans, "I'm coming, Mav." Well, I'll be damned. All it takes is three words out of her mouth and I'm about to snap. Her face isn't frenzied like it usually is when I use my fingers or mouth to fuck her. It's different.

"Come for me. Come on my dick. I want to feel you on me," I say, making sure I keep my dick moving at the same speed. I want this to be perfect for her. I try to think of every uncomfortable situation I've ever been in to keep from coming too early. Windsor grabs my ass and pulls it toward her, causing my dick to go all the way in, and then she explodes around me.

No amount of picturing horrible things can stop me when I feel her grabbing me like a vice grip over and over. I let go. I live in the damn moment because it is an epic one. The best one so far. Her head is thrown back and her face is beautiful in this state of ecstasy. I lean down and put one of her pink nipples in my mouth and I come. It tears from me like a fucking fountain, finally flowing after a century of sitting stagnant. My eyes fall shut and I ride the waves of this feeling, with Windsor still screaming my name underneath me.

My dick finally stops twitching and her pussy isn't clenching me every other second, but I don't pull out. I want to stay inside her as long as humanly possible. I want this to be where my dick is every second of every day. I don't think three times a day will be enough to satisfy this hunger I have for her.

"One word," Windsor whispers as she drags her hands through my hair. Love. Love. Love. I love everything about what just happened, about what is still happening.

I heave a sigh. "Finally," I admit. She laughs and the sound makes me even more delirious with love from my new position. It's like I'm inside of the sound and inside of her at the same time. "Your one word."

Her hands stop moving. Her breaths stop. She's going to tell me she loves me. She has to. I know that was just as mind bending for her as it was for me. "Ruined," she finally says, laughing.

What. The. Fuck.

Before I can ask what the hell that means, she says, "I know why every girl you've had sex with is obsessed with you. You are like a sex God, with your big cock and perfect sex manners. You ruin it for all the other men in the world."

"Sex manners?"

I feel her nod against me. "It's all about me. I didn't have to do anything and you knew exactly what to do. Was it as freaking fantastic for you as it was for me? I have to say, I've been thinking about sex with you for a long time and it's even better than my brain could concoct," she explains. I feel her gripping my dick. A few more of those and I'll be at full attention again in no time. She's wondering if sex was good for me? Was she not in the same room?

"Windsor, I had to think about horrible things so I wouldn't come the second my dick slid home." I lean up on my elbows and look into her eyes. She smiles a half smile. "That's the first time I've had to do that. That's for sure. That," I say, pushing my dick inside of her a little more, making her eyes flutter closed, "was the best thing that's ever happened to me. It was earth moving." How's that for a Mav ramble?

She moans a little from the pressure and my dick is officially hard again. Ready for a second round. That happened a time or two in high school, but definitely not anytime in the recent past. It's a testament to my new addiction. I slide out of her long enough to put a new condom on, and ease back into her tight warmth. Flipping her around without disconnecting our bodies, I position her so she's on top of me. A lusty smile inches its way across her beautiful face and then she starts riding me like a fucking pro. Her tits bouncing, her hair swinging, one hand resting on my new tattoo, and her blue eyes fixed on mine.

And maybe for the millionth time I change my mind about my favorite sight.

Chapter Eighteen

Windsor

His hands on my hips are so rough and feel so warm…almost as hot as the fire spreading through my veins. I am working him like I've never worked a day in my freaking life. Bouncing up and down on his humungous, thickness feels incredible. Not because it feels better than I imagined, but because he's looking at me like he's completely and utterly in love with my every move, every inch of my body—and me.

He's in love with me. He said so. And I didn't say it back. I'm not sure if I can. Because I can't describe what I feel for him—it feels like more than love. Until I can formulate it into words, without rambling, I'll keep my mouth shut. I haven't said it to a single soul since Nash. Now I'm not even sure love is what I felt for him.

"You ride me so good, babe," Maverick growls. His neck is strained and every damned, huge, sculptured muscle that exists inside his body is popping out to tell me hello. The sight of him under me is burned into my mind for eternity. Maverick changes the pace by controlling my hips with his hands. "Feels so good. Feels so fucking tight," he hisses. It is almost too tight. The timbre of his voice combined with the perfect pressure he's rocking me with is all it takes. A jolt shoots straight to my core and I close my eyes.

Fireworks and rockets red glare? Yeah, that's what having an orgasm around Maverick feels like. There is no controlling my screams, or the stream of obscenities that leak from my mouth. I feel his hands on my nipples, twisting, pulling, making my orgasm last that much longer. When I come back down from that thigh tingling, lusty place, I make a breathy plea, staring directly into his fierce eyes.

"Come, Mav. Come." He must have been holding back because the second the words escape my mouth, he bucks his hips a few more times and, with a roar befitting a beast, he comes. My gaze lands on his new "love" tattoo and a shiver laced with excitement and possessiveness rocks me to my core.

I slump down, leaving him inside me, and put my head on his chest so I can continue staring at my claim on his body.

"You're everything, Mav," I say, praying he knows exactly what I mean by it. I mean what he meant by it before he could say the actual word. I feel him nod against the top of my head. Finally, our breathing evens out the same time he pulls out of my body. It's this wordless comfort I have lying in his arms, all sated and my stomach full of butterflies. I have nothing to compare this to, because I was never in this deep with another person. I've never felt so proprietary about anything else. Maverick rolls the condom off and then retrieves the other used one off the floor with a grimace. I can't help but laugh. "It's yours. You can't really be that grossed out by it, can you?"

"I prefer it in the condom and not on the floor," he explains, eyebrows scrunched together. I jump out of bed, feeling light on my feet. He watches me with a smile and says, "I'll deal with it though. I'd deal with jizz dripping from my fucking ceiling if it means I get to do that, with you, every day of my life." Now he's laughing, because I'm grimacing. The jizz dripping image kind of gets to me. The dimples are out and paired with his exquisite naked body they war for my attention.

"I'm on birth control—just a posted FYI. And I haven't had sex," I say, pausing to consider what I should confess to. "For a really long time." I don't say since Nash because then he would have a visual of me having sex with Nash in his head, and I don't want that. I can tell he's jealous of me merely talking on the phone. He needs no reminders. "So, as long as you're comfortable and…" I stutter. How to ask properly?

"Christ. Of course I'm clean, Windsor," he says, turning around mid-step.

I shrug my shoulders and raise my brow. "How am I supposed to know that? Remember all I have to go by are rumors at this point," I say. He narrows his eyes.

"Even if I wasn't tested every other month for shit like that I'd be clean. I always use a condom. Always. Except for," he admits, cutting off the end.

"Except for what?" I ask, walking toward him.

He swallows, turns away, and heads for the bathroom. "Except for when I was in a relationship," he says, after what feels like an eternity. Well, that's surely new information. I fight back the sting of unwanted jealousy. *It's in the past Windsor,* I remind myself.

"When were you in a relationship?" Okay, that came out super catty. Shit.

"A long time ago. The point is I'm clean. You're on birth control and *we're* in a relationship now," he explains. He tosses the condoms into the trashcan and stalks back toward me. "You want to use your CPA skills," he says with a half one-dimpled smile.

I tilt my head to the side in question. "I use a calculator for work things," I say. "Or a program that does computing for me." I think my accounting skills are the furthest thing from his mind. His eyes heat, and my stomach jumps to my throat.

His white smile assaults me. "Cock Polishing Assistant. That's the title that comes to mind whenever I hear your job title," Maverick says, pulling me to him. He kisses the top of my head and inhales. I love when he does it. It's like he can't get enough of me. He wants me inside him. I let a small chuckle slip. I'll never think of CPA the same way again and it's my freaking job.

"Isn't that what my mouth does? That so counts as polishing," I fire back.

"Sort of. This," he growls, stroking in between my legs, "will do a much better job though." A small moan slips. His hand disappears after he strokes me a few more blissful seconds. He pulls my face up to look at him.

Then he kisses me senseless. Like that type of whole body kiss that shocks you from your head to your toes. It starts simply with his tongue in my mouth, and then it greets my heart, causing it to pound out a new, more frantic rhythm. Next it goes down to my tummy waving hi to the flip-flop sensation. And lastly it shivers all the way down to my toes. It's melty-electric and passionate at the same time. His hands stroke my face in the same spots where his stubble will turn me red later. He scoops me up and places me in the bed again. He scoots in next to me as I pull up the soft sheets to hide us from the world.

"I just want to kiss you like this," he whispers into my mouth.

"You know exactly what I want...sexual manners," I say back. All we do is kiss, entwined legs and hands on faces and necks. He uses those manners for a long time, not taking it any further even though my body is on fire for him.

Eventually we fall asleep. His body wrapped around mine, my hand over his heart.

*****

"I don't know how I feel about this. Won't everyone wonder what I'm doing there? I only know Morganna. It will be weird," I explain, a little wildly, one hip propped against his desk in his home office.

It's late afternoon on Saturday and he wants me to go to dinner; a-farewell-we're-headed-out-on-deployment dinner, with the guys and their significant others. I. Am. Terrified. I imagine Morganna times fifteen and my heart races like a freaking jockey in the Kentucky Derby. Logically, I know there won't be anyone quite like Morganna, I just fear the judgment that comes from dating a guy like Maverick. Will his friends think I'm a *Frog Hog*? Will the girls think I'm just easy convenience sex before he leaves for six months? I know I shouldn't give a shit and I could tell myself that a million times, but I still would. Mommy issues. It's like Daddy issues except worse. Mav sits at the huge desk, papers and non-fiction books stacked in organized piles, shirtless.

He shakes his head while he speaks. "You're mine now. You have nothing to be afraid of—the fact that your Morg's friend only solidifies that. No one will say anything rude to you. I mean, I've never been to one of these things as half of a *couple*, but I can't imagine it's that painful. You might even make some new friends. It will be good for you to have people who are in the same situation as you." Sell it, Mav. Sell it. "Go get dressed, please. I need you to be there with me," he says.

And I can't say no to that. He needs me. He wants me wrapped up in his world. I huff a little, which makes him laugh. I turn and stalk out of the room before I catch sight of his dimples and attack him for round four.

I'm dressed in jeans, a dressy top, and heels at Maverick's request and out the door two hours later. We had sex one more time before we left because he saw me naked after I got out of the shower. My core clenches when I think of the way he looked at me before even touching me. It was the hottest gaze in the entire universe.

Dressed in tailored jeans and a black button up shirt, Maverick looks divine. He opens the door for me, offering his arm to walk into the restaurant. I'm not nervous when he's near, when his body heat drips into mine and I know I'm okay, fearless. But then I see the two tables near the back. Separated into sections like Thanksgiving at Aunt Velma's. Girls at one table and boys at the other. He senses my freak-out and squeezes my elbow a bit.

"It will be fine. Text me if you really want to leave. There's Morganna," he whispers, nodding toward her. I see an empty chair next to her and breathe a sigh of freaking relief. Her red lips part in an exquisite smile when she sees us. Subtly, Mav pats me on the ass, sending me to a table full of vultures, eyeing me down like I'm fresh road kill. Bottle blonde heads laden with more extensions than a Hollywood red carpet turn in my direction.

I ignore them and head to my seat. "Windsor," Morganna exclaims a little too loudly. "Come sit. Fashionably late was fifteen minutes ago." By the gleam in her eye she knows exactly why I'm late. Friends always know a well-fucked look when they see one. I'm probably a step beyond well-fucked. I'm not sure what comes after, though. I've never been there until now.

"Sorry," I mutter, quickly sitting down. Morganna introduces me to the table full of women, most of their names ending in Y, and I know I won't remember a single name because they all look the same and are dressed similarly. I smile wide and exchange fake pleasantries like I do at work.

I glance over at Maverick as he greets his buddies with weird, contorted handshakes and back pats—lots of touching. He flicks a smile at me when he sees me staring. I smile back. Barely. The women chatter around me. It's only now that I see physical details about them. Standard fake. They have lollipop heads on tiny bodies with enormous breasts that chant the song of their people when in a gathering such as this. Every other guy in the restaurant is staring at them, which seems a little stupid seeing as they obviously belong to the guys one table over. They do *belong*, too. They spare me a tiny glance and continue talking about their husbands and boyfriends like they are talking about their own lives instead. Morganna texts under the table, and I'm blessedly reassured that she finds these mundane, vapid creatures just as boring and senseless as I do.

I sip my wine and smile when someone says something that's supposed to be funny. I don't offer anything, and it's because I can't. I have absolutely nothing in common with these women. They talk about their gym regimens and exercise classes like Christians speak of God. To be more specific, one of the Y's just compared *Lululemon* workout pants to baby Jesus. Others chatter quietly about their own, real babies and how advanced they are because of their father's obviously glorious sperm contribution. I cringe when a brunette with a huge mane of hair announces her plan for a weekly spouse/girlfriend meet-up while the men are deployed. She bats her huge, fake lashes a few times and says we should *do* lunch next time. What. The. Freak.

I clear my throat and send Morganna a text message, keeping my phone hidden under the table. *You're going to gag me with a spoon when this is over, aren't you?:) Wait! I know. It's a joke…It has to be a joke.*

She responds quickly, liking the distraction. She smiles. *No. Phillipe is going to do that to you. I won't have time. I had to clear my schedule for this waste of fucking time. Welcome to the Rosy Team, Win. Where the only thing the women love more than themselves is their husband's career.*

Rosy? I text her back. I gathered the rest just by listening to them talk.

Everything always looks "rosy" to the rest of the world.

That makes sense. *Shit that doesn't stink and all that jazz?*

Morganna grins and responds quickly. *Yes. Obviously they are more disturbed than Fifty…*

A reference to Mr. Grey—I'm impressed. *Whips and chains? :-O*

Worse. Straps on Pilates boards, a mascara wand, and charity events. I laugh out loud.

You're part of it, Morg. You're making fun of yourself.

Her response is immediate. *Bullshit. They don't mess with me. They're too scared. Don't let them see you sweat. Rule #4.*

Another rule. Fabulous. I'm still laughing to myself trying to come up with a witty quip when a female voice hisses from across the table. "Do we bore you?" I know it's directed at me because of the tone. It's not the bogus friendly voice you use with fake friends. It's the mean, petty one you use on the rest of the world who resides beneath you. My mom has the tone perfected.

I shock them with something they probably don't hear often. "Of course not. It's just work…you understand," I reply, waving my phone in the air. Most of them have no freaking clue about work. I watch their faces shift in confusion. Maybe they think I'm being a bitch, but I can't find it in myself to care. "I have a few deadlines to meet," I add on, just to drive the point home. Morganna snorts. I shoot her the side-eye, smirking a little. I text Maverick.

They hate me. I watch him check his phone. He meets my eyes, and gives me this perfectly planned wink paired with both dimples. Narrowing my eyes at him, I sigh and try my best to focus of the task at hand. I catch the eye of one Y and I notice she's looking back and forth between Maverick and me.

She raises her perfectly arched eyebrows and says, "Maverick doesn't date. What do you have that I don't?"

I pause, because I have to let that question roll around in my head before I can answer. She's implying she's been with Maverick...and he didn't date her. So he must have had hotel sex with her. "Excuse me?" I ask perfectly, politely.

"Do you habla English? Maverick. Girlfriend. How?" she snips. Giggles buzz around the table and unfortunately I can't help the shade of red I feel my cheeks turning.

Morganna clears her throat, ostensibly to see if I plan on laying into these women before she does. I miss the simplicity of Gretchen's friendship. I'd never be facing the wolf pack's Rosy Team with her—I'd be facing a lingerie rack with my arms laden with bras and garters.

"You should ask him that," I reply, shrugging my shoulders. The high road is a lonely one. Especially when I feel like taking the dirty, low one. She rolls her eyes and scoffs. I have to purse my lips to keep from slinging insults her way. Not only am I jealous she's had sex with Maverick, I'm angry I didn't know I'd be running into his conquests at this thing. I guess just because they're with other men now doesn't mean anything about before. It's a new fact to add to the weird ass list. They share. Everything. How polite of them.

"Shut the fuck up, Marney. Don't be a bitch. He wanted her here. Why do you care anyway?" Morganna grates. It's nice to hear her stand up for me, when most of the time I'm trying to stand up for myself against her. The table falls silent. Morganna is head bitch. That much is obvious. At our silence a few of the guys cast curious stares

251

our way. I try not to avert my gaze, to avoid Maverick. I'll hold my own without his help. I've got this. Actually, Morganna's got this, but it's my freaking heart that is pounding.

"It's just weird. That's all," Marney says, chastened. "I've never seen him *out* with a woman before. Aren't you the least bit interested in why he picked her? After turning away Becky and Freya and even Chloe!" My stomach churns. Marney fixes me with her glare and this time it's sincere curiosity.

I swallow. I take a deep breath. I fold my hands in my lap. I take another calming breath. Sometime during my exercise in control he crept up. Maverick stands right next to me, in between Morganna and I, sending shivers and panic throughout my body.

"Becky, Freya, and Chloe weren't for me, Marney," Maverick says tactfully. Actually, *now* my heart is pounding. He lays a hand on my shoulder. "Windsor isn't like them. She's not like anyone, because she is *the* one. *My one.* Why did I pick her? I'm lucky she picked me, honestly. She's real. I owe her more than rattling off the never-ending list of why she's the one for me, so I'm shutting my fucking mouth. All you need to know is I'm hers. Make her feel welcome." His fingers tighten on me.

Morganna cackles. The Y's, including Marney, are open mouth breathing, watching Mav. It's kind of nice, but I don't want him to defend me. I want to be the woman who stands up for herself. I might suck at it, but a valiant effort is always noticed.

Never let them see you sweat. I gaze up into his hazel eyes and then back at the group. "So we're clear. My business is my business. Not yours. Thanks for that, Mav, but you didn't have to explain yourself for their benefit." I wave my hand around the table. Nervous hair tosses catch my eye. "But I did enjoy listening for my own benefit." I bite my lip and give him my most suggestive smile.

He leans down and kisses my temple, then my cheek. I feel self-conscious, but not enough to stop him. He kisses me again, over my hair, but still on my ear. He whispers, "It wasn't for their benefit. I'll give you the never-ending list later." I shiver. "In bed," he rasps quietly. He straightens. "Let me know when you're ready to go," he says, walking back to his table.

The guys haven't even missed him. They're all wrapped up in some overtly loud conversation that requires the use of their hands to explain. It's sort of funny. They get away with so much more than average people. It's because they honestly don't give a shit what people think. The earth circles the sun. That's normal—it's a fact. These guys go through life on their own frequency, with their own agenda and their own...rules. I get it now—seeing them together fuses all the voids I wasn't sure of before. This is Maverick's family. That's a fact.

Marney snaps out of her trance and says, "Well, guess we all know the answer now." Hushed whispers start. Morganna groans, ready to dominate any conversation that sparks. I prepare myself for round two. With Maverick's touch still on my skin, I'm ready for anything.

"What exactly is that?" I ask, looking at each person in the eye one at a time. *Show no weakness.* I repeat the mantra of the strong.

"Maverick Hart is finally in love," Marney admits. The women laugh a little and it's not caustic laughter; it's genuine laughter stemming from disbelief. I realize whatever I have with Maverick is huge. The leaps and bounds of progress we've made in our relationship shifted from tiny skips to huge spikes. I never in a million years would have thought I'd be okay with being in this position again. I am, though. So much so, that I didn't even think about it. It was just a natural progression. Maverick and Windsor.

The air shifts and they no longer direct bitterness at me.

"Who would have thought," Morganna offers, shooting a fond look at Stone, who doesn't notice her gaze. "Who would have thought?" She glances at me, smiles wide, and then turns her gaze to all the Y's. Morg raises her glass and all of the others follow suit. Hesitating a few seconds, I wonder what I'm toasting to, but I do eventually raise my wineglass. We all clink, fake smiles perched on our faces like an expensive accessory.

And just like that…I'm in.

Chapter Nineteen

Maverick

With every day that passes, my apprehension about leaving grows. Never before did I give a shit about deployments—they are just part of the job. I accept it. It's usually a little fun…if there's stuff to do—bad guys to catch, lives to make a little harder.

This deployment will be different because I'm doing something I've never done before. Insane, I know. I'm leaving something behind. Not just something, but someone. And I happen to be madly in love, heavy on the "madly," with that person. My mind is a twisted fuck of a place to be. Having sex with Windsor didn't have the effect I thought it would. She didn't push me away; she pulled me closer. I'm not sure which is worse.

I've lost all hope of having a clear head before or after I leave. The only time I'm not thinking about Windsor or some part of her body, or something she's said, or something she's done is when I'm inside her. See that catch-twenty-two? It's a bitter bitch. I'm impossible to deal with at work. I can't stop calling and texting her just because I can. I won't be able to talk to her very much after I ship out.

And because I fucking think about calling her, I pick up the phone and slam my finger on her name.

Her picture pops up on my screen. She has a white sheet tucked under her arms and her hair is a tangle of perfection. I snapped the pic after we had sex for the second time in one night. Her lips are pink and swollen and her blue eyes scream *come fuck me again*. Contrary to popular belief, I will never get sick of being inside her. My dick gets hard just daydreaming.

The phone rings a second time. Windsor answers and says, "I'm never going to get anything done if you don't stop calling me." Her voice is playful. I take a deep breath. She giggles. I've done this five times already today. I'm packing, so I have thirty huge dead-hooker-bags strewn around my house in haphazard array. I call her to forget.

I sigh. "How many appointments do you have this afternoon? I want you to come home," I tell her.

"Mav, I have to work. I can't stay in your sex dungeon twenty-four hours a day," Windsor whispers. I chuckle. She told me this morning she wishes she could spend the entire day in my bed. I told her she should. I'm at this crazy breaking point of being absolutely insane. I'm scared I'm going to say something so ridiculous that she's going to freak out.

"What's wrong with the bedroom? You seemed to love it this morning." I smile. I wish she could see it through the phone. "Last night. The day before that. And the day before that, too." I hear a door shut. Her office door.

"I miss you, too. Let me get through these reports. I'll be home two-ish. Can you work with that?" Windsor asks. I look around my room at all the bags. I purse my lips.

"Yes. I can work you out then," I growl. I'll have to pack my shit quick. I want to be finished so I can focus on her as much as possible. T-minus four days. I close my eyes. "As soon as you can. Come home."

Windsor laughs. For a second I forget about everything except what makes me happy. Her laughter erases every fucked up thought that races through my brain. It's such a simple, ordinary, unoffending thing. Something I would have laughed at if you told me the same thing six months ago. I never would have believed it. Right now, I've never believed in anything more.

"You're crazy," she says, pausing. I know she's thinking. She didn't say enough. Windsor holds back when she's not admitting something.

"One word," I say, curious. She makes a little sucking sound and I'm one hundred percent sure she has her fucking lip in her mouth, eyes turned up to the ceiling. My cock responds accordingly, as if she were here in my presence doing the same thing.

"Sad," she replies, her voice low. Boner flat-line.

"Don't be," I say automatically. "We have four full days. I have plans for all of them, too." If I can convince her, maybe I can convince myself, too. Stone told me leaving Morganna is a bitch, that he misses her like he'd miss a limb if it got blown off. I never understood what he meant. I will soon. I missed my parents after I left and didn't look back. That's a different kind of miss, though. I chose not to care, and they chose not to reach out.

Her phone beeps. She has another call. "You're everything," she whispers before clicking off the line. I hold the phone against my ear for a few additional seconds.

I drop the cell to my side, balling it in my fist. "Fuck!" I bellow, my growl echoing in the vast expanse of my bedroom. Existing in this interminable state of *almost gone* is miserable. Windsor *almost* saying love is also a fucking drag. I don't fault her, because I feel her affection in every word she says to me, in every breath she takes—in her huge blue eyes when she gazes up at me. She needs time. I can give her that.

I drag one of the huge black bags into my closet. I've packed all my uniforms already, so I go to the side that houses my t-shirts. Scanning the hangers I pull off one that says *The Dude Abides*, another that has a huge mustache sprawling across the front, and another that says *Yo Mamma*. All exceedingly appropriate. I fold them the way you're supposed to fold a t-shirt and put them in my bag followed by a red poncho, a sweatshirt with an AK printed on the front, and a pair of Elvis sunglasses. My skintight, spandex American Flag shirt goes into the mix and I start to feel a little lighter doing what I do every time

I ship out. The familiarity of packing eases the burn a little. I feel even better when I pull out my leather, badass eighties rock gear.

The costume reminds me of Stone, so I dial him up to talk about what he's bringing and to make sure I have all the necessities on the pack-out list. He convinces me to bring *my* big screen TV because Morganna isn't letting him take their TV from their living room, and I have an extra for occasions like this. After that long, drawn out conversation, in which he forced me to listen to the new rock song he just wrote for Morg, I call Steve. I need to make sure they don't expect me to go to the bar hopping party. He tells me I'm a pussy—that I'll regret not tapping a few girls from the Maverick stock sex pool. I tell him he should bag them instead. He agrees and I'm off the hook.

A few hours later I'm stacking all my bags next to the front door, feeling a little excited to deploy, when Windsor rushes in. She has on a gray skirt and a black button up shirt, the top two buttons open. Her hair is up, but pieces have fallen down into her face. Her smile, like it always is when she first sees me, is God damned brilliant. She kicks off her heels and runs toward me. She knocks into me as hard as she can, but I catch her easily and pull her up so her face is level with mine. Her eyes say *I miss you. I want you. I miss you.* I could stare into them all day long.

Windsor shakes her head and says, "God, you're even hotter than when I left this morning. How do you do that?"

I let it rip—the big smile, because she's looking at me like I'm the fucking prize. Her gaze lands exactly where I want it. Almost immediately, she kisses me. Her eyes fall shut as I lower her to the ground and bend down to avoid taking my mouth off of hers. Reaching up, I release her hair so it falls down around her shoulders and fist it in my hands. Her fingers snake under my shirt and skirt up to rest on my chest, always one hand on my heart…over her tattoo. She loves it. I love her.

I help her take my shirt off. My heart races at skin on skin contact because it knows what comes next. Who am I to deny it? I unbutton her shirt, teasing her mouth with flicks of my tongue and gentle kisses. She tilts her head to get a better angle and joins in the competition to see who can dominate better. She wraps her hands around my neck and pulls me closer once her shirt is wide open. Skimming her wet mouth down over my jaw, my chin, and down the front of my throat, she licks my neck tat and sighs a happy little moan. I close my eyes and take it all in.

She sucks my neck, just enough to make it feel good, but not enough to leave a mark. "I don't want to leave you," I admit, tilting my head back to give her better access. She bites my collarbone.

Against my skin she murmurs, "So don't leave. I want you to stay with me, too. I don't even know what to expect when you leave. I miss you so much when I'm at work and that's only like nine hours. What does four thousand, three hundred, and twenty hours feel like? Torture." She kisses me where she just bit me.

"Did you work that out in your head?" I ask to avoid the sickening truth.

"Numbers are my thing. I figured it out around the fourth time you called today." Her full lips find mine again, but this time they don't help me forget. They are like the signature on my death sentence— or a drug I won't be able to have for a significant amount of time. She's right. It will be torture. Windsor strips her shirt off and then her pink lace bra. Her tiny nipples pucker at the chill in the air. I kiss them. I lick one and then the other as she clutches my head to her chest.

"I have to go, Win. I don't have a choice. You'll be here when I get back?" My tongue slides up the center of her breasts as I lick a trail all the way up her throat to her mouth. I whisper at her lips, "Promise me." Windsor darts her tongue out to trace my lips. She pulls my bottom lip in between her teeth.

"Like right here? In this exact same spot?" She says, her lips grazing mine as she speaks. I hate that she doesn't get what I'm asking. My addictive personality is about to rear its head. Fuck. Fuck. "Or are you asking if I'll still be yours when you get back?"

"Yes," I say simply, inhaling the scent of her cherry lip gloss intermingling with her shampoo.

She pushes me back a touch, so she can look at me face on. "Isn't that the way this works? Why would you even have to ask? Of course I'm yours. I'm yours forever. I'll be here. I'll be in this exact spot if that's what you want. Say the word," she says, pointing to the ground.

My stomach is a tangled fucking mess. This conversation just increases my inner turmoil. I've never had to have a talk like this. Not even with the blonde monster. But I never gave a shit about her, so I guess I wouldn't. This is the sissy stuff that attached people deal with. Not lone wolves like me.

I view attachments with a singular view. With each person you grow close to, you increase your odds of miserable things happening—whether it's friends or a girlfriend, or even parents having more children. With each addition of love to your life, the favor turns against you. You're more liable to have something stripped away. Cancer. A car accident. A broken heart. The horrific scenarios of loss are endless and more plausible with each attachment you form. Because that's the thing with attachments —you benefit from them, but they fucking destroy you. If you keep attachments to a minimum your risks stay low. I have Stone and my team. Now I have Windsor. An addition I know makes me vulnerable tenfold.

Stone told me I should talk about how I'm feeling with Windsor. I took his advice because number one, I always take his advice, and number two, he has Morganna, the impenetrable force field wrapped like a hard dick. You can't undermine that feat.

"This is new to me, Win. I've never left a girlfriend behind before. I just wanted you to know that I don't want to lose you because of my job. I don't want to lose you for any reason. I want you to be here, in my house, in my life when I return. That said, I'll understand if you can't. It's a lot to ask of anyone. You should know though, I'll never not want you. You're my *always*. And I do think I want you in this exact spot when I get back…maybe in the bedroom instead. We can negotiate if you're amenable." She has this huge fucking smile on her face as she watches me spill my soul.

"You're being dramatic. Six months is not that long to wait. Especially for the best damn sex of my life." Now she's teasing me. Christ, if my friends saw this pathetic show, they'd have a field day. "Also, I'd wait forever for you—you crazy man, you. You're my always, too. I'm in, Mav."

"All in?" I ask, pulling her waist toward the bulge in my pants. She raises her eyebrows when it bumps her stomach.

"All the way in," she purrs. Fuck yes. I glance at the bags behind her head quickly, distractedly. She follows my gaze and then narrows her eyes at me. "I think those bags need some action. Something to remember me by?" Windsor says, her tiny hands falling to unbutton and unzip my jeans.

I shake my head. "*I* need something to remember you by. Those bags don't deserve you." She's lost her skirt and her panties in the last few seconds. She gets the award for world's quickest naked woman. I want to be the one to congratulate her. Pursing my lips together, I cross my arms over my chest. Windsor takes a step back toward the bags. I slide my boxer briefs off and step out of them.

She clears her throat. "Well maybe you can both have me at the same time," she explains, her gaze trained on my cock. If I didn't know better I'd think she was talking about getting tag teamed.

Placing a hand on one of my black bags as tall as her waist, she strokes it reverently. I'll never look at that fucking bag the same again. That's the point, I think.

Windsor turns around, giving me a grand view of her narrow waist and round ass. Her long hair falls down her back, brushing her side when she turns her head to look over her shoulder. "Fuck me. Right here. On top of these bags," she commands, her eyes fierce.

My dick is the only thing I can think of. How hard it is. What her words do to me. I blow out a pent up breath and approach her. When I'm standing behind her, I put my fingers where my dick wants to go.

She is soaking wet and obviously ready for me. "I've been waiting for this all day," she breathes, throwing her head back to rest it on my chest. I kiss her forehead, watching her eyes grow heavy as I work her with my fingers.

She moans and my dick twitches. My mind is clear for the first time since I last touched her.

*****

Windsor

I love my back being pressed against his front. I feel every hard muscle bulging, controlling me, and owning me.

Being in his arms makes me delirious with lust and passion. I say things I wouldn't normally say; I just asked him to fuck me on bags. I'm pretty sure that never would have come out of my mouth before having sex with Maverick. The uninhibited person I am when I'm with him is freeing. It's a person I never thought I'd have the courage to be. It's me. It's Windsor Forbes unfiltered.

I spread my legs a little wider to give his hand better access to me, and stifle another moan. The tips of his fingers circle and rub, causing my slick sex to pulse. He dips a finger into me. I can't even stop my muscles from tightening around him. I do try to calm myself, because I want him inside me when I do come. His hand disappears, and I'm left panting, wondering what comes next. Lifting me by my waist and pushing down my shoulder blades, he bends me over the stack of bags.

"Keep your legs open for me, baby," he says, hissing when the tip of his dick presses into my sex. My face is pressed into his bag. It smells like new plastic. I guess it could smell like something worse. "You feel so good, Win. I'm gonna fuck you now," Maverick growls.

He pushes all the way into me, hitting the back. It hurts at first, but after a couple thrusts I'm used to his punishing rhythm. This isn't the sweet sex we usually have, when we're entwined with each other. This is frantic. He pulls me off the bags a little each time he thrusts, like he's trying to bury himself inside me further than he's ever gone. I grab onto one of the handles on the side of the bag to steady myself.

I know he needs this. I saw the way he looked at me when he asked if I was going to stay. It was the same look he wore when he looked at his packed bags. All I can do is trust him to trust me when I tell him I want him forever.

His strokes are more harried and out of pace as he reaches a hand around to stroke me. I feel everything, everywhere. How hot is cock is as it fills me, how his muscles strain as he pumps. I feel him shaking a little and know he's about to come. Maverick coming is the most erotic sight I've ever seen. Imagining what his face looks like right now is all it takes to send me off. I arch my back, and work myself back onto him as far as I can as I pulsate around him. Tingling shoots throughout my body and I ride it for as long as I can.

"Shit. Yeah," he whispers, smacking my ass. With a loud groan he pulls out of me and comes. His hot spurts land on my ass and all the way up my back, reaching my shoulder blades. "Fuck," Maverick mutters, between clenched teeth. "I got it in your hair," he says, panting loudly. I turn my head around so I can see him. I don't dare move though. Come would get everywhere. I'll have to play the run to the bathroom and not get it everywhere game soon.

I laugh when I see that he's actually concerned I'll be upset he got it in my hair. "It's good for it," I explain. "Really, I'm only concerned because this sort of makes me a *bag*, doesn't it?" I point at the one he just thoroughly worked me over on. He graces me with both dimples.

"You're my forever bag, baby. And I think I hate these dead hookers a little less." I'm not sure what that means, but he's looking at me with those black fringed, hazel eyes and I'm so done for. I don't care that he holds all the power, that he alone has the power to crush me into tiny bits. I'll fade like a dying star without him anyways.

"I wrote you another song," Maverick says, scooping me into his arms. He hums an upbeat melody as he carries me to the shower. Serenading me in the wet room, his sexy, growly voice breaks up the stream of the showerheads. I can only stare at him, in all of his glorious perfection as he looks directly at me and sings a perfectly lyrical love story. Luckily my tears mix with the warm water, hiding just how much I'm going to miss this sight.

And him.

Chapter Twenty

Windsor

The days passed too quickly. I tell myself I'm ready for Maverick to deploy, but honestly it's like readying for an execution too soon. No one, I don't care who you are, can be ready for that. I've already said goodbye to him in my head a million times. Maybe a billion? I feel guilty because I just want him to leave so it can finally be real—and so he can come back and it can be over. It's an odd mindset, but not nearly as odd as some of the other things Morganna tells me about.

Crying Sex is in fact, the act of crying during fornicating because your significant other's long departure is imminent and you realize how much you're going to miss them...and having sex with them. I found myself tearing up during sex with Mav the night after she told me about the bat shit crazy occurrence—because really, it makes perfect sense. Doggy style while tears run down my face? Epic moment, let me tell you. I've added it to the weird freaking list of things that are unimaginable to average people.

My emotions are all over the place. I'm not sure what to say to him about my feelings. I want to placate Maverick, to ease some of the hesitancy he feels about leaving me behind, but I can't tell him I love him now. He'd think it's because he is leaving. How fair would that be? *Oh, by the way I'm in love with you. I think you already know, but I'm just telling you because you're leaving for a dangerous area and might not come back. Ever.*

That would just make me a bad person. Plus, the last time I uttered the same words I can safely say I didn't mean them. I didn't love Nash. I loved the idea of what marrying him and settling down meant. It was comfortable. Nash merely represented what I wanted in life…at that specific time. I was desperate and blinded by what society told me was the next step in my relationship—and in my life. I truly love Maverick, but I want to tell him on my own terms without any outside pressures forcing my hand. It's a big deal. I told myself I wasn't going to say "I love you" until I knew it was forever.

Speaking of desperate and blinded, I'm semi-dodging my Mom's calls and texts. I know now that he's leaving I'll have to face Kathy down and actually visit her or, God forbid, have her come and visit me. I'm drowning in horrible thoughts, swimming—flailing in all directions when I feel strong, heavy arms snake around my waist from behind…an anchor to my seriously insane thoughts.

I lean my head back against his chest. "Is it always this miserable saying goodbye?" I ask, trying to keep my voice steady. The airport is buzzing with people, but they could be inanimate objects for how much they mean to me. We're as good as alone.

He clears his throat and whispers, "Probably."

I keep forgetting, while he's deployed a half-dozen times, he's never been in a relationship during one. It's comforting and scary at the same time. What if we both suck at the deployment game? I'm sure I can handle it. I'd handle anything life deals as long as I get to keep this loving, caring man in my life in some capacity. What if it's too much for him? How is he supposed to do his job, which is superbly demanding, while worrying about keeping a girlfriend happy?

"Thanks for bringing me to the airport, Win," Maverick says, pressing a long kiss on the top of my head inhaling deeply. He has a solitary suitcase and wears normal, civilian clothes. His departure looks like any other person's. Except it's not. It is anything but normal. Six months. Half a year will pass before I see him in person next. Four thousand and some odd hours will have to go by before he'll stand in front of me or wrap his arms around me again.

I turn in his arms and hug him, burying my face in his hard chest. "Seriously, as if I'd be anywhere else. This is my favorite place to be. It just feels so final. Like maybe I'll never see you again," I say, trying to keep my emotions under wraps. "You'll forget all about me and come back and be like 'Windsor who?'" I tease, breaking up the serious with a lie. Maverick chuckles against me, his chest rumbling. Another noise I'll miss.

His hands, hot against my lower back, ground me to right now—to this moment. My chest tightens.

"Even if that was remotely fathomable, it wouldn't be possible. We'll see each other on Skype as much as I can. Stone tells me this helps with the loneliness," he replies. I hear his smile through his words. Both dimples greet me when I look up. We've talked about what we should expect from each other. It's like a fully functioning relationship simultaneously disguised as something else.

Shaking my head, I say, "Stone would say that. Now I have images of Morganna naked burned into the back of my mind." She probably has equally disturbing images of me in her memory bank too.

He closes his eyes. "Great. Now I do too," Maverick sighs. I laugh.

"I'll do whatever it takes to combat our loneliness, though," I admit. One side of his mouth quirks up and he nods, slowly, watching me. His hand cradles my head as his thumb strokes the side of my face. The softness of his caress is opposing the fierce rigidity in his gaze. If I didn't feel the same way I'd probably be confused.

"I'll call you when I can," he finally says. I bite my lip to keep it from quivering. I promised myself I wouldn't cry. I'll keep my shit pulled together for as long as possible and break down in the privacy of my own bedroom, surrounded by all the comfort items from my former life. Everything that I loved before I loved Maverick. Before he loved me, changing everything.

I lean up on my tippy toes and he automatically leans down. I make the last move and press my lips to his. He clutches me to his chest like he needs me as much as he needs the air he breathes, but the kiss stays simple, pure. I shut my eyes and let myself feel everything I've pushed away. I hurt, I love, I want, I'm alive, I'm dead. I'm everything I once was when Nash ruined me, and at the same time I'm beyond that because Nash never loved me like Maverick does. My pulse skitters and my unsettled stomach flutters when I take a breath and smell Maverick—his cologne, his scent. The kiss slows, and I know it's almost time. His thick lips don't own me like they usually do.

They say goodbye.

I'm crying when he pulls away way too soon. It's not the ugly, jagged Kim K cry; it's more subdued. It's the type of tears that promise a freaking flood later. I'm heartbroken and completely in love at the same time if that is even possible.

I nod and sniffle. "Safe travels," I whisper. He smiles, but it doesn't reach his eyes. He can't even pretend enough to convince me right now. The artful actor is nowhere in sight. Maverick is stripped of his defenses.

He grabs the handle of his sleek, black suitcase. The tiny movement causes my heart to pound out a crazy rhythm. Catching my breath will be impossible.

My gaze darts up to meet his. "Please be safe. Please. Good luck. You're everything. You mean everything to me, Mav," I murmur.

"Always," Maverick says, voice light. "It's not about luck, baby. That's one thing I don't need." He presses his lips together in a firm line. "You're everything to me too. I love you, Win." He swallows and looks down at the ground, his black lashes fanning across his cheekbones. He turns and walks away. He doesn't even wait for me to respond. He knows I won't or can't. He turns his head, his black t-shirt bunching in perfection across his back. A small one dimpled smile crosses his face as he says, "You have a surprise waiting for you at home."

I cry and laugh at the same time. It comes out as an unattractive snort. I don't trust myself to speak, so I smile as a response. It's the last thing he sees. He turns again to walk toward the security line and I watch him for as long as I can.

He doesn't turn around again.

*****

I give ugly crying a new definition. Every single, freaking song that comes on the radio causes my vision to blur. They're all miserable songs about love lost. Even the rap songs for God's sake—even though the beat is a little happier than some of the other morbid choices.

I hit another pothole on the horrible highway. Between my tears, Virginia Beach potholes, and the sadness swelling in my chest, I'm not sure I'll make it home in one piece. My phone chimes with text messages from Kathy and Gretchen—both of them wanting something from me. I can't give any of them anything in my current state, so I don't plan on responding until I can sleep off my heartbreak hangover. Until I can work out an equation to compute just how much one person can miss another without dying.

I figure Kathy's dealt with her fair share of what I'm feeling, but turning to her for any kind of sound advice won't be my best bet. My Dad, God rest his soul, would know exactly what to say to me right now. He died in a car accident that was both utterly tragic and ironic. It killed him on impact, which I always looked at as a blessing. No suffering. He was driving one second and dead the next. If you have to go early, that's the way. A drunk driver hit him. I don't think Kathy's been sober a day since it happened. That's the ironic part.

Dad would have told me a story about a strong heroine who conquered the world, and then spouted off several relevant quotes about love and perseverance. Sometimes I think if I had him around when Nash and I broke up, I wouldn't have landed in a shrink chair laden with self-hatred. That's all psych's really are anyway—someone who listens and gives sound advice without judging.

I miss my Dad. I'll always miss him. I haven't died from missing him yet, so maybe missing Maverick will be easier. A college professor once told me that missing someone meant that you are fortunate to love someone in the first place. If you don't miss them, you don't love them. Some don't get that chance. Somehow, fortunate isn't any of the things I'm feeling.

My phone rings through the speakers of my car, scaring the ever-loving shit out of me. I slam the answer button to shut off the noise as quickly as possible.

Gretchen's screeching voice blares out of the speakers, "Where the hell are you? I thought you'd be home by now. Was it horrible?"

I sigh. I won't hit the green button next time. "Of course it was horrible!" I yell. Gretchen speaks to someone else, her mouth away from her phone. "Who are you talking to?" I ask.

"No one! I have to meet Benji...will you be home soon?" More whispered words and then I hear her say, "Shhhh!"

"I'm pulling on to our street now. Why do I have to be home before you leave? I don't really want company right now. Or today. Probably not for a week or so," I admit because, honestly, I don't want Gretchen to organize anything in my sad, sorry honor. It's totally something she'd do. Then I'd have to kill her in her sleep.

"Hurry up!" Gretchen snaps. She hangs up the phone. I sigh, leaning my head back on the headrest. As soon as I park, I flip down the mirror and wipe beneath my eyes in vain. I'm sure they'll be black and smudged for a few days—especially if the freaking radio doesn't stop scoring for the other team. I need to turn on *Pandora* on the get-freaking-happy station. Six months will go by in a snap if I can find things to entertain me in my spare time.

I obviously have plans to work like demon. Luckily tax season is coming up and I'll be working crazy hours anyways. Distraction is key. Morganna told me so. I have a brief urge to call her, then decide against it. She feels like I do. She doesn't want to talk.

I glance down to grab my phone and see a white envelope sticking out of the side of the passenger seat. My name is printed on the front in tiny capital letters. Maverick's handwriting. Definitely not reading this until my cry fest later.

I slam my car door and hit the lock button on my key fob. My feet feel like they weigh a thousand pounds each as I trudge up the stairs and push open my front door.

Gretchen squeals and a plaintive little bark echoes the living room. "Finally!" She says rushing toward me with a tiny, and I do mean tiny, tan hairball under one arm.

My eyes are as big as marbles when she thrusts the cutest thing in the world into my arms. "What the hell is this? I mean I know it's a Pomeranian, but why is it in our condo?" I ask. The dog wriggles in my arms and licks the salty tears off my face. Puppy breath. I melt. The dog is wearing a tiny black t-shirt.

"Maverick didn't want you to be lonely," Gretchen explains, looking at the dog with as much fondness as a mother would her newborn baby. "He got him from the shelter you always go to. Someone dumped a litter of Poms a few weeks ago. I've been hiding him at Benji's." Gretchen smiles wide. "I would never let you be lonely, but this way you at least have a guy sleeping in your bed every night." She scratches the top of his head, cooing in a high voice. "What are you going to name him? I've been calling him Bear because he looks like a fucking teddy bear, but I'm sure you'll be more creative," she says. I look down, still in shock at the warm little fuzzy mess, and see that the doggy t-shirt has the words *TOP GUN* printed on the back of it. I laugh a little and shake my head. "The shirt was at Mav's request. Obviously," Gretch explains.

"Goose," I say. "I'll name him Goose." I cuddle him up to my face and, amazingly, this little creature makes me feel better. Looking at him I won't be able to forget what I mean to Maverick. "Thank you, Gretch." I hug her, the puppy squirming between us. She pulls me in a little tighter.

"It will be okay. You'll see. I've never seen a man more in love or care about a woman more than he does for you. Six months really isn't that long to wait for the rest of your life."

"I hate it when you're right," I whisper into her hair. She squeezes my ass in both of her hands.

"I'm always right, bitch. Go snuggle with that puppy. He's like a mood enhancing drug. I swear it. He went outside to pee just before you got here, but that doesn't mean much because I think his brain is the size of a pea."

I walk to my room and set little Goose on my huge bed and just gawk at him. He's staring right back at me. The responsibility of owning a dog scares me. I pull the letter from Maverick out of my purse and trace my fingers over my name.

Win,

Stop reading unless you've seen Gretchen first...

You have him now? Okay, good. Surprise!

Courage is a strange thing. The more you use it, the more it consumes you. You didn't want to pull the trigger on a puppy, so I did it for you. Fear not, you will be the greatest dog mom ever. How am I so sure? Because you're good at everything (and I do mean everything). Usually things that involve your mouth and hands...but everything else too. You're so good that I popped wood just writing/thinking about the last sentence. See? So good. I wanted to get you a larger mutt, something that would latch on and then kill an intruder, but Gretchen stepped in and said something smaller and "cute" would be preferable for condo life. Look at that furry thing. He's adorable. That isn't a word I've ever used.

I pause reading and look at Goose. He huffs and stretches his back legs out like a frog. Freaking adorable as sin. Mav's right.

He'll keep you company and kiss you senseless until I come home and kiss you senseless in a better way. I miss you already.

Mav

Chapter Twenty-One

Maverick

"Goddammit! Toss me the bottle of *Febreeze*, man. It smells like a fuckin' whore house on a Saturday night," Stone yells.

Our room in this camp, if you can even call it that, is small and full of sand. At least it's not a tent. At least it has walls. Plywood forms the dividers and the floor. The door creaks because it doesn't shut properly. That fact doesn't matter much. Even if someone made it as far as inside our camp, which isn't possible, the second they step into this room they'd be dead. Not like, "hey man, you're dead meat," either. Like a bullet in between your fucking eyes dead. I pull in a deep breath and wince. It's hot here.

I throw the bottle at his head. "Like you even know what a whore house smells like, you pussy." Most of the guys do know the exact eau de skank scent of such a place. Stone doesn't. Believe it or not, I don't either. Standards, people. He catches it before it hits his head...the quick asshole.

The second I landed in this fucking dust bowl, something inside of me switched. It's time to work. Of course I miss Windsor and all the comforts of home, but I'm just as comfortable in this cramped shack as I am in my four thousand square foot house. Part of the glory package is dealing with such conditions. I gladly accept all the shit aspects to be able to do what I love. I was made for this life. Not many can say that.

I tell Stone to stop spraying the plywood with *Febreeze* because the *linen breeze* is giving me a damn headache. He tells me the stink is coming from the wood. Morganna's habits are so ingrained in him that he doesn't even realize when he's acting like her clone. Minus the tits, of course. When we've cleaned the room as much as possible, I hang a huge American flag. It takes up the entire plywood wall of our room—reminding me why I do what I do. It's my good luck charm, too. I never deploy without it.

With all the menial tasks done for the day, I let myself think of her. I hike myself up into the top bunk, because Stone won the arm wrestling match for the bottom bunk, and open my laptop. The Internet connection is always splotchy and doesn't work most of the time. I don't have enough bars to call Windsor on Skype so I type her an e-mail, which will be our main form of communication while I'm gone.

*****

Winnie Bear,

I can't call because too many fuckers are downloading ass fucking porn right now. I'm officially "home". I'm jetlagged and it's hotter than Dante's inferno, as I'm sure you'd expect. How is everything back in VB? How is Goose? I love the name you chose, by the way. The photo you sent of you guys in bed made me jealous. I want to be in between your tits licking your face. Keep the pictures coming. They make me feel like I'm there. I'll send you some if you want, too. Although I'll probably look pretty damn scary in a couple weeks with more facial hair than Borat and Bin Laden combined. Try not to cream your panties thinking of that. Come to think of it, maybe you just want dick pics?

I want to start up our game. I'll tell you one thing about me that you don't know and when you write back you tell me something about yourself. Scary, deep shit. Sound fair? Our relationship won't suffer from the distance, I promise. So here is my one: I want us to work, Win. I told Morganna that I wanted you more than I've wanted anything else. The words were true, but they surprised me because I honestly never thought I'd want anything more than I want my career. It's a big thing to do what I do. It gives me something that I know I'll never be able to get from another job. But when I jumped out of that airplane with you strapped to my chest, I knew that I needed to keep you there...close to me. Close to my heart. Because your honesty and trust gave me hope. Hope that one day I'd have more than just passion for my

career. I feel greedy sometimes. Who deserves the
job and the girl? I thought Stone was a weird freak
of nature for having "it all." Now I have it, too.
When I hold you, I realize how lucky I am.

My parents aren't good people, although they'd
like everyone to believe they are some upstanding
citizens with scrupulous morals. They did give me
the foundation to be a great man. But morals
aren't everything if it affects your own happiness.
I'm telling you this because your relationship with
your own mother reminds me a lot of...me. We're
both lucky. Life tastes sweeter because of our past.
Solid foundations are built with tough love.
Remember that when you deal with Kathy.

Stone just got in. He's twerking to get my
attention. I miss you already. The picture of you is
taped on the wall by my bed. It's the first thing I
see when I wake up and the last thing I look at
before I close my eyes. You're on my heart and in
it. Gotta go, babe. Tell me something.

You're everything,
Mav

Maverick,

Goose peed on the freaking floor three times
yesterday. Gretchen said it's because he has a
brain the size of a pea and I should forgive him,
but I'm not sure, although his cuteness makes up
for it (mostly). I wish you were snuggling with me

too. What will we do with Goose when you come home? He's going to get pretty jealous if he doesn't get the spot between my boobs at night. He might whine so loud we can't sleep! Tell me more about where you're living. What do you eat? What do you do all day?

Virginia Beach is good. The weather is changing. Not that I really appreciate it. I'm stuck in the office for fifteen hours a day. Don't worry, it's what I prefer. It helps the time go by faster. I have more appointments and paperwork than I can handle. Who's doing your taxes, by the way? I know a CPA who would love to polish your coc...work your numbers real good.

I almost feel like you were just some perfect dream. I'm going to wake up one day and all I'll have are memories of you and I'll wonder if they're even real. Does that make sense? I miss you so much. Not just because you're so good at sex, but because I feel like a little piece of me is missing. I'm always aware something isn't there. I'd compare it to forgetting your cell phone at home, but it's so much more than that. It hurts my heart.

I went out to "lunch" with the Rosy Team yesterday. Those women are ridiculous in good ways and in bad ways. Did you know there are twenty-five different ways to give a blow job? Or that one of the wives is writing a romance novel about Navy SEALs? Crazy, right? Another one, who will not be named, had to go to her car because she got a SF call in the middle of lunch. Know what SF means? Hint: not Special Forces. It means Sexy Facetime. I don't even want to know what she did in her car, in the parking lot of a restaurant. Can we do a non-public SF call? :)

Marney did give me some good ideas on what to send you in a care package. Do you want anything specific? Or should I just use my best judgment? I guess all of us "girls" are going out next month. It's supposed to be a big deal. Morg says I should start shopping for a dress and shoes now. I'm going to invite Gretch because she doesn't believe me when I tell her what these women talk about. Any idea what I should expect from a Rosy Team rager? Tips? Tricks to avoid back stabbing?

I love your "tell me something" game continuation. A way of pushing the relationship forward in the absence of...not being together. You totally made me cry with your one thing. Just so you know. It was very poignant because Krazy Kath is actually coming to visit me for a while. Number five still hasn't returned. She says she wants to bond with me, but hello? Everyone knows she's lonely and wants someone to harp on. Windsor is a perfect candidate. I may end up hurling myself off a tall building. Not really, but I'll probably wear headphones the entire time.

Which sort of leads to my one thing: I've been crying a lot since you left. Not just because you left and will be gone for a long ass time either. Things make me cry that shouldn't, because I'm not typically a crier. Kathy, of course, has that skill perfected, but commercials and rom com movies? Jesus, what is the world coming to? What is wrong with me? Everything is sad. Songs on the radio, too. I'm sensitive to everything around me. Morganna told me it's normal, although I've never seen her shed one tear her entire life. She tells me "it upsets me when Stone is away." I wish I could be as stoic as she is.

Your love changed some fundamental part of me. The wall I built around myself for so long is completely toppled down. I'm open. That's something even my psychiatrist couldn't achieve after years of therapy. You did it. It's all because of you. I like to think it has something to do with the fact that falling for someone changes a person, but I also know it's because it's YOU I fell for. I didn't expect to feel so strongly about someone after Nash. But being with you made me realize I didn't love Nash. He was my safe choice. My safety net—when the going gets tough, you want that type of person. But jumping into the unknown with you? It has been the best decision I've ever made. So as I sit here crying while I write this, know it's your fault. All of it. Touch your chest and pretend it's my hand.

Forever and ever yours,
Winnie Bear (That's pretty cute.)

P.S. Get a Facebook. Even a fake one. That way you can keep up with all the photos I post! Thank you for the flowers you sent to my office. And the six dozen you sent to my condo...and for the ones you sent to my mother's house even though you knew I wouldn't be there. So coy. They're beautiful.

Winnie Bear,

Out of your entire letter I zeroed in on one thing.
I'm a man, after all. Yes. Yes. Yes. Let's have a
naked Skype session, Facetime call—whatever.
You naked is my favorite sight. What happens
after I see you naked is my favorite thing in the
universe. I'm not sure how I'll handle the insanity
of seeing you naked and not being able to touch
you. That seems like a type of torture even I'd be
unwilling to deal out. Cruel and unusual. I'm
willing to deal with it, though. My hands are kind
of shaky just thinking about touching you naked.
See what you do to me? I better not think of you
when I have a gun in my hand. :) How about
tomorrow 7 a.m. your time? I know it's early, but
the time difference is a bitch. I have some training
to do the rest of the night. Stone will be gone, too.
Not that he wouldn't want to see you naked, but
I'd have to kill him if he did.

I got a Facebook account last night. I'm sure
you've already accepted my friend request. I'm
Julio Bigcock. My main photo is none other than
Bob Saget. I thought you'd get a kick out of that. I
hate to admit that you're right. I like the
Facebook. I got clicking and couldn't stop. The
picture Gretchen took of you after you got home
from a run, all hot and sweaty and delicious
looking, is my all time favorite. Send me a copy?
Also the one of Goose wearing the sign around his
neck saying "I peed on Mommy's briefcase and
liked it." Made me laugh out loud. Maybe doggy
training camp is in order?

We eat horrible cafeteria food here. Sometimes it's okay and other times it's bad. They have a salad bar that makes me nervous because I'm not sure how fresh the vegetables are, but it's better than the fried alternatives. Last time we were out this way, Stone got so puking sick from eating shellfish that now he refuses anything that doesn't come out of a can. It was pretty bad. Ocean dwelling seafood in the middle of the desert is a bad idea—always. Morganna is constantly sending him boxes of food so he doesn't starve. He's such a pussy. (He also says hi.)

My camp is safe. I'm sure that's what you really want to know. The second you leave the gates it's a whole different ball game. The locals don't want us here. Their bullets tell us so. They think we're the enemy. Which is a joke because we're trying to protect them from people who kill themselves without thinking twice. It's fucking sick, really. We're working on educating the people here (in between doing what we're really here to do.) Maybe it will be safer one day, though I'm not sure if I'll be around to see it.

A night out with the girls sounds like fucking trouble. You should go, though. They aren't all bat-shit crazy...I promise. If you're going out locally, I probably don't have to worry about every swinging dick trying to bring you home. With a group of women that hot most guys just "know" without having to be told. In case they don't, you should tell them your boyfriend packs heat—in the pants and on his hip and that he's killed for smaller indiscretions. If that doesn't scare them off, go get Morganna. Tell me more about these twenty-five blowjobs. Color me intrigued.

I'm sorry you've been sad. That's a fact I could probably go without knowing, but I'm glad you told me all the same if only for the reason that you realize you never loved Nash. That comforts me in a weird, fucked up way that I'm ashamed of. I want all of you, Windsor...now and forever. I can't control your past, but if I could, you would have always been mine to love.

Something you don't know about me: I have an addictive personality—emphasis on addictive. That spans all areas of my life. Some things you could guess, because of how wrapped up I get with the things in life I pursue. But others you won't know unless I tell you. Alcohol. I was the world's most highly functioning alcoholic. You know about my bad past with my parents. Stone finally admitted to telling you about how they don't agree with my life or my choices.

Don't worry, I'm not mad or upset. I'm almost relieved. It makes it easier to admit this now. I drank to remember, Windsor. It was the only way I could remember the days when I had a loving family without tainting the past with their estrangement and the following bitterness. I'm better now—mainly because Stone has kept me this way for five years, but partly because it almost ruined my career—the one thing that's always been steadfast and sure.

You're my new steadfast so I want to be honest with you. Looking for my picturesque past at the

289

bottom of a bottle only worked for so long. I was reckless with my life and the lives of those around me because of a fucking hang up. It even sounds ridiculous as I admit it now. At the time alcohol was the only thing that I felt I could control. I'd get really drunk and still be good at my job. It was like one more challenge I wanted to conquer. Before I knew it, I couldn't work or live or breathe without a drink.

That's when Stone stepped in like a muscular, tatted up, vagina-dicked angel. I love Stone for a million different reasons. He saved me when I couldn't and didn't want to save myself. I'll owe him for the rest of my life. That's what brothers are for though. I'd do the same for him. The person I am today wasn't the person I was five years ago, Windsor. It's been a progressive change leading up to the day I met you. The ascension of Thomas Maverick Hart was complete the night I looked into your blue eyes and you stuttered "no thank you."

Selfishly, I'm asking you to accept this part of me, because it will always be a part of me whether you know it or not, unfortunately. It hurts because I know you deal with a family member with an alcohol problem. It's not fair to you, but in the spirit of honesty—here it is…a snippet from my dark past. This got a little deeper than I intended. I'm better, but I'm not fixed.

My only addiction these days is you. I promise.

I wish it were your hand on my chest,

Maverick

P.S. I'll see your sexy ass tomorrow. What I have
planned for next week is even better than flowers.
Just wait. Oh, and Goose can whine all damn
night if he wants. We won't be sleeping.

Chapter Twenty-Two

Windsor

I never get up this early. Ever. I've showered, put on makeup, and checked my Skype messenger fifty times anticipating Maverick's screen name popping up. We've only spoken a few times on the phone over the course of the month. Mostly e-mails and small messaging chats here and there have comprised our communication.

He confessed some pretty dark things from his past that made me both scared and reassured, honestly. It doesn't bother me that he was...is an alcoholic. Honestly, it explains a lot. The way he was with women before me being one of the things. He seems like a changed man for the most part. I know firsthand how slippery that slope can be.

I'll be there for him though. As long as he needs me, I'll be here. It's also odd because it seems like Maverick is a person who could single-handedly save the world...and he needs saving. That's what scares me. The things-aren't-always-what-they-seem aspect of his confession. I wouldn't have guessed that "something" about him.

My mother turned to the bottle for so long that I never knew anything was wrong with it until I was older. Maybe that's it. It was never hidden. Maverick hid this from me. Did he hide it from everyone? From Stone? Did Stone stop him when he found out, or did he let it go on until it affected others? I won't bring it up, because it doesn't make a difference now. The past is the past. I, of all people, know that.

I haven't seen his face, outside of photos, since the day he left. I push the black lacy lingerie down my thighs and run my fingers through my hair. I'm more nervous than I was the night I lost my virginity in high school. And that guy? He shook my hand to congratulate me on a job well done. So, you understand just how unusual this feeling is to me. I miss Maverick so much. Not just him, but everything about him. The way he looks at me, the way he handles the world around him so effortlessly. I miss the way he knows what I'm thinking even before I know. His lack of presence in my world leaves a gaping hole.

I take two of the throw pillows on my bed and puff them together to make them bigger, and climb onto my bed to continue my wait. I slipped Goose into Gretchen's bed early this morning so I could have some privacy. He shouldn't see what's about to take place. Right?

TMH pops up on my list in a blaze of loud alerts and my stomach flips completely over. He types me a message the second he gets online.

TMH: You're up? Good.

WinnieF: I've been up for a long time. I'm so nervous. Is your Internet connection good enough for a face call?

Please say yes. Please say yes. And if he says no, please don't let me cry.

TMH: We're a go. The door is locked, which means I slid a heavy box in front of it and I kicked everyone off the wifi in our hallway just to make sure the picture would be clear.

More stomach flipping. I smile the hugest smile and no one can even see it.

WinnieF: I miss you. I want to see your face.

Old school ringing blasts through my computer speakers. *Accept* or *Decline* boxes pop up on my screen. Please…as if there were ever a question. *Click.* A medium sized black box pops up in the center of my screen and my pulse skitters like crazy. I narrow my eyes and watch closely for the Nano-second when Maverick's face appears. I realize he might be able to see me first so I make sure to smile. I cross my legs underneath me and take a deep breath. Maverick's hairy face appears and it's fuzzy at first, but grows clearer.

"I see you!" I squeal, clapping my hands together. His huge smile appears a few seconds later because of the delay.

"You are so fucking beautiful, Win. I can't believe we haven't done this yet. I need to see you all the time. Like this." He reaches a hand out, like he's trying to touch me and brings it down again.

I frown. "I can't see your gorgeous dimples under all that hair," I admonish. It looks kind of hot in a way that only a person insanely in love could rationalize. "Will it hurt to kiss you with all of that?" I ask. Maverick laughs, leaning back in his chair. His shirt is off. If I squint I can make out my tattoo on his chest. A part of me is with him there. My heart squeezes a little.

His full lips, because I can still see those, form a line. "What did you think of my last e-mail?" Maverick asks. I know what he wants from me. Assurance. Taking into account the delay, I start speaking before he even finishes his question.

"You couldn't scare me off even if you were a bearded, trained killer...oh, wait." I laugh and then finish, "Maverick, I'm glad you were honest with me, but it doesn't matter what happened in your past. We're moving on to the future. Our future together. Everyone has things in their past they wish they could erase—some more than others. You don't have to worry. Okay?" He shakes his head with a little smile on his face. I continue, "I won't worry either."

"How did I get so lucky?" The screen pixelates for a second, but I see him again a few seconds later.

"I'm asking myself the same question right now, Mr. Shirtless hulking eighth wonder of the world." I bite my lip, only because I know it drives him nuts. It used to be a bad habit to keep from talking back to my mother, now I use it purely for seduction.

"Speaking of shirtless. It's been a long time since I've seen you in that state," Maverick admits. The lip bite had the intended effect. I laugh and point the laptop camera at my very black, very see through, very lacy slip camisole. Maverick whistles, folding his arms behind his head. I aim the screen back at my face.

"I thought you might like it," I say. Maverick's smile fades, though I can barely tell with all the facial hair. "What's the matter?" His hands still perched behind his head, he merely stares at his computer screen.

"I just wish I was there…that's all," he sighs.

Oh, how I wish he were here too. Seeing his face and knowing how far away he is makes me miss him that much more.

"I knew I'd miss you, but your face…right there," he says reaching for the screen. "I didn't think it'd make me so…homesick. For you."

The sadness hangs between us, somewhere in cyberspace, or in the atmosphere both here and in Afghanistan. It's weird. It has a tangible quality to it. I can't touch Maverick, but the sadness is wholly formed and ready to be grasped. I don't want it to seep into this brief time I have with him and ruin it.

"Hey, I'm right here. We can Skype each other as much as your pervy friends let us. Tell them to curb their porn addiction so you can see your girlfriend." I slip the strap of my camisole off one shoulder. His lopsided grin appears a second later.

"I like the sound of that. The girlfriend part. Not the pervy friends part." He leans forward to see me better.

All of a sudden I'm nervous. I've never done anything even remotely this brazen. Well, what I'm *about* to do. Get naked in front of a webcam and do God knows what.

"Have you ever thought about being more than my girlfriend?" he asks seriously.

My eyes bug out of my head and my jaw drops. I wait a few beats, staring at him curiously. I stutter. "I mean…has it been long enough to be appropriate to think about that?" The logical Windsor steps up to the plate. I also added a trick of his: answer a question with a question.

"That's not what I asked. Drop your preconceived notions about everything you've been told about relationships and be truthful. Have you thought about being more than just my girlfriend?" He swallows as his chest heaves. I'd guess his heart is hammering a mile a minute.

I slide my strap back on my shoulder. This conversation took a detour into new, uncharted territory. *The truth, Windsor. Tell him the truth.* I can't say I love you to him, because I'm still sorting out that whole concept in my twisted mind, but have I ever thought about being more than his girlfriend? Yes. I'm female. A flash of a white dress, two point five kids, and a picket fence simmer to the surface whenever a woman dates a man. Even a first date so, watch out, guys. It's an uncontrollable response whether love is involved or not.

"Of course," I exclaim. I make it seem he's crazy for having to ask. Men don't know about the inner-workings of a female brain, though. I can't fault him for that. "Is that the right answer? Have you thought about me being more than your girlfriend?"

"If it's true, it is the right answer. I have. I hate that we're not having this conversation in person. I wasn't joking when I said forever, Win," he replies. My heart thunders and my breathing speeds up, my body responding to words from a man on the other side of the world. It. Is. Ridiculous. Maverick's hazel eyes land on mine. "I'm not good with words," he starts saying, but I cut him off.

"You are excellent with words. The song you wrote me? Perfection, Maverick. I wish I could tell you how I feel about you as easily," I say, looking over to my window to break the cyber eye contact. I hear him clear his throat. He won't push me to say or admit anything no matter how much his curiosity gets the best of him. I face the screen again. "How do you know when you love a person, Mav?" I take a deep breath. He's steered this conversation to this deep, scary place. Why not ask what I really want to know?

"I can't answer that question for everybody. I can answer it for me...about you," he says, pausing. "I knew I was in love with you when I wanted you more than I wanted anything else. I don't need you to live my life. I want you in my life to make it worth living." He clears his throat, nodding. "It started off as a challenge. I won't lie, Win. I wanted you because I couldn't have you. You were like this jagged mountainside that I had to climb to get what I wanted. I never anticipated wanting to open up to you and what that would lead to. The day you trusted me enough to jump out of an airplane, I took a leap too. I decided to go all in. I'm all in, Windsor. There's no going back from this, or pretending I don't want to spend the rest of my life with you. I know I love you because you're good. Your honesty is the most beautiful thing about you. You make me a better person without even trying. It's uncomplicated because it's innate for you. I'm just waiting for you to realize how amazing you really are and leave my sorry, fucked-up ass. I know I love you because of this," he says putting his fisted hand over his heart—over my tattoo. "It would stop beating if you weren't mine. I'm yours, Windsor."

I sniffle. "I told you about my crying problem and you go and do that?" I laugh, but it's broken up by a small sob. Maverick smiles a wistful smile.

"I'm taking your lead in the honesty department," he admits.

I love you, I think. I feel like a liar, not the queen of honesty he portrays me as. I wipe underneath my eyes. "You're not fucked up, by the way. You're sort of magnificent. So is your heart. Our connection is pretty soul shattering, isn't it? I'm yours, babe. I'm all yours," I say.

He chuckles. "So, you're mine? All of you? Every inch?" he asks, wiggling his brows.

"So, now you want to see me naked?" I tease. I'm still trying to control my rapid-fire pulse. I never anticipated making declarations like this at this early freaking hour. I was ready for smut…not love. I'm glad he brought this up. Hearing his confession makes it easier to sort though my own hang-ups over my strong, unexpected feelings for Maverick.

"I always want to see you naked. I just want to make sure we are okay," he says, his voice warbling with the worsening Internet connection. When he says things like this it shocks me. I bet he rarely needs reassurance of anything. Then I remember his past. His family totally abandoned him. Of course he needs to know "we're okay". He's far away with nothing to hold on to except words. Words are just words until they're not.

"We're okay. One hundred percent okay. Take off your pants and show me what you're working with," I command, sliding the camisole off both of my shoulders and down around my hips. His eyes widen when he sees my naked body. I tilt the camera so he has a perfect view of my breasts and the bottom half of my face. I bite my lip.

"How can I refuse you when you ask me like that looking like *that*?"

"See, that's the thing…you can't," I say, shimmying the scrap of lace and throwing it across my bedroom. I catch Maverick trying to touch me through the camera at least twice while I strip. I crawl toward the laptop and watch as he takes off his perfectly hot, baggy camo pants revealing his very large and already hard friend. "I wish it was in my mouth right now," I admit. A vision of *Chat Roulette* pops into my mind at the sight of a dick on webcam. Morganna and I had our share of drunken laugh fests in college with that creepy website. Maverick and his amazing member are anything except creepy. I love the double standard.

He groans. "Not more than I wish it was in your mouth. I guarantee that, baby. Lean back let me see all of you," he orders.

Here goes nothing. I try to remember what it feels like to be naked with Mav in person. How uninhibited he makes me feel. I make sure the screen is at a good angle and crawl to the head of my bed, making sure he sees my ass as I go.

Another loud whistle buzzes through my speakers. "Damn, woman. Damn. Do you work out?" I giggle at his joke.

Sitting, I turn around and face the camera my knees bent up, exposing myself. Maverick shakes his head. I say, "I want you to work out...right now. Let me see your dick." I have to speak louder because I'm further away from the mic and I want him to hear me clearly. I pray Gretchen is still in the REM stage sleep. Shit.

His camera points down to his lap. His huge hand is wrapped around the most ferocious looking hard-on imaginable. I'm immediately wet. The erotic sight does crazy things I wouldn't ever expect. I think it's because it's him.

"You're so hard for me," I purr. "Do you always think about me when you touch yourself?" His hand works faster.

"Always," he grinds out. "Always."

I let my legs fall open as I lean back on all the throw pillows men don't understand. Bet Maverick will now. I close my eyes and pretend it's Maverick's hand as I rub my nipples and slide my hand down in between my legs. "What do you think about exactly?" I ask him, peeking through my lashes.

"Your mouth on me. Your sweet, tight fucking pussy milking my cock." His breathing is labored as he replies and the sound turns me on even more. I move my fingers, finding the perfect rhythm, using my wetness to take it to the next level. "I think about fucking you in my shower, on my bed, in my car…making you scream my name as I fill you with my come."

Circling my fingers a little faster, a small moan escapes.

"Inside. Put them inside," Maverick growls. I do and it feels divine. I watch the computer screen and imagine it's his hot dick sliding into me instead of my own small fingers. "Yes. Like that. Just like that," he groans. He slows down his stroking to match the pace I'm working myself. He is the one screwing me now. It's hot. Everything about this sets me on fire. I feel my cheeks flush and tingles flash everywhere.

I come hard, moaning small pants as I float down from the epic high. I close my eyes to regain my bearings and when I open them, Maverick has his camera pointed back at his face.

"Hey," I breathe. "No fair." I sit up, wrapping my arms around my knees.

"Oh it was perfectly fair. I'm a fucking mess over here. I underestimated your virtual appeal." He points the camera down to his come-covered stomach and quickly back up.

"I like seeing you a mess," I say.

"I like seeing you come," he counters.

"I'm the newest fan of SF. Can we do it again?"

He tilts his head in question, eyes wide. "Right now?"

I laugh. "Not right now but another time?"

"Okay good. I'd love to beat it again while watching you writhe on your bed like the world's hottest porn star, but Stone will be back soon and I'm not sure I can be that quick again. Though, if you asked me, I wouldn't say no," Mav admits, smiling widely.

"I feel bad. I didn't even get to tell you what I think about when I use Bob late at night." I wink.

He presses his lips into a firm line. "Oh, come on, Win. You don't have to breathe a word to have me blowing my fucking load," he says. An uneasiness creeps onto his face. I frown.

"What?" I ask.

He shakes his head and says, "We both know exactly what *I do* want you to tell me."

The words die on my lips. *I love you*, I think once again. I open my mouth to explain or play dumb, I'm not sure which. I'll never know because the screen cuts to black and the Skype call is lost...or disconnected.

Chapter Twenty-Three

Maverick

We have a mission tomorrow night. We spent two months planning it. It's a big one and I'd be stupid if a little nervousness didn't mix with my excitement. It's all I think about. The scenarios flit through my mind like a Power Point slide show.

That's how it's supposed to be. I'm reassured knowing that Windsor won't cloud my brain as we storm a compound vice shack and kill some fucking bad guys, but she's always there in some form or another. She won't admit that she loves me. She tried to explain in an e-mail after the greatest Skype call of all time, but her explanation fell short.

Here's the thing: I know she's in love with me. I recognize it as the same thing I feel. It's in her eyes, in her words, in her heart. It's everywhere, blatantly staring me in the face, taunting me, because she won't say three words. I feel guilty after I get upset. She went through a lot with Nash and I can't get pissed about that. It's that jackass that ruined her to begin with. She's mine to fix.

I thought she'd be past him by now. It will be in the corner of the room for the rest of her life, I realize. It sucks. I know the feeling.

When I do let myself think about Windsor it's all consuming. I pull up the Facebook and Julio Bigcock sends Windsor a quick message explaining that he won't be able to talk or e-mail for a few days. She's always understanding when I can't write her. She's good at this…at deployment. It makes my chest well with pride. I hear stories about girlfriends cheating a week after we take off. This life isn't made for many men. It's made for just as few women, too. I found one.

Steve and Stone are in my room pacing around like a couple of caged panthers ready for their raw meat. I only hear snippets of their conversation because I'm scrolling through Windsor's Facebook page like a superstar stalker. I read what her friends post, I click on photos of people I don't know to try to figure out how she knows them, and then I scan through her newest photos. It's addictive. It's like glimpsing into her life—a life I'm not currently a part of. Sometimes she'll write little updates about missing me or private jokes that only I'll understand. I like that.

What I don't like is the tagged photos of her out at the bar with the "girls" from the night before. Her tight, navy blue dress is too short and she looks too stunning to be out without me. Her brown, wavy hair is loose, falling over her shoulders and down her back. Her blue eyes are a little glassy and she has a different drink in her hand in every picture that's posted. She gets drunker as I continue clicking. The other women are dressed similarly and are all inebriated, but they aren't mine. I don't care who looks at them. That's when I get to the last photo. It's a group shot.

"Fuck!" I roar. It's him...the fucking nightmare that will never leave me alone. John Nash. His arm is draped around Windsor's shoulder like it's always been there, like it belongs there. I see red. No, I see blood red. "Fuck!" I scream again. I breathe in through my nose and out through my mouth. I'm overreacting. I know it, but I can't control my impulses. She doesn't make me crazy; what I *feel* about Windsor makes me fucking crazy.

Through my bloodlust I'm aware Stone is beside me looking at the photo with narrowed eyes. "It's probably not what you think," he explains.

I shake my head. Calming down isn't going to happen right now. I scrutinize the photo further. The arm isn't the biggest thing. Windsor is looking sideways at Nash who is looking directly at the camera—a huge smirk on his asshole wiped face. She's smiling...or laughing? Looking at him. It's a look that is reserved for me...the person she's in love with except, fuck, there she is looking at him like he's God's fucking gift.

Stone bends down to look more closely and says, "I'm sure they are drunker than shit. Look at Morg. Her hair is flat…Windsor probably doesn't even remember taking this picture."

"And that's supposed to make me feel better? What if he took her home? If he fucked her, I'll kill him, Stone. So help me God I will annihilate everything he's ever touched. She's mine now. She's fucking mine," I growl. I know I sound like a raging, possessive asshole, but there is no controlling it now. I look up at Stone. He looks scared as shit as he gazes back at me. I don't see that look on his face very often and when I do, it isn't directed at me.

"Get your head straight, Mavvy. It's a photo. She loves you," he says, trying to bring me back down to Earth. "Send her a message or call her if you're so worried. She'll explain it. That's the thing with Facebook. Shit always looks one way when it's usually the opposite."

He's right. I've been able to gather that much during the brief time I've had an account. I take a deep breath and I pull up my messages after studying the offending picture for a few more beats. I tap out a message asking how her night out was and I let her know I'm thinking about her. And that I *love* her.

I feel better for a moment. Stone puts his hand on my shoulder. "You'll have to deal with the jealousy, man. They're out there in the world and we're here with the pause button jammed down. It's part of it. If you don't have trust, you don't have anything."

I suck in another breath, determined to calm my racing heart. Control. I need to be in control. I have a job to do—a large, very precarious important job to do. Getting insane over Windsor's life isn't a luxury I have. Especially now. Fuck. I'm mad I let a photo affect me.

"I just hate that asshole, Stone. I hate him and what he did to her. It's why she's so scared of me...of her feelings and yet look," I say pointing to the image one more time. "She gives him the time of day. She hangs out with him and he obviously makes her laugh—or happy. It's twisted and I can't tell her that. I let her do what she thinks she needs to do, but that's not healthy is it?" I ask, curiously. "She won't tell me she loves me and she looks at him like that!" I sound like a whiny fucking child. Luckily, Steve took my first outburst as his cue to leave.

"What's not healthy is your fuckin' attachment to this girl, Mav. It's making you act crazy. There is no gray area. Black or white—pick one and live your damn life. Trust her and be with her, or don't and walk away. If her friendship with Nash bothers you so much, break it off. Is it a deal breaker?"

My chest tightens. Nothing is a deal breaker. I'm fucking sick in the head. I'll take Windsor in any form. "No," I say simply.

I click on my messages again and find no new replies. I shut the laptop. "Let's go to the gym," I say. Stone doesn't say anything else about Windsor or my insane outburst. His silence is steadfast and comforting. It says he'll forget this whole thing happened. "I have to work this shit out of my system before tomorrow night."

Grabbing a set of ear buds from his bunk, Stone says, "fuck yeah you do." He follows me out of the shitty ass door.

*****

She deleted the photo. I came back from my workout and the photo was magically missing from her Facebook page. She sent me a reply message and didn't mention anything about Nash joining them.

Now, I'm not a fan of the saying "omission is a form of lying" because I'm a large offender. If you want to know something, ask. If it's something you don't know you should be asking—that's one thing. But Windsor knows I saw the photo. She should explain it. I messaged her back asking if any guys joined them. Her reply? You're my guy. Evasive. Guilty. Something must have happened between her and Nash. It's the only explanation. I've felt sick for the rest of the day, my stomach grumbling with fucking unease.

I remember listening to a teammate whine like a fucking baby because he couldn't trust his girlfriend back at home. He was all over the place that day, like a God damned loose cannon. I couldn't fathom something so stupid fucking up my game that badly. But it did. Now I know why. I can't think straight.

I've never wanted to not think about something more in my life. I'm ready to go earlier than I usually am. All my gear is on and double-checked, my guns are loaded, and

I've gone through my mental checklist three times. It pisses the other guys off when someone gets jocked up early because it makes them feel like they're behind. Everything is a competition in my world—even when it's not. All the guys are outside getting ready. Stone stands beside me, also fully ready to rock with his ear buds in. I hear screaming rock blasting into his ears, drowning out the sound of the 47's blades beating the hot night sky. His head bobs to the beat, his eyes straight ahead—he's in the zone. The sight of him gives me pause. He's ready...I'm not. My brain is somewhere in cyberspace analyzing my girlfriend's body language and cryptic messages.

A slight restlessness is still present when I go over exactly what I'm going to do tonight. I replay the favorable scenario in my head over and over in a methodical practiced manner. We've practiced tonight's mission over and over, every minute detail is fine-tuned, and if something goes wrong? I know exactly how to handle it. It's not a back-up plan; it's just option B, or C—all the way down to Z if need be. It's not about luck, it's about skill, and that I have. I can't listen to music like some of the guys. I need my thoughts clear. That's where I find my zone.

My thoughts clear even further on the short helo ride to the target compound. The adrenaline hits my system when the dust starts swirling at the helo's approach for landing. Our advance is silent by most people's standards, but the bad guys won't be sleeping after we land. They'll know we've fucking arrived. Apache helos swarm the air around us to protect the slower 47 we ride in. The noise is like death for those who know exactly what the sound means. To me? It lulls me—lets me know it's game time. The second the helo touches ground, our boots hit the ground too, breaking into a sprint.

By the time my eight buddies hop out before me, rushing to be the first in line to be the first on target, I'm there, in that perfect place where skill meets Thomas Maverick Hart. Stone is in front of me with his hand pressed by his ear, listening to the radio as we move, fanning the huge fucking compound. When the big, black two-rotor 47 disappears into the air, it leaves us in pitch-black darkness—our favorite way to work. Our specialty.

Silence wraps me as I move swiftly toward my goal. Like always, the bad guys have no idea we're coming until we're on top of them. Combine that with this quiet, dark night and we've got a perfect fucking storm—bad for them, good for us. The compound is exactly as intel said it would be. A large structure with smaller buildings surrounded on all sides by walls. Stone is point man for the smaller building we're headed into. I follow behind, covering him with my rifle up, methodically scanning around nearby and far off in the distance.

The other guys have already broken into groups to clear the buildings they are responsible for. This is the point where repetition kicks in. I've done this before. Maybe even something so similar that my mind goes on autopilot. The heavy nods, my night vision goggles, provide the perfect green view of everything around me. I see a few farm animals through the metal gate we're about to enter, but it's completely unguarded. The bad guys weren't quick enough. I smile. I make quick work of blowing the lock off and with a small clank, Stone and I are in and pounding dirt toward the small building. He stops, pressing himself against the wall when he gets to our point of entry. I join him a second later, our heavy breathing permeating the thick night air. Though we're used to all the gear we carry, it's still fucking heavy as shit.

Stone stoops to check the door and then places the slap charge by the hinges. A few gunshots break out in the distance, and though we ignore it as best we can, I know Stone is thinking the same thing as I am. *Someone's doing work.* Another small grin crosses my face as I scan the area surrounding us.

I don't have to see him; I know he is pausing, waiting for me. Focusing my attention on the door I drop one hand and squeeze the top of the back of Stone's thigh, signaling I'm ready, I'm here, and it's time to kick some fucking ass. We back up a few paces before the charge blasts and black dust blows in all directions. We ignore it completely and enter the building over the debris. It's quiet inside. Too quiet. It means the fuckers are going to hide. Luckily hide and seek is one of our favorite games. There's no question now, even if they were hard sleepers, they know we have arrived.

We enter a small room to the left. Stone slips in as I clear my corners, knowing precisely which areas he's responsible for and which I am. I know the exact speed at which my gun needs to travel, the way my feet need to be placed. A thousand specific details that were a bitch to learn are now coming together to form a perfect, stealthy killer. More than that, a protector for my point man. The room doesn't have very many places for people to hide and we soon discover no one is hiding in this room. *Count to ten, mother fuckers.*

Stone and I make our way upstairs and clear another bedroom without pausing. There's only one more room left. It's at the end of a long corridor. It's still pitch black—no light coming from the door. Creaky floorboards twinge under our heavy weight, but at this point it's no matter. We know the people we've come for are behind the door in front of us. We approach cautiously, ready for the gunfire that will surely blast through the door any second. Keeping to the wall, we stack up a few feet from the door, me behind Stone. I hear his breathing pace pick up as adrenaline spikes. For most people this would be a detriment. We require it. A small flash of light lands on Stone's boots, the light coming from the bottom crack of the door. Just as quickly, it's gone. *Ready or not, here we come.*

The door isn't locked. I squeeze the back of Stone's thigh. He turns his head, which breaks protocol. "Tighten your fuckin' towel, T.H.," he breathes, a goofy smile crossing his face. He calls me T.H. And that's all it takes to trigger it. *Windsor. Windsor. Windsor whispering T.H. into my ear. Kissing Windsor. Windsor and Nash.* Stone opens the door and gunfire litters the air like the Boston Symphony. *Windsor.*

I see Stone in front of me, in slow motion, firing his rifle into the room. I hesitate not even a half second, maybe not even a Nano second. *Windsor.* I pull the trigger and begin firing in succession at the bad guy who has a shitty table on its side as cover. I forget to the clear the corner, my corner. I turn to glance at Stone and I see it written in his tense body language. I fucked up. His eyes grow large, round in surprise. Because I don't fuck up. I don't fuck up because this is the only thing I've ever been good at. Another half second passes.

The bad guy, the one in my corner, shoots and I hear the familiar *tink, tink, tink* of a grenade, but I don't know where it's at because I can't take my eyes off of Stone who is on his knees, clutching his bleeding side with both hands, his face a mask of disbelief. Another second ticks by. Then another. I send a kill shot to the corner and watch the bad guy slump down the wall, staining it as he slides to his final resting place. I stoop next to Stone, my whole body trembling. He looks at me, briefly, and nods. In another slow-mo moment, I watch as Stone throws his arms out and falls forward over the explosive green oval, covering it with his own body.

And the grenade detonates.

You know that feeling I was trying to explain? About how death changes the air. I feel it now. It soaks into my awareness and wraps around me like dark clouds. It's different this time. No elation or adrenaline buzz. And I know this death, the one I sense right now, isn't like the others. I'm the one dying. Or my brother is. Maybe we both are. One fate is more preferable than the others.

I feel nothing. I know nothing. I deny everything. Darkness, the most helpless feeling, takes over. I want to feel Stone—to be close to him. Because I'm scared he's right.

My newest attachment not only made me crazy, she just pulled the fucking pin from thousands of miles away.

Chapter Twenty-four

Maverick
Present Day

I hold the letter in my hands like it's the most fragile thing in the world. I've memorized the size, shape, and weight of the envelope. I promised Morganna we'd open the letter together and it's the least I can do. It was like a never-ending nightmare when I woke up in the hospital.

First, I see Monica's face. And if that wasn't enough to throw me into an absolute fucking fit of rage, they told me Stone died. My brother—the only person who was there for me for as long as I can remember is gone forever. Denial would be the easiest way to cope, but even that doesn't fill the jagged hole in my heart.

Tiny pieces of the mission float back to me as the days pass and I'm finally at the point when anytime I close my eyes, I see my best friend sacrificing himself for me, bits of his body coating me as I lie on a dirty floor wishing I'd made the move first. It would have been easier to wallow in my pretend denial had my *darling* wife been absent.

After I threatened Monica, she left the hospital and promised to finally sign the divorce papers. Morganna gave them to her at least seventeen times in the past five years. It took seeing me shot up, in a hospital bed, looking her in the eye and telling her that I never loved her—that I will never love her, for her to see the light.

Monica never truly wanted me, she wanted my career...my community. I married her at a courthouse when she got pregnant five years ago on a trip back to my hometown with Stone. It was my pathetic attempt to win my family over by doing the right, moral thing. Of course her convenient miscarriage came two weeks after the wedding. She'd manipulated me into giving her exactly what she wanted.

When I found out she lied about being pregnant, I left her. It was also the very last time I did anything because society deemed it "right" or "moral". She's refused to divorce me ever since.

I pay her monthly. Partly to keep her mouth shut, and also because somewhere inside me I'm a good person. I loved the idea of having a baby. I wasn't fond of Monica, but the idea of a baby is one I eventually liked. The day I walked away from Monica, I distanced myself that much further from my parents. To them, my loser status reached new, unfathomable depths. Little did they know...little did they know.

Morganna blasts into my bedroom, wearing huge sunglasses and sweatpants that hang off her body. She's unrecognizable. She hasn't answered a phone call from anyone except the guys or me since *it* happened. I can't even think the words without feeling ill. Morg looking like hell is a reminder I don't want. I pick a spot on the wall and focus on it.

Taking a deep breath I say, "You look like shit. He'd hate it. You know he'd hate it." My voice is hoarse from rarely using it…and because emotion clogs everything.

She kicks off her shoes, pulls the covers back on the other side of my bed, and gets in, sunglasses on.

I roll to my side and truly look at her. "Hey," I say, clearing my voice. I lift her glasses to rest on the top of her head. "You actually have to go in public tomorrow, Morg."

The funeral. I shiver. Her sad eyes, rimmed with permanently wet, black lashes meet mine. What I find there crushes me. Dealing with my grief is one thing—I can internalize it—but Morganna's is quite another. It takes me a full three seconds to swallow.

"I can't do it. I really can't," she sobs. "It's not real, Mav. It's not real. I woke up this morning and I forgot for one tiny second. And then it hit me all at once. I can't breathe. I can't breathe without him…my heart," she whispers bringing both hands up to her chest.

I know exactly what she's feeling. It's a full-blown panic attack; except the misery is so overwhelming that it takes my breath away. I hug her close to my body and listen to her sobs, feeling her cry against my chest. I try to find the spot on the wall again, but I'm not quick enough. A solitary tear slips out and runs down my face.

"Have you talked to her?" she asks, looking up to my face. I shake my head. *Windsor.* The thought of her pains me. The thought of kissing her reminds me of death. Monica told me she was at the hospital. Driving away Windsor by letting her assume I'm married is the only good thing Monica has ever done. Because I don't think I can look at her without facing harsh reality. How much heartache can one person deal with before it drives them mad?

I'll soon find out. Morganna's assistant fields both of our phone calls. I haven't even asked him if Windsor's called or texted. Attachments kill people. I'm living, breathing proof. I may take breaths and my heart may beat, but I'm not alive anymore. The good part of me died in a dusty room far from home.

"He'd want you to," Morg whispers, trying to ply me with my own words. "You can't blame yourself."

A random stranger would be able to recognize the guilt that sits on my shoulders. I shake my head. I would have died for Stone in a heartbeat. He did what I would have if I were thinking clearly. I'm not sure which is worse. The guilt I carry or actually being dead. The latter seems preferable at the moment.

"He'd still be alive if I didn't fall for Windsor. That's a fact. I'm a fuck-up."

"You are not a fuck-up. She loves you, Maverick. You need people who love you around. She deleted the photo because she didn't want you to concern yourself with it. Johnny was trying to talk to her all night. You know what she said when she finally did talk to him?"

I haven't heard this story yet. Honestly, I fucking forgot about it. It's funny how something so insignificant becomes such a powerful catalyst. I nod, urging her to continue, though I've already made up my mind about Windsor.

"She told him she's so in love with you that she can't see straight. And then she thanked him for cheating on her because she'd never have met you otherwise." Morganna lays her head on my chest. I try to swallow, but it gets stuck in my throat. "I broke confidentiality and told her about that bitch, Monica. She was still angry you lied, but I bet you'd have a shot with her. You need her, Mav. Trust me, love like that only comes around once."

I kill her husband and she tries to salvage my relationship. It makes me sick.

I sigh. It's painful, and reminds me that I have to keep breathing. "I'll always love Windsor. She's the only one for me, but I can't be with her. We have each other. We'll get through this, Morg. We'll get through it." *Because I have to be strong for you,* I think. Stone would want that.

Morganna sniffles. "Don't make this more tragic than it has to be." Her wise words rattle around in my mind, but eventually peter out. I refuse to take things I don't deserve. I won't destroy another life. "We do have each other. But don't think I'll sleep with you." She smiles against me. I kiss the top of her head. My heart aches more than I thought possible.

Several silent, morbid seconds pass. We're both thinking of him.

"Come with me tomorrow. I need you," she admits. "No one knows what this feels like except you. You're the only one who understands. I miss him, God. I miss him."

I miss you too, Bro. If there was ever a time I believed in a God or a place after death, it's now. Because someone like Stone doesn't just stop. It's impossible.

"I need you too, Morg. I'll be with you all day tomorrow. I wouldn't be anywhere else," I tell her, hugging her close. Stone's sweatshirt still smells like him. He's here in bed with us. Smiling, I shake my head at the fucked up thought.

"I invited her. She'll be there," Morganna says. I'm still amazed how quickly Phillipe organized the funeral. Morg didn't have any part of it. She couldn't. Phillipe knew without asking exactly what needed to happen. I told Morg she needed to pay him more. She agreed.

I clear my throat. "Everyone will be there," I counter. Avoidance.

She changes the subject. "Read me the letter, Maverick. Read it to me," Morganna whispers.

We've put it off long enough. I know if I hesitate another second, I won't do it. Sliding my fingers under the flap, I open the envelope and pull out the two letters. I glance at Morganna, shake my head sadly, and open the perfect fold. Using more bravery than I've ever possessed, I read.

Morganna, Morg, my fuzzy kitten wrapped in canon ball metal:

Do you remember the time we went to Belgium? We spent a night drinking honey beer and talking to an old guy that kept showing us phone pictures of his half-naked, overweight girlfriend? I spoke French all night and you smoked stogies like a fucking Mafia lord. God, you are so fuckin' hot. What about the time I tried to teach you to surf on a long board? The sight of you riding that huge wave makes me smile. Remember what you did to me on our wedding night? You freak.

The smile you have on your face right now (I know you're smiling after that last question) is the reason I fell in love with you. If you're reading this letter you're gonna have to use that same perfect, fucking smile to trap another badass mofo. I know you will and you need to know that I want you to move on.

Because you saved me, Morg and if you never saved another bad seed it would be worse than my lost life. And because you saved me, I could save Maverick. You know what that means to me.

I want you to understand you are the reason I live and breathe. My world gravitates around you. That hot fucking sun rises and sets because you live on this planet. It's your face I see every time I close my eyes. It's like you're tattooed on the back of my eyelids. (Fuck, why didn't I think of that sooner?) Don't think anything different happened when I closed my eyes for the final time. I saw your face. In fact, when I get to the pearly gates, I expect to see your beautiful head residing on God's body. That's the only sight I want to see for eternity. If I don't get it, I want my fucking money back. I love you, Morganna Sterns. I love every single piece of your perfect body and twisty fuck mind. I love all of you.

Take care of Maverick. Take care of each other. You are the great love of my life. I'm sorry my life took away your love. It was the only thing capable of taking it—that's something, right?

I'm sorry for a lot of things if you're reading this. I'm sorry I didn't give you a rock-n-roll son, or a devious daughter with your beautiful face. I'll never get to see you hold our baby, or listen to you sing sweet lullabies with that hot southern drawl. I'm just sorry I went and got myself killed. I died doing what I love. I can say without a doubt that I *died with pride filling my body. But my heart? That's always only yours. Just yours. Nothing holds me like you do.*

Wear the tight blue dress to the funeral. Don't let them play bad music either. Pour Some Sugar on Me has to be included in the play list. I won't be satisfied unless my mother is mortified. Keep your head up and tits out. Live on, baby. This isn't goodbye— It's see you later.

Forever, crazy, endless love,

Stone

Morganna is crying, somewhere in between happy and completely destroyed. Before I lose my nerve, I unfold the second letter and pull Morganna into the crook of my arm.

Mavvy, Brother, Thomas twin:

We are seven years old standing on the roof of my parent's house. We have my mother's best bath towels wrapped around our fucking necks. Side by side, our arms wrapped around each other's backs. We counted to three and jumped from a second story roof. That should have been the first sign we were fucking crazy. We thought we could fly that day. I broke my right arm and you broke your left arm. We didn't let go of each other even when we hit the damn ground. We never let go. Our parents were so pissed. How many planes have we jumped out of since then (successfully)? At least 500? We never leave each other behind. You're reading this, so I must have left you. It's obviously against my will because I'd never leave you without a fight.

Life is short, man. It's too fucking short. Let go of all the hate. Reach out to your parents. They won't turn you away...I know it. How? I talk to them, bro. They care about you. Give them a chance to know the real you. The man who is strong, wise, and capable of anything he sets his mind to. The man who was my friend before I even knew what a friend was. You are the man who gave my life purpose with one sentence, "Let's be Navy SEALs." Thank you, Mav. Thank you.

Don't turn to the bottle, dude. I know that's exactly what you'll want to do. It may even be the first thing you think about after you finish reading this. I'm not at the bottom of a bottle. You are so much better than that. You never really needed me to keep you in line. You wanted to be in line. Give yourself more credit. And if you can't, I'm gonna sick Morganna on you. (Hear that, Morg?) I guess I can finally admit that I've always been jealous of you. You're a better fucking shot, your vagina dick is tighter, and those fucking dimples? You bitch. It feels so fucking weird saying goodbye to you. It's like saying goodbye to myself.

You're good, Mavvy. You're good. I love you, brother. You're the left to my right. Take care of Morganna. Don't let her swim in the shark tank for too long. And for God's sake— get the fucking girl. Tighten your fuckin' towel, bro.

If you fly, I fly

Stone

Chapter Twenty-Five

Windsor
Present Day

I have had the dream too many times to count. The elaborate church is filled with people all wearing black in some form or another. I'm in the middle of the aisle walking toward the front, kind of like what happens during a wedding. Except it's a black veil that hides my face, and no one turns to look as I pass by the pews. Their eyes remain forward, staring, weeping...trying to come to terms with their grief. I walk the long length alone, my gaze trained on the dark wooden coffin highlighted by a single spotlight. White flowers surround it like they're trying to hide the ugly truth. During the dream my chest hurts and my breathing never comes easy. Though I'm crying, my face is never tearstained. My high heels echo on the hard floor, the only noise other than the wails of anguish that break out every couple seconds.

I never understand the magnitude of my loss until I reach the coffin. I fall to my knees and that's when the tears come, wild and fierce and unstoppable. I lift my face to the ceiling and scream. The pain is unbearable. The loss cuts me inside and outside, and sears every good thing about my being. Resting my hands on the side of the sleek wood, I ask for another chance. I beg for another opportunity to do it all over while simultaneously thanking God for the time I did have. The pain of heartbreak is different when it comes hand-in-hand with death. There isn't an option of *maybe sometime in the future*, and second chances don't exist. This was of course, just a dream.

I sit in the very back choking on the memories of my nightmare as I watch Morganna Sterns, powerhouse, walk to the front of the church, tears streaming down her face so quickly that she wouldn't be able to stop them if she wanted to. They're the uncontrollable kind of tears that have a mind of their own. They won't stop until you're dehydrated or finally pass out from exhaustion. Her flat-soled shoes don't echo and she doesn't bother with a veil. Morganna is fractured, irretrievably broken by Stone's death. Maverick is by her side, holding her up, forcing her forward, toward the coffin. This is their reality. It's also the first time I've seen Maverick since the hospital. My stomach flips, without my permission. It's weird to be in love with someone who almost seems like a stranger.

I haven't spoken to Morganna since she invited me to the funeral. I didn't find out about Stone's death until after I got home from the fateful trip to the hospital to visit Maverick…and his wife. Morganna explained away the marriage easily, almost too easily, and I wondered what she got out of confessing these things. Surely breaking confidentiality isn't something she makes a habit of.

I'm not sure why I haven't called Maverick or why he hasn't called me. It doesn't matter. I know the man I love is gone. Sure, he may be somewhere inside, but his life song is altered indefinitely. People come into your life for different reasons. Some give you something you didn't know you ever needed. Others take things you didn't know you should give. Stone gave Maverick love. What happens to a person when the only person who gives you unending love dies? I don't know specifics. I'm not sure exactly how he died. I know they were together.

An older pair with silver streaked hair stand and hug both Morganna and Maverick. Phillipe leans over and whispers, "Stone's parents."

Maverick's back is to me, a fact I'm thankful for. I'm not sure what seeing his grief will do to me. Distancing myself from him has been hard enough. I'm sure I'll crack any day and forgive him for lying about his wife. Part of me thinks that it won't be enough. That some other unspoken grievance hangs over us. The urge to comfort him is overwhelming. Why doesn't he want me to do that for him? I respect Morganna enough to not hassle her for details. Keeping my distance is the only way I know how to react.

Kathy visited me for a few days after I came home from the hospital. We got along, surprisingly. I think it was because she sympathized with my plight. Or was happy she was right about Maverick. Whatever the reason, she was there for me in a way that still confuses me. Although she did leave after she got a phone call from Bill, number five, because he wanted to come back home. She wanted to be there when he got back from whatever "vacation" he claimed to be on. She didn't listen to me when I told her that's not what love is about. Spouses don't just leave and return whenever they please. She responded by shoving my life's mistakes back into my face. I obviously didn't know what love was either, or I wouldn't have fallen for a married man. My mom has me so delusional that I honestly question whether she's right. A person, who loves you doesn't just stop talking to you during a time of need. If anything they need you more. My mind plays awful tricks on me. I hope Maverick comes around.

I've planned what I want to say to Maverick a million times and changed it a billion more. I remember when my Dad died everyone said the same things to me because there are certain things that must be said. Not because they mean them. It's because it's what they think they're supposed to say. Some higher power dictates that. They hugged me awkwardly, and told me how sorry they were for my loss. I'm not sure if I hated them more or less for their hollow words. I play by the rules, so I had to respect that they were doing what they were supposed to do. Deep down I wanted to scream for everyone to fucking shut up and tell me what was really on their minds. My sensibilities won over today, and I compiled a few generic sentences to say to Maverick if I run into him. I don't want to make him even more upset than he already is. If possible, I want to be a neutral element in his messed up world. The impossibly cruel heartache I have over his whopper of a lie takes a backseat to Stone. Death always has a miserable way of showing you what is really important. I wonder if I promised never to take anything for granted if the grim reaper would be less nasty. Probably not.

I hold Gretchen's hand the entire service. Funny photos of Maverick and Stone flash across a huge screen. They make me happy and undauntedly sad at the same time. From the time they were children right up until the second he took his last breath, it's obvious that Stone loved Maverick like family…like a brother.

I cringe when Maverick walks to stand on the stage, the microphone in front of him like a weapon. He puts his hands on his hips, accentuating his much too small waist. His black uniform would look like sex-in-cotton-polyester-blend on any other occasion. Not right now, though. I cover my mouth as a sob escapes before he even says a word.

"Stone wouldn't want a lot of fanfare. Actually, I know he didn't because he told me so. He did want everyone to know that you shouldn't feel sorry for him, or say his life was cut too short. He lived. Oh, he lived. It may not be a full life compared to the average person, but his life was complete. And Stone was anything but average." Maverick clears his throat and stares straight ahead, his gaze focused on something high above our heads. "He had a life many would kill to have. He loved his job. He loved his wife even more," Maverick says, finally searching the sea of faces to find Morganna. I let my eyes fall to my lap. The sadness in his eyes when he looks at her is palpable. He goes on, "Thomas Sterns was a hero in every sense of the word. His honor and his love for his country is why, in his darkest hour, I am alive today. I could say that it was a debt for his country, or that he died doing something he was trained to do, but that would be a lie."

I watch his neck work, as he swallows. "Thomas…Stone died so that I could live. It sounds so selfish when I say it out loud. Like he chose me over his life. Over his wife…and over his career, but his act of selflessness shouldn't be undermined by my own feelings. He died so his brother could live. Every day I wake up and take a deep breath, it's because he is no longer breathing." Maverick balls a fist and brings it up to cover his mouth, his eyes wilting in the corners as he silently breaks down.

He looks down to the coffin. "You saved me more times than I can count, brother," he whispers, though it still echoes in the church. "I love you, Stone. We all do." He walks off the stage and finds his place next to Morganna. She envelops him in her arms. I'm thankful they have each other.

It's all I can be thankful for.

A memory is resilient enough to destroy the strongest individual. So much so, that nothing is left in its wake. Complete and total annihilation form in remembrance. Kathy's words about remembering ring true, in this specific scenario. I wonder how much longer I can fault her actions. I wonder if I should have ever faulted her. Because when I see what a single memory is capable of all I feel is guilt…and pity.

The lights dim and the spotlight on the casket gleaming with golden trident pins is the solitary focus. All of Stone's teammates banged their tridents into the lid out of respect. Maverick openly weeps, his face covered by both of his hands.

About those memories? Nothing but destruction.

*****

I didn't approach Maverick at the funeral. I hugged Morganna and told her to call me during a lull when Maverick was with the other guys. I'm a coward at best. I snuck out of the church and cried all the way home while Gretchen drove. I haven't cried in public like that for a while. I don't let myself cry for Maverick anymore. At least not in the relationship sense. I used up all the sympathy cards with Nash. No one should have to deal with Windsor's broken heart ever again. So, I don't let anyone know just how much I'm hurting. Today, I let the floodgates open because seeing the type of pain Maverick and Morganna are in is terrible. Mav once told me that funerals are commonplace in his community. He said most of the time he didn't know the person that well, but sometimes he did. He said you try not to be affected by death outwardly, that you deal with it and move on. Because who wants to have a job that has an expiration date? That's scary, and I don't care who you are or how much you bench press. Doom and gloom constantly take a toll on morale.

Goose greets me when I push through the door. I pick up my fuzzy dog and retreat to my room. I glance at the cards on my table. The week after Maverick sent a bunch of flowers, he had cards sent. Each one was valid for a long weekend away with him. I was so excited when I got those cards. Fate had other ideas. Fate is a bitch.

"Call him," Gretchen says from my doorway.

I kick off my shoes, shaking my head. "I don't even know what to say. I'm not sure what we are anymore."

"Even more reason to call him."

I shrug my shoulders. It would be the polite thing to do. Somehow I know he won't answer anyway. I pick up my phone and pull up my speed dial. I hit number one, because I refuse to remove him from that spot, and tap his name. It rings once, and then again.

Phillipe's voice says, "Maverick's phone." I scrunch up my brows and look at the phone. I definitely dialed Maverick and not Morganna.

"Windsor? Hello, Windsor?" Phillipe prompts.

"Yeah, I'm here. Why do you have his phone?" I ask.

"I'm fielding calls for both Mr. Hart and Morganna now. Do you want to leave a message?"

I shake my head. "Yeah, tell him Windsor called and that I want to…," I stutter. "Just tell him Windsor called." I can't force myself to utter the generic condolences. Phillipe voices noise of approval and I imagine him scribbling my name down on his pad of power. "That was so damn weird," I tell Gretchen.

Gretchen sighs. "Go to his house to talk to him in person. He's not giving you much of a choice."

I widen my eyes, already shaking my head no. "No way in hell." Gretchen doesn't say another word. She leaves my room, clicking the door closed.

Feeling sorry for Maverick and myself, I fall asleep crying, Goose licking my face the entire time. I wake several hours later to a pitch black room and my phone buzzing next to me.

Maverick's handsome face is on the screen, signaling his call. I hit the green answer button quickly and pull the phone to my ear. I hear Maverick breathing on the other end and it surprises me. I guess I expected Phillipe to pass along a message.

"Hello," I croak out. Maverick sighs long, and hard. "Are you there?"

"Yeah. I got a message you called today," he slurs. "And I just wanted to call you back to tell you…I got your message."

Maverick is completely shit faced. I've never heard him like this. While it warms me everywhere just hearing his voice, I know he probably won't even remember talking to me or calling me in the morning. "Are you okay, Maverick?" I realize how freaking stupid the question is the second I speak it.

"No," he whispers simply.

"Do you want me to come over? I figured you wanted space...you haven't reached out since...you know," I say. I palm my forehead. I sound like an idiot.

I hear liquid splashing and then he coughs. "I called to tell you not to call anymore."

"Okay. That's counterproductive; you could have just ignored the message, like you've ignored me for the past few weeks. I'm not stupid. I'd understand what that meant. I know you're hurting Maverick. I forgive you for lying about your wife. I wanted you to know that. Morganna explained everything. I forgive you and I miss you," I say, pushing Goose off my face for the thousandth time since I answered the phone. Maverick laughs bitterly. I sit straight up in bed—dread filling my stomach.

"*You* forgive *me?*" he rasps, coughing once again. He is absolutely sloshing drunk. "Well, I don't forgive you."

"What?" I yell. "I know you're drunk, Maverick. I can smell it through the freaking phone. You aren't making any sense." He cuts me off with another laugh.

"You killed him," he says. I hear him take a pull from a bottle. "I don't forgive you, Windsor. Don't leave messages anymore." As he says the last sentence he sounds stone cold sober.

The line goes dead.

I stare at the phone screen for several long seconds before putting it down and pulling Goose into my lap again. I'd like to think he's just drunk and talking crazy, but deep down I truly believe he thinks his accusations are truth. Who am I to tell him he's wrong. I fall asleep for the second time in one day with tears streaming down my face.

It will be the last time I let myself cry over Thomas Maverick Hart. Tomorrow I plan to move on with my life, knowing I made another mistake. This time though? I'll learn from it.

Chapter Twenty-Six

Maverick
Two months later

"Get your fucking ass out of this bed, out of this room, and out of this house. Go to work, Maverick," Morganna screeches. I crack one eye. She's dressed, her blue tooth already installed in one ear. She yanks the blankets down, unwrapping me from my warm cocoon. I stretch my arm to my nightstand to grab the beeping alarm clock. A whiskey bottle and a full glass fall off and spill all over the hardwood.

"Shit," I murmur, slumping over the bed to pick up the bottle. "I'm up. I'm up. What day is it?" I ask, clutching my aching head, but masking it by rubbing my hand through my hair. I put the bottle to my lips and tip it up to drink the remainder.

"It's Saturday. But you need to go in to workout. You are a fucking disgraceful slob. I have four meetings today and I can't babysit you," Morg says, bending over with a towel in her hand to mop up my mess. "I've let you wallow long enough. Stone is rolling in his fucking grave right now." She looks up to the ceiling and crosses her chest.

"You're not Catholic, Morganna," I say.

"I'll turn myself into fucking Ghandi, Buddha, Lord our Savior if it means you'll flip the switch. Don't think I won't! What if you lose your job?" she seethes. I know I only have a certain amount of time before she gets really mad. I thought it would be longer, though. I'm not ready to give up the bottle. It's the only thing that dulls the pain. She snatches the bottle out of my hand and throws it on the ground. It shatters. I'm impressed she has enough strength to break it.

"Nice. That's thick glass," I admit. Her chest is rising and falling like a dragon. She still hurts. She's still broken. She hides it better than I can. I hold my hands up. "I'm sorry. Fine. I'll go in to work," I say. I have zero plans to go in to work. I want to appease Morganna so she'll get off my nuts. I want to drink. I want to drink all fucking day. Until I can't see straight and I'm not sure if I live in reality or a dream.

"Liar," she says. "I know you're lying which is why I told *her* to come over later. Maybe she can talk some sense into you." She can't be serious. She sees the shock written on my face and nods, a calculating smile on her lips.

"Why the fuck would you do that?" I stand up and start pacing. I haven't seen or spoken to Windsor since a hazy, drunken phone conversation the night after Stone's funeral. At least something I did was successful. I pushed her away completely. Not so much as an e-mail in how long has it been? I wrinkle my brow.

Morganna reads my thoughts. "It's been two months you idiot and surprise, surprise—Windsor is dating. She's dating, Maverick. You are going to lose her for good if you don't pull yourself out of this," she waves around the room grimacing.

My stomach sinks. I sit down on a chair, putting my head in my hands. I remember Windsor's small hand brushing the top of this very same chair and my heart starts pounding.

"I thought maybe you'd like to know that. I've tried to tell you a million times that life goes on, Mav. The sun keeps rising and setting no matter how you feel or what's going on inside of your head. You'll never get these two months back. They're gone. I'm a miserable piece of shit without him. I know not to waste my life because of it, though. This is it. This is all you get. She'll be here at four."

My pulse is all over the place and I feel like I'm suffocating. "At four?" I ask, my voice trembling. I can't see Windsor. Better put, I can't let Windsor see me like this. I'm already trying to come up with something to deter her.

Morganna clacks up to me, hands perched on her hips, and says, "Don't mess it up. You wouldn't believe how much convincing I had to do to get her to agree—

everything except my first-born. I did this for you, because if you push her away any longer, you're going to lose her to some fucking accountant with bad hair who gets hives at the mention of skydiving. Is that what you want for her life? You spew all this bullshit about not loving her and not giving a shit about what she does. You've concocted this wild notion that she has something to do with why Stone is gone. It's all in your head. You love her and that's changed you. It changed you for the better, for your information. Take what is yours, you stubborn asshole."

Fuck. She's right. Morganna is right. I know it with every fiber of my being. But I'm not finished punishing myself. I'm not sure I'll ever be.

I try to clean the house a little, but it's useless. Two months of being so drunk I can't remember how to use a dishwasher has taken its toll. Morganna gave up cleaning after a few weeks, telling me that I was depressing her even more than she already was. I thought about asking Tawny to come clean, but didn't because I didn't want to end up with an STD in a drunken stupor. I don't remember my nights. Which is just how I want it.

Steve walks in when I have a broom in my hand cleaning up some mess of unknown origin. "Hey dude, you coming in to work today? Morg said you wanted to work out for a little bit," he says stretching his arms over his head. Everyone pussyfoots around me, like I'm some baby that has to be watched very carefully and their words finely monitored. It drives me crazy.

"She's coming over here this afternoon and I don't know how to stop her," I say. Steve knows who *she* is. Everyone does. He winces a little. He feels sorry for me, obviously. "Don't look at me like that, fucker. She's dating," I admit.

"So what? You don't have to let her in. You don't have to do anything you don't want to do. You don't want her here, right?" Steve asks.

I do and I don't. Actually I don't. Seeing blue eyes will only fuck with my mind.

"Why are you so hung up on a chick? Dude, I've been telling everyone this for years. No one ever wants to listen. You can't trust anything that bleeds for a week and doesn't die. Forget her, man. Go back to your fan club. Those girls won't fuck you over. They'll just fuck you senseless. We miss you on the dark side."

I could do that. Maybe it would make me feel better. I wouldn't be drinking by myself every night and slipping into oblivion.

I smile at Steve. Not because I agree with him. Not fully, anyway, but because he gave me a brilliant idea. "Call as many tens as you can. Maybe get some of the guys over here. We're going to have a fucking party. It starts at three. Make sure everyone is here on time, fucker. You hear me?" I ask. Steve grins, nods, and pulls out his cell phone, dialing numbers like a madman. "A pool party," I add. I need the perfect scene.

I continue cleaning, and drinking straight liquor until I'm making more of a mess than cleaning. As I'm showering, I catch sight of Windsor's pink, empty bottle of shampoo in my shower. I can't throw the fucking thing away. I used it until it was gone. I didn't want to think about her, but smelling her kept me from doing something really stupid. It was a reminder that good does exist in this world, even if I don't deserve it.

Deep down I know she's not the reason Stone is gone. It's just the easiest thing for me to assume when I can't come up with better reasons for his death. The bottle reminds me of the best night of my life. A piece of plastic is the only thing I have left of the woman I love.

I swat it, making it bounce in the wet room. I don't pick it up. I dress in a pair of shorts, not even bothering to put a shirt on. Looking at myself in the mirror is hard. The shell of a person staring back at me is unrecognizable. I'm a good twenty pounds lighter than I was when I saw Windsor last. My face is gaunt and the bags under my eyes are sunken from drunken sleep. It's not real sleep, you know? Passing out doesn't count. The REM state of sleep isn't reached. Fuck. I look horrible.

I rub the tattoo over my chest. I don't regret it. I'm actually proud of it. It proves that there was a time in my life that I wasn't this fucked up. It was a very short-lived period, but it was real. Windsor is real. She just isn't mine anymore. My heart aches. Morganna's words replay in my head. *You're going to lose her forever. She's dating, Maverick.* Although I panic at the thought, honestly I'm fucking relieved she's moving on. I second-guess the "scene" I'm setting up for her to witness. I may not even need to go through the trouble. She could be over our relationship already. I swallow down the emotion. It's too much, too soon.

I walk into the living room and see all of the half-dressed women. Well, if Windsor's not over it, she will be very shortly. Steve made sure of it. Hot women litter my house like they've always been here. A few of them are lounging on my leather couch. I grimace, remembering performing Windsor's song and her sitting in the same spot. It's strange to see all these people in my house. A cute blonde in the corner smiles and wiggles her fingers at me. I smile. I mouth back "hi" and pour myself a glass of whiskey.

Steve walks over. "Morganna is pissed. She found out. Just thought you should know. I tried to keep it from her, but it's like she lives in my fucking head. She told me this was your last chance."

All I need is one more chance. I will blow the remnants of my heart into dust.

"Is she my mother?" I bite out. "I just invited some friends over to party." I take a sip of my strong drink. I think of Stone. How he would always pass me cups of water or diet soda so no one would know I wasn't drinking. I cough. "I just want to get this over with."

"I blamed you. I didn't want her wrath. You understand," Steve explains. I narrow my eyes at him. He backs up a step, holding his hands up.

"Why?" I ask, setting my cup down on the counter. "Why do you care if she descends upon you like a smiting warlord? It shouldn't matter," I accuse. I see the look in his eye. "Unless you want her," I whisper. Steve shakes his head. "Do you want Morganna, Steve?"

"No. Jesus, of course not. I just don't want to be on her bad side. What's your problem, dude," Steve responds.

I'm angry for no good reason now. That's what drinking in the company of people does. I'm a mean drunk. I show no mercy. The bad part is, I'm completely aware it's happening and I can't stop it.

"Good. Don't even think about touching her. I'll kill you," I say. Steve walks away, shaking his head. Like I'm the crazy one? The fucking nerve of some people.

The doorbell rings and I know it can only be one person. Everyone coming to a party just walks in. This isn't someone who's been invited. Not by me, at least. Windsor. My heart leaps up into my fucking throat. I haven't seen her for months—six months? I never saw her at the funeral. Not that I would have acknowledged her anyway.

I look at Steve and he angrily raises his glass in my direction. No fucking help from him.

Swaying on my feet, I walk to the front door and open it just enough to see her without exposing the contents of my house. Windsor and her scared blue eyes focus on my face. She looks so damn beautiful that I catch my breath. My memory of her faded over time, and it didn't serve her right. She is the most gorgeous person I'll ever see. Inside and out. I know it. Which is why I have to let her go.

"Hi," she says, her gaze traveling down my chest and back up to my face. She's seeing the miserable exterior of a deconstructed man. I'm hideous.

I can't bring myself to do it. Not yet. I want to pretend for a second that she's still mine. Before everything in my life was taken away. "Hey," I reply, trying and failing to smile. A tiny half smile lights her face a second before a small bark pierces the air. I look to her car.

"Goose is pretty upset I didn't bring him," she explains, looking over to her car with an adoring face. She loves the dog. I take a deep breath. The life I could have had is right in front of me and I can't take it. "How are you Maverick?" she asks. She knows I'm not good. She's just going through the pleasantries I'd expect from a stranger.

I lie. "I'm doing better. On the road to a full recovery," I say, mispronouncing the last word in a slur. Fuck.

Her pursed lips raise in a fake smile as she nods, eyebrows raised. "Good. I'm so glad. I've been worried about you," she says, her gaze darting behind my head. I close the door a little more, feeling sick about the scene behind me. What was I thinking? I wasn't.

"Morganna said you wanted me to stop by. I'm not sure how much of her pleas is fact or fiction, but I'm here for you in you need a friend, Mav. I know you don't want a relationship with me anymore," she whispers, biting her lip. "Maybe a friendship would work out better? I'd like to try because..." her words trail off.

"Because why?" I ask, my heart hammering like a God damned drum in my ears. She shakes her head. My anger grows. Still, even in proposed friendship she can't speak what's in her heart or her mind. I can't take it anymore. My hand, the one holding the door, shakes. I'm losing control. "Why?" I demand, louder this time.

"Because I freaking love you, Maverick! And I know words are just words, but I'm so sorry about everything and I love you. You don't love me anymore and I understand that, but you have to be in my life. Maybe I can help you...or make you feel better. Be my friend," Windsor says, her face red and bottom lip trembling.

I nod. She did it. She fucking finally did it.

Too little, too late. "Blow me," I say, a sarcastic grin spreading across my face.

Her perfect bottom lip drops in shock. I take in a deep breath. This is it.

"Those were the only three fucking words I wanted to hear from you," I slur, and it's unfortunate because it'd be more poignant if I were sober. "And you say them now? That's shit and you fucking know it. So, you want to make me feel better? Blow me, Windsor Forbes. Get down on your perfect knees and blow me."

Her face crumples. I close my eyes and let my trembling hand open the door so it's wide enough for her to see inside. She brings her delicate hand up to cover her mouth. That's right—*all these women in my house. In my world. You aren't special, Windsor. You were never special.* I stare at her, committing her pain to memory as punishment for all time. I have no doubt this will be the last time I see her. She shakes her head in disbelief as she surveys my living room full of women.

"Christ knows no one else holds a dick sucking candle to you," I say. Her gaze flicks to mine. I see the moment she writes me off forever.

It's odd. I like it. More punishment. Her hand still covering her mouth, a heavy tear drips from one eye. She walks away like it was nothing. Like I'd said "see you later," instead of the horrible things that I actually spoke. She didn't lower her chin or bat an eyelash, but her proud tears fell all the same. Those tears told me she knew this would happen all along. She knew I'd fuck up...that our demise was inevitable. That hurt worse than the quiet indifference spilling down her face. Because it wasn't supposed to end like this—no.

It was never supposed to end.

Chapter Twenty-Seven

Windsor

Two more months later

"He's the cutest dog on the planet. I don't care what anyone else says," I say, pausing as I watch Goose prance around the dog park. "Do you think I should put him in doggy modeling? He's so well behaved he could star in a movie. Like those kids' films full of animals?" I ask Gretchen while nodding at the women currently ogling my dog.

Gretchen sighs, a long and drawn out noise. "Stop transferring and being evasive. You're talking about Goose and his cuteness as avoidance. I mean, I agree, he's cute, but he's late Windsor. Your date is late to your weird ass doggy park date…with your best friend. I don't even understand how this is an actual date. People do this type of thing all the time? So weird," she exclaims, rolling her eyes.

I admit it's weird. I wanted to do things differently this time though. No bar or club trolling. I'm thirty now. My dating life needs refinement. I forced Gretchen to come because she doesn't believe me. I guess it's a hard thing to believe.

I hear him in the distance. "I'm sorry. I'm sorry I'm late! Windsor!"

I smile, narrowing my eyes at Gretchen. Thank God he's finally here. I turn and look at him. His hair flops as he runs, awkwardly. His turquoise polo shirt matches the seersucker stripes in his shorts. He's waving his arms, which seem to be filled with all sorts of stuff, emphatically. I wait but the butterflies don't come. More time. I just need more time.

I push all the hesitant thoughts away. "Told you," I hiss under my breath. I stand and greet him, wrapping my arms around him in a loose hug. He smells like he always does—like *Crew* hair product and Armani cologne. He's used the same products for at least a decade.

His eyes work their way over my body and land on my face. "You look beautiful, Winnie. So sorry I'm late. I wanted to get some…presents," he says. I look at the bags curiously. "For Goose. It's a dog park date. The gifts are for the guest of honor," he explains, flashing his lopsided grin. I nod and grab the bags he holds out for me.

"Goose thanks you, I'm sure," I reply. "Hear that, Gretch? He brought Goose presents." I take a deep breath when I hear her approach.

"Well, what if Goose doesn't want presents, Windsor?" she asks, stopping right next to me. I take another deep breath. I hate that the tension is still so crazy. It's been months of trying to defuse. It's why I want her here. Maybe they'll eventually work out...my past. *Our* past.

"He loves presents," I say through my teeth. "And his manners are far better than yours." I shoot her a pointed look.

After an exaggerated sigh, Gretchen says, "Hi Nash. How have you been?" I tilt my head and smile a fake serene grin.

"I'm great, Gretchen. Sorry I'm late. I didn't want to show up empty handed," Nash explains, raising his eyebrows. "Should we play with the toys now?" He's trying. Good Lord is the man trying. Almost embarrassingly so.

"So much better, Gretchen." I pat her arm and grab Goose. "Look baby, you have new toys and a new collar," I say pulling a bunch of random shit out of the bag. It's obvious Nash does not have a dog. Or a pet of any kind. Gretchen groans, and wanders over to a bench and pulls out her cell, her fingers flying over the keys. I'm keeping her from Benji, but a girl needs her friend every once in a while, too. I get the animosity, as does Nash. He keeps telling me that all he needs is more time—to win over *everybody.*

"There's treats in there too," Nash explains, leaning over to grab the box. His face comes so close to mine that I can feel his breath on my cheek.

Automatically, I pull back, stumbling a little. I may be going out on dates with Nash, but I can't bring myself to be the least bit intimate with him. I can't. You might think giving Nash another chance is the most idiotic decision I could make. I never dreamed I'd be in this situation, but Maverick taught me something. Sometimes second chances, if you work for them, are deserved.

I didn't tell Mav how I felt for him until it was too late. I wasn't granted a boon. Even cheating scum can reform. There is also the fact that this time Nash is…well, Nash is different. He likes that I make him work to earn my time. He's respectful. He's kind. He plays by my rules. He's not the guy he was when I almost married him. The best way to put it is he's grown up. I'm not even sure you can call what I do with Nash dating, really. It's more of a process of gaining my trust back. It's an implied friendship with a torrid past. That's how my therapist explains it. Nash even comes to sessions to help me better understand everything. The key word? Understand.

Distracting myself with healing this relationship is the easiest way to dull my feelings for Maverick. He made it quite clear exactly what I meant to him, but my heart? It's still clueless. My heart also questions me on a daily basis about what the freak I'm doing with John Nash, cheater extraordinaire. Maverick is a risky choice in life, but his volatility was one of reasons I fell in love with him. But I couldn't live with that for the rest of my life comfortably—always wondering if he's going to flip out and kick me to the curb. My gaze slides to Nash. He's throwing a squeaker toy for Goose to chase. He's what I always thought I needed. Safe. Steady. If he can keep his dick in his pants, that is. I have no doubt I'd be watching him chase our toddler around this park right now if he hadn't cheated on me. The thought makes me wince. What's the saying? Six one way, half a dozen another? Pick your poison? At least I'm not completely alone living with a house full of cats. There are worse fates.

Morganna tells me it was the alcohol talking that day, that Maverick's a wreck without me. *He regrets his word choice immeasurably* were her exact words. He hasn't apologized and I don't bring it up to Morg anymore. Her hands are full with life after death and God knows what else. She's kept her breakneck pace as a distraction, I'm sure. The heartache that came with Stone's death won't go away—maybe it never will, because that heartache is the reminder that you loved in the first place. That's one of the few good things I took away from my father's death. The very last thing I want is Morganna worrying about me, or trying to play matchmaker when the dead horse is not coming back to life.

Nash clears his throat. "I was hoping to talk to you alone today," he says while glancing over to Gretchen. "It's been a couple of months and you know that I'm fine with these dates, I love them, but I have to ask—can I make you dinner? Not at my house," he exclaims. He adds the last part because my eyes are the size of planets. "Alone. Just you and me." I stare at him, waiting to feel something...anything that lets me know what I feel for him or what he's asking of me. Maybe an *alone* date will help me figure it out. Or it will be a disaster. Because both of those things are helpful, I smile.

Nodding, I say, "Sure, dinner at my house sounds great, Nash. Like old times." A million dinners followed by romantic nights flit through my mind. It's both comforting and sickening at the same time. *Get over it, Windsor. This is your reality now.* "I'll make dessert. You have to promise not to make Mexican food. That's a deal breaker." I smile. Laughing, he grins wide. Out of habit my gaze lowers to his mouth. No dimples there.

He winks. "Promise. Tonight then?"

"Tonight," I say. I call Gretchen over and tell her of our new *alone* plans. She scoffs, her new Windsor special, and types out another text message. Nash is still smiling like he's the luckiest person in the world. It's a side of John Nash that I'm still getting used to—while still keeping a huge cup of skepticism nearby, of course.

Gretchen's phone rings. She doesn't greet the person on the other end. "Unfortunately, I'm not joking," she says, pursing her lips at me. "Tell me about it. Oh, I know…" Gretch trails off as she turns on her heel to finish her conversation away from prying ears. I lower one brow and smirk at Nash. We walk around the park watching the dogs play like we're the happiest couple in the world. Goose chases his tail and we both laugh out loud.

Now Gretchen is stabbing the air with a finger and stomping her foot like a child. "I wonder who she's talking to," I groan. Shrugging, he wraps his arm around my waist. I don't flinch. He pulls me closer and I lean my head onto his shoulder and put my arm around his back. We continue walking. Our embrace is comforting. It's familiar. It's a place I've found comfort and shelter so many times in my past.

Most importantly, it feels absolutely, positively neutral. And I'm okay with it.

*****

Wearing sweaty running clothing, I point to cabinets that contain things he needs to cook dinner. He watches me move around the kitchen like I'm stripping instead of explaining. If I'm being honest, it creeps me out a little bit, because I know exactly what's going through his mind. I know him. I know that look. That's the thing about dating someone twice. "I'm just going to shower. You know where everything is at now," I say.

Shaking my head, I scoot around him and out of the kitchen as quickly as possible. He laughs at my not-very-covert-maneuver and catches my hand in his.

"Hey. Thank you," he says almost reverently. His tone makes my stomach flip. It's his serious, business voice.

I clear my throat. "For what? You're the one cooking tonight," I reply, jokingly because I'm acutely aware this conversation is about to get serious.

"No." Nash shakes his head. "Thank you for giving me another chance. I don't deserve it...I know I don't. I'm waiting for you to realize what you've done—and run far,

far away." Placing his hands on his hips, he sighs. "I was so stupid, Windsor. I know it's going to take a long time for you to really grasp this, but I will never take you for granted again. If you give me a chance or keep giving me chances, I will spend the rest of my life making up for the foolish asshole I used to be." His eyes close and he hangs is head. His words don't comfort me; they cause me to freaking panic. Every word he uses is every word I dreamed of hearing him say during my darkest most depressing period. Coming out of his mouth right now? They're a jumble of confusion.

Lifting his chin with one finger I say, "I'm not some fragile piece of glass, Nash. I'm not going to lie, I was sad for a long time. I got over it eventually. It wasn't even the...cheating that was the worst part. I was mourning a loss of a life. No one died, but it was just as confusing and difficult to work through. We were supposed to be marrying, building a house, and having babies. Those dreams had to die right alongside our relationship. Because I was wrong about one thing...you. The rest of my life fell into shambles and needed to be put back together." Nash presses his hand to his face. Shaking his head, he exhales, our entire relationship playing out in his mind no doubt.

"You were a freaking foolish asshole. You were selfish, sneaky, manipulative, deceptive, insensitive, caustic, out-of-touch, and lucky for you I've decided those are the type of people who should be given the chance to right their wrongs. Because people like that don't get breaks. People like that rarely make the same mistake twice. People like that appreciate more. They love more. They admit they're wrong, and never take a second for granted. So, you're welcome…for the second chance. I'm not promising you anything, Nash. This," I say motioning between the two of us, "may never be more than friendship. I forgive you, even though I'll never be able to forget what you did. Remembering is powerful. It might not work out because of it, but you're welcome for this." I take both of his hands into mine, my chest light. I finally said all the things he needed to hear and I needed to say.

Nash blinks a few times, looking at me like I'm a stranger. "I can respect that, Winnie. I'm willing to work for it. For us. For however long it takes for you to decide it's right. We aren't the same people anymore. This will be a fresh start. I'm so sorry."

I cut him off with a hug. I don't want to hear him apologize ever again. It just reminds me of his mistake. Nash pulls me against him, hard and squeezes. Burying his nose in my neck he inhales. "I know you're sorry. You can make it up to me by making dinner," I tease. "My stomach is eating my intestines as we speak." I pull away. His eyes focus on my lips and I know he wants to kiss me. I also know he won't. Because this is the new Nash and he really, truly has changed.

"I'm doing a real fine job of convincing you to keep me around. Go shower. I'll cook quickly," he admits, eyes still locked on my mouth. I smile and turn to walk away, feeling his gaze bore into my back.

When I get to my bedroom I close the door and slump down the back of it, heaving a huge, disgusting sigh. The conversation was painful. Fixing things with Nash is supposed to make me feel better. *Why doesn't it?* I wanted him to be the old Nash, that's why. I didn't want to find this reformed person that I wished he were years ago. No, this isn't fair at all because so much has happened in between the scandal and now. Most importantly, I fell in crazy love. I wish I guarded my heart better

I take my time in the shower and take even longer choosing something to wear, my stomach no longer caring about food, my mind a mess of disproportionate madness. After fumbling through my closet and dresser for longer than is polite, I tie on my robe and head for the laundry room for the one chaste, unflattering dress I own.

Nash's iPhone is blaring some sultry song through the speakers in the living room. I smile. He has always had the weirdest taste in music. I'm sure the next song will be just as odd. His singing, which happens to be horrible, breaks out from the confines of the kitchen. "Hey, Pavarotti the hounds of hell can hear you! Keep it down!" I yell down the hallway. Nash pokes his head out and grins when he sees me.

The doorbell chimes.

"It's Gretchen," I yell.

She told me she was going to ring the doorbell so she didn't interrupt our alone time when she got home. She didn't even seem as bitter as usual when she left earlier for a date with Benji—even going so far as telling me to have a good time.

I fluff my fingers in my wet tangled hair. Opening the door I say, "I would have texted if we were doing it on the dining room table, Gre…"

Maverick. He's breathing hard and wearing workout gear. His eyes buzz up and down, taking in my appearance while surveying the room behind me at the same time. His shirt is soaked with sweat and a light dewy sheen glistens on every perfect inch of exposed skin.

"Maverick," I whisper. My heart and stomach do a flip-flop at the exact same time.

Rocking back and forth on his feet he says just as quietly, "Win. I was hoping I could talk to you." His eyes dart down to my thighs.

I tighten my robe in response. What I really want to do is rip it off and attack him. My brain catches up…eventually. "You already said everything that needed saying. Unless there's something you left out before. Maybe you want me to write a manual on how to give you the perfect blowjob? I'm sure your girlfriends would appreciate it. Or, did you need to talk to me about something else?" I ask. Maverick's eyebrows pull in as he shakes his head.

"We need to talk."

"I'm busy right now," I say, looking behind me when the song changes to some 90's power ballad.

"I know," Maverick deadpans.

Nash's soulful, out-of-key voice grows closer until he finally stops beside me, clutching Goose in his arms. I don't even bother looking at Nash. I know what he looks like. Plus, the emotions flitting across Maverick's face are so raw and blatant that I can't look away. It'd be a crime. He obviously had no idea I was hanging out with Nash, tonight or otherwise.

When Maverick's shock abates, his angry hazel eyes meet mine. "Him?" He works to swallow. "Out of all the worthy men in the world, you pick the one who already proved unworthy. Him? Really?" Yeah, that seems to be everyone's logic. I get tunnel vision. All I can see is Maverick. I hold up one finger in the air.

"First off, this is not what it looks like." I gesture to my robe and then to Nash, unsure why I care what the hell he thinks. I do, though. "And secondly, people deserve second chances. That's actually a normal occurrence in the realm of good people. Lastly, when you're ass backwards wrong about so many things, you question your initial choices. That's what I'm doing here. Giving him a second chance and wondering why I made all the stupid ass decisions to begin with."

Maverick nods. It's scary, captivating. "Stupid ass decision?" he asks pointing to his broad chest. Nash walks away and I'm thankful to hear him slam a door somewhere in the condo.

I bite my lip to keep from saying something I'll regret. I choose my words carefully. "You blame me for your best friend's death, Maverick. You just walked away from me…from everything without so much as a backwards glance. Sure, it took me longer to tell you how I felt, but that's because what I felt for you was so much more than love." Maverick takes a few steps away from me.

"Felt?" he rasps.

I ignore his question. "Am I a stupid ass decision, Maverick? Stone would still be here right now if you didn't make that choice. Right? Or is Monica the only stupid ass decision you made?" He shuts his eyes. Guilt rears up. I shouldn't bring Stone into this. Pain is etched into his every feature. I take a step toward him, but he throws out his hand. "I'm sorry. I shouldn't have said that," I whisper.

"Don't come any closer, Windsor. Are you with him?" His whole face wilts as he asks. "She said you were dating. Morganna told me you were dating. She didn't tell me it was that asshole."

"If you're asking if I'm with him like you're with all of your hotel bags, then no. Not this go round, at least. Why does it matter? You got what you wanted from me. I was wrong about you just like I was wrong about Nash. You aren't a one woman man now, just like Nash wasn't back then."

Maverick smiles meanly. "For someone who is wrong so frequently that's a huge leap to make. But hey, you're probably right about him." He pulls his knee up to his chest to stretch it out and then the other. "He may be magically cured, but since the day I met you I've been a one woman man."

It can't be true. I saw the women with my own eyes. He has no reason to lie. Grabbing the back collar of his shirt he pulls the sticky material up and over his head. My traitorous eyes immediately seek out my tattoo. He notices. Dimples pop, my pulse skitters.

He shrugs and says, "Good luck with him, Windsor." Maverick disappears down the hallway at a jog, while I'm left catching my breath. I want to cry and laugh and have sex at the same time. Neutral Windsor, meet positively charged, insanely in love Windsor. The latter also communicates with stupid Windsor frequently.

I close the front door and go find Nash.

Chapter Twenty-Eight

Maverick

John Fucking Nash. I pour four fingers of whiskey and slam it down. Nashhole gets her. I don't know why I'm so surprised. I throw the glass into a wall and watch it shatter. I take the whole bottle and go outside. I need to breathe. I haven't had a drink in weeks. I was trying to get sober for work and for Morganna. If I don't have one, or a whole bottle right now, I'll do something really stupid. I want to kill him. For taking what I couldn't. For taking what is irrevocably mine. Windsor can pretend all she wants. I saw her eyes when she looked at me.

I knew walking away from her would be hard. Keeping her away is proving more challenging than I planned. I know what the asshole is capable of and she deserves so much more than that. I swallow down more alcohol and savor the burn as it eases down my throat. *I don't deserve her either.* Maybe I can deserve her. I can clean up my act and turn this shit train around. For her, maybe I can.

I amble down my long driveway to my automatic gate and punch in the code to open it, and walk out into the main road. The security lights flick on and my yard shines like it's fucking day light. It's a façade—the perfect house and cars, and then me with my almighty career. None of it means anything. I'm a fucking puppet controlled by addiction and guilt. The road tonight is deserted, not a car in sight. Taking another huge sip from the bottle, I sit down in the middle of the fucking road.

"What the fuck now?" I scream to the damn stars. The whiskey warms my stomach and the familiar drunk sensations start coursing through my numbing body. It's the feeling I'm after. It erases. "What the hell do I do now, Stone?" I whisper. I speak to everything and nothing at the same time.

Leaning back, I let gravity pull me down until I'm lying, shirtless, on the cold rough pavement. One hand on the bottle, I shut my eyes praying for a huge, heavy truck to come barreling down the road. I'm so sick of the pain. I'm sick of forgetting he's gone. I'm sick of reliving his death over and over like fucking *Groundhog Day.* Tonight I add I'm sick of seeing Windsor from afar, but mostly I'm sick of everyone saying how lucky I am.

I tip the bottle to my lips without spilling a drop. "When does my fucking luck get to run out?" I shut my eyes when a pair of headlights register and tighten my hold on the bottle. It'll break it any second...the whiskey bottle...and me.

A car door slams. Someone approaches. "Get out of the freaking street right now!" Windsor yells. I've never heard her so angry, lethal. I open my eyes. She's standing over me, eyes wide like some sort of rabid angel.

With the headlights beaming I can't see the blue of her eyes and I wish I could. It's the only thing that chases away the bad. She came after me. Windsor is here. I'm not looking at her from afar, or spying on her when she has no fucking clue I'm around. She's here.

"I said get out of the fucking street, Maverick!" She's also furious.

With great fucking effort I sit up. The alcohol owns the gravity. It wants me down. Windsor reaches down and helps me to stand and hobble over to her car, and then into the passenger seat. I lean against the leather seat and close my eyes.

"How is it possible you got that drunk since you left my condo? What the fuck is wrong with you? I came straight here. Did you drink a few bottles on your jog home? Jesus, Maverick. Seriously, what's wrong with you?" I hear her tears coming. I'm scaring her.

I let my head roll to face her and open my eyes. "You," I say.

She slams the brake pedal and I jerk forward, slamming my face on her dash. Bitch move. "Bullshit," she whispers, a smile gently playing on her lips. "You do this to yourself. I'm sick of you blaming everyone else for it." She pulls into my driveway and stops in the parking spot she always used to park in. I don't even try to get out. She opens my door a few seconds later. "Your face is bleeding. Fabulous."

I ignore the blood—I can't feel it. "I can't believe you're with him," I say, because it's the only lucid thought I have. Thankfully I can see her blue eyes now. A little of the pain in my chest diminishes. *She's not yours.* I take a deep breath to calm my nerves and my stomach.

"I'm not with him," she replies, pulling me out of her car and helping me into the house. Her hands are all over me so I take my time, relishing in being this close to her. It surely won't last long. "I told you I forgave him and I'm merely giving him a second chance for a friendship…or possibly more, depending," Windsor stutters, pushing me down into a leather chair.

I catch onto her hesitance immediately. Even drunk Maverick wants her confessions. It's uncanny how quickly I can sober up enough to hear what she has to say. I can't believe this is how it's going down. I finally get her back in my fucking house and it's nothing I consider *ideal.* I never pictured this scenario. Her coming to me. I wrote it off because I thought she wrote me off. I should have known better. She's too good.

"Depending on what?" I slur.

Her gaze slides all over my body. Her pupils dilate as she forces her lips into a firm line. I throw my arms out to the side, propping them on the arms of chair. May as well give her the view she wants. I smile the big fucking smile.

She pulls off my sweaty running shoes and tosses them across the room. She says, "I'm offering you friendship—if you want it."

"Depending on what?" I ask again. She rolls her eyes. It's infuriating because I see how much she's hiding even in my piss drunk state. "This again? I thought you got over this. If you want it, say you want it. You know what? Just fucking take it, Windsor. Take it. Take it all," I hiss. Windsor shakes her head, still not speaking. "You want my body? My mouth? Just fucking take them, will you? You already have the one thing that I give a shit about." I thump my fist on my chest, right on my tattoo. "But you're too damn naïve to see that. Aren't you? God forbid you see anything other than what you want to see."

She looks unaffected by my words. I'm not sure whether that's good or bad. She leaves for the kitchen and comes back holding a glass of water and a damp cloth.

She presses the cloth against my bleeding forehead. "Actually I see perfectly clear. Any ounce of naïveté I had fled the second you left me. It's friendship or nothing. It doesn't matter what I want or what you're trying to offer. That's it," she exclaims. "Take it or leave it?" She shoves the glass into my hand. I drain it quickly.

Why did I drink? Why can't I be completely sober right now? I'm a fuck-up. I swallow down the bitterness and narrow my eyes at her.

"I can't be your friend, Windsor. I'm supposed to watch you date…fall in love? Then what? Get married? I can be your best man? It's not in my nature to stand by and watch other people take what's mine. I look at you and I want you. I wake up and I want you. I breathe and I want you. How do you suppose I go about being friends with the only person I've ever wanted?"

Windsor's eyes widen and her pink bottom lip drops down. "You said you...were done. That you didn't feel that way about me anymore."

I shake my head. "No I said blow me. You never asked if I still loved you. I never stopped. You're giving him another chance. Give me one, too."

She springs at me, finger pressed into my chest, face so close to mine I can smell her hair. "No. You don't get to say stuff like that anymore. I know you've been through hell, but you get to make the decisions in your life. You're making bad ones." Windsor breaks her gaze and looks to the glass spread on the floor from my earlier outburst. Shaking her head, she whispers, "I can't watch you destroy yourself. It's not fair to ask me to," she says, voice breaking the second her anger dissipates.

She's breaking down. Her mother. She watches her mother do this same thing to herself, and I'm the asshole serving her second helpings. I stand up, pulling every ounce of sober Maverick from his hiding place. Her breathing speeds up.

"Do you still love me?" I'll change. I'll pull it together if she picks me. If she says yes, I'll do anything.

"If I say yes, will you let me go?"

Anything except that. Her eyes are sad. I cup her face in my hand. It's so soft compared to the hardness in her eyes. She's asking me to let her go. Like I haven't been trying for four entire months.

I lean down, buzzing my lips around her ear, and I whisper, "If that's what you want. Is that what you want?" I meet her gaze. She swallows. The air changes and I know she's about to say something that will rock me to my core or bring me to my fucking knees.

Her lips brush mine when she whispers, "Love doesn't die, Maverick. I love you." She shakes her head. "But I can't be with you. We're too different. You're toxic." My heart thumps unevenly and my stomach tightens. We may be toxic for each other, but I'm lethal without her. Windsor leans away.

"We'll be friends who are in love with each other, then. Brilliant." I sneer. One way or another, I will get her back. Right now I have absolutely no idea how that is even possible. Love isn't enough. She looks unimpressed with my solution. With a hard shove, she pushes me back into the plush leather chair. I won't be able to get up again.

Spreading a blanket over me, she shakes her head. "I'm not going to leave you by yourself."

I watch her move around my living room scouting pillows and blankets for the couch. My eyes get heavy, but I keep them open because I know when they open again it will be morning and she'll be gone. Her hair fans over the pillow when she turns to look at me from her bed on the large sofa. It looks like it's swallowing her.

"It didn't have to be like this," she says.

Instead of responding I close my eyes to black. I want to fall asleep with her face in my mind. That way I can dream about the way her lips brushed mine when she told me she loved me. And also so I can spin a fictional tale for my subconscious about how different my relationship with Windsor would be if Stone didn't die.

*****

The vomit rises from my stomach through my chest and finally out onto the floor, mingling with shards of glass from the night before. "Fuck," I whisper. I never vomit after drinking. My stomach is like a steel trap. I can't even force myself to puke. My mouth tastes like bitter beer and stomach acid. I wince.

A towel hits me in the face. Morganna and Windsor stand over me.

Morganna sneers. "Clean that shit up. God, you are despicable."

Windsor turns away. I'm so fucking embarrassed.

"You were doing good, too. Which is the only reason I sent him over last night, Win. You have to know I didn't think this is what he'd do. When I spoke with Gretchen earlier yesterday, she told me things were progressing…in your relationship and I needed to intervene."

Great. "Jesus Morganna is nothing sacred? My head is pounding. Can I just talk to Windsor…alone?" She didn't leave. She's still here. That has to be a good sign.

"You should probably brush your teeth first. I'm going to work in the office," Morg responds before answering her shrill blue tooth, walking away to one of my back rooms she's set up as a small office. Windsor crosses her arms over her chest, averting her gaze completely.

"I'm sorry for last night. Fuck, you know…I'm just sorry in general," I say.

She clears her throat. "I'm so sick of hearing apologies. I wish the people in my life would just stop fucking up." She glances at me, but then quickly away.

I start cleaning up my disgusting mess. Windsor holds out a bottle of cleaner and sits on the coffee table while I work. My head feels like it's going to explode.

"That said, of course I forgive you. I forgive everybody. Maybe that's my problem. I told you not to lie to me…remember what happened? I ended up verbally accosted by your wife, Mav. You were…are married. I've tried to concoct a lie worse than that—I can't."

I freeze. "Never say that. The fact that you're so forgiving is what makes you different, Win. It's you. It's one of the reasons why I lo—" I look at her.

Her sad forlorn face is broken. I'm not even sure what else to say. I can't finish what I was going to say. She smiles. It's a weak attempt at *I'm okay.* I see through it because her eyes say *I'm broken.*

"Monica was never my wife in the true sense of the word. She was my last ditch effort to do the right thing by my family." I tell her everything. Sitting on the floor, next to my mess I let the horrible story pour from my mouth in its entirety. I tell her things I've never told anyone else because she deserves the full truth. I admit the only reason I kept it from her was because I was scared to lose her. She points out I did that all on my own without Monica's help and that I made a promise not to lie. "I omitted a half truth. That's all it was. I'm sorry for that. I am. I can't imagine what you faced in the hospital with her. She's always been a little…catty."

"Thank you for explaining. Consider yourself absolved of all wrongdoing when it comes to her. It's already in the past. I'm sorry, too. You know? I can't take back the things I never said," she continues, but her eyes are focused on the floor. I nod even though she can't see me. It's all I can do. I don't trust my words. "I have to get going. I have plans today. Goose is probably wondering where I'm at, too. I didn't want you to wake up alone."

She has plans…plans that probably include John Nash. I'm still wrapping my mind around the fact that she's giving him another chance. She wouldn't be Windsor if she didn't though. That's the catch twenty-two with someone like her.

"We should have plans. What about our plans?" I ask, desperate. I need her. She has to see how much I need her. I've never truly needed anyone the way I need her in my life right now. In this moment, as she looks at me with a face full of remorse and eyes full of love, I know she will be the person to bring me back to life. "He has plans with you today so give me plans tomorrow. I want tomorrow."

I'm sharing her. That's what this fucked up situation has deteriorated to and I have no one to blame but myself.

She shakes her head. "I had years to get over my failed relationship with Nash, Mav. That's why it's easy to begin a friendship with him. With you...I'm still raw and confused. I need some time to figure out how to be your friend. I'm here for you. If you truly need me, then call. I'll see you later, okay? I have to go talk to Morganna." She looks down at me, still on the floor cleaning my mess. "Stay sober, Maverick. And don't do it for anyone except yourself," she demands. Windsor looks like she wants to say something else, but she doesn't. Disappearing into the same room as Morganna, she closes the door behind her, leaving me alone with a disaster.

After I finish cleaning and shove leftovers down my protesting throat, I shower and get ready, actually giving a shit about my appearance for the first time in months. When I exit my bedroom to head out to the garage, I hear hushed whispers coming from the office down the hall. Then a small, very recognizable sob—Windsor's crying. A few seconds later Windsor runs from the room. She heads to the front door barely looking at me as she rushes away, some sort of paper in her hand. The horrified look on her face freezes me to my spot. "What's the matter Windsor?"

She shakes her head, wipes her eyes, and runs out of my front door. A guilty looking Morganna appears a few seconds later. "She just needs a push in the right direction," she admits, swallowing hard. She's said something. She's done something.

"What did you tell her? Why is she so upset?"

Morganna fidgets, pushing her black dress down as Steve barrels in the front door.

"Whoa, angry bitch alert. Windsor almost ran me over on her way out. What the fuck did you do now, Mav?" Steve asks, eyes darting directly to Morganna when he realizes I'm not alone in the room. He smiles.

Windsor wasn't angry. That's the thing with Steve. If a girl isn't horny or telling him "yes, do me", she's angry. He needs some lessons. That shit isn't my job.

"I don't know," I rasp, glaring fucking daggers at Morganna. But she's not looking at me. She's looking at Steve through narrowed eyes and scrunched brows. Like she's trying to see something else...or someone else. It makes the hairs on the back of my neck stand up.

She looks directly at me and murmurs, "You'll thank me later." To Steve she says, "Hey, what are you up to?" Raising her eyebrows she waits for a response.

Steve replies, "Making my daily rounds at the psych ward, you know?" He warily glances at me. I force a smile to my face and slowly nod. One friend has handed guard duty over to the other. This is my sick new norm. I don't want it anymore. I want to be alone.

"You guys should go grab something to eat. I know Morg is hungry and I have some stuff to get done," I say.

Steve throws his hands out in an offer. Morganna shrugs and says, "Maverick doesn't have any food in his house and I am starving. I want to go to Captains." It was entirely too easy. For a second I wonder if that was their plan all along.

They leave without another word. Cold prickles my skin and I swear to God that *he's* in the room right now. Telling the whole world to move the fuck on already.

So I do. I make a plan to move on with my life and get my fucking girl back because Stone, with his obscene wisdom, once told me something. He said sometimes you have to make snap decisions and do things that seem irrational to make sense of the bigger picture. You have to trust your instincts and just go with it. That something or someone else is out there swaying in the atmosphere, looking out for you. It made perfect sense when it came to work, but not life decisions. I thought it was bullshit. But there is no going back on the plan I just decided upon. Like everything in my life, it's all or nothing. Unlike most decisions I make, I have no fucking clue how it will end.

The only thing I know for certain is that I've never been surer about anything in my entire life.

Chapter Twenty-Nine

Windsor

It's been a week since Morganna gave me the wrinkled envelope containing something that is supposed to *change my mind about Maverick*. It's sealed and she's told me she didn't open it. I haven't opened it. I leave it inside my desk drawer at work because I don't trust myself with it at home. I don't want a piece of paper to sway my mind.

Maverick and I have been texting back and forth during the days, and he seems better. Morganna said he's better, too. That he had a coming to God moment where he realized how much he was throwing away. He's eating, going into work, and functioning on a level consistent with that of the old Maverick.

I told him I wanted some space to sort through my feelings. If I'm going to keep him at arm's length, I need to figure out how to put a damper on my freaking libido and my heart. I feel guilty even admitting this to myself, but it's unfair to Nash. This time is supposed to be his to prove himself. To have my ex-boyfriend meddling at every turn is just wrong. See how twisted that sounds? If Nash wasn't in the picture I think I'd still be hesitant to jump feet first back in with Maverick. I feel like a skittish cat…in heat. I miss him.

Hannah's voice blares through the speakers. "Your mom is on line three!" The jarring buzz scares the crap out of me.

"Thank you," I say, pressing the intercom button down.

I pull up my e-mail to make sure I haven't neglected to e-mail her back or something. I'm not sure why else she would call me at work. Our relationship is shaky at best, and I haven't even told her about Maverick. It's a conversation more complicated than I'm willing to have right now. I hit the red blinking button and tap on my blue tooth headset.

"Hey, Mom. What's going on? Is everything okay?" I get it all out of the way in one swoop.

"I'm fine, honey. I have some company over and we're just sitting down to tea. Funny thing, you're the person we've been talking about."

"Jesus, Mom. Don't gossip about me with your cranky friends. Isn't five back? Don't you have husband-pleasing duties to perform? I'm at work," I whisper shout. I'm pleasantly surprised she sounds sober and she's drinking tea instead of vodka. Who knows, maybe she has vodka in her tea. Isn't that a thing? Maybe I should ask Maverick.

"Well this guest only has wonderful things to say about you. He came all this way to apologize to me for putting my daughter through a rough time. How gentlemanly is that? He also scared the living shit out of Bill. I doubt he'll leave again in the foreseeable future. Isn't that nice, Windsor?"

The room seems to be spinning as I process her words. I lay a hand on my head and take a deep breath. "I'm not sure what you mean, Mom. Should I be happy Mr. Apologizing-scary-gentleman scared the shit out of your husband?" I hear muffled, supremely male giggling—if that's even possible.

"Windsor," he says my name. Or makes love to it. I'm embarrassed he spoke it like that in front of my mother. That's a feat in itself. It's merely a name—*my* name dripping from *his* lips.

I sigh, trying to collect my thoughts. Why the hell is he at my mother's house. How am I supposed to react to this? "What are you doing there, Maverick?"

"Well I think your mother explained it quite nicely. I have amends to make…with many people. You are the first one of course. Think of it like my six step program if you'd like," he explains. I hear him ask my mom for more tea and another photo album.

"Do not look at the ones from middle school. I swear I will rain dark, acid blood down on you right now if you so much as peek at those horrible albums," I threaten. "And isn't it twelve steps?" He laughs and continues a dual conversation with Kathy and me at the same time. They banter back and forth about me, and my trials and tribulations when I was an unruly teen.

"She just finished telling me the story about the Pimp and Ho party you attended in tenth grade, complete with a detailed description of your prostitute costume. I have to say, I never thought you'd dip that dark. I want to see that," Maverick whispers and I know for certain my mother didn't hear that comment. He pauses a few beats and then says, "I'm sorry again, Windsor. This is the beginning of my restitution trail."

Although I'm still baffled that he's sitting in my mother's kitchen, gleaning more knowledge about me than any one person should have, my heart flutters. With Maverick it always does, even when it isn't supposed to. Because that's what love is. Your heart beats along frantically and compassionately for that individual, even when the same person rips it out of your chest. Funny how my fluttering heart reminds me why I need to keep my distance.

"What exactly are you doing?" I ask quietly.

He breathes out a long sigh. "I'm proving to you that some things don't have to make sense. They're just right. You think we're wrong for each other, but we're not. I can't lie to myself anymore and you shouldn't either. And I also need you to realize you don't want to be my *friend*."

"I do want to be your friend," I reply. *I also want to jump your bones and make sweet blissful love to you at the same time.* So much for not falling feet first into the Maverick pool.

"And that's what I need to fix. Wait until you see what I have up my sleeve. I'm going to be the man that deserves you. Deserves more than friendship with you. I fucked up, Win. I'm sorry I wasted so much time. I'm going to make up for it now. I have to go. Kathy and I are going to play Bunco with her friends. Oh, and Windsor?" I'm afraid to respond. What else can he one-eighty me with?

"Yes?" I hold my breath. Silence.

"I think you look sweet with braces and glasses."

"Ugh."

"You have to be in the same room to rain dark, acid blood on me. You headed this way? I miss you." He laughs. I lean my forehead down on my desk.

I groan. "Bye Maverick. Look out for Carla. She'll rob you blind." Well, she won't rob Maverick blind, not in one day at least.

"I'll see you soon." He clicks off the line. I'm left sitting at my desk with a gaping hole of guilt. I have to be up front with Nash as soon as possible, before whatever crazy thing Maverick does next affects all of us—like a big, happy dysfunctional family. The confusing thing is right next to that guilt is a huge well of sheer happiness. He's making an effort. More importantly, he's pulled himself out of the swirling grief hole. I'll do whatever it takes to facilitate his healing process because I know how important lifelines are. The thing about lifelines though, is if you jumble them up enough, they fail.

I sort files into perfect stacks in order of importance on my desk and fill out online forms, stamping my electronic signature like a notary on speed. I distract myself with work while I gain the courage I need to dial up Nash.

When we first started dating back in my early twenties he would always tell me how fun and adventurous I was. We fell into a routine very quickly and I know the exact moment our relationship took a nosedive, and not just because I know when he started cheating on me. It's because I remember when I, myself started feeling bored. I sat on the couch in my frumpy pajamas wondering if it was too early to go to bed on a Saturday night. Nash went out that night without me. And I didn't care.

The irony about the situation now is that I'm acutely aware of how much my leaping-no-holds-barred relationship with Maverick changed me...and that's what's drawn Nash to me again. Who should I give the credit to? Maverick for changing me? Or Nash for pointing out my flaws to begin with?

My plant, which never stood a chance in fiery hell, is wilting in the corner. I look at the brown leaves morosely and decide it's time to throw it away. With that depressing thought, I finally dial his number.

When he answers in that chipper, businesslike tone, I falter. "Hey Nash, it's me."

"Hey, Winnie. What's up?" I hear him winking at me. It's all in his tone.

I decide honesty is the best policy. "I can only be your friend. I think even from the beginning I knew I wouldn't be able to be with you again. Or at least, how we were together before. And it's not because I think you haven't changed, because you have and that's sort of it…because if you were the person you are now back then—well then everything would be rosy and we'd be married right now. We're not though. I said I would try, I said I would be open to the possibility of more, but I can't lead you on anymore. We've both changed. Even as right it feels to be with you and as comfortable as it would be, I don't want that anymore, Nash. I never did, really. Sometimes shit things happen for a reason and they don't make sense until later," I ramble. Maverick said almost the same thing to me.

Nash's end of the phone is dead silent except for his steady, even breaths. "It's him. Isn't it?"

"He is the sole reason you're attracted to me again, Nash. Someone else instilled that indescribable quality that draws you to me. Isn't that the least bit disturbing or disheartening? I'm not even sure I can be with him either. Or if he even truly wants to be with me. I have no idea, but I'm telling you what I do know. You're a good guy now, Nash…but," I trail, choking on the generic words I can't force myself to say.

He finishes, "But I'm not the one for you. It's okay to be honest. I half expected this sooner. At least you don't hate me anymore. I can sleep at night knowing I tried to get you back. And if you do end up with a guy, it should be the one who broke my nose as punishment for wronging you. I'm here for you if you need someone, Win. Always," Nash promises. I don't doubt him for a second. I still wince.

I sigh. "We've repaired us enough to be friends? Like real ones that call each other when they have mom problems or tax questions?" I joke. But deep down I'm serious. Repairing this kink in my life means a lot to me. For it all to be for naught would be horrible.

He chuckles. I picture his smile in my mind. It's sweet. It gives me a straight-up platonic vibe. "Of course. Though I'm sure Kathy will be upset she doesn't get to plan another wedding," he says, teasing me right back. My mom loves him. But, I'd fathom a guess her current Bunco partner is feeling the love, too.

"Planning gives her hives anyways. Thanks for being understanding."

"It pains me to say this, but thank him for me."

I blanch. "Thank him for what?"

"For bringing out the best in you. In record time, no less. I guess I never could quite do it." His voice cracks. Instead of saying anything else, he hangs up. If he'd asked I would have told him I couldn't be with him, because I never loved him. Not the way I was supposed to. He didn't love me either. Our relationship died when it was supposed to. It went down in a flaming rush of gory destruction, because something else was coming together. Good things fall apart so better things can come together. And you know what? Even if I'm never with Maverick again, he's changed me. I didn't even drag my feet or submit kicking and screaming. It just happened. I think that's the best kind of change there is.

*****

He just asked me for your clothing sizes and what time Gretchen gets off work, Morganna's text message reads. I roll my eyes and look to the sky. A few seconds pass.

Ping. Another text from her. *I told him.*

Of course she told him. Maverick only talks to me about our friendship. He talks to my friends about everything else. I haven't told him about my decision to sever the pseudo relationship with Nash, but something leads me to believe he probably knows. He knows everything. I haven't Googled, but I think it's a SEAL thing.

I send Morg a message. *If you're just going to tell me everything anyway, just tell him to ask me.*

You unappreciative stodge. Be that way. Stay in the dark. Did you open it yet?

I giggle. I wonder if she has Phillipe texting for her as per usual. He's rolling his eyes at word choice. *No I didn't open the envelope. I told you. I'm not going to. If you want to give me details so badly tell me why he needs my sizes. P.S. I'm here.*

She responds, *Didn't tell me.*

I push open the front door to her house and lock it behind me. She never leaves the doors open unless she's expecting someone. The large foyer is devoid of all clutter, the marble floor immaculate. The only sign a woman lives here is a pair of sky-high heels off to the side. They were obviously kicked off upon entry. I slide off my own heels and head for her office.

"Hey Windsor. Morganna is in her room." Phillipe's light voice echoes in this fortress of a house. I make small talk with him for a few minutes. It's obvious he's been staying here constantly. His bare feet and lounge pants speak volumes.

I turn and head for the stairs when he takes a personal call on his cell. I wonder how his boyfriend feels about his boss's needy status. My feet squish into the plush hallway carpet as I approach the huge French doors at the end.

I take a deep breath and push into the room. Morganna is sitting in the middle of her California King sized, four-poster bed. The dark wood envelops, hiding her. I set the bag of take-out on a table. "Is this monstrosity really needed?" I swing around one of the posts and land on the bed next to her.

"Stone liked it," she says, petting the blankets around her. She has on a pair of black boy shorts and a ratty college t-shirt. Her face is completely bare. She's stripped of Morganna Sterns. Now, she's just a woman who lost her husband. The sadness in her eyes diminishes when she falls back to lie on the bed. "Plus I can sleep sideways, upside down, or regular," she explains. Honestly, it just looks lonely.

"Your room is a mess," I admit, glancing around at clothes, bottles of water, and makeup shit everywhere. It truly is wince worthy. This is the new Morganna—the one that was born of Stone's death. I'm still getting used to it.

To the rest of the world she's the same bull nose. Which is how she wants it. She shrugs. I pick up a drawing sitting next to her on the bed. It's Stone's lobster tattoo. She takes it from me.

"I'm trying to get all of his tattoos drawn by the artists. You know…so I don't forget." I think she wouldn't mind forgetting this one, but I nod and give her a small smile. My chest tightens. How do you remember and let go at the same time? Is it some precarious method of blocking certain things and grasping onto others? How do you choose? I'd want everything.

"Maverick is trying to get you back, Win. By now you've realized that. Before he died…Stone told me you were the one that would give Maverick a life. He's only ever had things. A great career, all the material possessions a guy could ask for, he's good at things, but he's never had what you give him. Stone believed that people's lives intertwine for reasons out of our control. I always told him that was nonsense, just as Mav did, but can't you see that it's not? It's real. I know he hurt you. I know Stone's death turned him into a different person, but you have to let the person he used to be speak for him now. That's the fair thing to do," she says staring at the ceiling. She catches a tear that leaks out of the side of her eye. Propping both of her tiny feet up on a bedpost she laughs. She sounds maniacal. But I don't care because it saves me from responding.

I lie down next to her and stare up. "I'm afraid to ask what's funny."

"The swirls on our ceiling had to be repainted three times. They weren't geometrical. It drove Stone nuts." It sounds just like something Maverick would do. They are like the same person.

"Stone *was* nuts," I say, laughing. She grabs my hand next to her on the bed. We stare at the white swirls, both trying to find a lopsided swoop.

She whispers, "He was. Wasn't he?" The silence stretches on and on, and it's comfortable because this is Morganna moving on. I feel it. She's taking pieces of him and locking him away in the part of her heart that will always belong to him.

She tightens her grip and says, "You should go home now. Enough time has passed." I shake my head. *I'm swamped, can you bring me some dinner?* My ass.

"I should have known you didn't want to hang out with me. What did he do now?" I ask. I turn my head toward her. She's still staring up, lost in thought. She looks at me, tears rolling off her nose.

"I always want to hang out with you, but I have no idea. Only that I needed to thwart you for a little while so he could perform another step of his master plan." She walks me to the door and down the hall. I ask her if she knows what the last step of his grand plan is, but she just smiles. I'd shake her if I didn't feel so sorry for.

I remind her of the time her college ex-boyfriend wanted to take her to a farm for a date. It was her worst date ever. That was a surprise. She isn't budging, though—insisting I need to go along for the ride. Phillipe is waiting for us at the bottom of the stairs. He's holding out the pair of Morg's shoes.

"Clean up your mess, you hag. My boyfriend will be here in ten minutes. So, you may want to put on some pants," he says, eyes roving her nearly naked body. "And maybe a bra while your at it." Morganna laughs, snatching her shoes.

"I'll just put these on and call myself proper," she jokes, dangling the designer heels off her fingertips. Phillipe shakes his head. That exchange just took place. What. The. Hell. I look wide-eyed to my friend. She throws her arms out to the side. "What? He's off the clock at five. The rest of the time he's just my friend. I hate being here alone."

I would, too. It's big. But the Morganna transformation just took on a new, unexpected facet. She's changing more than I can comprehend. I throw on my own shoes and walk to the door.

"Don't be scared, Windsor," Morganna says—standing in the middle of the marble foyer, in her underwear. The shoes she's clutching are the only remnants of the old Morganna—her old life. "Let him love you. It's worth it every time. No matter what happens. They never make the same mistake twice." Her tone is pleading. Like her life hangs in the balance. My heart pounds out at a frenetic pace for Morganna...and her loss.

I tell her I won't be scared and that I'll do everything she says. Not because I'll actually do it, but because the sight of her right now, holding those shoes, is enough to spike the air with loss…and I don't want any part of it. I'd say anything to get away.

When I slide behind my steering wheel, I just sit there a couple of minutes calculating everything that could go wrong…or right if I do this. I slip my hand into the side of my briefcase and pull out *the* envelope. Clicking on the overhead light, I flip the smooth paper over a few times and watch my name written in tiny block letters appear and disappear. I tear it open because I just want to get it over with. I can do this. I want to read this. The only thing that's kept me from it before is fear. I unfold the top flap and then the bottom. My throat constricts when my gaze lands on certain words. I read it.

Windsor,

From the very second I looked at you, I knew you were different. Not just because you were the hottest fucking woman on the planet, but because of what you made me feel without even trying. I never thought to ask for more out of life other than what I was already given. Asking for the perfect woman was out of the question. I mean how much luck can one man have? But there you were, like a freight train with a heart of gold and a body made for speed. I wanted you. There was a difference between you and every other woman I've been attracted to. I wanted you to want me back.

Initially I thought you'd be this unobtainable goal, but then I realized you weren't unobtainable...not really. My brain just labeled you that way because it saw the fucking DANGER signs posted around you. "Slippery slope. Will fall into fucking oblivion." Or something like that. I never listen to fucking warnings. Maybe I should have and perhaps you wouldn't be reading a grave letter right now. I don't regret going after you, Windsor. You're the best detour my life has ever taken. You are merely the best thing. That's an all-encompassing statement.

I can't write you this letter like I'm already gone, because I'm not. I'm still thinking of you and picturing you in my mind and living my life one day at a time to get back to you. To hold you. To kiss you. To love you. So while I may be dead as a doornail when you read this, I sure as shit wasn't when I wrote it. I can still feel your lips on mine. I know what my name coming out of your mouth does to me. I'm aware that I've left the likes of the Hope Diamond out for the taking. Maybe it's naïve to think because I love you so much no one else will touch you.

Maybe not. You give me hope in a fucked up world.

I want to give you everything in life. Everything and more because that's what you deserve, Win. Not just material possessions either. I know that shit doesn't mean anything to you. I want to give you laughter that never ends, understanding, acceptance, gratitude for taking a chance on the wild card, love...oh, boy do I want to give you that. I'm not sure that I know how to love you properly. All I know is that you have all of my love and somehow it grows each and every day. It fills me up until only you consume me. Things have consumed me before....my career and the rush of a fast-paced lifestyle, the glory of being a SEAL, but Windsor consumption can't be compared to anything else.

It's not going to be me to give you those things, because I'm gone. My chest aches thinking about it. Heartache beyond death is possible. It's right here—In these words. Fall in love and don't be afraid of anything. Life is too short to calculate everything. Don't settle for anything less than perfect love. The person might lack certain things, or be some crazy asshole, but if the love is perfect that's what matters. Everything else is just white noise in the background, lulling along the emotions. Sometimes you just have to leap without looking first. Take a chance, Win. Always. Always. Always take the fucking chance.

I will love you forever and then some. It's your hand over my heart, not mine. I won't break rules and say goodbye. I'll say live like goodbyes don't even exist.

T.H.

Chapter Thirty

Maverick

I'm sorry. Those two words are never enough. I learned that the hard way growing up in the Hart residence. You show your remorse through doing better and proving your apology is sincere by actions. That's what I'm doing now. I could apologize a million times for the fucking awful lies I told Windsor. But they'd be just words from a person who doesn't deserve trust. I barely trust myself right now. I haven't had a sip of alcohol since the night Windsor came to me. She could have stayed with Nash that night, but she came. It was the only show of confidence I needed. It's strange how some small act creates so much forward momentum.

"She's been wanting that new couch for like a year. Windsor is going to flip out," Gretchen says excitedly. I asked what Windsor wanted if price wasn't an object, and she told me a couch. It's not the most romantic gift in the world by any stretch, but if it will make her happy that's all that matters. It's similar to the leather couch in my own home. "All the flowers were a little unnecessary, but I get the over-the-top apology you're going for. I appreciate the lack of goldenrod in these bouquets. Your *love* sent my allergies into a fucking tail spin the last time you went on a flower gifting rampage."

"Roses tend to be less of a trigger if you have allergies," I explain, looking around at every single table covered with glittering flowers. "I just want it to look like the last time…except better." I want to pick up at a place when everything was perfect. Before Stone blew himself up and before I pushed her away. This is the only way I know how. Goose prances, yes, the fucking dog prances over and hops up to his designated blanket on the new couch. I smile. He's easy to train. Windsor's just a softie.

Gretchen clears her throat. "Your kitchen timers are going off, oh skilled-at-everything-Navy-SEAL." I made dinner for all of us, but Gretchen explained that if she had to play third fiddle on one more date in Windsor's life, her head would explode. Exploding heads aren't conducive for what I need to happen tonight. She's going to leave us alone. I'm nervous Windsor won't agree to be alone with me and she'll be here any second. Morganna sent me a text a few minutes ago. A sheen of sweat breaks across my forehead.

I meet Gretchen's calculating gaze and say, "I'm not skilled at everything. I wouldn't have to grovel like a pig if I did things perfectly the first time. I'm sorry, Gretchen.

You're the person who has to deal with the aftermath of…everything. Thank you for helping me pull this off."

Tightening her ponytail, she slings her hands on her hips. "Nash doesn't deserve her. You fucked up less. What he did to her, in my eyes, is unforgivable. But Windsor being Windsor feels like everyone needs the benefit of the doubt. She's big into second chances, if you didn't notice. She was destroyed after you pushed her away, but you know she never let on? I'd hear her cry all night long, and poor little Goose had a wet, tear soaked head constantly, but she didn't want to affect anyone else with her pain. That's how she dealt this time. So, you know I didn't deal with the aftermath directly. She's thoughtful to a fault. Thank you for making this right. She deserves this and so much more. Just don't fuck up again," she says, eyes narrowed.

I'm already shaking my head. "If I can make this work. If I can get her back, I'll never let her go again," I say. Punishing myself by denying Windsor wasn't going to work for very long. In my short sober stints in between drunken blackouts, I surmised that much. Now I've wasted four months. I want the rest of her months to be mine.

Keys jingle as the front door closes. Windsor's heels click down the hall, and she peeks into the living room, her eyes darting to me immediately. She can't hide her smile. It's in her eyes and on her beautiful mouth. She looks a little sad, like maybe she's been crying, but her smile distracts me from everything else. The ache in my chest encompasses my whole body, relief washing over me. I felt close to her while visiting Kathy in Georgia because I was in her space, with her mother, but seeing her in the flesh right now is better than my wildest fantasies. I missed her more than I can quantify. Gretchen slips quietly past Windsor and out the front door. We're alone.

Flowers are everywhere, but her gaze is all mine, she doesn't look away. I swallow down the fear. "I'm a stupid man, Windsor Forbes. I've said things I can't take back, I've done things that are even worse. I let alcohol step into my shoes and run my life for me. I let it take away the only good thing in my life. I let it take away the one thing that makes me feel alive. I'm so, so sorry." I pause because I see her blue eyes glassing over. She merely nods. I'm just getting started though.

I close the distance between us and grab her small hands in mine. She doesn't pull away. If anything she leans toward me, wanting me closer.

Time to play the honesty game. "I'm not honest. I'm trustworthy though. It sounds like fuck-all bullshit, but that's it. That's me. It's all I can offer, Win. The dark places stay dark places. You'll never have all of me. I don't expect you to be happy about that fact. I just want you to love what's in front of you. Because what you see, this person I am when I'm with you? It's the best version of me and it's all because you didn't run from the other me. I love you. I love all of you. Now, I'm asking you to love me back, but only the part that deserves your love. This guy. Right here and right now. I'm offering you what's left of me. It's not much, but it's all I have to give. Look at me. Look at my life. I'm fucking crazy, and maybe I'm a little bit deranged and over-the-top. But you? You're good. You make me good." I pull her to my chest, because the inches between our bodies feel like oceans. Her arms wrap around me and her face finds that place on my chest that only she can fit into—like a puzzle piece.

"I love all of you, Maverick," she sighs against me. The feeling buzzing around inside me right now is why I drank myself into oblivion. It was absent. "You're not deranged either. Maybe just a little compulsive and set in your ways, but not deranged. I'll take what's left of you. It's more than I could have hoped for. I have to admit though, I'm afraid." She shivers.

I pull back to read her eyes. "Of what?" I'll crush any fear she has.

"Of loss," she says. With one word she's explained everything that's wrong with my life. It's undeniable. It's the one thing I can't promise her. It's part of me. My loss. Her loss. The whole damned world's loss. I can't protect her from that. "I see what loss has done to you and Morganna, and I'm not that strong."

I tip her chin up and will her to see everything inside my mind. How I think she's the strongest person in this world...in this universe. Silent strength. Passionate strength. The strength to forgive. The strength to move on in the midst of her darkest hours. She's stronger than me. Fearing loss is the worst way to live. It's worse than actually dealing with it.

"You just have to live, Windsor. Worrying accomplishes nothing. Tomorrow isn't promised. All we have is today. Right now. This moment is what's left. Loss only exists because you had something worth losing in the first place. Do you know how stupid I feel for wasting four months of tomorrows?" Her blue eyes look fierce as indecision lights her face. A moment later Windsor leans up and presses her lips against mine, twining her arms around my shoulders, her body against mine. I've had a lot of great moments in my life. This one tops the list. I deepen the kiss, running my hands down her sides to rest on her small hips. If lips could heal, Windsor's would be my type of treatment. I forget about everything. It's just her and I and our blistering, fucking amazing, crazy love lighting the entire world on fire. That's what it feels like, anyway.

I bring a hand up to grab her chin. She automatically opens further, letting my tongue dip inside to meet hers. "Miss you," she says against my teeth. Her body is so warm against mine, her tits pressing on my stomach. She has morphine-laced lips. Her kiss numbs all the bad. Delirious happiness rages inside me. I want her. How did I stay away from her for so long? I was a fucking drunken idiot. I want to punish myself for punishing myself.

"I missed you too," I say, not breaking our mouths apart. It's more than mere *miss,* though. I want to stay attached to her forever. I don't want this to end. I thought it did end. I thought it was fucked forever. I should have known better.

Love doesn't die. No matter how many bullets you put in it. It breathes on its own without oxygen, without need for anything else. It exists, swirling in its own form of gravity, ready whenever you are, to be consumed by it.

I hold her gorgeous face in my hands and with a great effort I tear my wet lips from hers. I only stop because if I let this kiss go on I know I'll have her naked on the floor in minutes, and that's not what this is about. Well, it kind of is, because I want her…and I haven't had sex since her, but that's not part of my great plan. I wasn't even expecting her to surrender her lips to me tonight.

"I made dinner," I explain. Her eyes are wide, pupils dilated, and the soft pink of her cheeks are the telltale sign—she's ready right now. That fact flips a switch. I want her in all fucking ways. Which means I'll need enough restraint for both of us. I focus on controlling my uneven breathing. Looking around the room, Windsor sees the flowers for the first time, and eventually the couch. Her jaw drops.

"This is what you were doing? You bought me a couch?" she asks, her voice loud. I can't determine whether it's a happy or a what-the-fuck question.

"If you don't like it we can switch it for something you do like," I say, thinking the couch was a horrible idea. She shakes her head, her hair swinging across her back.

"No, I love it. Thank you. Gretchen must have told you I've wanted this one for a while. It's too much," she says, sitting down on it next to Goose. She picks him up and cuddles him against her chest, rubbing the leather with her free hand. She makes a few exclamations about how much she likes the sofa and then follows me into the kitchen. The couch isn't nearly enough. She doesn't know that yet, though.

"You didn't have to do all of this, Maverick. You had me at *I'm a stupid man, Windsor Forbes.* It's a version of *I'm sorry* I haven't heard yet. You get beaucoup points for creativity."

I exhale. Easy. Being with Windsor is easy. I think any other woman wouldn't forgive this easily. But then again, if they aren't Windsor, I don't need or want their forgiveness in the first place.

We eat dinner in a sexually charged atmosphere, eyes fucking when our bodies can't. I can taste it in the air. The need to be close to her in any capacity is stronger than anything else. The conversation is light and flows effortlessly. When you have months and months to catch up on, I guess that happens.

She's also relentlessly curious about my time spent with her mother. There really isn't much to say about that. I wanted to get to know the woman who raised Windsor. They are polar opposites, something I'm sure Windsor is grateful for. I know I am. Behind every single insult Kathy slings her way, behind it all, is undying love. It's just her weird, fucked up way of showing it. Knowing that fact comforts me. It gives me hope for my own parents. I called them and we talked. It was minimal and just the basics, but the lines of communication are open. If I was going to take Stone's advice about Windsor, I want to take all of his advice. Sober Maverick is going to attempt to fix everything.

Her eyes are downcast as she whispers. "I'm glad you feel better, but you can't be magically cured, Mav. I saw what drinking made you do. Even if I didn't see it, Morganna gave me first hand accounts of the situations she dealt with. You know, when you didn't want me in your life. My love for you isn't some magic pill. I saw exactly how intoxicating being intoxicated was for Kathy. Is it the same for you? Should you get more help?"

Heavy words—heavy, but so true. I don't feel like drinking right now. When I have to go home to my empty house tonight, I'm not so sure what I'll feel like. I know I can control myself. The problem is wanting to. What happens when I can't fall asleep because I can't stop the memories? "It's a work in progress, Win. You give me a reason to stay sober. When Stone died, a lot of fucked up shit crossed my mind. Drinking got it off my mind. I told you I have addiction problems. I need you to trust me. I can do this. We can do this. Tell me I can't and watch what happens," I say, smiling big and wide. Windsor laughs, exposing her perfect white teeth.

She stands, sauntering over to sit directly in my lap, her legs dangling off the side. I groan and laugh at the same time. It's so unexpected and so right at the same fucking time. Wrapping her arms around my neck, I feel her answer. She says it anyway. "I trust you. I just don't want to be the reason you quit. I want you to want it for yourself. If I were to drop off the face of the planet tomorrow, I'd want to drop knowing you'd be okay." She kisses my cheek. She kisses my ear. She runs her fingernails through my hair.

"I'm okay now. I know that I'm okay now," I whisper, closing my eyes, feeling her on me and around me. It's not a lie. I'll be okay if I always have this. Windsor's steely blue gaze is trained on me when I open my eyes.

"This plan?" Windsor asks, narrowing her eyes and biting her bottom lip. Fuck. "Does making out on the new couch come next?"

No. "Yes," comes out instead. She squeals as I pick her up, cradling her in my arms. "The plan is whatever makes you happy," I admit, pulling her down on me, sinking deep into the sofa. I want to know she's mine before I take her again. This time I'm going to do what I should have done the first time. The thing is, there is no way I'm telling her no...maybe not ever again. Our legs are entwined and I feel every body part that touches hers. She props herself on her elbows and looks down at me, her brown hair spilling over her shoulders. My heart starts pounding the second it recognizes the look in her blue eyes. There's no guessing about it. I know what she's thinking.

"I love you," I say, beating her to the punch.

A half-smirk inches its way across her beautiful mouth. Eyes smiling she says, "Blow me, Maverick."

She cuts off my laugh with a kiss, her hands sliding under my shirt, lifting it as she goes. I pull it over my head and toss it to the floor. She sits up, straddling my hips, her knee-length skirt rising to accommodate. My eyes are immediately drawn down.

"Whenever I couldn't sleep, when I was upset after you left, I would think about this," she whispers, laying a hand over her tattoo over my heart. "And the day at your house when I went to see you…" She swallows. I move my hands to rest on her hips. "I saw the tattoo and I knew that if I ever meant as much to you as you said, then we'd find a way to each other. Then Nash came along, a changed freaking man. I hoped that if you ever came back to me, I'd be able to forgive you…and that I'd be the same person you remembered."

At the mention of Nash, my hands tighten on her hips possessively. I blow out a breath through my mouth. I sense she isn't finished so I remain quiet as she drags a finger over my chest.

"One word," Windsor says, finally glancing back up to my face.

I don't lie. "Nash."

She sighs, placing her hands on top of mine. "I forgave him for the altar dash. I felt a little bad because the bimbo left him. I know that sounds crazy because of what he did to me, but there it is. He needed my forgiveness and part of my messed up mind wanted to give it to him. It's a clean break, Maverick. We were just friends getting to know each other again," she explains. She tells me how much he's changed and all the things he's said and done for her when I was busy in drunk mode. It makes me feel a little bitter.

It also makes me feel a little sick that he was there for her when I wasn't…because I chose not to be. If he honestly changed as much as she thinks, wouldn't he be the better choice for her? My ego won't let me believe it, so I push the thought away. I'm the man for Windsor. Kathy even said I was good for her. She told me how Nash was just a placeholder until the great love of her life showed up. She told me I was it. I'm not sure how she surmised as much, but I'm glad she said it.

"I was never supposed to be more than friends with John Nash. I told him so."

Relief courses through me. Though that had to be a hard conclusion to come to, after all those years spent pouring herself into something that never happened.

She puts a finger over my lips. "Before you say anything else, I need to know why you need my clothing sizes. Morganna told me," she says, cocking her head in question.

Morg, the blabbering bitch is going to ruin everything. I shrug. She didn't give away any pertinent details. That I know of, at least. "We're going on a long weekend," I say nonchalantly. I say it like she doesn't have an option either. If she doesn't agree, my plan will go up in flames. I need for her to see me prove myself to her. Her brows wrinkle in confusion. It's so cute. I smile.

She shakes her head. "I can't just take off work."

"You can. I already requested it off for you when I went to talk to Hannah."

"Of course you did. Anything else you did for me? Where are we going?" I notice she doesn't ask hypothetically. We're going. We're fucking going. I pull her close to me for a kiss just because I feel like I might explode from happiness if I don't use her as an outlet. It's the first moment in a long time that the grief doesn't rear and funny enough…it makes me feel guilty. I slam my eyes shut and kiss her harder.

She bites my lip as she pulls away. "Your boss was pretty amenable about the whole situation after I explained…and after I told her that you'll be managing all my accounts when you get back, she couldn't argue. Expensive time off, Win. Better get ready to have some fun. Plus, I have seven long weekend cards to use if I remember correctly." That was my plan if she shot me down all night. I was going to argue that she had to honor at least one of them. I was going to tell her that if she wanted, if it was what she wanted after I'd laid it all out on the line, it could be the very last time she saw me. Luckily, she's going to go along without kicking and screaming.

"You're so crafty. And manipulating. Trying to buy my love again, I see?"

"The first time I was trying to buy a date. Now I'm trying to buy your love," I admit, smiling. "Want to see the clothes I chose?" She hops off me and pulls me to stand. She swats my hand when I reach for my shirt.

Trailing a finger down the center of my chest down to the button on my jeans she whispers, "No shirts. You want my love…no shirts."

"You have a shirt on," I fire back, raising one brow. Windsor unbuttons her shirt unmercifully slowly, taking her sweet time sliding it over one shoulder and then the other. When it's all the way off and her black bra is all I can see, she throws her shirt in my face. Pissed she covered my view, I throw the shirt to the ground.

"Not anymore," she says, backing up, heading for her bedroom. It kicks in—the adrenaline…the fight or flight response that's wavered in fucking neutral since the mission. Fight. I'm not running anymore. Not in my head. Not in my life and definitely not in my relationship with Windsor. She's giving me another chance and, for fuck's sake, I'm going to take full advantage of it. My paused life is officially in drive.

She unzips her skirt and steps out of it at the entrance to her room. I close the door behind us. I hesitate a second, studying her black thong, and then lock it. She laughs.

"Goose can't do doorknobs," she says, smiling, eyes roaming my body like I'm her favorite sight in the whole world. I run my hands through my hair self-consciously. She glances at the closet where Gretchen hung the new dresses all in garment bags. A crease forms between her eyes as she tries to decipher what they mean for our weekend destination.

I clear my throat. She startles.

"I'm not used to having men in my room. But I'm very glad you're here." Windsor nods toward the dresses. "We going to the Grammys or something?" I unbutton my pants and let them hit the floor. No underwear tonight. Her eyes widen. Now it's my turn to laugh.

"We're going to the bed," I demand, flicking my gaze to it and back to her. I'm in front of her in the next second. "If that's what you want, of course."

I palm her bare ass in my big hands, and pull her against my hard dick. She kisses her tattoo on my chest, rubbing her hands up my biceps and shoulders. Her touch is so reverent, meaningful. I won't make the first move though. It feels like the first time. There's just one thing I need from her.

"You know you're mine, right?" I ask. She nods. I lightly touch her chin and force her wandering gaze to mine. "Forever," I say leaning toward her so she gets my implied meaning. I can't be any clearer.

"Make love to me, Maverick Hart. I'm yours forever. And you? You're mine for eternity," she whispers grabbing me in her hand. That's a green fucking light. Her words hit me square in the chest.

I have the remaining scraps of lace on the floor and her in my arms before we even hit the bed.

A realization dawns on me—falling in love hurts. Existing in it is bliss.

Chapter Thirty-One

Windsor

There's no hesitation on either side. He's kissing me like I'm oxygen and he can't breathe. I'm kissing him like he's a condemned man on death row. I take it. He gives it—all of it. I forgot how delicious his lips taste when they slide over mine. The way his cologne and body wash seep into my awareness cause heat and wetness everywhere it's supposed to be right now. Lust. Love. They both battle for the front position. I want him to slide into me and finally be connected to him again, but then again I don't. Because that means it will be over sooner.

"Don't leave me tonight," I say when Maverick buzzes his nose down my neck on his way to my chest. I tilt my chin up and arch my back to give him better access. I peer down at him through my lashes as he closes his mouth around a nipple. His grin is deliciously devilish. I missed this so much—this connection that shakes the world around me. I can't get close enough quickly enough. All the beautiful words from his letter solidify everything. All of my fears and preconceived notions about our relationship dissipated after he confessed everything face to face. Love is louder than anything else. It comes before anything else.

"I want to stay," he growls, his mouth pressing kisses into the skin on my stomach. I run my fingers through his hair to feel him near me. It's almost unreal to have him here in my world after everything that happened. I gently pull his head to bring his lips back to mine…exactly where I want them.

I feel him smiling against my mouth. "What?" I ask, pulling myself up to kiss the tattoo on his neck with my tongue and then each dimple.

He presses his hot lips on my neck and trails them over to my ear. Goosebumps break across my entire freaking body. One Maverick move sets me on fire. "It's been a while," he whispers. "I'll try to remember how to do it."

"Let me help," I say, taking his shoulders to hoist myself up. I push him back on the copious amounts of throw pillows and smile. It reminds me how badly I wished he were with me when we had our sexy Skype call. He tosses a few on the floor, never taking his eyes off me. "What should we do next? It's been a while for me, too," I admit. He licks his lips. I suck my bottom lip.

Maverick groans a painfully turned on noise. He is standing completely erect, pointing at the ceiling like a compass needle points north. The sight of it reminds me how wet I am. Which is basically the state I live in when he's in the same vicinity…naked or otherwise. I straddle his knees and lean over to let a strand of spit fall from my mouth onto the head of his sex.

"No one can hold a candle, right?" I ask, flicking my gaze up to meet his. He's stopped breathing altogether and his hazel eyes are transfixed on me, on himself. His mouth drops open a little more when I let my head fall closer to where he wants it to go. His hips automatically thrust up to meet my lips. He closes his eyes when I take him in deep and delicately wrap my hand around him, and start moving both at the same time.

Careful not to use my teeth, I swirl my tongue and rise and fall at a slow pace. I see Maverick's fists bunching my quilt out of the corner of my eye. He mumbles nonsense and I hear my name thrown in every few words. His face is that of pure, unfettered ecstasy. Suddenly his eyes fly open to meet mine.

"Okay," he breathes out. "Enough." He slides me up to straddle the top of his chest. I can feel his heart hammering away against my core. It turns me on so much that I can't see straight. "I want to taste you," he rasps, his heavy, hooded eyes letting me know he's telling and not asking. I place my index finger on his thick bottom lip and pull it down. His eyes are pleading now. With the same finger, I circle his mouth and dip my finger inside. He sucks it, flicking it with his tongue. My muscles clench in response.

"How do I taste?" I ask as I pop my finger out of his mouth. Grabbing my thighs, he guides me forward until my sex is directly on his mouth. He kisses it lightly, letting his tongue dip inside. I sigh because it feels so freaking good, pleasure blasts through every nerve ending in my body.

"Fucking mouthwatering," he replies, lifting his head to lick and suck more aggressively. I try to keep my hips from rocking, but I can't. Maverick puts his hands on my ass to try to still me as he works. I glance down and the sight of how turned on he is makes what he's doing even more pleasurable. Kissing turns to licking, which turns into his skilled tongue flicking just the right spot at just the right pace. I throw my head back and close my eyes. When his mouth pulls away I peek down. He's pushing my hips down his body. Foreplay is over. His lips, glisten with me as he says, "It's gonna be quick so I didn't finish you off. Are you close?" Maverick asks, positioning me over his throbbing member.

"I'm close," I whisper, moving his hand aside. I slide the tip inside me. "And you totally have perfect recall. No problems with your memory there," I say, sliding down his shaft until it's all the way in, hitting the back, filling me completely.

Maverick's eyes close as a hiss escapes his lips. "I did actually forget how amazing you feel," he growls, taking my hips into his huge, hot hands. He pulls me up using only his biceps and pushes me back down...hard. It feels so good that I throw my head back and scream his name over and over. Like it's my new mantra or something I don't want to forget. He impales me repeatedly until the rhythm is so perfect I know I won't be able to hold back much longer.

He flips me under him so my back is pressed on the bed and he keeps up the same pace, except the angle is different, and I cry out from the pleasure blasting through my body. I come and I come and I come, tightening around him, and losing all thought process. I wrap my legs around his waist as he pounds into me at a furious pace, taking me, claiming me as I spasm around him. A few more strokes and he's coming inside me, hot and intense. I feel each strong spurt as it blasts into me as deep as it can possibly go. He rocks his hips a few more times as his orgasm jerks through his body, and then he collapses on top of me, a sweet, sweaty mess of perfection.

"Holy shit," I whisper, burying my face into his neck. "I love you, Mav." His face, which was buried in a pillow, turns so he's looking at the side of my cheek.

"Say it again," he demands, voice raspy.

I turn my own head to meet his gaze. "I love you. I love you. I love everything about you."

"Because I just rocked your fucking world?" His dimples pop. He looks so freaking hot right now, freshly fucked, and with love oozing out of every pore that I can barely stand it. He's still inside me so I rock my hips to feel him deeper. I feel him watching me. My eyes flutter closed. He rocks into me again. I hear him laugh. He knows exactly what he's doing to me. "Can't even give me a straight answer huh?" He pulls out and rolls to his side next to me. I roll to my side too, so we're face to face—heart to heart. I stare into his eyes and just breathe, coming down from my post orgasm high. I smile at him as he watches me.

Maverick cups my face in his hand. "You say you love me. Why? Why do you love me? How can you love me? Convince me," he says, curiosity lighting his face. He doesn't think I'll be able to do it...with good reason, too. A year ago I would have no idea how to respond. I don't think I even knew what love really was. He still thinks I don't. But I do. I trace his lips with my fingers and bring my hand down to rest over his heart.

"I love you because behind the steel plates, narrowed eyes, and perpetually convincing 'tough guy' act you put up, you are soft—soft in all the places that matter. I love you because when you love something, you do it with all of your heart. Halfway or a quarter of the way isn't an option. It's all or nothing. I love that when you make up your mind, that's it...the decision is made. I wish I could have an ounce of that ability, but I don't need it when I'm with you because we balance each other out. I love that when you start a hobby, it becomes your passion. Passion is rare, and I can't even calculate the amount that hums around you at any given moment. I love the way you look at me like you know exactly what I'm thinking, even when you don't. I just love the way you look at me—like my eyes or face will fix something inside you. With a man like you, I feel helpless to contribute anything to our relationship. It drives me crazy. Then I realized I don't have to match you stroke for stroke. All I have to do is love you. And I do. I love you. More than I even thought possible. Being away from you is torture. I want to fight with you and make up with you and live life with only you. I don't need you in my life, Maverick. I want you in it to make life worth living."

I've shocked Maverick Hart. He's wide-eyed and gaping when I finish. Holding my head in his hands, he kisses me. Long and deep, just lips and breaths.

Into my mouth he whispers, "Thank you, Win." It's his only response other than his kiss. And I'm glad I finally had the nerve to admit it.

I should have told him that the second I figured it out. I know his thank you is all-encompassing and I don't ask him to explain. When he breaks our kiss, he trails his hand over the side of my body, gliding over my hip and ending between my legs—his fingers rubbing the insane wetness between my thighs. I prop my knee up so he can look.

"It's like truth serum," Maverick says. "I like me in you." He watches as he fingers glide in and out easily. A small sigh escapes my lips, drawing his gaze back to my face.

"I love you, Windsor."

I lean in and kiss his nose and then his lips. "I love you, T.H."

My words give him pause, his mouth stops working against mine. A few heartbeats pass, and he begins the kiss again, forcing me to lie back on the pillows as he buries himself inside me at the same time.

His face in my neck, he pushes in and out of me slowly, making love to me instead of fucking me senseless. I'm already hypersensitive so it doesn't take long before my thighs tingle and I'm clenching around him. He muffles my cries with his lips, watching my eyes as intense waves of pleasure cause me to shiver. He comes seconds later. There are no words between us as his warm body lies on top of mine, our chests heaving, trying to catch our breath.

He licks my neck and inhales by my ear, breathing me in. I'm his. We stay connected as he rolls us to our sides. We fall asleep that way, joined as one and as close as we can possibly be. He's mine. In all ways.

*****

"I still can't believe we're in Vegas. You're crazy. You know that?"

Maverick chose the one destination that I never would have expected. He's a recovering alcoholic for God's sake. Embracing the mindset that he can do anything he wants to do without being tempted, and in order to prove to me that he's in control of himself and his actions, he chose Sin City. The city of addiction of varying degrees. It's also one of the few places where people are drunk on the streets at eight a.m...from the night before. I put all of the glittery cocktail dresses he bought to good use at Cirque du Soleil shows and eating at upscale, delicious restaurants. It's our last night here, and it's Sunday. I figured Sunday would be a less crazy day here, but I was wrong. I think Saturdays and Wednesdays hold the same appeal.

"Oh, come on. You have to go to Vegas at least once in your life. Plus, what better way to convince you of your magic pill capabilities," Maverick says, taking my hand and leading me through the insanely loud casino lobby.

I'm still wary about his drinking. How could I not be, with Kathy as my mother? Surprisingly enough Maverick's told me she's stopped drinking, too. I try not to talk to her about her issues just to avoid conflict. I guess Maverick didn't avoid anything during his time spent visiting her and Bill. He's like a go-between now. I've never had that before and it's…nice. I still don't think any one person can be a magic pill. Until he proves me wrong, I'll trust him to do what he thinks he needs to do.

Machines ding and lights suffocate the eyes at every turn, no matter the time of day. We've played at the slot machines a few times just because I asked him to. I couldn't go to Vegas and not pull one of those filthy handles at least once. No alcohol or any other addictive substances, other than my body—multiple times a day—have even piqued his interest. Not even at the restaurants where a glass of fine wine is almost mandatory. If it's bothering him being in this atmosphere, I would never be able to tell. Maybe that's the point to all of this. It also makes me wonder how much acting he's doing. Heaven knows he's at expert level in that department.

A blackjack table catches his eye. "If you're good at probabilities and have a great memory, you can beat the dealer. I've done it before. It just takes a lot of patience and more nerve than most people have. It's ballsy to try," he says, winking at me.

Oh, I bet it's ballsy. Everything Maverick does is ballsy and unbelievable and honestly...unexpected. Now I'm almost certain SEALs function on a different frequency that no one else can tune into. It's like a cult. Kind of. It's definitely out of the realm where most people understand. I like that I don't fully get him. It keeps me on my toes— like this morning when I woke up naked, wrapped in soft cotton sheets, to the sound of a guitar. He sang me a song that rivaled my first song. This time he did it in a pair of boxers, with his impossibly irresistible bed hair tousled. He looked me straight in the eye the entire time. It's how he conveys what he's feeling when normal words, in his opinion, don't make the cut. I melted like I was standing on the face of the sun.

He points out the different games as we amble through the brightly lit aisles, while I flounce in my five-inch heels and a gold sequined dress that is probably more appropriate for Vanna White. It sparkles a million different colors. It really is beautiful...for a Vegas dress, that is. And Maverick loves it. So much in fact, that he removed it the second I put it on tonight and delicately placed it on a chair before screwing me against the huge plate glass window of our penthouse suite. My knees get a little weak thinking about it.

I glance over at him as we exit outside, the buzz of the people around us significantly quieter than the sirens and bells of the casino. He is so dashing in a tailored suit, his muscular form evident even in clothing. Every single woman in a fifty-yard radius stares. They don't try to hide it either. Some look to be about sixteen and others look like they could be my Grandma's age. His appeal knows no bounds. No one is attracted more than I am. Not just to his looks, but to what's inside that perfectly structured body. His broken heart mending a little bit everyday, his will to move on in the face of loss…that's the most attractive thing about him. He's a survivor. We're two souls cut from the same cloth. I swallow down the lump in my throat. My thoughts always wind back to his letter. How strong his feelings about life and taking chances are cause me to understand him better and love him more.

He grabs my hand in his and smiles just for the sake of smiling. He has no clue how appealing he is. Not anymore, at least. He doesn't even notice the attention he gets from random strangers, waitresses, or even the girl who checked us in at the hotel front desk. When I mentioned it, he shrugged and said it didn't matter who looked at him as long as I was looking at him too. I laughed it off. The man is all mine. There are no doubts how in love he is. I think that's the thing—I know how much he loves me…I feel it. That's what makes it real. That's what makes me so confident in every aspect of our relationship. I try to form a mental image of my relationship with Nash, paired with mine with Maverick, and it's insulting to the years I spent thinking Nash was *the one* for me. Love equals confidence. Bravery. Leaping without looking. Maverick Hart.

He looks both left and right, eyes scanning our surroundings. "I wanted to show you something," he admits, peering down at me. "It's just around the side here. We have time before our dinner reservations." He pulls me against his side and kisses the top of my head.

"As long as I don't end up getting road rash, I'm game," I tease. He tried to cajole me into having sex…in his driveway. Oh, did he try. His baritone laugh wraps around me, making me reconsider road rash as a bad thing.

I wrap my arm around his back and look up. His face is blank, but his eyes are full of worry. He doesn't know I'm looking. He peeks down and sees my case study.

"Everything okay?" I ask, pulling away to see his whole face. He bites his lip and nods.

"Being around this many people. It's a cluster. My brain won't turn off," he explains, like it's a normal thing every human being feels. He ushers me toward the side garden by the hotel. We took a walk through here the other morning so he knows where to lead under the dim moonlight. It's less busy here. There isn't any alcohol or gambling. It makes sense. The path winds around beautifully manicured bushes and trees that I'm sure require some sort of weird tools to keep up a la *Edward Scissorhands*.

"Are you going to grow claws and cut my name into this bush? Don't scar your face though," I say pointing to a large lion shaped topiary.

"Do you want me to do that?" A light on the walkway lights the side of his devastatingly handsome face. I see one dimple and white teeth and a hazel eye.

I shake my head. "Nah, but I do like that movie," I say, sitting down on the stone bench. My feet already hurt and we've barely walked—the price of freaking beauty. I put a pair of roll up flats in my tiny purse because I do not want to go home with another blister or Band-Aid. As it is, I'll be wearing UGG boots to work with my skirts for two weeks. I cross my legs and let one of my heels pop out of the shoe for relief.

Maverick looks up toward the hotel and checks his watch, his free hand fidgeting by his side. "Your feet hurt already?" It's been the ongoing joke all weekend. I look around as small spotlights flick on, lighting the patio that we're sitting in. I narrow my eyes at the onslaught of white light.

I look up at Maverick. I lie. "My feet are perfect. What did you want to show me? The timers on these lights have perfect timing." He runs a hand through his hair as he stares at my face, my eyes. Looking for something, no doubt. When he doesn't speak, I smile. He smirks.

Then he hands me a small jewelry box. My heart starts pounding. Not just pounding, but like rocking against my chest in a crazy rhythm that matches my stomach flipping. My mind goes blank, like absolutely black as I take the box from his palm. When I finally tear my gaze from the black box, I glance at him.

He chuckles. "Go ahead. Open it. You can see it now…in the light," he says. I watch as he swallows, his neck working. He's nervous which makes me nervous. With shaking hands I fumble a bit, but eventually flip open the lid.

It's a necklace.

To be more specific, it's a gold trident. The same symbol he wears on his uniform—the symbol that marks him a SEAL. It's an eagle clutching a rifle and a trident. It's beautiful. Its significance isn't lost on me. This is Maverick giving me part of his world. It's him asking me to be a part of it. It's also him asking me to accept all of him—even this part, the one that takes as much as it gives.

"Flip it over," he says, clearing his throat. On the wings on either side of the pendant are tiny, engraved coordinates.

"I know what these numbers mean." I rub one wing. It's the same longitude and latitude that reside on Mav's chest. The exact moment he fell in love with me. My stomach flutters as I take in a deep breath. "But what are these?" I rub my thumb on the other side, where the unfamiliar coordinates are etched. I look up to Mav. Scared freaking shitless would be the words I use to describe him right now. His hands shake by his sides, and his eyes are a little glassy. His usual cocky confidence is nowhere to be found—It's extinct like the dinosaurs. The man standing before me now is stripped of all of his defenses, transparent as glass.

"It's the exact location you said yes," he replies, his voice rising at the end. He gestures to the garden around us.

"Said yes to what?" I ask, looking around. Did I miss a question? Is a pack of rabid animals about to attack us? Why is he acting like this? He just gave me a beautiful necklace. Maverick should be happy, secure. Not whatever it is he's feeling. After peering around the garden I turn my confused gaze to Maverick. He wipes his palms down the sides of his black pants. I glance down at the necklace one more time and back up to him.

Dropping to one knee he swallows once and says, "Will you marry me, Windsor Forbes? Make me the happiest man in the world. Marry me? Say yes. Please say yes." He pulls out a second beautiful black box from his jacket pocket and opens it. A huge, and I do mean huge, glittering diamond shines up at me. Seconds pass as I try to formulate a response. When his hand wobbles, I throw myself into his arms and clutch him as tightly as I can while still keeping us from falling over. The happy tears come.

I pull back and look into his huge, shining eyes. "Yes," I whisper. "Yes. A million times yes." He slips the enormous emerald-cut stone on the finger that it will ostensibly be on for the rest of time. He kisses it, looking at it with such reverence. Then he takes the box from my other hand and clasps the necklace around my neck. Both gleaming objects signaling his claim to me—more importantly they're symbols of my acceptance of him.

I bring my hand up to inspect the ring more closely. "It's so beautiful Mav. It's so beautiful," I say, voice shaking with raw emotion. "We're engaged!" I exclaim. The word sounds odd, because I never dreamed Maverick would be proposing to me. But like everything he does, it's perfect and unexpected in the best way.

"It's not nearly beautiful enough to compare to you. You said yes," he says. Of course I said yes. Our love is perfect. "We're engaged," he repeats. The excitement on his face is palpable. A kid on Christmas is less excited than Maverick in this moment. I don't have answers about the future. All we have is right now, though. And right now is the best moment of my life. "I'll make you happy, Win. I'll be the husband you deserve. I'll be a man worth your love. I swear it."

"I never doubted you would be. Of course I said yes. Was there even a question?" I ask through happy tears. He kisses me, sealing our deal. My ring catches my eye as I cup his jaw. Butterflies invade my stomach. He draws back and looks at me—at my face and my necklace, while running his hands down my arms.

The spotlights fade and the dim lights illuminate our secret garden. Maverick shakes his head, laughing. "There was never, not for one second in time, since the day I met you, a question."

Chapter Thirty-Two

Maverick
Six Months later

We didn't get married in Vegas like you'd expect. I wanted to juxtapose the person I once was with the person who I'd become, so I proposed in Sin City. Windsor deserves the huge wedding she's always dreamed of. I'm the lucky fucker who gets to give her exactly that. And pretty much whatever else she wants.

I'd do about anything to see her smile. All she does these days is smile. Even with the pressure of wedding planning, she laughed and smiled her way through the big decisions like they were easy. When I asked her about it, she said that as long as I was standing at the end of the aisle when the wedding march started playing, the rest were just measly details that didn't matter. That statement is pretty much why I love her. It's also why I haven't so much as looked at a drop of alcohol since the bad time in my life.

I've been seeing a therapist, at Windsor's insistence, and it's helped me understand why I drank to begin with. He said I wasn't addicted, per se. I craved the numbness and I'd take it anyway I could get it. Distancing myself from Windsor after Stone died was another thing I used to numb my emotions. If I didn't feel love or happiness, my sadness and grief diminished as well. I shut out everything. Healing was easy with Windsor by my side, feeding me every single good thing I never knew I needed. For the first time in my life, I'm living a full life in every respect. I've got the fucking world by the ass. I just had to lose myself completely to get a better grip. Something the doc told me was normal. I'm okay with the normal label when it comes to that.

The Monica monster signed the divorce papers, freeing me from that abhorrent woman for the rest of time. Morganna probably threatened her life or something else Morganna-like, but whatever she did worked. I've never appreciated the sanctity of marriage until right now. When marrying the woman of my dreams for all the right reasons. Not because I have to, not because I think it's right, but because *it is* right. Nothing is more right. I'm like a firecracker with a short fuse. I'm so excited to marry Windsor—to make her officially mine.

This day, our wedding day, couldn't come soon enough. I would have whisked her to a courthouse to seal the deal the second she said yes, but I used restraint. I'm standing at the front of the huge fucking church, the same church where I spoke at Stone's funeral, and I'm hit with conflicting emotions. Good, bad, sappy and everything in between. The rows and rows of wedding guests are all dressed in bright, cheery colors, wearing smiles and happy tears. White and pink flowers are everywhere, stuck in arrangements, hanging from the ceiling, down by my feet, in every nook and cranny that is large enough to fit a flower. It's pretty. It's what she wanted.

My parents are here today, in the front row, beaming at me like I finally did something right. I guess I did do something right to have such a great woman in my life. If that's what it takes to get them back in my life, I'm okay with it. We've been talking, patching things up over the past months at Windsor's suggestion. Stone would be proud, I think. It's something he always hoped for me. You always have to start somewhere in any type of relationship. Sometimes in a noisy bar with a wet shoe, sometimes at a wedding. I smile when I catch my mom's eye. She wipes a tear and I hope she's proud of me. I hope she thinks I'm doing something honorable and right. I hate that I want that approval, but I do. I always will. My father wraps his arm around her and whispers something in her ear. He nods my way. I tilt my head in his direction. Mending burned bridges takes time.

Steve claps me on the back and whispers, "you fuckin' got this man. You locked that shit up." I smile and nod, hoping Windsor's Grandma in the front row didn't hear his foul mouth. We are in a church, after all. Steve's my best man. I can't help but get a little emotional when I think about who should be standing behind me today, but I know he's here. Wafting in the rafters, with a towel wrapped around his fucking neck, smiling like an idiot. God, do I miss Stone. Every day. Every second.

Windsor sent Gretchen with a pair of cufflinks and a letter this morning while she was getting ready, a process that takes entirely too long in my opinion. The cufflinks were polished gray stones. I got a little choked up when I read the letter. The simple gift is the single most thoughtful present I've ever received.

I rub one of the stones when *the* music starts playing. The entire congregation stands and looks toward the doors, backlit with streaming sunlight. Goose prances down the aisle and stops halfway, and turns to look back at the door. Laughing, I call him. Obediently he trots over to me, while small bursts of laughter ring out. I untie the rings from the little pillow strapped to his neck and hand Windsor's to Steve. Morganna struts down the aisle by herself, a huge grin plastered on her face. Her pink dress swishes as she walks. Steve clears his throat from behind me. I turn to give him a mini-glare. He laughs. I hand Morganna my ring and she takes her place on the other side, followed by Gretchen who sweeps Goose up into her arms.

The doors open a final time and they appear. Windsor, clutching onto Kathy's arm, starts down the long aisle. I can't see past the huge, happy smile on her face and in her eyes. She didn't wear a veil, because that was my only request. I wanted to see her blue eyes the entire time. My stomach feels like it might implode while every single hair on my body rises. She's mine. This beautiful creature is mine. It's unbelievable. Her eyes meet mine and I know what she sees. The fucking dimples, which are probably out so hard they'll be engraved there for the rest of time. Her simple wedding dress hugs her body and flares out at the bottom, accentuating every curve I'm so obsessed with. Simply put, Windsor is perfection.

As the wedding march plays, she gets closer and closer. I see smaller details. Her necklace, the trident—that means so much to me. I see her understated makeup and the loose waves of hair that fall over her shoulders and down her back. Her beauty takes my fucking breath away. No one will ever be more beautiful in my eyes than her. It's a fact of life.

Kathy leans over and whispers something into her ear before placing her hand in mine. It's poignant. This moment is so significant. It's Windsor telling her mother that she loves her, no matter what. It's Kathy telling Windsor that she's always been number one. Always. It's forgiveness. It's second and third chances. It's new beginnings. Windsor kisses her cheek and then she focuses on me. Blue eyes glass over. And the tiny fragment of my heart that I held back is hers. Forever.

The pastor goes through the motions, saying things I don't hear because I can't tear my gaze, or focus off of her. I'm sure I'm supposed to respond to something because I feel Steve nudge me from behind. He hands me the ring.

Vows. I stumble through the words that the pastor tells me to repeat, ending with, "I do." And me slipping the delicate band of platinum on her finger above her engagement ring. "I love you, Windsor," I whisper when I look into her eyes. Do I ever. They weren't scripted words. They burst from me on their own accord.

She sniffles and tears up through her vows, and as soon as the dark titanium band is in its place on the second finger on my left hand I feel immeasurable relief. I smile wide and wipe a small teardrop from beneath her eye. I pull her against my chest. She's my wife. Windsor Hart is my wife.

"I now pronounce you husband and wife. You may now kiss your bride," the pastor says. I do hear that much and I do exactly as I'm told.

I kiss my fucking bride. Then I kiss her some more because I just can't stop. The roar of applause breaks out and I feel Windsor's smile against my mouth. She pulls away to break the kiss and squeals in delight, covering her mouth with her free hand. I raise our joined hands in the air and Steve lets out a huge whoop from behind me. Manly shouts from the rest of my uniformed teammates break out, and it's complete and utter chaos. The best kind—the Team kind. My brothers. I swoop up my wife and walk down the aisle with little Goose close behind.

The music starts up again, but I've already got her outside the church alone. And all mine. I put her and all the layers of her dress down on the steps in front of the church. "Mrs. Hart," I whisper.

"We are married. Oh my gosh. You are my husband," Windsor exclaims, rubbing my wedding band. "It was perfect, Maverick."

I lean down and kiss her. For real this time. With tongue and passion, tilting her head with my hands to get the perfect angle. She moans into my mouth and her small, cold hands come up to cup the sides of my face. I lift her off the ground, pulling her against my body, but keep kissing her.

I hear a female throat clear from behind me. Windsor's head darts at the noise. It's Morganna. "The masses will be out here any second and this looks like it's about to turn into wedding night festivities a little early," she says, her southern drawl stringing out most of the words.

"Why Morganna. Your country is showing!" Windsor says excitedly with a fake country accent. "We can fornicate on these steps if we deem it appropriate."

I laugh. God, I love her. She kisses my neck. Then my jaw. I capture her lips with mine.

"He would be happy. You know that right?" Morganna says, smiling.

My stomach knots. "I know he would. He wanted this to happen when I wasn't sure if I deserved this to happen," I admit sadly, trying to keep my emotions at bay. I put Windsor down, but keep her close at my side. I touch one of my cuff links and close my eyes.

"Tighten your fucking towel, Mav. You have a reception to put on," Morganna says before disappearing into the mass of people who swarm around us. I swallow back the memory and focus on the happiness in my heart. The happiness that I get to enjoy because he's no longer here. His sacrifice indirectly gave me this. Windsor.

Everyone congratulates us with huge smiles. They shake my hand and hug Windsor. I kiss the top of her head, to remind her I'm still here while well-wishers swallow her alive. Everyone tells her how beautiful she looks and what a lucky man I am. They are all generic phrases that people say at weddings.

Except today they aren't generic at all. I am so fucking lucky, for so many reasons. For this reason, I'm going to live my life like the luckiest son-of-a-bitch alive.

For myself. For him. But mostly for her.

*****

The reception went by as quick as molasses. I'm sure no one else thought it was that long. I did because the only thing I could think about was how quickly I'd be able to get her out of the wedding dress. I want to make love to my wife. It's going to take a while to get used to saying that. Or even thinking it. It won't feel absolutely real until tomorrow after we've spent an entire night doing exactly what our vows said: loving and cherishing.

"How tired are you?" I ask when we're finally alone in the back of the limo. She kicks her feet up into my lap and I take off her high heels, which I know for a fact have been killing her all night. She won't admit to it though. I love that she thinks I don't know.

She scoffs. "Tired? Honey, I'm just getting started." I ask her what her favorite part of the day was and we both agree it was the vows. She admitted she didn't really hear what the pastor was saying either. I wonder if that means we're not technically married because neither of us paid attention. The night was awesome, the food was good and all our friends were drunk as skunks when we left. That's a successful party. Both Gretchen and Steve's speeches were upbeat and happy, not mentioning anything about any hardships. I was thankful they both gave Win happy memories of the night. I didn't want anything to taint her day. I even talked her into inviting Nash to the wedding. He declined, thank the deities above. But I think she was proud of herself for extending the invite nonetheless. It's something she's able to bury in her past and let it be just that...the past.

Windsor didn't have anything to drink at the reception, and I obviously didn't either. I wouldn't fault her had she wanted to drink all night, though. I just don't extend that kind of offer to myself. Nothing will cloud our wedding night together. I want to feel everything tonight. When the limo pulls up to the hotel valet, I hop out before the driver can open our door and offer her my hand. Slipping back into her shoes, she takes it, her face already flushed, her eyes all fucking mine.

I checked in earlier in the day so all of our stuff would be here already and so I could make sure everything was perfect for when Windsor walks in for the first time. This is like a transitioning night. Starting tomorrow she'll be living in my house all the time. I wanted her to move in with me after Vegas, but she resisted saying that we've gone this far, we might as well keep her an honest woman. Which was sort of a joke because I've defiled that woman every day since I proposed to her. Sometimes even multiple times a day. She stayed with me most nights because I needed her to. I couldn't sleep without her. When she had early mornings I would spend the night at her house. Practicality wasn't really on the top of our list when she decided we wouldn't live together full time.

"I know you're supposed to carry me over some threshold or something, but maybe you should, like, dangle me over the threshold by my ankle to break tradition or something? What do you think? You game?" Windsor asks when we stand in front of the suite door. She has her hands on her hips as she stares at the door like it's going to bite her.

"I'm game. You carry me," I offer. I scan the key card and kick open one side of the French doors, exposing the expansive suite the size of a house in front of us. Her mouth drops open. This was a surprise for her. I'm sure she expects flowers, but what I've done is even better.

"How did you get all of these photos? And blown up this quickly?" she asks, eyes wide. I motion for her to hop on my back. Her eyes dart around taking in everything at once.

"I'll piggy back you inside. It's not technically carrying," I explain. She has to hike up her dress to get up and I get a small peek of her black, sheer garter. It sends a shock directly to my groin. Keeping her on my back, I walk over to the first series of huge canvases. She slides down, holds my hand, and puts her free hand over her mouth, her eyes teary.

Julio Bigcock made a return to Facebook to steal every photo of Windsor he could get his fat hands on. Cropped portraits of her smiling face, photos of her and Gretchen, and the rest of her friends. He even went back so far as to get a photo of her and John Nash when they were dating. The photos are larger than life. Literally. They are huge.

She walks slowly from each image to the next. I stay where I'm at, by the door, and watch her expression as she takes in each one. Windsor gets to *the* photo. The one I never told her I saw. It's the group shot of her and the Rosy Team on their night out with Nash. She laughs a little and moves on to view a black and white photo of her and me. She's sitting in my lap gazing at me with a look of love on her face. It's not the same as the look she's giving Nash in the previous photo and that's the point. That nothing is really as it seems. Different types of love look different ways. A photo of her mother and her when she was in middle school comes next, then one of her and her father at a father-daughter dance taken a few weeks before his accident. At the very end of the row is a photo of all three of them. Her family. Her mother is looking at her father with that same substantial look.

I wrap my hands around her middle and pull her back against me as she cries happy tears. "My family," she says. I turn her away from the photo and face her toward the largest canvas in the room. It's six feet tall and leaning against the bedpost. It's the first time I've seen this one. Windsor looks fucking stunning in this one.

It's a photo from only six hours ago. The photographer snapped it seconds after we sealed our marriage with a kiss. Our hands are entwined and raised to the sky. Her face and that smile are the happiest things I've ever seen in my entire life. I vow in this moment to make her that happy every day of my life. Ironically, in the photo that I had no part in choosing, I'm looking down at Windsor with a huge sappy smile on my own face.

I turn her around in my arms and whisper, "Our family." I wipe a few spilled tears with my finger. "This is our family now," I say. She leans up and I lean down, and we kiss.

"Thank you, Maverick. For all of this. Thank you for our family," she says reverently. They're photos. This was easy. Well, the wedding photo wasn't easy, but anything can happen if you offer the right price. Windsor has given me so much more than photos. I smile.

"I know how you can thank me," I whisper while reaching over to the side of her dress where I know the zipper is. During our first dance as husband and wife I mapped that shit out real quick. I know exactly what needs to happen. "I just want you," I amend.

"I think we can safely say," she murmurs while fluffing out her gown, "that is the one thing you got today with absolute certainty." Windsor pulls her bottom lip into her mouth and cocks her head to the side. Devilish move.

"And if you ever wonder how I feel about you, all you have to do is look at that life size canvas of me smiling like a crazy person, wearing a wedding dress, clutching *your* hand." Her gaze wanders back to our wedding picture. "You kind of love me," she says, sighing.

I use her distraction to unzip the dress. She lets me unsnap the top clip, too. The gown pools around her feet like a billowy carpet. Only then does she look back at me. I'm not looking at her face anymore. *Sorry, babe.*

I lace my hands behind my head and pace backward a few steps. "You're trying to kill me off on our wedding night. It's the only explanation," I say, my voice terse as my eyes rove the black-as-night lingerie she wears under her pure white wedding gown. No bra. Only sheer black panties and her black garter. I glance between the wedding photo and her current state, and can't form coherent words. I get the best of both worlds. I fucking get *it all.*

Glancing down and back up quickly, she shrugs. "I wouldn't dream of it and this old stuff? It's no big deal. You are supposed to take this off," she points at the garter with a red fingernail, "with your teeth. No hands allowed. It's seven years of bad luck if you touch me before your mouth gets it off," Windsor explains. My man brain gets lost somewhere in between teeth and touch, but I get the gist.

Loosening my tie by yanking it side to side, I plan my attack. I look at my wife's body like a challenge. A hot fucking challenge.

"Oh and to make things interesting…here." She slides the black thong down and kicks it to me. All she wears is the trident necklace, her wedding rings and the black garter—all things that link her to me. The primal male rears to the surface, beating his fucking chest in victory. "Let me help," she says, reaching for the buttons on my shirt. My hands reach for her automatically. She *tsk's* me, while beaming a huge triumphant smile, all teeth and full glossy lips.

I take the shirt out of her hands. "I got it," I fire back.

She puts both hands up and says, "Fine. Fine. Have it your way." I strip down to a pair of black boxer briefs while Windsor walks around the suite looking at all of the canvases again. She pauses in front of a wall of glass that overlooks the ocean, her back to me. I drop the stone cufflinks onto a table so I don't lose them and approach her quietly. Not quietly enough. She spins on me, her gaze darting down to my dick.

"Seeing as we both obviously want touching privileges while also obtaining a lifetime of good luck I'm going to get to work," I tell her while dropping to my knees in front of her. She points her leg out while reaching down to raise the garter up higher, until it's almost level with her God damned freshly waxed pussy. Shaking my head, I glance up at her and raise one brow.

She hikes her shoulders. "Just leveling the playing field. It's an easy task, right? Maybe the more you work for it, the better luck we'll have?"

I don't respond. I take the garter in my mouth, blowing a mouthful of hot air on Windsor as I get a grip with my teeth. I smile when I see her skin raising in response. I flick my gaze up to find her watching me, no smile, parted lips, and heavy eyes. I smell how turned on she is. Pressing my palms against the glass beside her ass, I shimmy the scrap of lace down a little further and blow again. This time she whimpers. Let's be honest. I could have this thing off blindfolded, anesthetized, underwater, at the beach, during a tsunami in mere seconds. She made it a game first. So I take my time.

When I finally get done a few minutes later, teasing and blowing all the way down to her calf, she says, "Okay good job. Touching commences now." I come away with the black garter in my mouth. Windsor grabs it out of my teeth and flicks it across the room. It lands on the table where I put the cufflinks. *Stone would appreciate that*, I think.

"Touching now?" I ask. She nods reverently, leaning her body against the glass. Well, it is right there. I grab both of her legs and sit them on my shoulders. She wraps her legs around my face and I finally get to taste her. Windsor moans at first contact and I love that I know she always does that. I hope she always will. I also hope there's no one down on the beach watching me go down on my wife right now.

"That feels so good, Mav. Yeah, just like that," she pleads, her voice breathy and so fucking turned on that it causes my dick to twitch. "Bed. Bed. Bed," she repeats.

I look up to make sure she does indeed want me to stop. She nods, so I disentangle myself from her and stand. She leaps at me, almost taking me down to the ground. Her mouth is fierce, her tongue probing, like she's trying to taste her on me. Wrapping her legs around me, I grab under her ass and carry her to the huge bed, passing our wedding picture resting against one of the bedposts.

I fall down on top of her, breaking the fall with my arms. "I want to make love to my husband," she explains, reaching between our bodies to grab my dick. Her small, soft hand strokes up and down. The word "husband" coming from her mouth makes my heart pound. I get to be her husband. I'm going to wake up from this dream any second I'm sure of it. My dick brain takes over for the moment and agrees with Windsor's statement whole-heartedly—especially because I haven't been inside her for days. She was busy with wedding stuff and the night before the wedding she spent away from me. I need this more than food, water, breath...more than anything else. I move a couple fingers to her sex and hot wetness greets me. Sliding one finger in, I feel her gripping me, wanting more. With the wet finger I circle her clit and watch her gorgeous body writhe with pleasure. I lick up the front of her neck and across the bottom of her jaw, over to her ear.

"I'm going to make love to you now," I whisper before biting her lobe, probably a little harder than I meant to.

She grabs my face in her hands. "Yes," she says before pressing her lips against mine, eyes open, blue eyes gazing into mine. I slide home and her eyes flutter shut.

"Open your eyes." She does. I rock into her slowly, softly, deliberately. She moans softly and I know I've got the right pace going for her. She raises her hips each time I thrust into her. The world is silent around us except for the sounds of her breathy moans, my heavy breathing, and the rhythm of my strokes as they slide in and out of her tight body. Her hands are around my neck and her lips don't leave mine as she climbs higher and higher. I know the moment she's about to come. I'm right there with her this time.

"Come with me, baby," I say. She bites my bottom lip and nods. The sharp pain of her bite shoots me over the edge. She grabs my ass to hold me in, as if I ever wanted to leave, and I drop my hips a few more times and explode inside her.

Her head tips back and she moans, "Mav." I feel her flexing around me over and over as I pump inside her, heavy and strong. I roll so she's on top. Windsor slumps over on my chest, her head resting on my heart. No words are needed, but we still tell each other how much we love each other. She tells me how at peace she feels now that we're married. More specifically now that our new family is officially formed.

Our past and our future merged into one huge thing that seems tangible, but it isn't really. It's something inside of us, some unspoken knowledge of healing and love and forgiveness. Life is about taking what you want and giving even more. Not because you think you should. Because you want to. Love isn't easy because life isn't easy. You have to fight for the things you want. Sometimes you win and sometimes you wish you'd lost instead. Other times it feels like you're already dead and gone. That's always when the best part comes, like some avenging angel who evens all the scores no matter who you are or what you do. I won't lie, it does help to be a little bit of a badass.

Charles Bukowski once said, "find what you love and let it kill you." I say, "Rise from the ashes and take it back."

Epilogue

Windsor
Four Years later

"Daddy's hanging upside down out of the tree again. 'Cept this time he has that tool. It makes a lot of noise," Luke says, bounding through the front door.

"The chainsaw," both Morganna and I say at the same exact time. I roll my eyes and look at her. She laughs.

"Go tell daddy, Mommy is going to go all white-trash-barefoot-and-pregnant on him if he doesn't get in here and help me get the food ready for the party," I demand. I know he'll probably only relay half of that message. It'll be pretty funny to hear what Maverick hears. Is it so wrong we like to play telephone with our three year old? Luke, who is actually another Thomas, flies out the door repeating my message to himself over and over.

"I can't believe you talk like that to him. He's going to…" Morganna pauses, looking up to the roof in thought.

I scoff. "He's going to turn out just like his father? There's no stopping that, Morg. I've embraced the fact that in a few years he'll be swinging in trees doing whatever it is that men do outside," I explain. "Speaking of, where's Steve? Will he be making an appearance to the *Fantastic Mr. Fox* bash? Luke will be pretty upset if there aren't enough tough guys at his party." I air quote on the words "tough guys", because Luke has no clue what they do. He knows they are big and have cool tattoos and everyone else thinks they're cool, too.

"He had some sort of huge disaster in the garage when I left. I told him to clean it up or I'd shave off his eyebrows and hide all of his money in offshore accounts if I saw a drop of grease on the floor when I got home. He said he'd show up at some point, though," Morganna says. She's putting Steve through the freaking ringer. Which is what anyone would expect, so I can't feel that bad for the guy. He knew exactly what he was getting into when he asked her out on an official date a few months ago. He's been after her for years, but Morg just wasn't ready. I'm not sure she's ready now. She's trying though. And Steve? Well, he's been trying for a long time. They will happen…eventually.

Maverick's shirtless, sweaty chest makes its way into my line of vision. He leans over and says, "You're going to do what with me in a trash can? And the barefoot baby is going to join us? Don't fucking tease me, Win baby. Give it to me straight," he jokes, using his sexy voice that still drives me insane…with lust.

I laugh because this game of telephone just turned into the best one yet.

He gives me a sweaty kiss, lingering longer than he should in mixed company. "You want to come help me cut some branches? Know what I mean?"

Morganna groans and hurls a dishtowel at his head. He catches it before it makes contact and rubs it down his chest. I watch it, jealous it gets to touch him and I don't. Not right now, anyway.

"She's about to pop out your spawn and you can't think about anything else?" she says pointing at my huge stomach. It looks like I swallowed a watermelon. I promised myself I wouldn't have the baby today. Not on Luke's day. It shouldn't be his fault that his parents are obviously fertile at the same time of year.

Maverick wipes his hands off and pulls me in for a short kiss, rubbing my stomach as he does. His eyes are big and round when he pulls away. "It's because she has my spawn inside her that I want to be inside of her," he tells Morganna.

I blush. I can't help it. This man is still so crazy about me that I'm not sure how I got so lucky. Maybe because I love him way more than he loves me? It's a constant influx of passion and love, mixing together to coat the bad days and singe the good days. Maverick is happier now than

I've ever seen him. The dark shadows don't chase him here, in our home with our small little family.

Goose trots into the kitchen. Morganna picks him up and kisses the top of his head. "I'm going to help Gretchen and Benji with the balloons. I don't want to be standing near you when that balloon pops from the combustible heat he throws off," Morganna says, pointing at my pregnant belly and then Maverick with a sly smile.

"You want some heat, Morg?" Maverick calls out to her retreating back. She shakes her head, laughing under her breath. "You know what they say about heat and the kitchen," he says. I swat him on his solid, sweaty shoulder. He picks up a fox mask and secures it to his face with the elastic strap, rendering him absolutely ridiculous looking. "What? I can't convince my own wife to go cut down branches with me—even when I look like wildlife. What am I supposed to do? Plus, no one can fluster Morganna. I've been trying for over a decade."

I can't stand it anymore, I pull him as close as my belly allows and kiss his neck. He pretends to purr. "Foxes don't purr, Maverick." I look at the tattoo over his heart that now has additional coordinates: where we got married and the hospital where Luke was born. The two new, neat vertical lines reside next to the longitude and latitude where he fell in love with me. Our daughter's place of birth will be next. I feel wistful, blissful, so in love with our life. We've made this together.

"How do you know? No one knows what the fox says," he quips. I groan at his bad joke.

I sigh, narrowing my eyes. "Maybe I do have a few minutes to help you cut branches, if it means you'll act like an adult. Only adults cut branches. You need a shower too." I see his white teeth poking through the fox snout. Lifting the mask, he smashes his lips against mine and backs me up to the refrigerator. It's still all or nothing with Mav; he'll never change. I don't want him to.

Kathy enters the kitchen, takes one look at us, and leaves again saying, "I'm going to dress Luke in his costume. The cake will be delivered soon and I don't want him to see it." Translation: if you're going to have sex for the second time today, you better make it quick.

"I love you, Mav," I breathe against him, his scent intoxicating to my pheromone-ridden body.

"I love you, babe. You're everything," he replies, before kissing my nose, my cheeks, my eyelids. We hear a throat clear behind us.

Maverick turns to look and startles a little. His parents. I grab the fox mask off his head for him. He smiles his thanks and turns back to greet his parents. I should be watching the sweet exchange between Maverick and his parents, but the moment warps into something larger. Everything comes into focus. How all of my decisions have led me to this exact moment in time when everything is seemingly perfect.

The hurdles and bad choices all ended working in our favor. If one small thing shifted in our past we may not be right here, in our kitchen, getting ready for our son's birthday party. I wouldn't be pregnant with our little girl.

I rub my hand over my stomach when I feel her kick as if on cue. Maverick may not be talking to his parents. If it weren't for Mav, my mom might not be the mom and grandma she is today. If I hadn't had my heart broken, I wouldn't have taken the leap with Maverick. If Stone didn't save him, he wouldn't have died inside and then risen wiser and stronger. Everything is connected. By time. Or by space. Be it by people merely making stupid decisions. Once in a while, right in the middle of death, love lives. Love always lives.

Maverick interrupts my thoughts. "I have to shower. Can I have a rain check on that manual labor?" I shake my head and chuckle.

"Anytime," I purr.

He cocks his head when I don't elaborate. I hit him with one of his tricks first. "One word," I ask. Sometimes it's amazing how alike we think. I wonder if he's feeling as nostalgic as I am as our well-fought-for fairytale wraps around us. Our love story isn't ideal; in fact most people don't have to lose everything to come together. I'm glad we did. I'm so glad we did.

Dimples appear first and laughter is second. "What if I need more than one word to describe? I might need three," he says. I roll my eyes. He always plays by the rules when he's the one doing the prying. I give in to him. Because I cherish and believe every word that comes out of this man's mouth.

"Fine. Leniency granted. Three words," I sigh.

He kisses me softly once. "Happily. Ever. After."

Acknowledgements

This book would not be possible without my own real-life Maverick. I love you, C. Thank you for being my own kitten wrapped in canon ball metal. Your help and assurance during this rollercoaster ride is what kept me writing when my keyboard was salty-wet for four chapters. Thank you for fact checking my romance novel. Thank you for leaving me witty SEAL banter in comment bubbles. Thank you for being you. You balance my crazy with good, baby. One word? How about two? Better together.

My beta readers are so awesome. They really, truly are. Sarah, April, Adrian, Julie, and Belle: the input and suggestions you gave were invaluable. You cheer me on and force me to finish chapters when I really just want to sleep instead. You tell me when a scene is trash, and I weep in silence…and then realize you were right and hit 'delete'. When my husband told me there were too many sex scenes, you told me he was wrong. Thank you for that (if only for the reason I can say he was wrong about *something*). Belle, you ventured into the depths of the unknown to research "moose knuckle" and "The Goat". You're the winner—all day every day. The epilogue is for Adrian because I made her catatonic with the 'mission' scene first. See? All happy now, A.

My editor, Wendy Callahan. I wrote the story, but you turned it into a readable novel. The sharpness of your eyes shouldn't be underrated. Super hero power, maybe? You edited all the F words and the P word (that I would never say in real life) and didn't tell me to pull back. You even let me have judicious exclamation points(!) You're the best!

Tatum, you turned my vision into real life. You are amazing and beautiful, and best of all you reside on the same slice of awesome atmosphere that I do. So we're like creative twins. Thank you times a million!

Last, but certainly not least *The Guys.* If one of you happens to pick up Crazy Good and make it this far, thank you for doing it all, for our country. You look good doing it. Your wives are pretty damn awesome, too.

I'd mess up a salute, so my hand is on my heart for *you.* And for those who gave all, we remember. We always will. Because love *never* dies.

Other titles by this Author:

Escaped: A Samantha Scott Novel (Eternal Press)
Embraced: A Samantha Scott Novel (Eternal Press)
Six (Eternal Press)

Visit Rachel Robinson online.
www.racheljrobinson.com
https://www.facebook.com/racheljeanrobinson